Quest for Valhalla

Book 3 of

The VIKINGS! Trilogy

Jay Palmer

All Books by Jay Palmer

The VIKINGS! Trilogy
    DeathQuest
    The Mourning Trail
    Quest for Valhalla

DEDICATION

To my SCA squires (past and present):
Carl Kurfess (Karrel der Ermutigender),
Leith McCombs (Master Leith Abranid),
Sean Troupe (Baron Sean McGurn),
and
Tony Burtis, (Karl Redstone, Einherjar).

Chapter 1

Cracked

KARL

It was a tree.
It was a tree.
It was a tree.

Karl staggered and fell backwards, still gaping upwards. His mind reeled, unable to comprehend; *trees couldn't be this big.* It was ... *impossible, unthinkable.* Yet they were standing on its roots, helpless, like tiny black ants begging to be squished.

Barely aware of the hands that grabbed and lifted him, Karl felt only his whole body tremble, his voice strained from his own screams. Horrible nightmares assaulted Karl, and then darkness enveloped him.

When Karl came to, he was clutching Eloise, who lay unconscious, her back to him, with Roselyn pressed warmly against his back, snoring softly. They were sleeping under the torn red and white striped sail, which was hung over part of their wrecked dragonship, bright stars shining through a hole punched through its wooden hull; illuminated from outside, the red stripes lit everyone with a pale, crimson glow. Fortunately, the sail hid the horrific, giant tree. Karl felt slightly relieved; he knew that the monstrous tree was still there, but he didn't want to see it again.

Seren sat between Rafe and the Seer, sharing a whispered conversation. The Seer looked like a living corpse; being comatose for a week had taken a heavy toll.

Why am I here? Karl asked himself. *How did I come to this?* He'd never really believed that a 'crack in the world' existed. Even his days fleeing from his parent's house were better than being stranded in an alien world.

"I don't like leaving the ship here," the Seer croaked, his voice raw and raspy.

"It would be pretty obvious," Rafe said. "We might as well leave a sign saying 'Here's the crack in the world'. But moving this shipwreck won't be easy."

"Do you want to explain to Titania why we didn't move it?" the Seer asked.

"We did promise to keep it a secret," Rafe sighed. "It's mostly just sliding it downhill into the river; that would take it over the brink ..."

"Down to oblivion," the Seer said. "No tale tells what's beneath Yggdrasil ... and now I know why."

"I never want to look over that precipice again," Rafe said, and he shuttered violently. "Eternal doom; that's what's down there."

"The Abyss," the Seer agreed. "Imagine falling into it, never reaching bottom, slowly starving to death ..."

"Don't speak of it!" Rafe hissed, and he crossed himself. "Let's just slide the ship down to the water and let the current carry it ... away."

"We'll have to wake the others," the Seer said.

"I'm awake," Karl whispered.

"Then we'd best get started," Rafe said. "Prepare yourself; the view hasn't changed."

"Where are we?" Karl asked.

"Yggdrasil," the Seer said. "The Norse Tree of Life which, according to their legends, always was and always shall be. It's the foundation of the Norse universe. Here is Asgard, where the Norse Gods live, and Valhalla, where we're going."

"Sorry I asked."

Karl eased out from between the sleeping women and crawled out of the sail-awning. He tried to survey their situation without looking up or thinking about where they were. Their dragonship was shattered, most of it lying in two heavily-splintered sections, with broken boards lying all around them, along with some of the contents of their hull. Rafe reached down and lifted up one end of a long piece of broken rail.

"We can use these larger boards as levers," Rafe said.

It didn't take as long as expected. The fore-section had most of its hull missing, broken apart during their wild ride before they crashed onto shore. Their food supplies had been in the fore and were lost forever. Roselyn and Eloise were awakened by the sounds of the work, but they mostly helped gather up all the numerous small pieces of wreckage and carried them down to the rushing water. Seren busied herself by sorting through their few remaining supplies, selecting things that they'd have to carry.

The larger sections of the hull were heavy and kept losing more boards as they levered them, but the men slowly inched each heavy section downhill and out into the water until the rapid current floated it downstream and finally pushed it over the falls.

"What did you see when you went over there?" Karl asked Rafe.

"Nothing that I can explain," Rafe replied with a slight shudder, "and nothing that I ever want to see again."

Karl decided not to risk it. If it was worse than the horror of the vast tree, then he didn't want to see it.

It took them another hour to collect all the debris and toss it in the river. The Seer, in his poor condition, wasn't much help. He fell often, and struggled to rise each time, yet he insisted on helping. Eloise wouldn't watch as they threw in most of her dresses, and Rafe cursed as he tossed in the last of their saddles, the ones that they'd ridden on since Bristlen.

"That's about it," Karl said. "Now what?"

The Seer looked askance at him.

"After all that we've talked about, do you still need to ask?" the Seer sighed heavily. He pulled out his blessed moonstone: a trail of glowing yellow 'V's appeared, leading towards the trunk. "I checked for them when I first awakened. My spell upon Eric, which only half-worked, from what Rafe tells me, failed the instant that we came into this world. Eric's a ghost again, wandering to his doom. He'll lead us to Valhalla."

Karl frowned. The Seer seemed to delight in making him feel stupid; *someday Karl was going to break the little snob's nose.*

They gathered up their things and put on their cloaks. Since their food was lost, Seren had stuffed their packs with three folded dresses and a few extra tunics, and filled their four canteens with water from the river. Karl's helmet, mail, and sword she'd found wedged in the dragon's broken frame. Rafe still had his new mail, sword, and Eric's helm, but both shields had been packed against the broken hull and were gone. Roselyn had her father's armor, but her bow had gotten broken

9

when their ship wrecked, so her full quivers were useless. She dressed in her father's armor, but tossed the broken bow and useless arrows into the water. It wasn't cold, but they all wore their cloaks because it was easier than carrying the heavy cloths in their hands. Everything else they tossed until nothing remained to mark their presence.

They began walking uphill. Karl tried not to think that they were on the roots of a giant tree, walking like tiny insects upwards toward its trunk. Karl focused his eyes on the glowing yellow 'V's, chagrined that these wavering magical symbols were now all that was still familiar to him.

The Seer soon collapsed. He was just too weak, too injured.

"Here," Eloise offered.

She held a canteen to his lips and helped lift his head so that the Seer could drink. His lips were still gray, badly chapped and torn, and his skin looked like aged parchment.

Drinking, the Seer suddenly coughed. Eloise pulled the canteen back, but the Seer seized it and took another sip.

"What's this?" the Seer asked, surprised.

"Just water," Eloise said. "We refilled it at the river."

"What was in here before you added water?"

"Nothing. It was empty. That's one of Farmer Tiller's canteens."

"Give me another," the Seer said.

Seren handed him another canteen and he tasted it.

"Is this water from the river?"

"Yes; we filled them all."

"What is it?" Karl asked.

"Taste this," the Seer offered.

Karl hesitantly took the canteen, sniffed the water, and poured a bit into his hand: it looked like any other water. Then Karl tasted a sip, and quickly swallowed a mouthful.

"Wow!" Karl said. "What is this?"

"Water," the Seer said, "but it's not like any water on Earth. There's something special about it; pure, as if it were newly-made."

"It's delicious," Karl said, and he took another swig, then passed it to Rafe.

"Like a white wine, but with no flavor," Rafe said as he wiped his chin.

"More than that," the Seer said, and he leaned his head back and poured the water onto his face.

"Athelwynne!" Roselyn scolded.

The Seer laid back and let the water soak in. When he finally shook his head and wiped his sleeve over his face, they all gasped. The Seer's face was much improved, his lips less chapped, almost healed.

"What is this?" Roselyn asked, holding up a canteen.

"The Water of Life," the Seer said. "I've read about this in mystical texts. To those who live here, it's probably just ordinary water, but to us ..."

"What can it do?" Eloise asked.

"It's reputed to quench thirst like no other water, and hasten healing. Vitality and strength flow from it; I already feel better."

Suddenly the Seer rolled to his knees and sat up, moving far faster than he had since waking up. They all drank some, and a new energy filled their legs, and their burdens seemed lighter. Eloise threw up her arms and began to dance, laughing delightedly.

"I don't know how long these effects will last," the Seer said. "We'd best get as much use from them as we can."

They resumed their trek, marching over Eric's glowing tracks. Their path grew steeper, but they went faster and no one complained.

Finally they came to a narrow ridge where the trail split. To the right, the trail seemed to extend all the way around to the other side of the tree. To the left, it led to a tall opening, like a giant oval knothole, and onward, past the knothole as far as they could see. The knothole was about twenty feet above the wide tunnel that the river was pouring out of, the one that led back to the 'crack in the world'; Eric's tracks followed the left fork and vanished into the knothole.

The Seer led the way up, following the glowing tracks, into the knothole. Inside, Eric's prints illuminated a smooth, oval, wood-walled tunnel, leading a winding path deep into the base of the tree. They entered slowly: the wood seemed very old, rubbed smooth, its floor, walls, and ceiling equally polished. The Seer tread slowly, peering around each bend and twist in the passage. In some places, their tunnel rose steeply up, in others they slid down slippery slopes, and it branched many times with side tunnels equally polished. The tunnel wound like the intestines of some monstrous beast, yet Karl wasn't bothered by its strange course as much as by being inside of a huge tree.

"I hate to point this out," said Rafe, who was trailing last, "but we'll never find our way out of here. We should've brought some pebbles or sticks to mark our trail."

"Too late now," Karl said.

"Use your swordpoint," the Seer said, ignoring Karl's comment. "Scratch some marks on the floor."

Karl fumed in silence. Rafe drew his sword, stabbed the point into the floor twice, and repeated his marks every few paces.

They stopped to drink twice, but mostly because they needed to rest. At last, they curled up in their cloaks and slept. Despite the magic water, all were hungry and exhausted. The last thing that Karl remembered was the tiny sleeping room in Farmer Tiller's, and how much he wished that he were there ... or anyplace ... except where he was. He fell asleep wondering if he would ever see his world again.

Jay Palmer

Chapter 2

Monsters

ELOISE

Eloise awoke stiff and sore. Sleeping on the smooth wooden passageway was even worse than the dragonship; the deck planks had been hard but the whole ship had rocked with the waves, a serene, comfortable motion, and she'd felt like a baby in its mother's arms. Being inside the tree Yggdrasil, sleeping on its hard, cold, unmoving floor felt unfamiliar and uncomfortable. Eloise was also starving, but there was no help for that.

It was pitch-black, so much that Eloise couldn't tell if her eyes were open or not; the Seer must've put away his moonstone. Eloise pushed back the hood of her cloak. She smiled in the darkness; she'd seen no moon; perhaps here she was safe from the curse of the Wolflord; that thought warmed her like a hug. The terrible transformations had hurt excruciatingly, and vague feelings of hate and bloodlust haunted her afterwards.

Quietly Eloise located and uncorked a canteen. The water tasted so good, so fulfilling, that she drank far more than she needed. It was intoxicating, yet wholesome; Eloise had never felt so glad to be young.

Yggdrasil was terrifying, but Eloise tried to keep some perspective; she'd seen Yggdrasil from its roots. What would Earth look like if seen from the Great Brink, where the waters of the ocean poured over the edge of the world? Would that sight not be equally as awesome as Yggdrasil? The Seer had said that this world would be much like their own; she'd wait and see. Yet she couldn't help but marvel at the majesty of Yggdrasil, and wondered what other worlds existed. The Seer had also said that he could teach his magical secrets, although it'd take years, and that she had an affinity for magic. The idea of having mystical powers deeply interested her, but here and now wasn't the time or place; Eloise was their leader and had to keep them going, staying on their quest. If the company stopped now, if they really asked themselves why they were doing this, then they might end up trapped here forever ... or worse: *separate.*

"Wake up!" Eloise said loudly. "We have to move on. Drink some water and let's get going. There has to be food here somewhere."

Roused but grumbling, the others slowly awoke. The Seer pulled out his moonstone and the faint glow of Eric's tracks lit the tunnel. Eloise passed around her canteen, making sure that everyone drank. The water had the same effect as before; energetically they returned to following Eric's trail.

Hours later, past countless twists and turns, their tunnel ended abruptly onto a wide, flat shelf. Unlike the smooth wooden walls of the narrow tunnel, the shelf was wide, flat, solid rock, and seemed to be the floor of a monstrous cavern. Its ceiling was lost in shadow; they could barely see the tips of huge stalactites hanging from the darkness above. Eric's glowing tracks led straight across the wide stony cavern, and the company tentatively followed. For hours, they marched straight ahead over miles of barren, featureless rock, drinking often to keep from succumbing to exhaustion.

A great stone wall appeared suddenly as the moonstone illuminated the glowing 'V's near it. The massive wall stood thirty feet high, built of huge, rough stone blocks, heavily overgrown with ivy and moss, but all of its foliage hung brown and dead. The wall seemed infinitely wide and vanished in the distance in each direction. Eric's glowing tracks led to a wide, high arched opening, an open doorway through the wall, with no gate. From just inside its entrance shouted a familiar voice.

"Karl! All of you! Go back! Run! Flee!"

"Eric!" Karl shouted in disbelief.

Eloise gasped; under the high arch stood Eric, not a wavering ghost but real and fleshed-out. Eric ... *alive again!* Eloise squealed with delight and started to run forward.

"Look out!" Eric cried.

A giant shape pounced from the darkness. Vast, slavering jaws breathed hot steam upon their faces. The companions cried out, stumbled, and fell, overcome by its threatening presence. Fierce red eyes glared menacingly down upon them. Eloise screamed.

It was a wolf, but far more menacing than the Wolflord. This wolf was huge, bigger than the largest horse ever born; it towered over them. The rumble of its growl shook the rocks beneath them. Eloise cowered, certain once again that she'd fail before a horror in wolf-shape.

"Garm, no!" Eric cried.

Huge teeth bared, its great red eyes focused on Eloise. Eloise cringed, too afraid to scream, lost in terror. The massive head lowered, its moist black nose pressed close, and the huge wolf sniffed her. Eloise curled up upon the rocky ground and covered her face with her hands, ready to die.

"Eloise, pet it!" the Seer cried.

"Don't move!" Roselyn shouted at the same instant.

"Eloise, listen to me!" the Seer said. "You bear the wolf-curse! This thing must sense that, or it would've devoured us all. Pet it, quick!"

Eloise opened her eyes. Great red wolf eyes stared back at her. Its monstrous paws clawed the rocky ground on either side of her. The others quietly scrambled away, ignored by the giant wolf. The Seer's instructions were insane; Eloise could do nothing but tremble.

"This way!" Eric shouted. "Everyone, inside the gate!"

"We can't!" Roselyn cried. "The wolf's in our way!"

The red eyes turned to Roselyn at the sound of her voice. Its terrifying mouth opened and a deadly growl roared from it.

"No!" Eloise cried as the giant wolf tensed to leap toward her friends, and its wolf-face turned back to her. Slowly, shaking, Eloise reached out her hand and touched its nose.

A giant slimy tongue licked her arm.

"Eloise, don't move!" Eric shouted. "It's Garm, the Guardian of Niflhiem, son of Fenris the Master-Wolf. Don't do anything!"

Eloise swallowed hard; nothing was all that she could do.

The giant muzzle lowered and brushed against Eloise. Garm wasn't like the Wolflord; Garm looked just like any other wolf except for his size, which was greater than any beast that she'd ever seen save for the dragon in the lake, if its body matched its head. Garm's fur was long and soft and Eloise shivered as it brushed against her.

No one spoke ... and the wolf didn't eat her. Slowly Eloise reached out and stroked its furry muzzle, and Garm bowed his head. He kept sniffing at her, and eventually Eloise recovered enough nerve to sit up. The wolf panted hot breath upon her, but he licked her tenderly.

"He likes me!" Eloise exclaimed.

"Stand up very slowly ... and move away," Eric said. "Garm's not wild; he's one of Hel's pets, but he's very dangerous. Don't alarm him."

Eloise slowly stood. Garm rubbed against her and pressed her backwards, but gently, and Eloise scratched her fingers through his thick fur. Garm seemed to enjoy it, hanging his long tongue and wagging his giant tail. Slowly Eloise moved away from the gate, and Garm followed.

"That's it!" Eric said. "Slowly, slowly!"

Walking backwards, one hand petting the giant wolf, Eloise drew the giant beast away. It took one step, then another, opening room for the others to run.

Suddenly a tremendous spout of green flames exploded, blasting from the rocky ground to the high ceiling; Seren and Roselyn screamed as the fiery roar deafened them all. The emerald flames vanished as quickly as they'd come, leaving only wafting smoke. Inside the smoke stood the figure of a giant.

This giant wasn't anything like Skaldi; he was almost as tall but lean, his crisp green wool tunic immaculate, his hair closely cropped and combed, his thin beard neatly trimmed. The giant wore tall, polished black boots, baggy gold-striped trousers, and a wide black belt with a huge golden buckle. He looked to be the very epitome of Norse culture and sophistication. He stood straight and still, and light radiated from his very being, yet his eyes glared brightest, a menacing glower beaming power and strength such as Eloise had never felt before. The force of the giant's stare almost knocked Eloise down.

"Congratulations!" the giant shouted, displaying a perilous smile. "You've done it! After all these centuries, Loki shall rule Midgard again!"

"Loki?" the Seer gasped. "The Norse God?"

Loki turned his gaze to the Seer and the Druid winced, raising his arms to shield himself from the radiance of Loki's stare.

"God I am," Loki said, his powerful voice booming across the wide cavern. "Loki, whom you mortals worshiped in elder days. Now those days shall come again. Loki shall return to Midgard, assume the throne of Earth, and all mortals shall bow before me. Bow!"

The force of his command struck them like a battering ram, glowing from his eyes, radiant, irresistible. Eloise crumpled, falling to the rocky ground, unhurt but beaten, as if crushed by Loki's poignant will, as tangible as a spiked mace. Garm growled but stepped back.

"Master!" the Seer cried, who alone had managed to keep from falling, although he was straining, as if being blown by a great wind. "Great God Loki! Honored are we to stand in your presence! How may we serve you?"

Loki towered over them. His words struck like knives.

"Where is the Hidden Portal, which you call the 'crack in the world'?"

Eloise gasped, fighting to think clearly. The crack in the world, the one secret that they mustn't reveal, was all that Loki wanted, and the one thing that they couldn't give him. Her mind raced, trying to think of a response, but none came to mind.

"Forgive us!" the Seer cried, staggering. "We're under oaths to keep secret ..."

Suddenly the Seer screamed. Loki focused the brunt of his eyes upon him. Terror masked the Seer's face, outreaching pain. The Seer fell backwards as if battered by Skaldi's fist and writhed in agony on the ground.

"Speak, puny mortal!" Loki shouted. "I didn't bring you here to be silent!"

"No!" Eric shouted. "Loki, I led them here!"

Loki turned his glare from the Seer to Eric, but nothing happened. Eric paled and flinched, but otherwise stood unharmed inside the Gate of Niflhiem.

"Speak not to Loki, deadman," Loki ordered. "You'll do my bidding soon enough! Were you not hiding in my daughter's realm, already you'd be nothing."

"I'm their leader," Eloise croaked, fighting just to look at the God in his anger. "Leave them alone; I speak for ..."

Eloise screamed as Loki's potent glare fixated upon her; only his deep voice penetrated her agony.

"Where is the Hidden Portal?"

Loki reached down, seized and lifted Eloise. Eloise screamed and writhed under his glare, helpless in his grip.

"Tell me now or I'll crush your life!"

With a fearsome snarl, suddenly Garm pounced full upon Loki, biting deep into his godly flesh. Loki howled in pain and Eloise fell from his grasp; Eloise hit the ground lost in torment, burned by even the memory of Loki's eyes, but soft hands quickly grabbed and lifted her. Eloise forced her eyes open just as Karl and Rafe carried her inside the arched Gate of Niflhiem. The furious struggles of Loki against Garm deafened them; infuriated Norse curses rivaling savage feral growls.

Thunder exploded behind her; the column of green flames burst again toward the ceiling. Garm yiped and fell back, his massive jaws dripping with blood. The emerald fire instantly illuminated the great, high cavern's ceiling and endless stone wall, and then abruptly died away. Loki was gone, vanished.

"Garm wounded Loki!" Eric gasped.

"Good for Garm!" the Seer sneered.

"Wolf save us," Seren said.

"At least Loki's gone," Rafe said. "What's with his eyes? A spell?"

"Loki doesn't need spells to deal with us," the Seer said. "He's a God, a Power unto himself."

"What did he mean about 'bringing us here'?" Karl asked.

"He must've ensorcelled the Valkyrie to reject Eric's spirit," the Seer said. "I've wondered about that. The only alternative was that the Lady manipulated her, but I doubted that, since the Lady doesn't force Her will upon others."

"We can't tell Loki where the 'crack in the world' is," Roselyn said. "We swore to Titania."

The Seer lifted the white crystal talisman that Titania had given him and looked at it.

"No, we can't break faith with Titania," the Seer said, "but we'll be hard pressed to refuse. Loki's a God and we're in his realm. He could easily kill us ... or much worse."

"He didn't seem to have power inside Niflhiem," Eric said. "We may be safe here."

Eloise turned around to see Eric's familiar face, his big teeth smiling amid his long gray moustache and beard. Overjoyed, Eloise leaped to embrace him; Eric was real, solid, just like before.

"You're alive!" Eloise shouted, burying her face in Eric's leathers.

"No, I'm dead," Eric said, embracing her, "but this is Niflhiem, and here I'm as real as when I left mortal life. But why are you here? Why have you followed me to this wretched place?"

"To get you into Valhalla," Karl said. "The Valkyrie told me that, should I present your arm to Hel before the Gates of Valhalla, then you'd be admitted, just as you wished. Well, we're here, and the Seer has your dead arm, sword and all, in his leather case. All that we have to do is find Hel, and you can finally enter Valhalla!"

"Karl!" Eric shouted, but his eyes welled with tears. "Never did I guess what great friends I had! Never will this tale be forgotten, the day when the living traveled to the Netherlands for the sake of the dead. Honored I am, and all honor is yours! But Karl, you should've heeded the Valkyrie more carefully! You need to reach Valhalla! This is Niflhiem! You've come the wrong way!"

The wrong way?

Eloise staggered. After all their travels, all their suffering ... *they'd failed?* Eloise turned and glared at the Seer, who looked aghast.

"Oh, no!" the Seer cried. "Lady, no! After all my planning, how could I blunder ...! I've failed my Lady!"

"We can go back," Rafe said. "I used my sword as a cane and marked much of our path."

"No food," Seren reminded Rafe, taking his arm.

Eloise tried to think. Karl angrily balled up his fists, and Eloise knew that he'd been waiting for an excuse to payback the Seer for his barbs and insults; if that started, then they'd be truly finished. Eloise was still baroness, their leader; it was her duty to take charge.

"Eric, we need food," Eloise said.

Eric startled.

"You've grown, little princess, since I died," Eric said.

Eloise gazed back at him, and for the first time her eyes followed his arm down to his empty stump. Eric's right forearm was still missing, the arm that the Seer carried in his case.

"I don't know what food's here, but there must be some," Eric shrugged. "Hel must eat, even if all of her subjects are dead. Garm must eat, too. We'd best go to Eljudnir, Hel's hall, and see what we can find."

Eloise relaxed; she may be baroness, but Eric was here again, and he knew these lands better than anyone. She'd follow Eric wherever he led.

Leaving Garm at the gate, the company followed Eric deeper into Niflhiem. Garm whined as Eloise wandered away; she called for him, but he only stared longingly at them through the narrow doorway that Garm was too big to push through.

"He'll be alright," Eric said. "Garm can't enter Niflhiem, I suspect; legends say that Garm prowls outside the walls of Niflhiem, never inside of them. But you'll see him again ... if we can find food."

Eloise followed Eric, but looked back at Garm with regret, feeling oddly guilty for leaving him behind. Even in the distance, Garm's red eyes stared at her through the gate.

Niflhiem wasn't pitch dark nor well-lighted; a faint red glow reflected from above, as if the light of a distant fire shined, reflected against its glistening rocky ceiling. The dim red glow cast gloomy shadows over everything. The ground inside Niflhiem wasn't smooth and flat; abundant small hills and valleys of shattered, broken, jagged rocks surrounded them. Nothing alive or growing showed, not a single tree or blade of grass, and the thin, unusually cold mists around them stank of death and decay.

Niflhiem wasn't abandoned; dead men and women, even children, filled its stony plains, silently standing or aimlessly wandering about its vast wastes. As the companions marched deeper into Niflhiem, the numbers of walking dead grew alarmingly. Many dead folk turned to look at them as they passed, and some silently followed, but most paled and turned away. The dead were ghastly, displaying the semblance that they'd worn on their deathbeds. Some, like Eric, bore marks of their deaths; open wounds or newly-missing limbs. Eloise tried not to stare at the walking corpses and clung tightly to Eric's sole arm. Hundreds of dead followed them as they walked through the chill, arid barrenness.

The rocky ground suddenly surged beneath their feet. Eloise stumbled, as did most of them, even the dead, as the ground quaked.

Frightened, all of the dead ran away. The stone ground trembled, then surged, as if suffering an earthquake. Most of the dead fled instantly; only a few remained, unable to quickly move their injured or missing limbs, or simply uncaring about their continued morbid existence.

"What is it?" the Seer cried.

"Don't wait to find out!" Eric shouted. "Run!"

Behind the fleeing companions, the rocky plain burst upwards with the roar of a thousand oceans. A massive dragon's head pushed up through the stone, high into the thick cloud of dust that it had churned up. Several dead folk screamed, but most seemed oblivious, trying to flee the horrible behemoth.

"Nidhogg!" Eric cried. "The Devourer of the Dead!"

"So huge!" Rafe exclaimed.

"Run!" Karl shouted.

They ran to a safe distance, where many corpses stood watching Nidhogg, and then stopped and looked back. Nidhogg was no smooth water-dragon as they'd seen in the lake; his skin was covered in thick, rough scales, pale gray as if he'd never seen sunlight.

Nidhogg's head was hoary, blocky, as if made for breaking through stone.

"Eric, how many dragons are down here?" Roselyn asked.

"This is an ancient land," Eric shrugged, "far older and wilder than Earth. Here dwell many horrors of old, too tough to kill, too wild to tame. Most are known only by vague rumors; Nidhogg's said to tear at the roots of Yggdrasil."

Some of the dead beside Nidhogg were crawling away as fast as they could, while others just stood there, looking weary and uncaring. Nidhogg snapped pike-long teeth upon them, scooping up many victims, and then he disappeared down inside the dust cloud with another deep rumble that shook the ground beneath them, and Nidhogg vanished beneath the rumbling rocky land.

"No!" Seren screamed, almost hysterical. *"Monsters everywhere!"*

"It's okay," Rafe soothed Seren, and he wrapped his arms protectively around her. "It's gone. We've got to go on ... to find food."

"No ...," Seren whimpered, but Rafe led her on and she didn't resist.

All kept their eyes open, wondering what new terror would suddenly appear.

In the distance, Eloise saw bright red lights. They approached an enormous hall built around four great towers, and atop of each tower was a huge bonfire.

Crackling flames reflected light off of the cavern's ceiling and the massive hanging stalactites towering over them, illuminating Niflhiem. The hall itself was brightly lit, but of such dark ruin and dilapidation that it was difficult to see how it remained standing.

Two great doors marked the only entrance to its hall. The companions walked up to the doors.

"What now?" Karl asked.

"I guess we should knock," the Seer said.

No one objected, so Karl banged his fist against the door. After waiting expectantly for several minutes, Karl banged on the door again.

"Maybe no one's home," Rafe said.

"Hel must be here," Eric said. "Eljudnir's her home."

"There's no lock," the Seer said. "Maybe we should just ... go in."

"Maybe wait here," Seren said.

"Maybe wait until we starve," the Seer said. "Then we can stay here forever."

"We can't wait," Eloise said. "If there's food in there, then we have to purchase it, no matter what the price. Karl, open the door."

Karl grabbed the bottom of the huge iron door ring and pulled hard. The door slowly opened enough for them all to squeeze through.

Eljudnir, Hel's hall, was brightly furnished compared to the rest of Niflhiem, with glints of silver and gold sparkling from all over, reflecting the burning torches set in sconces on every wall. Eljudnir was thick with dust, and cobwebs buried its corners; no one had cleaned this hall for years, maybe centuries. In the center of the room was a great firepit with a huge, roaring bonfire that poured black smoke out of a wide hole in the ceiling. Two people stood there, a man and a woman; alive they looked, although their resemblance to the dead couldn't be mistaken. They stood frozen, unmoving, like statues transformed by a Gorgon's stare. Several large wardrobes, elaborately carved, rested in one corner beside a many-pillared bed shrouded with lace curtains.

"Warm," Seren commented, rubbing her arms after the chill outside.

"Hello!" Eloise said to the strangers, but neither moved nor spoke, as still as corpses.

"Under some spell, I suspect," the Seer said.

"Perhaps," Eric said.

"So, what do we do?" Karl asked.

"We wait," Eloise said. "We should get some rest, if we can. Hel, or whoever owns this hall, must come back soon."

They piled their belongings just inside the door and sat in a circle around them. No one spoke, and some drifted off to sleep. Eloise tried to stay awake but failed utterly. They'd been marching all day and terrified by Garm, Loki, and Nidhogg. Eloise quickly fell into an exhausted slumber despite the rumbling emptiness of her complaining stomach.

Jay Palmer

Chapter 3

Hel

SEREN

Seren awoke as Rafe jostled her.

"Wha ..?" Seren forced her sleepy eyes open.

"Shhh!" Rafe shushed her. "Look!"

Seren looked; the vast hall seemed the same. Even the great bonfire didn't seem to have changed, as if its wood burned forever and never needed to be replenished.

"What?" Seren whispered.

"Those people!" whispered Rafe. "Weren't they ... did they change positions?"

Seren looked. The frozen man and woman, still as statues, had moved. Both now were looking straight at the companions and had one arm extended, pointing behind the firepit.

"Moved," Seren gasped. "What ... they point at?"

"I don't know," Rafe said. "But we'd best wake the others."

Quickly they woke everyone, and the companions jumped to their feet.

"Hello!" Eloise repeated, but to no response.

Slowly they approached the man, who stood closest. His eyes never moved, just stayed, his gaze fixed upon where they'd been sleeping. He was an old man with thinning gray hair wearing plain black robes, ancient and worn. A thin layer of dust sat upon his head and both shoulders. The old woman looked almost exactly the same.

Then Roselyn gasped, and they all looked in the direction that she faced.

Behind the great bonfire lay a golden bath, built into the floor; gold steps led down from all sides to a small, deep pool. But no water filled the pool; it was deep crimson red: *fresh blood.*

Standing in the center of the pool, waist deep in grisly blood, stood a woman that could only be Hel. Hel was pale white with raven black hair, and utterly beautiful, her every line and curve sculpted perfection and more, for she radiated, almost glowed, as her father Loki had, and Hel's eyes glared, although not as strongly as Loki's. Hel stood naked before them, her large breasts round and firm, hovering as if weightless over the

34

pool of slimy blood that covered from her thin waist down.

"I assume that you wanted to see me," Hel frowned.

Rafe spun around and faced away, his back to Hel's nakedness. Karl mimicked Rafe. The Seer bowed and averted his eyes. Eric stared but hid behind the women.

"Please forgive," Seren said softly.

"Yes," Eloise said. "We humbly apologize; we'd never have intruded upon your ... bath."

"What do you want?"

"That's rather complicated," Eloise said. "Perhaps we should wait outside until you're ... prepared for company."

"Stay," Hel ordered. "You're alive; why do living mortals haunt my realm?"

"As I said, it's complicated," Eloise said.

Hel said nothing, merely stared at them.

"Us go," Seren said, and she turned to leave.

"Stay!" Hel commanded again. "Approach me, all of you. Face me."

Hesitantly the companions approached Hel and looked down at her. Seren felt a tinge of envy; traveling with Eloise and Roselyn, both of whom were young and exceedingly beautiful, was bad enough. Hel was gorgeous beyond description, dazzling, more perfect in form and figure than any mortal woman could ever hope to be, and more; Hel was Loki's daughter, a half-goddess, radiant with divine loveliness, and darker, more mysterious than forgotten legends and myths of terror. Seren had seen Madrone's prettiest whores unclothed; none held a candle to Hel.

Hel haltingly climbed up the hidden steps of her bath. Blood sickeningly splashed in her pool as Hel sloshed through its gore, which cascaded off of her as she climbed its steps.

Seren gasped in horror. Hel was heavenly from the waist up; the ideal woman, divinely beautiful. Below Hel's waist, her flesh was ruined and rancid, brown and gray and green. Her legs were corpselike, more decrepit than any of her subjects. Tendons flexed against visible bones, and rotting skin hung like rags.

"I must bathe in blood," Hel explained as she emerged to stand naked before them. "Blood alone keeps my legs supple and flexible. Without blood, in mere days my legs would dry out and become hard and rigid."

Hel reached toward a tall chair beside her; upon it lay a thick black robe. Hel slid her arms into it gracefully, and then slowly pulled it closed, concealing her nakedness. Then she regally sat upon her chair and faced them.

"Now, why have living mortals come to Niflhiem?"

"The Valkyrie told us ...," the Seer started.

"She instructed me," Karl suddenly interjected, "when Eric died."

Seren winced, hearing the enthusiasm in Karl's voice. Seren turned to look at him; Karl seemed excited.

"The Valkyrie spoke to me on the battlefield where Eric fell," Karl continued. "I showed her Eric's severed arm, still holding his sword, and she told me to bring it to you."

"Did she?" Hel asked. "Whatever for?"

"Why ... so that you can free Eric," Karl explained. "So that he can enter Valhalla."

"Presumptuous Valkyrie," Hel calmly said. "How dare she speak for me? Did she mention why I'd do this?"

"Uhh..., no," Karl stammered. "She just told me to present you with Eric's arm, and then she flew away."

"Not exactly," the Seer interrupted. "She said to present Hel with Eric's arm before the Gates of Valhalla."

"What an odd thing to say!" Hel said.

"Forgive us, Great One," the Seer said. "Perhaps you should hear our whole tale, not just one piece of it. But our tale's long, and we haven't eaten in some time."

"I see," Hel said. "I will hear your tale. Ganglot! Ganglati! Prepare a feast for our guests!"

Seren glanced back. The two figures, Ganglot and Ganglati, still appeared frozen, but had again moved, as if they weren't statues at all but people moving so slowly that it was hard to detect. They didn't even respond to Hel's command but stood there, motionless, looking at her.

Hel gestured for the companions to sit, which they did, careful not to touch the gruesome bath with its wet trail of pooling blood that marked Hel's footsteps out of her pool. Hel's gory pool reeked, but little worse than all of Niflhiem.

"I started everything, Mistress," Eric said, bowing deeply to Hel. "I was in Norway, preparing to sail the next day, when Thorland, my friend King Svenson Two-Sword's only son, attacked me. It was a bar fight, and we were both drunk. The fool youth drew his sword, and in defending myself, I killed him.

"Svenson would've killed me; I apologized for killing his son, but he wouldn't listen. It was a matter of honor: I had to die or he'd be disgraced. So we agreed on a hunt: I promised him that I'd sail to Castle Bristlen in England, and there we'd begin the chase."

"Castle Bristlen was where I met Eric," Karl interrupted, enthusiastically taking over the story.

The great tale repeated, moment by moment, speaker by speaker. Each of the companions spoke in turn, telling of their part, leaving out only that which no one wanted to admit. Yet it was obvious that there were strong feelings between certain members of the company; Seren guessed that Hel understood all of the parts that went unmentioned. Hel sat imperiously before them; she was older than all of them, although she looked only slightly older than Roselyn. Seren knew the advantage of age and experience, how simple young men and women seemed to her, how easy to understand and predict, and Hel was immortal, ageless; one couldn't live for centuries without gaining perspective. Seren disliked Karl's forwardness to Hel's immortal beauty: the last thing that Karl needed was an attraction to another woman. Yet Seren wondered why he did it; Karl had seen her dead lower half; *what kind of relationship could they have?* But about love and sex, all men were stupid.

Seren knew, or guessed, Hel's purpose. Being an expert at her trade, Seren recognized Hel's subtle manipulations; Hel was an ultimate master of manipulation, especially of the men.

Hel often interrupted their tale with questions, but she mostly listened as the companions took turns, describing various events and details. The Seer scowled while they retold of Grusshire, his parent's village that the companions had sacrificed before he was aware of them. Eric spoke up during it, willingly assuming all blame for the deception, and the Seer glared hatefully at him. Roselyn and Eloise glared when Karl described their beauty while riding naked to save him and Eric from the Viking assassins. Eloise revenged herself by telling in great detail how Karl became The Jester and sat mute while Charles the Tinker flirted with Roselyn.

Their story-telling lasted more than an hour. Seren kept glancing at Ganglot and Ganglati. Each time that she looked, they'd moved only a little, and appeared as still as statues. Seren glanced at the one empty table that they'd set up by the time that Eloise described their battle against Skaldi, painfully aware that her stomach was empty. It would take them hours to set up enough tables for a feast.

Hel seemed extremely interested in Roselyn's description of the fairies and Titania. The Seer kicked Karl when he absently mentioned the 'crack in the world', describing their quest after leaving the swamp. Hel ordered him to continue, explaining that she already knew of the legend of the Hidden Portal.

Seren kept mostly quiet, letting the others speak, save that she told of their return to Grusshire, of their fight against the undead, and of Eloise's first transformation. All the while they spoke, Hel's gaze cycled across each of them; Seren could feel her gaze tingle, although it lacked the force of her father's eyes.

The Seer skipped over their days at sea, describing only how he'd linked his life-force to summon Eric, who alone could save them from the storm.

"Forgive me if I don't speak of the Hidden Portal," the Seer said to Hel. "Besides the fact that I was unconscious and never saw where it lay, we swore to Titania never to reveal it."

"I've no interest in the Portal," Hel said. "Niflhiem is my domain."

Rafe spoke last, of their terror of Garm and Loki's sudden appearance. Here Hel sat up, listened intently, and asked many questions. When Rafe told her how Garm attacked Loki, to defend Eloise, Hel actually laughed. All of Niflhiem seemed to alter as Hel laughed, to grow lighter, warmer, and less oppressive. But when Hel's laughter failed, so did its effects; Niflhiem again became a harsh, dark, cold and dismal graveland.

"You were lucky," Hel concluded. "Father doesn't tolerate humans well; to him you're like Fairie, easily crushed and vanquished. I'll have to reward Garm for this; it's been too long since I renewed our friendship. But I'm not surprised by Father's interest in the Hidden Portal; Father has always sought secrets which others avoided to weave into his plots and mischief."

"We're worried about that as well," the Seer said.

"While in my queendom, you worry needlessly," Hel smiled. "For now, we must see to your immediate needs. I don't have food that any of you can eat, so you must go where food may be found. It's outside of my realm, so I'll send Garm with you, to hasten your journey and protect you. But Garm can't carry all of you; I'll send three of you to bring back food for the others."

"What about Eric?" Karl asked. "I know that this isn't the Gates of Valhalla, but you're here, and so is Eric, and we have his sword to prove that he died in battle."

"That's a matter of grave concern," Hel said, "for it affects many events which have not yet come to be. I'll consider your request, but it will take much concentration and time for reflection. I'll give you my answer as soon as I may."

The companions thanked her many times. Then Hel rose and led them out of the doors of her hall. Many dead were crowded around her doors; they stepped back, clearing a path for Hel, and many bowed or knelt.

Hel led the companions through the thick throng of countless dead. Soon they approached another section of the massive stone wall, but here the wall was vastly higher. The main gate of Niflhiem was fortified by real gates, massive bars of iron elaborately wrought and towering, fortified with crenellations shaped like grinning skulls. Hel led them through her gate onto a drawbridge that spanned a mighty river.

"This is Gjoll, the river of Niflhiem," Hel said. "Nothing lives in it, for its waters are icy cold, so you must travel to the Well of Hvergelmir, the River-birther, where fish are plentiful. My subjects will provide you with a net, and you may cast it into the churning waters, but do so wisely, for the currents of Hvergelmir pull beyond mortal strength. Catch all that you can carry, and bring it back; then we'll feast."

Hel turned and faced away from the Gates of Niflhiem. Silently she looked out upon the rocky plain, and soon a drumming sound approached; the great wolf Garm loped into view. Hel greeted the giant wolf with open arms, and he nuzzled her and wagged his tail as she affectionately scratched between his eyes.

"Garm, I have a task for you," Hel said. "Carry three of these mortals to Hvergelmir, wait for them, and bring them back safely. Do as I command and I'll reward you well."

Garm's expression was unreadable, but he rubbed against Hel and panted like an excited puppy. Hel chose Karl, Eloise, and the Seer to go with Garm, and without warning, Hel picked up Karl, still wearing his heavy mail, with no more effort than if she were lifting an infant. Hel boosted Karl onto Garm's back and sat him upon the giant wolf as if it were a horse. Then Hel lifted up the Seer with equal ease, and set him behind Karl. Eloise went next, and Hel slid her in before Karl to sit upon the great wolf's shoulders. Then one of the dead came forward, holding a large bundle; a huge, folded fishing net wrapped in coils of rope. Seren wondered why they needed such a large net to get fish out of a well.

"There!" Hel said. "The leader, the warrior, and the mage; you should be enough to accomplish your task. Fish are plenteous in the water, and gather your pick of the many edible plants that grow around the well. Hurry back; cook-fires will be waiting. Fare well!"

Garm suddenly bounded off of the bridge, carrying Karl, Eloise, and the Seer away in wide leaps. Seren watched them vanish into the distance apprehensively; she disliked seeing them go alone, although none could ask for a better protector than Garm.

Hel stood in silence and watched as they rode off into darkness.

Chapter 4

Hvergelmir's Feast

THE SEER

The Seer clung desperately to Karl's shoulders, digging his soft fingers into the hard links of Karl's mail. Garm's gait was smooth but rolling, strong and swift. Dim light seemed to glow from the river itself, and a thin fog wafted off of its icy waters. Garm followed the river Gjoll upstream along the Wall of Niflhiem for some distance, then curved away, leading up into barren, rocky hills. Scrub brush peeked out of crevices in the wasteland; away from Niflhiem, they soon approached areas where life existed. The ceiling, if they were still in a cavern, was lost in the gloom above.

The Seer silently berated himself; he'd known that they needed to go to Valhalla, and that all Norse dead not chosen by the Valkyrie went to Niflhiem. But he'd been so fixated on following Eric through the 'crack in the world' that he never connected the obvious: their final destination was different than Eric's. An absence tugged at his soul alarmingly; the Seer had felt nothing of the Lady since entering this realm; he feared that he'd failed Her.

Yet self-recriminations couldn't quell his excitement; *he'd made it to another realm!* If he ever got back, even the Druid Council would have to bow before him and acknowledge him as the greatest mystic of all time. He'd experienced wonders that few ever imagined, seen gods, dragons, and creatures of legend in their native lands. He'd drunk the Water of Life. The things that he could learn here dwarfed all the knowledge of Druid lore and could lead to more power than he'd ever dreamed of.

If he lived, the Seer reminded himself as Garm took a bounding leap. He'd never imagined the dangers that he faced now, or had faced since joining this cursed company. Every day their lives seemed in greater danger. The Seer missed his cozy home in Madrone, delicious foods served by silent retainers before a warm fire. Yet he wouldn't trade this experience for anything.

The fog grew thicker, yet still Garm ran uphill, and the three companions hung on for life. The Seer clung tightly to Karl, although not willingly. All his youth he'd been bullied by fools like Karl, big and strong with nothing but luck of their birth to claim superiority. To Karl, he'd never be anything but a small, skinny man, beneath contempt. Even their rivalry seemed one-sided; training on the Isle had taught the Seer powers greater than Karl would ever know, but Roselyn and Eloise never looked at him the way that all women looked at Karl.

The Seer cursed himself for his weakness. He'd given up such petty concerns years before; *why had they resurfaced? Because of Eloise and Roselyn?* Both were beautiful and strong-willed, like steel lilies with razor-sharp petals. Their touch had ignited coals in him that he'd thought long extinguished. More, they accepted him, and they weren't afraid of him, even after seeing his magic at its fiercest. He'd never met women like them, never dreamed that women would take him by the scruff and force him into pleasures that he'd long ago tried to forget. The Seer feared to fall in love with them; his duty to the Lady had to come first, and while he never doubted his courage, he wasn't certain that he was strong enough to deny love, not even for She who was his life.

A great light shined ahead of them. The Seer glanced over Karl's shoulder, through the blowing strands of Eloise's hair, while trying not to bang his forehead against Karl's steel helmet. Ahead of them rose a great mountaintop, and brilliant light beamed down upon its top. Garm loped uphill, never slowing, ever closer to the light.

Tall plants grew around the mountaintop, and
Garm pushed into them. The Seer was amazed to see
strange plants of all sorts fly past them, as if all the plants
of every world gathered here in the bright light of this
mountaintop. A strange roaring noise echoed, and the
warm moisture in the air fell in heavy drops.

Suddenly Garm slowed, and with a mighty leap,
he jumped up onto a wide, weather-beaten rock into the
great stream of light. The three companions sat
unmoving upon Garm's back and stared down at the
source of the light.

The Well of Hvergelmir was huge. Hvergelmir
looked as if the top of the mountain had been sheared
off and filled with deep water, frothing and churning as it
crashed in great waves. From beneath the water beamed
a bright white light, splashing into thousands of rainbows
before their blinking eyes. Tall spumes of foam burst
skyward from the violent, thrashing waves, and its steady
rain fell upon them. The far side of Hvergelmir was
almost too distant to be seen, hidden by tall waves and
rainbows. In seven places, vast waters spilled over its
rocky walls, out of the well; one poured nearby and fed
the river Gjoll, which flowed down past the Gates of
Niflhiem. The Seer stared amazed, and seriously
wondered if the Well of Hvergelmir was the source of all
the rivers of Yggdrasil.

The roar of the waters pouring out of Hvergelmir
was deafening; they had to shout to be heard.

"We're supposed to fish in this?" Karl shouted.

The Seer shook his head; *why did Karl bother asking questions when he already knew the answer?* Was Karl baiting him ... or asking to be derided in front of Eloise? The Seer didn't hate Karl; he could never forgive Grusshire, but Eloise and Roselyn had also been part of that evil deed, and he couldn't bring himself to hate them ... not anymore.

The Seer didn't answer Karl but grabbed two handfuls of Garm's thick, wet fur, and slid down off of the monster. Hel had sent them here to find fish and he doubted if she'd be wrong.

Hel deeply worried the Seer; Hel was a monster more dangerous than any dragon. Unlike Nidhogg or the Guardian of the Underground Lake, Hel was beautiful, poised, and cultured. It was easy to run from a horror that breathed fire and bore giant fangs. With a creature like Hel, crafty beyond mortal cunning, you never knew when to run ... until it was too late.

Perhaps it was already too late. He'd foolishly led their company into Hel's domain, and now they were her prisoners. Hel had let three of them go, but with Garm as their only protection, what hope had they but to return, unless they wanted to face her father, Loki, who'd be furious after his wounding by Garm? And, with pets like Garm and Nidhogg, they'd be trapped in Niflhiem unless Hel gave them leave to depart.

Karl handed the Seer the heavy net and then helped Eloise dismount before he slid off. Garm stood there, sniffing at the rocks.

49

"I'll see if any of these plants are edible," Eloise shouted, fighting to be heard over the roar of the waters.

"Don't eat anything until I examine it," the Seer shouted back. "Stay close, and call for Garm, if you need him."

Eloise met his eyes and she smiled at him; beautiful and youthful, almost glowing in the brilliant light. The Seer's heart melted. Then the Seer watched as Eloise smiled at Karl. The Seer bowed his head; no one could miss the desire in Eloise's eyes when she looked at Karl.

Suddenly Eloise stepped forward. She grabbed the Seer and kissed him, then pushed him away and kissed Karl in the same manner. Then Eloise turned her back on both of them and scrambled down the rocks, out of the direct shine of the light, into the forest of tall plants.

The Seer turned to look at Karl, who stood looking back. A confused moment passed, and then both men shrugged.

"We'd better get started," Karl shouted.

Together they approached the frothing Well of Hvergelmir, climbed down onto its giant slippery rocks, wet with spray, and in some places thick with moss and green slime. The huge rocks seemed tiny compared to the vast, agitated lake. Near its churning surface, its roar deafened, and shouting became useless. With pointing fingers they signaled to each other as best they could, until they climbed out onto a huge boulder overlooking the wild waters.

Karl laid the net down and began to unfold it. Despite Karl's obvious annoyance, the Seer took one end of its long rope and tied it to a large outcropping of rock. Then Karl took firm hold of the other rope, lifted the net, and threw it into the water.

Instantly the water snatched up the net and tore it from Karl's grasp. The rope whipped far out and vanished beneath the waves. Karl stood there, blinking stupidly, and the Seer sighed. Slowly he tapped on Karl's shoulder, and then he pointed to the other rope still tied to the outcropping of rock.

They hauled the net back in, pulling together as hard as they might, and tied the other end around the same outcropping. Then they cast the net back in. The pounding waves of Hvergelmir pulled hard, but the net stayed lashed to the rocks. Slowly they pulled with all of their strength combined, and several times the waves almost pulled them both into its waters. When that happened, they had to release the net; no mortal could swim in the Well of Hvergelmir.

When they finally pulled out the net, many large fish wriggled, trapped in it, beside other strange aquatic creatures, most of which they'd never seen or imagined. Quickly they sorted through their catch and tossed anything that they didn't recognize back into the deadly waters. Still, they had a mighty catch, with several big salmon and fat tuna among them. They wrapped the net around the large flopping fish, and it took both of them to carry it back.

As they started to ascend, a great wave crashed over the rock and slammed against their backs. But they held on and quickly climbed out of reach of the angry waters, although still bathed in the light of the Well.

"Perhaps it's the still-beating heart of Ymir that churns the waters," the Seer shouted. "Ymir, the evil giant, was the first being in the Norse mythos, and that brightness could be the Light of Creation itself."

"You don't really believe that, do you?" Karl shouted.

"Who knows?" the Seer shouted. "Who cares? Look where we are! How many mortals get to see a sight such as this?"

"More than I want to see," Karl shouted. "Let's find Eloise and get out of here!"

The Seer shook his head, but helped lift the heavy net, now filled with wriggling fish, and carried it back. Garm still stood there, with Eloise, who was petting the massive wolf. At her feet lay a huge pile of fruits and vegetables.

"You won't believe it," Eloise shouted. "There's plants here of every kind, so many that I couldn't count. They all seem to be ripe. I found these easily, and many others that I couldn't identify."

"More than enough," Karl shouted, and he held open their fish-filled net. "Drop them in, and let's go!"

The crowd that greeted them as they returned to
Niflhiem was vast, larger than any gathering that they'd
ever seen. The dead crowded inside the Gates of
Niflhiem by the tens of thousands, and all cheered as the
companions rode up onto the bridge. The Seer was
deafened by the noise of their cheering and amazed by
the sight: he could see no end to the crowd, no break in
its multitude save for a single wide path back to Hel's
hall.

Deposited by Garm upon the drawbridge over
the river Gjoll, the Seer and Karl carried the heavy net
back to Eljudnir with Eloise in the lead. Eloise walked
proudly, fearlessly, bowing to the festering corpses as if
she were their rightful sovereign. The Seer wondered
where Eloise found the courage; the dead couldn't harm
them against the wishes of Hel yet, even with all his
training, they were ghastly to look at.

The Seer, Karl, and Eloise entered the hall of
Hel like victorious champions returning from the wars.
Many tables with benches had been set up, most filled
with dead men and women seated on benches. All
stood and cheered loudly as Eloise entered. Karl and
the Seer trailed closely after her, carrying their bundle.

A group of dead women approached from the
side and took the heavy net from them, and then
vanished into the crowd with their food.

Hel was seated center at her table before the
ever-burning bonfire with Roselyn, Rafe, and Seren.
Three empty chairs were set closest to Hel, and Eric was

stood behind her. Unlike the tables of the dead, their table had dishes and platters upon it, although there was as yet no food. Many bottles of wine sat in buckets of Gjoll's cold water, and several bottles were already half-empty.

"On the count of three, bow to Hel," Eloise whispered to Karl and the Seer. "One..., two...,"

Together they bowed; Eloise performed an elaborate curtsy, and Hel stood and raised her wine glass. The dead fell instantly silent.

"Welcome back, my friends," Hel said with a bright, godly smile. "Come, sit with us, and tell us of your mission. Were you successful?"

"Indeed," Eloise bowed, and the dead cheered again.

Hel glanced at her dead and their cheering subsided.

"You must forgive my subjects," Hel said. "Here they have no needs and are beyond all wants. To see others toil with the daily requirements of life, such as they once had, is a great joy to them ... when all other joys have failed."

"We are pleased as well," Eloise said. "We brought many kinds of fish and fresh vegetables, but I fear that we didn't bring enough for everyone."

"The dead don't eat," Hel said. "I seldom dine, but tonight I'll break my fast. This is a great day for me, for all of Niflhiem, when the love of one dead has proven so strong that the living leave their world and journey to the aid of one fallen. Never shall this day be forgotten; we must mark it with great celebration, and as soon as my servants prepare our dinner, with great feasting!"

The dead cheered again. Eloise repeated her curtsy, and Karl and the Seer awkwardly bowed behind her. Then they circled around the tables; Hel directed Eloise to her right and the Seer to her left. Karl took the chair on the other side of Eloise, next to Roselyn.

Together they told of Hvergelmir and their journey each way. The dead listened intently, hanging on every word. The Seer asked Hel many questions about Hvergelmir, but she reported that she knew little more than what the legends told.

The dead women-cooks returned, not a moment too soon, carrying steaming platters whose smell perfumed the rotten air of Eljudner. The largest salmon was placed in front of Karl, the fat tuna in front of Rafe. Both were beautifully cooked and heavily garnished with freshly-baked vegetables. Other platters held smaller fish, surround by various kinds of vegetables, all steaming and cooked to perfection.

Despite their hunger, they waited for Rafe to recite a blessing over the food, and then they ate slowly, painfully aware of all the eyes. The dead watched each mouthful, each swallow. The Seer found eating difficult, but he was too hungry to care. He had three helpings of tuna and many yellow squash, which Hel told him was one of her favorites.

The Seer tried not to stare at Hel, but whenever their eyes met, her stunning beauty amazed him. The power of her eyes was entrancing, mesmerizing. He often found himself blushing, forcibly tearing his eyes away from her.

"I'm always interested in knowledge," the Seer said to Hel. "I've read two eddas on Norse history, but I'd love to hear it told by one who was there."

"That's a very long tale," Hel smiled warmly at him. "Don't worry; I remember it clearly, and I'll teach you all that I recall. It takes a long time to tell, but there's no hurry; you'll have plenty of time to learn it ... and anything else that you wish."

The Seer grinned, trying to mask his concern. *Plenty of time?* Exactly how long was Hel planning on keeping them there? Her offer wasn't without attraction: *what great secrets he could learn from the daughter of a God!* Yet, what would he do with those secrets if he never escaped Niflhiem? Hel met his stare, her dark eyes shining clear and bright into his, and the Seer forced a confident smile in return, but he felt like a trapped mouse being toyed with by the most cunning of vipers.

Chapter 5

Hel's Audience

KARL

Karl stopped short, snagging the tip of his sword in Rafe's mail.

"Good," Rafe scowled.

"Stop relying on your shield," Karl said. "Use your whole body; turn sideways and your shield will follow; you'll expose less target."

"I liked Eric's big shield better than this one," Rafe said. "Let's take a break."

"Get some water," Karl agreed, and he stood still while his old friend limped to the bench, his heavy arms hanging as if his sword and shield were lead weights. Seren helped Rafe disarm so that he could remove his helm, and she forced a fresh cup of the Water of Life into his hands. Rafe drank greedily, sweat pouring from his face. Karl was almost as exhausted as Rafe, but he waited in silence; the appearance that he didn't need as much water was a psychological tactic against any foe. Rafe was getting better, but he had much to learn. Rafe still wasn't a challenge to Karl, but Karl had to concentrate; if Karl gave Rafe an opening, then the horse-trainer would take it.

"My turn," Roselyn said.

Standing in her father's bright armor, Roselyn held the long sword that Hel had lent her in front of her with both hands. Karl took several deep breaths, trying to bring down his body temperature; Roselyn was still a rank novice with little strength, but she was fast, agile, and determined.

Seren had started their lessons, asking Karl to teach her to fight, and then they all began training. Karl showed them his basic moves with long bones that Hel provided: they didn't ask where the bones came from. Yet Seren and Eloise were terrible and quickly quit; Eloise had no desire to learn to fight, and Seren lacked the strength and stamina; Karl suspected that she had started the lessons just to give them something to do.

Roselyn stabbed, almost reaching Karl's face.

"Slower," Karl said. "This is practice; we don't want to kill each other."

Roselyn nodded, but held her sword pointed at Karl.

"Is Hel still watching?" Roselyn asked.

Karl stepped to the right, forcing Roselyn to pivot. Behind Roselyn, Karl saw Hel seated upon her throne, her radiant eyes fixed upon them. He could've just glanced over, but Karl knew better than to take his eyes from Roselyn's sword; he'd taught them that on their first day.

"She's still watching," Karl answered.

"When is she going to decide?" Roselyn asked, sliding her stance, raising her sword. "It's been three days!"

"She has no reason to hurry," Karl reminded Roselyn. "How often does she get company in Niflhiem?"

"Well, the fish are starting to go bad," Roselyn said. "Soon you'll have to get more. Then what? Will she build us a house? Do we start a garden?"

"Do you want me to talk to her?" Karl asked.

"No!" Roselyn said fiercely. "She already has you wrapped around her finger."

"*What?*"

Suddenly Roselyn stabbed inside of Karl's borrowed shield, stopping with her tip just touching his mail shirt.

"Easily distracted," Roselyn commented, smiling wickedly.

"You didn't mean that, did you?"

Roselyn paused and frowned. "Not yet."

"I-I ...!" Karl stammered, but Roselyn suddenly walked away.

Karl glanced at Hel, feeling self-conscious. *He wasn't attracted to Hel!* Hel was undeniably beautiful, even when dressed, but he'd seen her dead legs; every day they left Hel's hall and stood outside while she bathed. How could he love a woman like that? *How could Roselyn think that he ...?*

Karl sighed and walked over to the bench. The Seer was sitting there, downcast, his face in his hands. They'd spoken little since the feast, and Karl was glad of it. Yet the Seer spoke to Hel more than the rest of them combined, staying up late each night in deep discussion. If anyone knew her mind, the Seer did.

"When's Hel going to decide?" Karl asked him bluntly.

"Eh? Oh, that," the Seer said. "It's complicated. She has a lot to consider."

"Like what?"

"You wouldn't understand."

"Meaning that you're too stupid to explain it?" Karl smiled.

The Seer glared up at him. "You've no right to call others stupid."

"Let's see how stupid you are," Karl said. "Insult me again and I'll cut out your tongue."

"Don't blame me if the truth is insulting," the Seer sneered. "You wouldn't understand Hel because you don't know Norse legends. Norse faith is very fatalistic; it clearly predicts the end of their world, of all worlds, including ours. Eric's tale of the final battle doesn't end well: Norse legends say that, at the end of Ragnarrock, a fire-demon call Black Surt will come from Muspell, and from his sword shall pour great flames, and all the worlds of men and gods shall be consumed by fire."

"So?"

"How easy that is to ask that when you're mortal," the Seer said. "We'll both be long dead by then, but what of Hel? What happens to Hel when flames consume Niflhiem? Doesn't she have the right to survive, to fight for her survival, as we do? Her part in the Norse myths has yet to come; when the God Baulder dies and enters Hel's realm, then Odin himself shall come before Hel. She's only a half-goddess, yet she must stand ready to defy the King of the Gods, if need be."

"Why?" Karl asked. "What will the King of the Gods want?"

"Odin will ask of her the same thing that we're asking," the Seer said. "He'll want her to release Baulder, the dead God of Nobility, who will then be one of her subjects."

"Will she do it?"

"Who knows? It could happen tomorrow ... or thousands of years from now. Hel would gladly spare him, if it happened today, because she wants to survive. But the Norse legends come from the Norns, the Stygian

Witches, whom the Greeks called the Fates, and my masters called the Wyrd. They say that Hel will refuse, and they're never wrong. Something must happen to make Hel change her mind, although she can't guess what that will be. She may need to refuse Odin, and her reasons may be valid at that time.

"That's why she hesitates to release Eric's soul," the Seer explained. "Her challenge to Odin's request will seem powerless if she's already given up one of her subjects ... to a group of mortals ... simply for friendship's sake. But she hasn't refused us yet, and we mustn't hurry her."

"Why not?" Karl asked.

"Because ...," the Seer started, but then he faltered, staring as if he hadn't considered rushing Hel.

"And you call me stupid," Karl said. "She's manipulating you like a toy, dangling ancient magics before your eyes."

The Seer glared up at Karl, but then he lowered his head.

"You may be right," the Seer said reluctantly. "Hel's ageless, and far more powerful than I'll ever be. She may be toying with me ... and I'll never know ... unless she wishes for me to perceive it."

Karl stared horrified at the Seer. The Druid had never spoken to him like this before, as an equal, and never looked so depressed and defeated.

"You wouldn't be telling me this if things weren't really bad," Karl said.

"It's the Lady," the Seer confessed. "She's gone ... or ignoring me. I've always felt Her listening to my prayers, but now ... all is silent. I've failed Her, and I fear that She's abandoned me."

Karl sat in silent reverie. If the Lady had led them here, then he'd assumed that She would lead them home. What if She abandoned them? Without Her help, they were trapped in an alien world; even if they could escape Niflhiem, where would they go?

Karl recalled the rapids pouring out of Yggdrasil, the river that had almost carried them over the brink. Perhaps Titania could walk upon those rushing waters, but no boat could ever sail up that river. The 'crack in the world' was a one-way entrance, not an exit that mortals could use. Without the Lady, they'd never see Earth again.

They all went outside while Hel bathed, but none wandered far from Hel's hall. Several of Hel's newest subjects entered; the Seer explained that Hel would bleed them to fill her bath. Soon they departed, looking much paler, and the companions walked around or sat upon the hard rock for an hour.

As always, Eric told them when Hel was finished. Then Eric entered Hel's hall with them and stayed during their meal. Their fish was still good; Karl suspected that they were storing them in the icy waters of Gjoll.

"The Seer has spoken to me of your urgency," Hel said as they ate. "I don't share such feelings; years to you are but moments to me. I'm still undecided about Eric, and I must know more about each of you before I can determine this matter. Therefore, this evening I'll hold an audience with each of you individually. Perhaps together we can resolve this issue to everyone's benefit."

Karl swallowed hard. Hel seemed nice enough, and he liked the idea of talking to her without the other's listening, but Karl felt anxious, a little afraid of being alone with her.

"Karl, you met Eric first, did you not?" Hel asked.

"Yes."

"Then you shall be my first audience."

Dinner lasted far longer than the food. Eric recited the ancient tales while they ate, legends of the Norse Gods in the early days. Hel was mentioned rarely, but Eric told how she was born of Loki and Angrboda Giantess, with two brothers, Fenris the Master-Wolf and Jorgamund the Midgard Serpent. Fenris was a wolf far surpassing Garm, such that he defied the strength of all of the Norse Gods combined, and had to be bound in a magical cord to be kept from devouring everything. Jorgamund was a great serpent, so dangerous that Odin cast him into the sea, where he grew so long that he encircled the entire Earth and could hold his tail in his great, fanged mouth. Karl shuddered when he thought about it; with such terrible monsters for brothers, what was Hel?

Finally Eric's tale ended, although Eric had recited only the earliest parts of the legends. Then Hel excused herself, wishing to dress for their audiences, and they all went outside while she changed. The wait seemed to take forever.

"You may enter now," Eric said to Karl.

One massive door to the great hall swung slowly open, just wide enough for one person to enter. Karl slipped inside and the door closed behind him. Eljudnir was just the same as he'd seen it moments before, the large fire and torches endlessly burning, their black smoke filtering through the thick cobwebs and out of the hole in the roof. The remains of their feast were gone; Hel must have cleared them, for it was too soon for the eternally slow Ganglot and Ganglati to have finished. Then Karl noticed: Ganglot and Ganglati were nowhere to be seen. They hadn't exited the main door; they were simply gone.

Only one table remained before the bonfire with one chair before it, and Hel's throne sat opposite it. The table was clear, with not even a glass or wine bottle atop it. Hel was standing in front of it, dressed in a fancy gown that Karl had never seen.

"Welcome, dear Karl," Hel said. "Come, join me."

Karl approached cautiously. Hel stood by the table wearing a gown of red, looking very different from her usual black. This dress was long, low cut, and a red spiderweb necklace covered with sparkling gems hung from Hel's slender neck. She was radiant, resplendent, and very ... human.

"Please sit, Karl," Hel gestured to the empty chair beside her.

Karl walked closer, feeling awkward. Just out of arm's reach, Karl stopped and bowed slightly, and Hel laughed. Her voice was musical, echoing with delight, and Karl felt her delight wash over him. As before, the gloom of Niflhiem faded momentarily as Hel laughed, and slowly returned when she stopped.

Hel gently reached out, took Karl's arm, and drew him to the waiting chair; Karl went worriedly, recalling her tremendous strength, which he'd only felt once; today Hel seemed weak and soft, almost delicate. Karl sat and watched as Hel walked around the table to her throne, mesmerized by her willowy sway. Hel sat upon her throne with silent poise and smiled brightly at Karl. The invisible force of her eyes seemed doubled as she focused entirely upon him. She leaned forward, set her elbows on the table, and cupped her chin with both hands.

"Tell me about yourself," Hel grinned.

Karl tried to lower his eyes out of the tingling glare of Hel's half-goddess stare, but then his gaze fell upon her voluptuous cleavage, and Karl quickly closed his eyes, although their image seemed frozen in his mind. Karl forced his eyes open and met Hel's potent stare, preferring it to blatantly staring at her chest.

"Um ..., what?" Karl asked.

Hel smiled widely, narrowing her eyes.

"Start with your mother. Tell me about her."

"My mother?" Karl asked.

"It's as good a starting place as any," Hel smiled.

Karl began speaking, describing his mother, how fussy she was about dirty hands at the table, and her fine cooking. He ended up telling Hel more about his father, who was very strong, and stories about growing up on a farm. He eventually described his brother and their neighbors, and the places that he'd go to escape from chores.

Hel asked many questions and laughed often. At her sly queries, Karl confessed about his dalliances with the neighbor's wife, and why he'd run away. Then he quickly changed the subject and told her of his first real fight at Ferny Creek, which had seemed like a great battle at the time, although it seemed almost childish now. Then he told her how Captain Sir Gunderson had hired him to be a guard, and of Bristlen and Demril.

"How interesting," Hel said, fascinated. "What was Demril like?"

"I really didn't see much of it," Karl smiled. "I only went there once, got drunk, and then ... robbed."

"Where in Demril did you get drunk?"

"The Bent Hook, Demril's only tavern."

"What did you drink?"

"Just beer; I think it was all that they had."

"Did you get the beer yourself?"

"No, the beermaids brought it, once I'd given the ale-master two coppers."

"Beermaids? Were they pretty?"

"Well, yes."

"Were they as pretty as ... Roselyn?"

Karl hesitated. He'd been talking freely, absently, and suddenly felt unsure.

"I don't know," Karl lied. "They were just ... pretty."

"Were they as pretty as me?"

Karl foundered. His mind raced to find a suitable answer but none came to mind.

"Um, well ...," he stammered.

Tears began to drip down Hel's smooth cheeks.

"Then ... I am ... ugly," Hel said, and her face twisted with grief. Hel began to sob, and Karl trembled, not knowing what to do.

"No, Hel, don't ... cry! You're not ugly! How could you be ugly? I ... don't know what to say; you showed me your ..." Karl waved one hand under the table, indicating her legs, "but what I see now is beautiful beyond description, more beautiful than I can say, so beautiful that it hurts just to look at ...!"

Karl froze, realizing that he'd said too much. *Why did he always blather when he was confused?*

"Y-you're ... not ugly," Karl stammered, averting his eyes.

A single finger reached out, touched his chin, and turned Karl's head to face her. Hel was smiling triumphantly, almost beaming. The moisture on her cheeks gleamed in the firelight, reflecting flames off of her milky skin.

"I'm pleased," Hel said smoothly, smiling widely. "My upper half, at least, you find appealing. Am I truly that beautiful?"

"Yes," Karl admitted, trapped in her gaze.

Hel inhaled deeply and exhaled heavily, her deep cleavage flexing.

"Dear, sweet Karl," Hel said. "You may not believe this, Karl, but that's the first time that anyone has ever called me beautiful, and I'm far older than you can imagine. Odin cast me here when I was only a child, and my life has been very lonely. The dead are poor company; they slowly go mad, until I must feed them to Garm and Nidhogg. They have no will unless I give it to them. It's been an effort to keep Eric as free of my influence as possible, in case I choose to release him. But I am afraid, Karl; very, very afraid."

"Of what?"

"Of everything," Hel said. "I know nothing of life outside of these walls."

"But you can leave anytime," Karl said. "I saw you walk out of the gate."

"I'm condemned to remain here, a prisoner, just like you," Hel said sadly. "That's why Odin banished me here."

Karl looked questioningly.

"My legs," Hel hissed through clenched teeth. "I killed a man, for his blood, so that I could heal my legs. I need my bath, Karl. Without it, I'm nothing, an invalid ..."

Hel began to cry again, harsh, racking sobs. Karl jumped up and ran around the table to her.

"So lonely!" she wept. "So lonely!"

Karl wrapped his arms around Hel and held her tightly. Hel cried against Karl's chest, lost in despair. Long they sat, embraced, and Karl felt pity well inside of him. Hel had lived a hard, lonely life with no one to care for her, born of an evil father and cast away from civilized folk, with a giantess for a mother and monsters for brothers. Karl tried not to notice the warmth of her womanly flesh or her soft touch that tingled him all over. He tried to think of Hel's dead legs, hidden by the drape of her gown. But even that evoked only pity from Karl's heart. Hel was trapped in this land of walking dead, to suffer eternally, with no hope in sight.

"Please, help me to my bed," Hel begged him.

Karl helped Hel stand, and slowly they moved away from the table. Hel's walk was stilted, with subtle, jerking movement, and Karl held her tight, fearful that she might fall without his support. Gently he held her as they crossed the great hall to her tall, covered bed. Hel reached out and pushed aside her shimmering black lace bed curtains and let Karl help her sit.

"Don't leave me," Hel whispered. "Please, stay with me. Talk to me."

Karl looked down at Hel's sad, tear-streaked face. She was so beautiful, so desirable, that Karl couldn't resist her. He knew that he should, although he couldn't recall any reason strong enough to draw him away from Hel's soft, clinging arms. Hel held him with a strength that he'd never felt before, soft yet irresistible, and she firmly drew him closer.

Fighting to resist her, Karl closed his hand upon the black lace curtains. Slowly, against his own will, Karl slid the curtain between them, hoping to break the fire of his lust, her immortal longing, and their overwhelming desire. But the dark, open lace was thinner than spiderwebs, and its sparkle only intensified Hel's entrancing beauty, her dark mystery. Karl's will evaporated.

Karl kissed Hel hard, ignoring the shimmering web between them. He seized her, pulled her against him, and her fingers squeezed against his back. They melted into each other, a moment frozen in time, lasting an eternity. Karl drew back just long enough to push away the mysterious curtain, and then they fell onto her bed, hungry mouths pressed, demanding and yielding. Long they kissed, entwined, and never had Karl felt so alive as in the arms of the Goddess of Death.

"I'll make you happy," Hel whispered. "We can live here together, forever! I'll give you golden apples that'll keep you young, and teach you things that no mortal knows. You'll be powerful beyond your imaginings. Oh, Karl! I can make you a God!"

Karl kept kissing Hel's smooth, white skin, but he never closed his eyes. She was so beautiful, divine, a Goddess; Karl had no power left, no strength to resist, and knew no reason why he should. Lost in the moment, Karl willingly surrendered. Karl closed his eyes, enrapt, and whispered back.

"I love ..."

Roselyn!

The thought leaked into Karl's mind like a forgotten dream. Love was what he felt for Roselyn, and suddenly all of the light inside him turned to shadow except for a tiny glow around her name. Hel was beautiful, more than Roselyn could ever equal, greater than human, and willing to give him all that she had. Karl desired Hel, cared for her, pitied her; would do anything for her. He was willingly Hel's. He wanted nothing but to be hers forever.

But Roselyn!

Slowly Karl's kisses faltered. Gritting his teeth in anguish, Karl pulled away, agonized, torn between desires. Inch by inch, Karl extricated himself from Hel's fiery embrace. Numbly he pulled free and pushed her back.

"No!"

Hel began to cry. She seized his wrists with a strength that even the Wolflord couldn't match.

Her touch seared and drew him, but he couldn't submit. Deftly Karl resisted, finally pulled loose, and pushed back her glimmering bedcurtains. Slowly he rose from her bed, fighting to ignore her pathetic sobs, his flaming desires, and Hel's unquenchable beauty. Fighting his own muscles, Karl slowly limped away from her bed, across the wide hall.

Blinded by tears, Karl struggled for each step, trying to focus on Roselyn, but the delicious taste of Hel's kisses, the memory of her perfect form, invaded his thought, combated his reason. Karl stumbled, then kept staggering until his hands pressed against the heavy wooden doors. On the doors Karl pushed and banged his fist, but to no avail; the doors wouldn't budge. Hel commanded her doors; Karl couldn't escape.

"Karl!" Hel called from her bed, her voice strained with sorrow. "Come back!"

Karl struggled as if every muscle that he owned wanted to push away from the doors and run back and leap into Hel's warm, passionate embrace. Karl tried to picture Hel's legs, to remember her father, her brothers, any reason that would sustain him, that could strengthen his resolve. But all that Karl recalled was her sad, immortal tears, Hel's ultimate loveliness, the tingling magic of her touch, and the heat of her ardor. Karl wanted Hel more than he'd ever wanted anything before.

But Roselyn!

Slowly, as if it too were fighting, the door moved. It creaked open, just a crack, and Karl fell through it onto the rocky ground outside. Hands quickly grabbed him, accompanied by worried voices that Karl barely heard over the pounding of his own heart. His ears heard only Hel's pleas, his eyes saw only the perfect vision of her.

Slowly the door closed behind him like the lid of a coffin upon all his dreams. Karl had lost ... or won; he couldn't tell.

Chapter 6

Hel's Audience 2

ROSELYN

Roselyn let out a stifled scream as Karl fell out of the door. Eloise reached him first, but stood aside so that Rafe could help lift him. Karl was sobbing uncontrollably, inconsolately trembling, unhearing their pleas as they held him and begged him to answer. They drug Karl away from the door and set him against the wall; Roselyn held him on one side, Eloise on the other, and the others crowded around, save Eric, who stood sadly watching.

"Karl, snap out of it!" Rafe shouted.

"What happened?" Eloise demanded.

"I suspected as much," the Seer said. "Hel's audiences aren't as simple as they sounded. We may each face a challenge."

"What did she do to him?" Roselyn asked.

"Only he knows," the Seer shrugged. "It was never a life-or-death struggle; if Hel wanted us dead then we would've been killed the moment that we arrived. I can't even say if Karl survived his challenge or not."

"What she want?" Seren asked.

"Don't you know?" the Seer asked. "Hel wants us."

Roselyn cradled Karl in her arms. What had Hel done to him? What could they do to stop her, if she did it again? Roselyn had never seen Karl so traumatized. But what could mortals do against a half-goddess in her own realm, surrounded by legions of walking dead? The bones of Grusshire were nothing compared to the vast population of Niflhiem, and Hel had Nidhogg and Garm, either of which they'd be helpless against.

Slowly Karl recovered, but he refused to say what had happened inside Eljudnir. Half an hour passed, and then the door slowly opened again.

"Roselyn," Eric said, looking ashamed, as if he didn't want to utter the words. "Roselyn, it's your turn."

Roselyn sat on the ground, almost uncomprehending. *Go inside?* After what Hel had done to Karl?

"You might as well go," the Seer said. "We'll all have to, eventually. Even a beggar is master in his own house, and this is Hel's domain."

Roselyn took a deep breath and steeled her resolve; Hel may be a half-goddess, but no one hurts Roselyn's companions with impunity. Glancing at the others, Roselyn turned toward the door.

"Remember me!" Karl said suddenly, desperately.

Roselyn looked down, surprised. Karl's frantic eyes were almost pleading. Roselyn swallowed hard, and then she stormed inside. The mighty door closed behind her.

"What did you do to Karl?" Roselyn shouted as she stomped angrily toward Hel.

Hel said nothing, seated imperiously upon her throne before a single table, looking surprised as Roselyn stormed up. Roselyn stamped right up to her table, faced Hel defiantly, and glared her angriest stare.

Hel slowly smiled.

"I kissed him."

Roselyn staggered. *Hel ... kissed Karl?* Karl kissed Hel? The Goddess of Death, a half-living, half-corpse ... *Karl kissed her?*

"You love him, don't you?" Hel asked.

Roselyn stammered an incomprehensible response.

"Dear child, don't worry," Hel smiled, laughing softly. "I wouldn't steal your love. But Karl is a handsome man, isn't he? Do you know how many centuries it's been since I kissed anyone? Forgive me; I couldn't resist. Come, let's not quarrel. Sit and talk with me."

"What did you ... do to Karl?" Roselyn asked again, although her vehemence felt wounded.

"Karl and I talked."

"About ...?"

"Now, Roselyn, it was a private conversation. Karl may tell you, if he wishes to, but a poor host I'd be to command private audiences and then make them public. You may ask Karl later. Please, sit and talk. You're not afraid of talking, are you?"

Roselyn considered as she glared at Hel; Hel was unnervingly beautiful. On Earth, kings would gladly war over her hand. But Roselyn wouldn't be intimidated; she understood the effects of beauty, the power that it wielded. Hel wouldn't have that power over her. Roselyn glanced at the single chair and sat down.

"Nice dress," Roselyn scowled.

"Do you like it? I had it made years ago, and the necklace is dwarven. I think I look best in red, don't you?"

Roselyn frowned. "What do you want to talk about?"

"You, my dear; even if I wanted to, I couldn't release Eric's spirit to strangers. I must know each of you, intimately, your histories and purposes. But I mostly wished to see you. You're very beautiful; something that we have in common, I believe."

"I'm mortal."

"Sadly true," Hel frowned. "What a pitiful doom mortal beauty is! Mortal beauty is transitory, is it not? Beauty sprouts with youth and blossoms in the morning sun. Then beauty withers and fails, leaving only its stem, a pale memory of a greatness which never returns. Perhaps that's part of mortal beauty, that it's a gift for the young who know not what to expect of the mirror when those days are past."

"You're not young," Roselyn said.

"My beauty isn't mortal. Yet, what good does beauty do me? My subjects can't appreciate anything; they're my possessions, their very thoughts subject to my will. How many men's eyes have you turned, Roselyn? How many doors has your loveliness opened? Doors don't exist for me, save only the gates that trap me here. You, Roselyn, know beauty far better than I."

"It's vain to worry about the ravages of time," Roselyn said.

"How little you understand of time," Hel said. "To me, you were all born yesterday and won't live past tomorrow. Ages fly past me, alone and untouched. Yet there are ways to cheat time. Golden apples exist, golden apples that preserve. Youth dwells in them, unchanging, never aging, growing in secret places all over Yggdrasil. I have them; they're my chief meal, the favorite of all the Gods. With golden apples, even mortals may live forever. Eternal youth, free and without obligation, all in the bite of a single golden apple.

"I eat one a month, and I never age. Frigg, Odin's wife, eats one every day. It's a pity that golden apples have no seeds or I'd plant groves of them. They're the most prized possession in Yggdrasil, jealously guarded. No one knows when, or where, a new tree will sprout, but they never die, so each goes on growing apples forever."

Hel reached down and cast back a black cloth at the foot of her throne. Beneath it was a silver bowl filled with golden apples. Hel lifted the bowl and set it on the table between them.

"Pretty, are they not?"

Roselyn's eyes widened. Each apple shined as if made of precious metal; like ordinary apples, save that they were colored metallic gold. Even their stems and leaves were bright gold.

"Have one," Hel smiled.

Roselyn hesitated. The apples looked so good; like Hel, they almost glowed. Roselyn's mouth watered; *eternal youth and beauty? Was Hel really offering her that?*

"Go ahead," Hel urged.

Slowly Roselyn reached out and took one. They were firm but not hard; like any other apple save for their shiny skin.

"Will they do anything else to me? Anything ... unnatural?"

"No. These apples keep you young for a short while, nothing else."

Roselyn lifted the golden apple and bit into it. It was sweet, ripe and flavorful, pure and wholesome like the Water of Life, only more so. Warmth seeped into Roselyn's body and she felt light and heady.

"How long will it last?"

"Who measures such things? Not forever, but even those who only occasionally eat golden apples never age. We don't grow heavy with years or wrinkled by cares. I only have one tree in my realm, but I eat sparingly, so I have plenty to spare. As long as you're here I'll share them with you."

"As long as we're here?" Roselyn asked. "You want us to stay, don't you?"

"Isn't that obvious? I'm trapped here, alone, with legions of dead and the two slowest servants in history. Having guests is my greatest pleasure, and I'm ... limited in such areas. I'd even have welcomed a lying scoundrel, and I was lucky enough to meet the most-honorable group that I could've hoped for. I won't hold you prisoner; I'm the jailor of the dead, a title forced upon me against my will. I won't be a jailor of the living as well. Were you in my place, a lonely prisoner, wouldn't you welcome friendly company?"

Roselyn took another bite of the apple; its vitality surged through her. Yes, in Hel's place, good company would be a priceless treasure.

"Tell me about your mother."

"What?"

"Your mother; tell me about her."

"Why?"

Hel smiled.

"Actually, it's a question that I've learned to ask when I want to know someone. Most people's earliest memories center around their mother, and by asking about her, they tend to talk about everything in their childhood. Unless they stop, they talk past their youth, often telling their whole life story, which was what I really wanted."

"I don't talk about my childhood."

"I understand. Your father, isn't it? Trust me; I know what it means to have an evil father. Nasty man, chasing his own daughter across England ... and torturing her friends. A pity that he's not Norse; when such men come to me I instruct Garm to play with his food.

"But you need fear him no more. All of the armies of England are nothing compared to my legions. You've only seen a fraction of my realm; Niflhiem is vast ... and crowded. Here you're protected, even from Loki."

"We can't stay ..."

"You most certainly can stay, although you don't have to. Think of what you're turning down. Look at the prize in your hand; I have enough apples for all of you, and I can bestow countless gifts. Treasure, power, and wisdom: all could be yours. I could build you a palace in any style that you wish, and you'd be together forever. You would have Karl ... forever ... and never grow old or ugly."

Roselyn glanced at the golden apple in her hand. Immortality and eternal beauty; *what woman could ask for more?* She and Karl could be together forever. *Where did she have to go, anyway?* Roselyn could never return to England, and they had no treasure to purchase a villa in France. Their villa could be here, with thousands of servants, and a half-goddess as their friend.

"I ... don't know," Roselyn stammered.

"That's all that I ask," Hel said. "I just want you to consider staying. You don't have to make up your mind right now. Take a year, or take a century; you won't age. Then you could go home, after your father's long in his grave. Stay ... until you've decided."

Roselyn struggled, confused. Hel was right; everywhere else was danger, poverty, old age, and death. With Hel's golden apples, they could live here for a thousand years and leave only when they tired of Niflhiem.

"You should finish that apple," Hel said. "It's wrong to waste such a gift. But perhaps you should finish it outside. It's late, and I need to speak to the others. Send in Eloise, if you will. And ... thank you, Roselyn. I look forward to us becoming close friends."

Roselyn slowly stood. She tried to utter some polite response but was too lost in her thoughts to continue. *Could she really live in Niflhiem?* Hel, with her legions, could provide them with anything. She could stay young forever and grow wise beyond mortal capacity until she was like Hel, a half-goddess. *Why would she want to leave?*

Slowly Roselyn walked to the door, which opened as she approached. She stepped out with a dazed expression.

"Roselyn?" Rafe asked. "Are you all right?"

"What she say?" Seren asked.

Roselyn looked at them, but she couldn't answer. *How could she tell them that she was considering staying? That she wanted them all to stay?* The others exchanged worried glances, but Roselyn said nothing.

Chapter 7

Hel's Audience 3

ELOISE

"Eloise," Eric said, "Hel will see you now."

"Roselyn?" Eloise ignored him.

Karl took Roselyn's right arm, the Seer took her left, and Rafe stood in front of Roselyn and softly called her name. Roselyn didn't seem as stunned as Karl had, but she looked visibly shaken.

"Eloise ...," Eric repeated.

Roselyn reached out to Eloise and placed a reassuring hand on her shoulder; Eloise didn't feel reassured. She looked at the doors of Eljudnir fearfully.

"I'm sorry," Eric whispered, and he laid his hand on Eloise's other shoulder.

Eloise looked at Eric and took a deep breath. She had grown indeed, she thought, if Eric was able to notice it. She was no longer a victim. She'd be strong, even against Hel.

Forcing each step, Eloise entered. The huge door closed behind her and Eloise found Hel, in a beautiful red gown, standing just inside the door.

"Welcome," Hel said. "I know that you're afraid. Believe me; I only want to talk."

"I'm not afraid," Eloise said.

"Good," Hel said. "Let's sit together."

Eloise saw a table with a wide bench before Hel's throne, near the great firepit. They walked toward it together, side-by-side. At the table, Hel sat upon the ornate bench and invited Eloise to sit beside her. Eloise did, and they faced the huge doors, their backs to the table.

"What did you do to Karl and Roselyn?" Eloise asked.

"Just talk."

"Just talk?"

"Not all talk is easy," Hel said. "News may stun as heavily as the hardest maul. I told them truths, some of which they weren't prepared to hear."

Eloise fell silent, wondering what truths could shatter her companions so.

"You've done well, leading the others to Niflhiem," Hel said. "I'm impressed."

"My mistakes have cost us," Eloise said gloomily.

"All mortals make mistakes," Hel said. "Mortals that never repeat a mistake are considered wise. If you've learned from your mistakes, then an even greater leader you'll be."

Eloise fell silent; she had to be wise against Hel.

"Tell me of your mother."

Eloise's eyes opened wide with wonder.

"My mother?"

"You knew her, did you not?"

"Yes, but she was taken away by Vikings when I was very young. She didn't come here, did she?"

"Only those who believe in an afterlife may enter it. You're a Christian Saxon, so I assume that your mother was. Unless she fully adopted the elder faith of the Norse, she'd never come to me."

"What about me?" Eloise asked. "I know that you exist, but I don't want to spend eternity wandering mindlessly about Niflhiem. I'm a Christian, but I've learned to honor the Druid Lady ... and you. What happens to my soul ...?"

"I can't say," Hel said. "Your soul is torn, the path of your life too short to show its complete route. Here I'll always welcome you, not as a subject, but as my friend. We are friends, aren't we?"

"I'd like to think that we are ..."

"Good, for we are much alike. You want what's best for your companions. Within my realm, my powers are far greater than you realize. There's much that I could grant you, if I knew your mind. What are your current plans?"

"We haven't discussed them," Eloise said. "I'd like to go home; if I don't claim my heritage soon, the king will take it, and my people will suffer."

"It seems that you must choose," Hel said. "Whose safety do you value most; your barony ... or your companions?"

"Why must I choose?"

"Look at what you dared by venturing here," Hel said. "Do you think that the journey back through The Portal will be easier?"

Eloise paused, considering. Hel didn't know that the 'crack in the world' was one way; even if they could swim or paddle up the rushing rapids, when the 'crack' opened, they'd be washed back by the waters of the underground lake, or they'd have to face the fire-breathing dragon that guarded it. Even if they escaped the lake-dragon, that path would lead them up more tunnels to the whirlpool, and then to the barren, frozen wasteland of the North Sea, to starve and freeze.

"Is there another route?"

"Bifrost, the Rainbow Bridge, leads to the lands of mortals," Hel said. "But not even a God may sneak past Heimdall's ever-vigilant eyes. Only the Valkyrie ride that bridge at will, but they carry passengers only toward Valhalla, never away from it. Even riding their winged steeds, you'd find danger. My father isn't a kind man; he'll kill you all, once he's torn the secret of the

Hidden Portal from your lips. Don't be deceived; Loki knows tortures such as would loosen even the tongues of Gods. No matter how much you fear him, you don't fear him enough."

"No route is safe, and the instant that we leave Niflhiem we'll be assaulted by Loki?" Eloise asked. "What other choice do we have?"

"You needn't choose right away," Hel said. "My father will soon tire of waiting for you and look elsewhere for ripe furrows to plant his seeds of malice. You may rest here until then, and I'll have my subjects build you a great hall, a palace for the living, and serve you until you're ready to depart. Here you'll be safe, even from Loki, until a secure path may be discovered."

"What if a safe exit is never found?"

"Then ... you'll be with Karl. That is what you want, isn't it?"

Eloise looked away. *Karl:* if Eloise had to choose one companions to stay beside her always, it would be Karl. Rafe had Seren now, and the Seer wouldn't want to stay with them after what they did to Grusshire. Roselyn ... well, they'd find a way.

Slowly Eloise thought about it; a home, here, safe from danger. Hel was a half-goddess with powers that could protect them forever.

"My mother wanted me to rule du Harmonn," Eloise said. "Yet I don't see how that's possible. Whichever way you decide, our quest is finished; if you keep Eric, then we can't continue, and if you release

Eric, then our quest is accomplished. I want to return home at once, but I see no safe route, nor do I see any way to maintain political control if I do get back. Earl Sir Guldwin will force me to marry and become a slave in his house. The king wouldn't let my mother rule; he'd gladly sell me to the highest bidder. I want to spare my company from harm, but I also want to honor my mother's wishes, and I can't do both."

"Your mother was a great woman, wasn't she?"

"She ruled du Harmonn amazingly well after father died, before the king sold her to Sir Vandislidge of France. She was very wise, beautiful, and commanded with a gentle voice ..."

"Poor Eloise! Lucky you were, even for so brief a time, to have a mother like that. Are you certain that she died?"

"No, but I suspect it," Eloise said. "If she were only a captive, then she would've sent word to me."

"Eloise, I can never replace her, but let me offer what I can. Let me be a mother to you now. I'll build you a great palace beside Gjoll, with gardens and fields that I'll have planted and irrigated. You can stay there with your friends, and I'll visit you every day."

"I'd have to ask the others."

"You're their leader, are you not?" Hel asked. "Their lives are in your hands, as their blood will be, should you fail. I can't give you du Harmonn, but would even your mother's barony be worth it if your companions die? What if Karl died, trying to get you home? How happily could you rule ... mourning the one that you love most?"

Eloise fell silent. She had no argument. *How could she lead her friends back into danger just for the unlikely chance of recovering her barony?* Hel was offering her more than safety. Here Eloise would never become ... the Wolfqueen. Here they could live together, safely, with no Viking or Saxon army chasing them, no magical giant attacking them in the night. They'd be free, as they were aboard ship, to live and love however they chose. She and Roselyn could share Karl and the Seer, and never let rivalry divide their friendship. Living in a magical world, the Seer would certainly be happy. Rafe and Karl ...

Rafe and Karl; *how happy would they be?* They'd be trapped inside these walls, never to leave, with nothing to do. Surrounded by miles of empty rock, filled with legions of dead, with Hel as their only friend; *would they ever truly be happy?*

"I don't know," Eloise said. "We certainly can't go anywhere without a plan for evading Loki. That may take some time. But I can't say how long; a day ... or a year? I'm not even sure where we're going. But I want to thank you, Hel. You've opened your home to us and given us shelter when we needed it most."

"You've given me more," Hel smiled. "Friendship and companionship in my loneliness; you'll always have my protection, even if you stay forever."

Eloise wrapped her arms around Hel, warmed by the tingle of her godly touch. Hel held Eloise tightly, slowly rocking, and Eloise felt like she'd returned to the arms of her mother.

"I can't say what we'll do, or when we'll leave," Eloise said, "but I'm in no hurry. If you like, I can recommend that we stay, at least until Loki stops chasing us."

"I'd like that," Hel said, and Eloise felt Hel's arms tighten around her.

Chapter 8

Hel's Audience 4

RAFE

"We are not staying!" Rafe said loudly as he stormed inside the door.

Rafe stopped as he saw Hel, standing just inside the door in a striking red gown with crimson spiderwebs sparkling about her neck. The huge door closed swiftly; it sounded to Rafe like cell doors in the dungeon of Castle Bristlen.

"I never said that you would stay," Hel said after the doors closed. "I offered, not insisted. Does my offer offend you?"

"I know what you said to Karl and Roselyn," Rafe said.

"I'm trying to protect them," Hel said. "Leave here and my father will kill you. You've defied him once and lived, which is more than any other mortal has dared. He won't give you the chance to defy him twice."

"You want us to stay to keep you company."

"Yes, I do."

Rafe glared at Hel, and she sighed.

"I intend no deception," Hel said. "Roselyn asked me as much, and I told her the same. Of course I want company! Do you blame me?"

Hel turned her back to him and spoke softly, her voice tinged with sadness.

"Year after year, century after century, here I've waited, imprisoned. For what? Until my loneliness drives me mad? Until the end of my world? What will I have then? A life lasting eons, each day as boring as the next, until I die at the end of time? Immortality is my curse, far worse than any malformation beneath my skirt.

"I'm not your jailor, Rafe. Loki's your jailor. Odin's my jailor. You share my prison, not by choice but by design of fate. If I leave, Odin'll cast me back here. If you leave, Loki'll kill you. I don't want you to die; does that make me your enemy? I only want what's best for everyone.

"How can I make you mortals understand? You've been trapped here only a few days. I've been here countless centuries, enduring beyond your comprehension. I know what it means to be trapped, more than you ever shall. Am I to blame for your imprisonment? How can you ... *shout at ... me?"*

Hel's voice cracked. Rafe stood shocked; Hel's shoulders suddenly slumped and her body began to shake. Confused, Rafe stepped to Hel's side, amazed to find tears streaming down her cheeks.

"I'm sorry!" Rafe said. "I thought that you were ..."

"You don't know, can't imagine, how long it's been," Hel sobbed. "Alone, always alone! No friendly voice, no conversation ..."

"Easy!" Rafe said, and he caught Hel before she collapsed. Rafe pulled Hel's arm over his shoulder and slowly helped her limp to her bench.

"Th-thank you," Hel whispered, and then she looked up at him with tear-filled eyes. "You have no idea how long it's been since I said 'thank you' to anyone. Who's here to thank? The dead have no choice but to obey. My servants are so pathetic that there's nothing to thank. Do you blame me for welcoming company?"

"I didn't mean to ...," Rafe fumbled an apology.

Hel leaned on Rafe's shoulder and kept crying. Rafe scolded himself and held her tight in his arms. *He should've understood, been more attentive.* He'd resented Hel; her claim to be a half-goddess defied every precept of Christianity, and to prove his faith he'd behaved as unchristianly as possible.

"You have to understand," Rafe said, "how difficult this is for me. Your very existence belies all that I believe ..."

"Why?" Hel sobbed. "This isn't your universe! There's no Christ here."

"The Bible says that the spirit of God is everywhere."

"You're outside of everywhere," Hel said. "You left your world behind, and your God with it. Don't expect me to sympathize. Once my people, the Norse Gods, freely traveled to your world. Now your new God has supplanted us, and only the Valkyrie may still travel across Bifrost. Our summer has passed. Now is our fall, and soon our winter shall come."

Rafe smiled. *His faith wasn't false;* the power of God was true, strong enough to drive out the old Gods.

Then Rafe looked at Hel. She was beautiful, each strand of her long black hair as perfect as the rest of her. If not for her dead legs she'd truly be a Goddess. Yet her tingling touch didn't frighten him. For all her power, Hel was trapped in this dead, miserable prison. He'd thought to protect his friends, but instead he'd scorned the one who most deserved his pity.

"I'm sorry," Rafe said. "I ... misunderstood."

"You don't like me," Hel said.

"I barely know you," Rafe said. "I just don't want you convincing them to stay."

"Why not?" Hel asked. "Because you don't want to stay? Because you wish to leave ... and not depart alone?"

"Yes," Rafe admitted. "You're world ... is too bizarre. We came here for a purpose, out of love for Eric. I came ... because I wanted to be with my friends. Valhalla and Valkyrie: Christ is what we should be seeking, and I'm a poor Christian if I don't lead them to His church."

"I won't stop you," Hel said. "I'll have my subjects build you a church, any kind that you wish. But you can't blindly run out of Niflhiem! Loki's waiting, and watching all the gates to my land. He'll force your secrets from you and then kill you. How will you fight Loki? Garm can't leave my walls for long. And the danger to Christians here is even greater; what happens to your souls if you die in this universe? Will you be able to reach Heaven? Even I don't know."

"I'd hoped that we could sneak out ...," Rafe said.

"You dare to believe that you're sneakier than the God of Mischief? Your faith has made you presumptuous! If not for Garm, do you truly think that you'd have survived your first encounter with my father?"

"No; we couldn't even endure his gaze."

"His gaze is the least of his powers," Hel said. "Oh, Rafe! I know that we're not close, but I would grieve if something dreadful happened to you."

97

Rafe held Hel close, comforted her and soothed her tears. Hel melted into his embrace and cried softly. The tingle of her touch thrilled him, but Rafe felt a distant tug, as if from a memory that he'd forgotten long before. Despite her beauty, Rafe didn't desire Hel; *hadn't he resisted the advances of Eloise and Roselyn, both captivating beauties?* Something was amiss, but Rafe couldn't name it.

Hel clung to him. Rafe wondered at this; he wouldn't have expected a woman of her wisdom to be so frail or to crumple so completely. Rafe knew the wisdom of age and marveled that deathless Hel could humble herself like this.

"Hel, I must ask," Rafe drew her up and stared into her black eyes, "are these tears real?"

Hel stopped crying abruptly, her smooth face becoming severe.

"How dare you question my motives!" Hel said imperiously.

Rafe pushed her back.

"Fraud! Deceiver!"

"In many ways, yes," Hel said, sitting up straight, facing him. "I'm trying to convince you to stay in any way I can."

"So that you don't have to be alone ...!"

"Loki isn't playing a game; you won't stay out of fear; you'll march out of here like children, knowing the danger, wishing too late that you'd heeded my wisdom. You will die, Rafe; I'll do whatever I can to prevent that.

"I understand the pride that'll lead you to this folly. I would've spared you that pain, giving you other reasons for staying. Now you must face the truth: outside of my realm, Loki shall always be watching, and after he pries your secrets from one of you, he'll kill all of you. I'm just a half-goddess; I can't stop him. You're imprisoned here as surely as I."

Suddenly Hel's sparkling eyes burned upon him, and Rafe staggered, closing his eyes and gritting his teeth. Sensations flooded him, not pain and fear, such as Loki had radiated, but of crushing weight, as if he were being pressed under a great stone. Rafe fell off of Hel's bench onto the floor, seeing nothing, hearing nothing, feeling only the weight of Hel's gaze upon him.

The pressure eased and faded away. Rafe rolled over and tried to sit up, but found that he was exhausted.

"My glare is but a fraction of Loki's potency," Hel said, "yet I can easily overcome you. You defied him; Loki will never tire of seeking revenge. Now tell me, Sir Rafe Horse-Trainer, how far will you get from Niflhiem if you walk out of my gates? What will happen to those whom you love, if they go with you?"

Rafe looked up at her. Hel wasn't angry; if anything, she was frightened. At least, she seemed to be.

"How do I know if your concern is real?" Rafe asked.

"You don't," Hel said. "I'm eons older than you; I could make myself appear in any guise that I wish. Humble, fearsome, accommodating, demanding; all are masks that I may wear at will. I did wish to deceive you, but for your good. Use your own judgment, if you're so wise. Will you tell your companions the truth ... and doom them ... as I'm doomed, without hope? In time they'll go mad, as I've suffered many times, only to recover centuries later.

"It's your choice, Rafe. Hope is the best gift that I have given you all, but you may take it away. Reveal the truth, if you think it best. I won't try to stop you. But think before you do this: you're wise, Rafe; I marvel that you perceived my deceptions. Use your wisdom here: will your truth aid ... or hinder your companion's confinement?"

Rafe sat silently upon the floor of Eljudnir. They were trapped in Niflhiem, and knowing that only worsened his doom. *What could the bitter truth do but torment his companions?* Hel was right; she'd given them the one gift that she hadn't: hope. Hope might not last long, but it was better than nothing.

Loki! Rafe silently cursed. They were nothing compared to him. Mosquitoes may bite, but the hand that slaps them ends their life. Rafe doubted if they could even draw Loki's godly blood.

Rafe looked up into Hel's beautiful, radiant eyes. He hadn't felt like a child for four decades, but suddenly he recalled childhood's simplicity and the confusion of innocence. Hel was so much older than he; Rafe wondered if she saw them as lost children ... or as pets like Garm and Nidhogg.

"I'll ... keep your secret," Rafe sighed.

Hel reached out her hand, and as Rafe took it, she lifted him to his feet with ease, and then she stood before him.

"You're a good man, Rafe," Hel said. "I've never met a Christian before, and now my opinion of them is great. I'll keep my promise. Plan your church, your house, and your farm, including a big stable. I have some items worth trading, and I can barter for seedlings, horses, and any other necessities. I'll build you all that you desire, and ask nothing in return but the pleasure of your company."

Rafe bowed his head. He'd entered Eljudnir full of steam, intent on confronting Hel's lies. Now he was a part of her lies; Rafe felt wholly defeated.

Chapter 9

Hel's Audience 5

HEL

Sadly Hel watched Rafe walk away from her, and she willed her door to open for him. Rafe was a good man, noble and thoughtful, wise in his limited way. How wonderful it would be to have such a man beside her, as a friend and confidant, perhaps even a lover; how terrible it would be to lose him. Hel hated herself for doing this, but what choice did she have? In time, they'd feel at home in Niflhiem, and she'd give them every comfort, if only they'd stay.

Hel closed her eyes, still feeling the warmth of Rafe's arms around her. How lucky they were: Seren, Eloise, and Roselyn! If only they understood how precious a loving touch was, how many people seldom felt it no matter how long they lived. Perhaps, if they knew, then they'd understand her needs ... and why she couldn't let them go.

Hel banished these thoughts; if she was going to succeed then she had to continue. The Seer was next, and he'd be her greatest challenge. The stage had to be set that would benefit her best; she'd replace the bench with a single chair and greet him from her throne.

Suddenly the Seer appeared, walking in as Rafe exited. Hel paused, but only for an instant; the Seer was taking the initiative, trying to catch Hel off-guard. Hel wasn't amused, but she wouldn't let him control her.

Hel could order the Seer out, and then call him back in again, but there seemed little purpose in that. He was a fool to think that he could outwit her. She would let him think that he was succeeding, like a hooked fish tiring himself out before the fisherman reels him in.

Hel sat motionless on her bench and watched the Seer approach.

"I'm here," the Seer stated.

"So you are," Hel said. "Do you know why I summoned you?"

Hel fought not to smile; he'd come unsummoned, but she'd declared him otherwise, and he couldn't refute her; she'd commanded these audiences.

"You wish to convince me to stay," the Seer said. "That's what you've done to the others."

"I take it that you're resolved to go?"

"I am."

"Through which gate will you leave?"

"That depends on you," the Seer said. "I have several ideas for evading your father. My preferred choices would require your cooperation. Of course, I suspect that you'll decline ... with a good excuse."

"Why would you suspect that?"

"You have no intention of releasing Eric."

"I said that I would think about it. I shouldn't, but I'm giving myself some time to think of any reason that would let me do so safely."

"Have you thought of a reason?"

"Obviously not."

"Then I must conclude that you won't help us."

Hel sat quietly, neither aggressive nor passive, and stared at the Seer from her bench. The Seer probably guessed that she was cornered, but she couldn't assume such against him. He was using blatancy as both his attack and defense, knowing that her wisdom was beyond him. His thoughts were deep and subtle, but the Seer was a mortal ... and he didn't even know what that meant.

"You said that we could leave, if we wanted to ..."

"You may leave," Hel said. "You may also feed yourselves to Garm and Nidhogg, if you wish. Death by them will be less painful than by my father."

"Loki may be harmed and deceived," the Seer said. "Already I've witnessed both."

"Loki's the Master of Lies," Hel said. "He isn't easily fooled. You must learn your limits, Seer, if you would live in this universe."

"I never said that I could deceive Loki," the Seer said. "You are best qualified for that."

"Me?"

"You know him best and are wise beyond mortal cunning."

"I'm not a slave to flattery."

"I wasn't asking, merely stating a fact," the Seer said. "You're our best hope for escaping your father. You know Niflhiem as well as you know him; I suspect that you already know how we could leave in safety, although you haven't spoken of it."

Hel glared at the Seer, forcibly restraining the intensity of her eyes. She showed no sign, but the Seer's compliments had hit their mark; Hel didn't hear compliments often. Tears would've flowed from her eyes were she not strong enough to hold them back. The Seer was a worthy opponent, more like her than any of the others. Although she was too strong to let it show, Hel admired the Seer ... and desired him most of all.

Hel couldn't let the Seer know that he was right. There was a secret exit, so ancient that even Loki would've forgotten about it. Hel had to change the topic quickly; once he learned of it, the Seer's desire to leave would overpower him.

Yet Hel sat silent, just looking at the Seer, admiring his smooth, angular face, his pale skin. In time, she could teach him secrets that no mortal had ever known, and his self-mastery would make him strong enough to rival even some Gods. Yet such learning would take centuries, here among the rotting dead; Hel doubted if she would accept such an offer, but then, she was a trapped half-goddess. The Seer had only mortal powers, but he was free.

Hel shook her head and scolded herself. *Now wasn't the time to dream!* They still didn't know of the secret exit, and she had to be careful not to confirm or deny its existence. If they caught her concealing its existence, then they'd turn against her. Hel had to keep them off balance as long as she could. If they stayed there long enough to learn all about the land, then they'd be trapped. Her power was greater than they knew; she'd string truths across them like unbreakable silk strands, and then they'd be caught in her net. The longer that they stayed, the less likely it was that they'd ever escape.

The Seer only needed two things: he needed to know how to escape Niflhiem without rousing Loki's attention and he had to convince her to let them go. She had to manipulate him carefully and deny him both.

"They love you, Hel," the Seer said.

Hel stiffened, radiating surprise; he'd struck her hard where she was most vulnerable. Centuries of loneliness rose in her throat, but she clenched her teeth and forced a gentle smile. Hel couldn't reveal the depth of this wound.

107

"Love is a strong word," Hel said, trying not to show her anger.

"They love easily," the Seer said. "They even love me ... well, some do. They like you, although they fear you as well. I expect that love isn't far behind."

"Why are you telling me this?" Hel asked, fighting to change the subject.

"As a warning," the Seer said. "As easily as my companions love, they can hate. Eloise's kidnapper, whom they call the Wolflord, they hate. Skaldi the Giant they hate. Roselyn's father they hate. Their hate is as strong as their love."

Suddenly Hel laughed loudly, leaning one arm back against her table. Peals of merriment poured from her lips and the oppressive nature of Niflhiem vanished.

"You seek to manipulate me? How funny! Do you not understand who I am?"

"You're the Goddess of Death," the Seer said. "A monster, no less than your brothers Fenris the Master-Wolf and Jorgamund the Midgard Serpent. They're monsters because of what they are. You're a monster because of what you do. You kill, Hel. You murder people for their blood. You feed like a vampire to keep your bath full, to soften your legs."

Hate blasted from Hel's stare, too strong to be contained, but the Seer stood firm, resisting as he would a gale wind.

"How dare you?" Hel shouted angrily, her control lost. "Mind your place, Druid! You're a mortal magician, a student of petty spells and incantations that I learned as a child. You're but one step above your teachers, and lord over all as if power justifies arrogance. Dare you match wits with me? I am such that you should bow to, and know secrets that only Odin shares."

"The Nine Secrets of the Dead," the Seer said knowledgeably.

Hel slowly forced herself to relax and quelled the vehemence in her breast. *The Seer was better at this than she'd expected.* He was antagonizing her on purpose, trying to get her to reveal her true purposes. He'd broken her composure, despite that she was older and wiser. But Hel didn't want to kill him, which she could easily do. She had to be more careful; Hel wanted him as her lover, not one of her mindless subjects. She had to control her temper or she'd lose her only chance for salvation.

"I was there," Hel said. "Odin hung himself from the limbs of Yggdrasil with a rope around his neck and his own spear thrust through his heart, and he died, just to learn the Nine Secrets of the Dead. But Odin was young then, in his prime, and such was his strength that he fought his way back to life, and eventually recovered his health. I alone share this knowledge with him, for the dead have no secrets from me."

"Against such power," the Seer said, "even Loki couldn't prevail."

A silence fell between them. Hel had to assert control. The Seer was too young to understand the depth of her loneliness, the anguish that she held inside her. He was playing with forces that could eradicate him, if she lost control.

"I won't give you the Secrets of the Dead," Hel said. "You must earn them, and grow more powerful than any mortal before you could use them."

"Tempting," the Seer said, "but I'm not fool enough to doubt your power. If I chose to stay, even for a little while, then you'll keep me here forever."

"Would that be so terrible?"

"I must leave ... and take the others with me."

"You won't get far."

"By all reports, this is a wide land. It'd be easy to become lost ... or travel secretly."

Hel glared at him. He was right again, and she couldn't allow that.

"Why must you leave?"

The Seer smiled, but then he faltered. He looked as if he had an answer prepared, but suddenly he couldn't voice it.

"Your service to your Lady has failed," Hel said. "She hasn't answered your prayers, and you can no longer feel Her inside you. She's vanished from your heart, where She's always dwelt. She's abandoned you."

"No!"

"Where have you to go now?" Hel asked. "Once you leave Niflhiem, since I can't release Eric, your mission will be over. You failed your Lady; you can't return to your Magic Isle without the mockery of your peers. Even with your magic, you can't safely search for your mother; she's somewhere in Earl Sir Gulcwin's lands, and he'd kill both of you, if you lead him to her. He's ransacked your house and put a price upon your head. You won't be safe anywhere in England, once word of your presence becomes known. Again you've been cast out, and again you can't go home."

Hel watched his every movement. The Seer was fighting to remain stern, but she'd hit him hard. He couldn't sense his Lady here; Her power didn't extend into this universe where She'd never been, but if the Seer believed that She'd abandoned him, so much the better. Hel would withhold that secret forever, if she must.

"The question is," the Seer said suddenly, "why do you stay? Others have lost the use of their legs and not given up on life. Surely your powers can more than compensate ..."

"Mortals they are," Hel said angrily. "I'm a Goddess, the daughter of Loki. I won't crawl like a beggar or be chained to a bed. I need blood, fresh blood, human or divine. Question not my purposes ... or you'll find a foe worse than Loki before you!"

The Seer stepped back, almost blown over by her glare, and Hel realized that she was pressing him harder than she'd intended. Hel relaxed, lessening her stare.

"I didn't mean to challenge you," the Seer said. "But I'm aware of your greatest power. Compared to you, we're infants, and the longer that we stay the stronger your hold becomes. Our only hope is to escape you soon, or we'll become nothing more than your subjects."

"Do you truly believe that I wish that?" Hel asked. "Fool wizard! Don't I have enough mindless subjects? Immortality is mine to grant, as is knowledge such as your petty Druid masters never imagined. A God I could make you! Power I offer freely! Will you reject that, which you crave most, just to be free of me? Why shouldn't I be insulted?"

"Niflhiem is a prison, and no offer of yours can change that," the Seer said. "You want us to share your confinement."

"These walls don't imprison me," Hel said. "I ordered their construction. I can destroy them at will. Even Odin, King of the Gods, didn't imprison me in Niflhiem. He forced me here out of pity, where my need for blood could be harmlessly fulfilled. It's the Norn witches who condemned me to Niflhiem. They named me the Goddess of Death and ruler of this land."

"Why not defy them?"

"Their predictions happen, and disaster falls upon all who dare their wrath. Once I left, riding Garm, and escaped Niflhiem. We spent weeks happily riding across glorious green fields under the sun. Then a madness took us both. Mindless we became, and when our senses recovered, we were here, led by the insanity of the Norns back to this, our prison. Garm will never again bear me forth, nor do I blame him; the anger of the Norns would be far worse, if defied twice. Their madness could return, never to leave. When Ragnarrok approaches, I must be here to play out the part that they've commanded, willingly or not. No one can defy the Norns. Even the Well of Mimir can't escape their power."

"The Well of Mimir?" the Seer asked. "Isn't that where Odin tore out his own eye and cast it into the water for news of Ragnarrok?"

"Yes, the Spring of Wishes," Hel said. "Mimir is a powerful foreseer, a sorcerer beyond all others. His head was severed and placed on a rock beside the well, but he still lives, and those who pay his price may ask almost anything. Odin wished to prevent the end of all worlds, but even Mimir couldn't grant that."

Hel leaned forward, noting the slight dip of the Seer's eyes toward her deep cleavage, the reflections of her necklace sparkling in his pupils. *He was still a man, full of fire, and all that she had to do was offer him enough wood ...*

"Stay, Druid," Hel said. "I can offer you anything that you desire. You won't be trapped here forever; the powers that I can teach you could make you my equal, able to leave whenever you want."

The Seer said nothing, but he looked frightened. Hel relaxed; he had no arguments left. Hel had won again, as she knew she would. This victory had done what the others had, planted in their minds the wonders that they could have if they stayed, and the fears of what they'd face if they left. It would be an ongoing argument for years, but if her seeds of doubt took root, then their fruit would give her what she wanted most: living friends to end her loneliness.

"I'm only a half-goddess, and only half of a woman," Hel said softly. "Still, all that I am, I freely offer to you ..."

The Seer crumbled before her eyes. Hel knew that he'd been offered many things, but never everything. People had often paid for his skills and wisdom, but never for his companionship. She'd struck where the Seer was weakest, shaken him to his core, and if he complied, then she'd reward him in ways that he could scarcely imagine. Hel liked and admired him, and his companions, but she was slightly concerned; they could become her weakness, once she came to love them, but it'd be worth it. Hel wasn't lying to him ... not fully. She could make a God of him ... and there were some things ... that every Goddess needed ... that only a God could provide. In time, they could even ... *mate.* Hel purposefully looked sad, defying the urge to smile. The Seer was hers, but now wasn't the time to consume him.

"Thank you for coming," Hel dismissed the Seer gently. "Please ask Seren to join me, if you would."

The Seer looked up at her and Hel smiled warmly. Hel understood the power of beauty over men; *let her smiling face linger in his mind and destroy the last of his defenses.*

Slowly the Seer turned away, and he stumbled toward the door, broken and defeated.

Jay Palmer

Chapter 10

Hel's Audience 6

SEREN

Seren's heart froze as the huge door creaked open and the Seer emerged. The Seer looked haggard, downcast, as if he'd suffered a great ordeal.

"Your turn," the Seer mumbled as he staggered past Seren.

Seren buried her face in Rafe's shoulder.

"Afraid ...," Seren whimpered.

"It's alright," Rafe soothed her. "You don't have to go. Eric?"

"Hel must see each of you privately," Eric frowned and bowed his head.

"You know why she wants us to stay, don't you?" Rafe demanded.

"Isn't that obvious?" Karl asked. "She's lonely ...!"

"We've been through all of that!" Rafe shouted. "But is that all that she wants? How will we ever know, unless we stay? She needs blood; maybe she wants ours!"

"An immortal needs no reason besides loneliness," Roselyn said. "Besides, she's a half-goddess. Other than our company, what have we got to offer?"

"She won't hurt us," Eloise said. "She wants to care for us, like a ... a mother. Go on in, Seren. The longer you that wait, the worse it'll be. But we stay, or go, together! No one leaves, or stays, unless we all do. Agreed?"

All nodded in silent accord.

Slowly Seren kissed Rafe, and then she entered the doors of Eljudnir. Seren trembled slightly, but she was determined. Hel couldn't defeat her because Hel had nothing better to offer than what Seren already had. What Hel wanted was obvious, but it wasn't the same as what Hel needed.

Hel sat upon her throne with an empty table between her and a single empty chair. Hel rose as Seren approached. Seren envied her beautiful dress and sparkling necklace; Hel looked regal, god-like. Seren felt even worse; she was all disheveled and didn't even have a comb for her long gray hair. Yet she wasn't daunted. Seren wasn't as old as Hel, but she knew many old women, some more than eighty years old. Age didn't insure wisdom; *she wouldn't be Hel's pawn.*

"Welcome," Hel said. "Please, don't be afraid. Sit and talk with me."

Seren sat upon the chair. Her dread didn't lessen, but she didn't turn away. She sat demurely, but matched Hel's stare with her own.

"Are you angry with me?" Hel asked.

Seren paused before speaking, quietly making the half-goddess wait on her.

"Seren stay with Rafe," Seren said.

"I wouldn't have it otherwise," Hel said. "But why do you glare so?"

"Afraid," Seren said, hoping to deceive her into relaxing.

"Of me?" Hel smiled reassuringly. "Have I done anything to threaten you?"

"Hel no need do," Seren said. "Hel frightening."

"I don't mean to be," Hel said. "Life in Niflhiem has driven deep shadows into me, more than I desire. I can't help being what I am, or who my father is. Surely you can relate to that."

"Why?"

"Why, because you ...," Hel stammered, and then she fell silent.

"I whore," Seren said flatly. "Whore honest, no hurt anyone. No look down on others."

"I'm what I was born to be, through no choice of my own," Hel defended. "We're both products of our birthright."

"Hel look down upon Seren," she said. "If we same, no do."

Seren stared at Hel as the half-goddess acted surprised. *How could she compare their lives?* Hel was immortal, powerful, the daughter of a God. Seren's unknown father was one of her mother's hundreds of clients, as her own children were fathered by her clients. Seren was born in a brothel, on a bed of hay, and raised in the narrow, dangerous streets of Madrone; they couldn't be more different.

"I have no choice of what I am," Hel said.

"Seren not divine," Seren said. "Seren choose look up to Hel or not. Hel choose to be Hel, choose look down upon us."

"Don't think that I know nothing of your life," Hel said. "When boredom grows too great, I call upon my subjects to entertain me. I've heard the life-stories of countless thousands from the lips of those that lived them; princesses and slaves, kings and thieves, whores and ladies. You'd be surprised how similar they all sound; grasping for momentary rewards, arguing petty disputes, and fighting pointless rivalries. Do you really think that your life is vastly different from theirs?"

"What Hel feel like ... to be powerless?" Seren challenged.

Hel paused, seeming surprised. Seren said nothing more, unwilling to let her question go unanswered, giving Hel no distraction, no chance to avoid her challenge. The two women faced each other across the table ... and Hel finally sighed.

"I've no idea what it feels like to be powerless," she said. "Not according to your definition of power."

Seren relaxed; *Hel had submitted to her.* Perhaps this audience wouldn't be as frightening as she thought.

"What does sex feel like?" Hel asked. "How does it feel to have a man inside your warm, living flesh? What is love?"

Seren stiffened, biting back unchosen words. Seren knew a life that Hel would never experience, countless lovers that Hel would never know. In her youth, many had fallen in love with her. Some she'd loved, while others were simply business. Her mother had loved her, as she had loved all of her brothers and sisters. *Did Hel's parents love?* Remembering Loki, Seren doubted it. Yet she couldn't let Hel control her. Seren held her tongue, not speaking until she was ready.

"We different," Seren said.

"Indeed," Hel said. "Of all your companions, I understand you the least."

"Me?" Seren asked. "Talk like this on purpose; hard to talk like normal, after whole life."

"On purpose?" Hel asked. "Why would you choose to talk stilted?"

"Work for soldiers and tradesmen. Them no want smart girl; bad for business."

"You misunderstand me," Hel smiled. "I don't find it hard to understand your words. I find it hard to comprehend your decisions. You left your world, all that you had, for the love of a man whom you barely knew. You must've loved Rafe almost instantly. Can you imagine how much I envy that ... that level of trust?"

Seren swallowed hard. She'd tried to change the subject, fearful of revealing too much.

"Madrone be prison, like Niflhiem," Seren said. "Rafe be escape."

"Surely there were safer opportunities."

"To what?"

"I see," Hel said. "You didn't want to be a whore anymore."

"No! Whore life great!"

"Really? Then why ...?"

"Goddess no understand," Seren said. "Seren alone."

Hel paused and looked down.

"I understand loneliness."

"Madrone men with money want young girls. Men without money want whore for free. Rafe want wife; he good man."

"Ironic," Hel said. "You risked your life for security."

"Better die soon but loved."

"Then ... you do know what love feels like."

Seren bowed her head, but her thoughts were racing. Possibly Hel didn't know what love was, and that thought frightened her; *those who've never loved can't be trusted because they don't know what real trust is.*

"I can give immortality to all of you."

"Seren stay with Rafe, whatever he choose."

"You do love him."

"Love good for business, bad for whore. Rafe strong. Karl strong. Trust them keep Seren safe. Not know where they take Seren until too late, but Seren no afraid."

Seren forced her smile away; Hel wouldn't catch her unprepared. A long moment passed.

"Tell me about your mother."

"What you not know about whores?"

Hel frowned and another long silence followed.

"I can give you many things ..."

"Give Eric," Seren said. "Let company go home."

Hel made no answer.

"When Hel be honest?" Seren demanded. "No answer same as answer no."

Seren saw Hel's eyes widen slightly and knew that she'd hit her target.

"Hel want us trapped, as she trapped," Seren accused. "Hel want company, do anything to keep. Company admire Hel, but soon won't. Prisoners no like jailors."

Hel jumped to her feet, her eyes glaring painfully into Seren.

"I am not your jailor!" Hel shouted. "You could spend your puny lives anywhere, and soon you'll die! Here you could live forever with everything that I have to give, and I have powers that you can't imagine! Why not live here?"

"Would Hel live here, if given choice?" Seren asked.

Hel fixed her gaze upon Seren and the old whore looked away, unable to bear its intensity. Seren felt as if she were too close to a great fire, pressed by wafts of heat strong enough to push her back or burn her to a cinder. Seren sat terrified, but she'd done it; angered Hel to the point of recklessness.

"Why Hel no release Eric?" Seren demanded.

Hel's relentless visual assault continued, but slowly it softened. Hel sighed and slumped down on her throne.

"You don't understand," Hel said. "Loki said that he brought you here. You may believe him, but I can't afford to. He's a master of lies, and Odin's just as bad ... when he wants something."

"What Odin want?" Seren asked.

"To prevent Ragnarrok," Hel said. "His death in the final battle has been foretold, and he'll delay that day forever, if he can. He'd gladly sacrifice me, if it suits his plans. I can't play Odin's patsy, a fool to his game, unless I know what that game is."

Seren faced Hel, amazed.

"Hel afraid," Seren said.

Hel glared at Seren, but the power from her eyes failed. Hel looked weak, empty, her beauty a hollow shell.

"Of all your companions, I thought that you'd be easiest."

"If Rafe stay, Seren be easiest. No want to leave."

Hel looked at her.

"I wish no harm to any of you."

"Seren know."

Hel sighed.

"Thank you for speaking with me," Hel said.

"Until leave, Seren glad talk to Hel."

Seren rose, but she didn't leave. Seren walked around the table to stand before Hel's throne. Hel looked surprised, unsure, but then Hel stood imperiously before her, richly gowned and gleaming with gems. Seren looked straight into Hel's godly eyes and smiled.

Slowly Seren extended her arms and hugged Hel. The half-goddess hesitantly accepted her embrace; Seren's arms were warm and soft, comforting and sincere.

Suddenly waves of emotions burst forth. Seren felt Hel tremble and start to push away, but Seren only tightened her grip. The Goddess of Death shivered and struggled, but Seren wouldn't let go.

Hel finally broke down. Hel sobbed on Seren's shoulder, harshly, wringing real tears. Seren held her, feeling untold centuries of torment wash out of Hel.

"It okay," Seren soothed Hel's tears. "No hurry now."

The audience was over. Seren remained long afterwards, whispering small comforts while Hel whimpered in her arms, but secretly she was proud. Where all the others had failed, she'd won. Whatever Hel wanted, all that she really needed was a true friend. By giving Hel even that one small token of friendship, Seren couldn't lose.

Chapter 11

Hel's Resolution

THE SEER

Where was the Lady?

The Seer paced back and forth just outside of the massive doors of Eljudnir. He'd been unable to sleep, fitfully tossing and turning while the others dozed. Finally he'd pushed back his blanket and crept outside to look around.

Why couldn't he feel Her?

Hel had said that he'd failed Her, that the Lady had abandoned him for his disappointing end to Her mission. Yet was Hel to be trusted?

He had to think! In all the stories that he knew of the Lady, She'd never abandoned Her people. Why would She abandon him? Had he failed Her that badly? Was he lost to Her, so greatly that She'd rejected his spirit forever? Why couldn't he feel Her inside him as he had since childhood?

Perhaps it was a test. Perhaps he should go on and attempt to complete his quest in the hope that She'd come back to him. How would he know? The Seer barely understood what his quest was. For some reason, the Lady seemed to want Eric's spirit admitted to Valhalla; he'd accepted that strange notion as fact and come all this way because of it. Now his journey seemed in vain. Had he misread Her visions?

Could the quest go on? Hel would refuse to release Eric; of that the Seer was certain. But something else was bothering him, like a flea hiding in the folds of his bed sheets. He needed more information: that was the usual solution to most mysteries.

Perhaps Hel had given him the clue: the Well of Mimir, the Water of Wishes, was here, somewhere. If he could get there, then the greatest Norse soothsayer would be his to command. He could ask for the true purpose in the Lady's quest and learn how to win back Her favor.

He recalled the words of the Valkyrie:

"The bond is broken," she said to Karl. "Only Hel, should the arm and sword be brought to her before the Gates of Valhalla, could admit him now!"

They'd come the wrong way. They needed to go to Valhalla, but they'd come to Niflhiem instead. Yet the Seer couldn't understand the riddle: Hel never left Niflhiem, so she'd never go near Valhalla, never stand before its gates. How could he present Eric's arm and sword to Hel at someplace where she'd never go?

If Hel were human, then his task would be simple. The Seer could magically bind her and carry her there. But Hel's magic vastly exceeded his, and she had Garm, Nidhogg, and who knew what else? She also had an army of deadmen, slaves who'd do anything for her. His simple Druid magics couldn't force Hel to do anything.

Yet she had a temper, and she could leave Niflhiem temporarily, until the Fates punished her with madness. With the right bait, perhaps he could lure her away.

The Well of Mimir was a long shot; what if the Lady had abandoned him forever? The instant that they left Hel's protection, Loki would kill them, even if they freely told him where the Portal was. Was it worth the risk? He could stay here and become the most powerful mage of all time, live forever, and know every luxury that Hel could afford. Was he to give up all that he ever wanted for the slight chance that the Lady would forgive him?

What about his companions? Could he willingly lead his companions into certain death? He'd barely known them in Grusshire when he'd raised the dead against them. Now, despite his feelings, the part that they'd played in his father's death seemed distant, almost forgivable. They'd accepted him and he'd begun to like them ... most of them. Even Karl had some good qualities, although he always spoke before he thought. Rafe was as honorable a Christian as he'd ever met, and Seren was unusually smart; he often wondered about her poor speech, noting that she never failed to make herself understood. Roselyn had nothing but admirable qualities, and his feelings for Eloise ... if she weren't vying with him for leadership of the company then he'd make his feelings for her very apparent.

The Seer kept pacing. He looked across the empty plain and wondered where Eric was. The dead were still gone; Hel must've ordered them away after her audience with Seren.

Seren: *how had she endured her audience so well?* Didn't Hel press her, as she had with him? She had endured the longest interview, yet Seren had walked out of Eljudnir as if she had just had tea with a friend, not been crushed by the will of a Norse half-monster. *What did they talk about that Seren wouldn't repeat?*

The Seer pulled out the crystal egg that Titania had given him, which he wore around his neck. He had no idea what it did, or if he could use it to help save Eric; he doubted it. Still, he'd taken an oath; if he didn't learn its secret, then he'd have to carry it back and drop it in Titania's well. The Seer put it back inside his robe and resumed pacing.

Hours resolved nothing. Footsore, the Seer joined the others as several dead women approached

Eljudnir carrying platters of food, including a large bowl filled with golden apples. The others were just waking up and welcomed breakfast gladly. Hel joined them and shared their morning meal.

"I've decided to make you wait no longer," Hel said. "I must let you leave now ... while I still have the strength to let you go. If you must leave, then you must go today. I don't want you to go, but the longer that you stay the harder it'll be for me to release you. There's an exit from here that Loki doesn't know of, but that won't deceive him for long. He'll know that you've left Niflhiem and begin searching at once. You may escape him for a few days, but not for long. If he catches you, he'll kill you all, and I can't protect you outside of Niflhiem. Yet I won't imprison you as Odin and the Fates have punished me. You don't have to leave; any or all of you may stay and live forever. Even if you do leave, you may come back; I'll always welcome you."

"Thank you, Hel," the Seer said, and the others chorused their gratitude.

"I don't do this willingly," Hel said. "Living friends we've become, the first that I've ever had. Even though you choose death, I'd have us depart as friends, a memory to ease my loneliness. I don't know what becomes of Christian dead in Norse lands. Perhaps you'll return as my subjects; a bitter celebration that will be. Yet friends I will have had, and that's why I must let you go."

"What of Eric?" Roselyn asked.

"His spirit means nothing to me," Hel said. "Gladly I'd release him if I were free to do so. Yet I can't; it's a precedence involving the Fates and Ragnarrok, and I can't risk the future of nine worlds, including mine, over the doom of one mortal. I'm sorry: Eric must remain."

"We'd like to see him before we go," the Seer said, cutting off Karl as he started to object.

"I'll summon him."

"Then we'd best eat all we can," the Seer said. "We've a long journey ahead of us."

The Seer picked up a golden apple and bit into it.

Eric arrived by the time that they finished eating, and Eloise and Roselyn rushed to hug him; it was a somber good-bye, and many tears flowed. Karl and Eric hugged long, Karl apologizing the whole time for not succeeding at freeing Eric from Niflhiem.

The Seer politely shook Eric's left hand and spoke a few words of respect, and then quietly backed away. He and Eric had never been friends, and the Seer had other concerns. He wished to be alone, to have time to think, but Hel approached him.

"See how they will miss him?" Hel asked the Seer. "That's friendship. Do you blame me for wanting such?"

"Popularity is a strange thing, is it not?" the Seer said. "Here am I, a powerful Druid Seer, and you, the

Norse Goddess of Death, and here we wait while a common mercenary soldier, no different than any other, inspires such loyalty that we stand forgotten in his presence."

"He cares for them," Hel said. "He cares deeply, far more than you or I. You can't fake caring or fail to recognize it; they see his caring and return it. That's the source of true popularity."

"I guess the real question is why," the Seer said. "Why don't we care like that?"

"It's not our way," Hel said.

"A pity," the Seer said. "There have been times when I would have traded all my training to be loved like Eric."

"As would I," Hel said. "Come. I have several questions that I must ask before you go."

They walked inside the doors, toward the eternal bonfire in the center of Eljudnir.

"Where will you go?"

"Bifrost, eventually," the Seer said.

"Heimdall won't let you cross the Rainbow Bridge," said Hel. "Why that way, not the Portal?"

"For us, the Portal is one-way," the Seer said. "Bifrost is our only way back."

"Then you're trapped here."

"If I am, I'll certainly return."

Hel smiled. The Seer smiled back, but he quickly lowered his gaze. He had to change the subject, to keep her from suspecting. *If she guessed his plan ...*

"Where will your exit deposit us?" the Seer asked.

"The troll caves," Hel said. "Trolls are very dangerous, but less fearsome than my father. Trolls live in the deepest caves, as far from sunlight as possible. If you can escape them, then you may climb into Nidavellir, the halls of the dwarves. Their works are amazing, but don't trust them. Bifrost can be seen from there, but not reached; you must go through Svartalfhiem, the land of the Dark Elves, to get to the surface. You'll emerge from darkness in Jotunhiem, the lands of Giants. From there you can journey across the wide lands to Bifrost, but it is far, near the Gates of Asgard."

"Asgard, home of the Norse Gods, with Loki chasing us all the way," the Seer scowled.

"There's still time to change your mind," Hel said. "I've little hope for you, if you go. There are no safe lands in the Norse underground, and few lands under our sun welcome mortals. And, as you say, there's still Loki."

"I must go," the Seer said. "If my Lady's abandoned me, then I must know. I can't abandon my faith; it's my life."

"When you return, I'll give you a new life," Hel smiled. "Be warned; trolls and dark elves live for violence, and Norse dwarves will betray you for a single copper. If they don't kill you, I suspect that they'll drive you back here. Call for me as soon as you see Niflhiem. I'll rescue you, if I can."

"You're a true friend," the Seer said, but he couldn't look into Hel's eyes as he said it.

Hel lifted her hands to the Seer's cheeks and turned his eyes to face her. The Seer looked at her closely, trying not to notice how beautiful she was, but utterly failing.

"I'll always be here, waiting," Hel said.

Slowly Hel leaned close and kissed the Seer. Her touch was electric, tingling through him. The Seer kissed Hel back, gently, tenderly. *What kind of man was he to do such a thing?*

Hel pulled back and took his hand. She led him out of Eljudnir, where his companions were still saying good-bye to Eric.

"It's time to go," Hel said. "There's an air vent in the roof of Niflhiem leading to an ancient series of tunnels where the trolls live. Nidhogg will lift you there, from where you can escape. Loki doesn't know of it, so you may be safe from him for a while. Fetch your gear; you'll need weapons, armor, and great courage to brave the tunnels of the trolls."

The others walked back inside. The Seer stood nervously beside Hel, his hand still in hers, Eric sad and silent before them. Nothing was said, but Hel smiled the whole time, her hand gripping the Seer's tightly. Eventually the others emerged, Karl, Rafe, and Roselyn wearing their armor, Eloise and Seren carrying their packs, one of which was stuffed with their few remaining vegetables. Karl brought the Seer his black case, the one still holding Eric's severed arm.

"Do you still want this?" Karl asked.

"Yes," the Seer said, trying to sound humble. "If the Lady does contact me, then I want to prove to Her that I had it when I came here."

Soon they were all gathered, ready to go. Hel hugged each of them tightly, and then she turned to face the barren plain.

"Nidhogg!" Hel shouted.

Suddenly the ground rumbled and shook. Rocks cracked, and not far away the plain burst upwards as Nidhogg, the stone dragon, Devourer of the Dead, rose from the roots of Yggdrasil. Nidhogg towered over them and the Seer gasped, realizing just how big it was.

"Nidhogg, I need you to lift these good people, without harming them, to the tunnel above my hall," Hel said.

The dragon roared, and then lowered its head. Hel grabbed Karl first, paused to hug him again, and then lifted him as if he were a child. On top of Nidhogg's massive head she set Karl. Then the dragon lifted its head and rose up to its fullest height. Moments passed, and when Nidhogg lowered its huge head again, Karl was gone.

"Karl!" Rafe shouted.

"I'm here!" Karl's voice shouted, and they saw him wave from a tiny crevice in the rock, high up in the cavernous ceiling of Niflhiem.

Rafe went next, and then the others. The Seer went last, and Hel hugged him the longest of all.

"I don't know what to say," Hel said. "I wish you luck, but I also wish you to come back to me."

"I, too, regret leaving," the Seer said honestly. He reached up and brushed away a single tear rolling down Hel's cheek. "You truly are ... so beautiful ... inside and out."

They kissed long, and then Hel seized his waist and lifted him with her godly strength. The Seer grabbed on to Nidhogg's thick scales as she set him on her dragon's head, and then the head lifted, carrying the Seer with it, swiftly towards the stone ceiling. The others were there, watching through the crack; the foul, chill mists of Niflhiem rushed past him as he rose.

Hands grabbed his robe and pulled the Seer through the crack. He had only one foot on the rock before Nidhogg's head lowered, and then they were overlooking a deadly fall from the top of Niflhiem. Hot, smoky wind blew past them, pouring through the crack; it was a natural chimney, venting the fumes of the land of the dead. Below, they could see Nidhogg bow before Hel, who reached out a hand to pet him, and beside Hel stood Eric, their lost companion.

"Good-bye!" Eloise shouted as she waved.

"Quiet!" the Seer whispered. "We're supposed to be escaping in secret, and trolls roam these tunnels."

"Easy," Karl said to the Seer. "This is the last time that we'll ever see Eric."

"Perhaps not," the Seer said.

The others stopped waving and turned to face him.

"It's not over," the Seer said. "Hel couldn't give us Eric, but that doesn't mean we can't take him."

"What?!?" they all gasped.

"We can steal Eric," the Seer said. "I still have his arm, and he's real here, not like at sea. I can bring Eric and his arm back together. That will draw Eric here, up here, out of Niflhiem. Once we have him, we can run. Even Hel won't be able to catch us."

"Why?" Rafe demanded. "What good would that do?"

"Our quest could continue," the Seer said. "By stealing Eric, we'll have betrayed Hel. Friendship is new to her, and I suspect that having a friendship betrayed will be equally new."

"Hel is our friend," Roselyn argued.

"Then you must choose between friends," the Seer said. "Hel or Eric; once we steal Eric, Hel will be furious. I suspect that she'll come after us."

"Why would we want that?" Karl asked. "You saw how strong she is!"

"We could still make the Valkyrie's words come true," the Seer said. "Hel will chase us, and we'll lead her to Valhalla. There, before the Gates of Valhalla, all of the components will be gathered: Hel will arrive, chasing us, and we'll have Eric and his severed arm. We can present the arm to Hel, as the Valkyrie instructed, before the Gates of Valhalla, and Eric will be admitted into his paradise."

"That's an evil plan," Rafe said.

"Yes, like when I nailed Eloise to that tree," the Seer said. "It won't be nice, but it's our only hope."

"Why?" Seren asked. "Why you do this?"

"For the Lady, of course," the Seer said. "Isn't that why we came here?"

"I didn't come here to betray a friend," Karl said.

"No, you came here to save a friend," the Seer said. "Will you stop now just because the method's distasteful? Eric can still enter Valhalla, if you agree to my plan."

No one spoke, looking at the Seer. The dim light from Niflhiem shone through the stone crevice, illuminating faces torn with doubt.

"We don't even have to go all the way," the Seer said. "Near Jotunhiem is the Well of Mimir, the Water of Wishes. There all of our questions can be answered. If we're wrong, then we'll turn around and give Eric back to Hel. From there it won't be far to Bifrost, the Rainbow Bridge back to Earth. We've no choice but to go that way; it's our only route home. But we have one chance to complete our task, to inter Eric into his afterlife of warriors, where he'll live forever, instead of rotting away in the land of the dead. I just thought ... it was a choice that you'd want to know of."

"How sure are you of this?" Eloise asked.

The Seer shook his head.

"How sure can I be of anything in this place?" the Seer asked. "But I see no other hope."

"What if Hel catch us?" Seren asked.

"What about Loki?" the Seer agreed. "What about the trolls, dark elves, and all of the other dangers that Hel warned us about? If we want to be safe, we should call Nidhogg to lower us back to Niflhiem and stay trapped with Hel forever."

"It's wrong to betray a friend," Karl said.

"Eric's still a member of this company, as far as I'm concerned," Eloise said. "What about him?"

"What about us?" Rafe asked. "What's your plan for getting us back to England?"

They all fell silent and looked at the Seer.

"As far as I know, there's no way back that we can travel," the Seer said. "We're trapped here for the rest of our lives. Yet I don't know everything about this land; I hope to find way home, if one exists. If we can, we'll ask Mimir."

The others glanced at each other, dumbfounded.

"I never said that it would be easy," the Seer protested. "I'm doing the best that I can. If one of you has a better plan, I'm listening."

The Seer took his turn, silently staring at them. None of them spoke, and most looked away.

"I'll decide this," Eloise said. "We've a long way to go before we can try to get home, so we should worry about that later. Eric and Hel are both our friends, and we must betray Eric by leaving him here, or betray Hel by stealing Eric."

Eloise looked at each of them, but no one said anything.

"Hel said that she didn't care about Eric," Eloise continued. "She'll be hurt by our betrayal, but Eric will be doomed forever if we leave him. His would be the greater betrayal."

"Then it's decided," the Seer said. "Are we all agreed on this?"

No one spoke for or against his plan, they just groaned and grimaced. The Seer understood: Hel had just learned the joy of friendship; the pain of betrayal she wouldn't take well. Besides, the Seer liked Hel; he wouldn't enjoy doing this.

"We'd best begin," the Seer said. "We have to do this while Eric's still in sight. Hold on to your noses; I have to open the black case and remove Eric's arm. While I perform the spell of joining, you'll have to hold his arm tightly, to prevent it from going to Eric. It'll pull with all of his weight; if you can hold on to the arm, it'll lift Eric right up here."

The Seer looked back down through the crevice as he fumbled with the lacings. Nidhogg had vanished, digging like a mole back under the plain of Niflhiem, but

Hel and Eric were still there, watching them. The Seer felt like a heel; he liked Hel more than he dared admit.

An abominable stench vomited from the black case as he opened it. Grimacing, the Seer reached in and pulled out Eric's stiff, rotting arm. It was putrefied and no one moved when he held it out to the others.

"Oh, come on!" the Seer complained. "I've been carrying this foul arm for weeks!"

Rafe took off his cloak, covered the rancid arm, and then took it from the Seer. Karl helped him hold it, and the women locked their hands onto the folds of Rafe's cloak.

"Be careful not to pull the sword from Eric's hand," the Seer said.

"Just do it!" Rafe complained.

The Seer placed both of his hands over the severed stump, trying to ignore the disgusting feel of Eric's rotting elbow. He cleared his mind, banished all other thoughts, and forced himself to concentrate on pure nothingness, on void. It was difficult, but he'd long ago mastered that state, even before he was an adept. Blocking out all other sensations, the Seer began to feel his subtler senses of time, space, and the flow of all things. The Spell of Reuniting wasn't difficult; it was natural for Eric's arm and body to be together. The Seer focused on that natural state and tried to enhance it. A prayer to the Lady whispered from his lips, but his mind was too enrapt in itself to notice. Slowly he gave himself over into the worlds of subtle sensations and became one with his spell. More words spoke from his lips, languages ancient and obscure, and then the Seer could feel their power flowing through him, and he began to direct it.

He chanted the sacred words, forcing the powers beyond time and space to merge with reality, to become one as he became one with them. Energy drained from him and he pushed harder. With his own mind, the Seer fueled his will into reality, heedless of the cost to his body. He could sense the connection growing stronger, stronger, *stronger!*

Sensing the climax, the Seer pulled back his hands just as Eric's body flew up through the crevice and his stump merged with his arm.

"Betrayers!" Eric shouted. "Give him back to me!"

Exhausted but frantic, the Seer realized that he'd fallen back against the cave wall. It had worked, but it wasn't over.

"Eric, it's us!" Roselyn said, shaking him.

"No!" the Seer shouted. "We're still in to Niflhiem! That's Hel talking through Eric! Pick him up and run! Up the tunnel! Go, or we're dead!"

"No!" Eric cried. *"Nidhogg!"*

"Flee!" the Seer cried.

The Seer paused only a moment to grab his empty black case, and then he fled, following the others up the narrow tunnel. These tunnels were coarse stone and soon led into darkness. The Seer knew a spell for light, but he was too tired and in too much of a hurry. They stumbled through the darkness, feeling their way up the tunnel.

A fearsome crash shook the tunnel and thundered in their ears.

"It's Nidhogg!" the Seer cried. "He's ramming the crevice, trying to crush us. Keep going!"

"Eric's struggling ...!" Roselyn shouted.

"Ignore him!" the Seer shouted. "Just go on!"

Several more times the tunnel crashed and shook. The Seer feared that the tunnel might collapse, but it didn't. They ran up its steep incline, which turned and wound freely, and finally leveled off. Suddenly he heard the others fall down and they all shouted.

"What happened?" the Seer demanded.

"Eric!" Seren cried.

"He's gone!" Rafe shouted.

The Seer reached inside his robe and dug into the pocket where he kept his blessed moonstone. When he pulled it out, the darkness vanished as Eric's ghostly form glowed into view, standing before them as he had in the dark courtyard of Castle Bristlen.

"We did it!" the Seer cried. "Eric's only physical inside Niflhiem! We've escaped!"

"Eric!" Eloise shouted joyously, and she tried to hug him, but her arms waved right through Eric's ethereal form.

"Do not be alarmed," the Seer said. "Eric's back to his spirit-shape, as he existed in Castle Bristlen. Eric has no physical form outside of Niflhiem, nor can he talk, but he's free of Hel's control. Eric, listen! You must follow us now, and stay close, because your glow's our only source of light. We're going to Valhalla again, but now we'll lead you. Stay with us, and help us, if you can."

Eric's ghostly form nodded.

"Hand me his arm and sword," the Seer said. "We have to put it back in my case. Hurry! Hel knows where we are, and I'll wager that she can summon her father at any time, if she wants to."

Soon Eric's arm was stowed, although its putrid stench still filled the air; Rafe threw away his cloak that they'd wrapped it in. They resumed climbing the twisting tunnel, fearing what might be lurking around every curve. In Eric's glow, they could see that the walls were thickly blackened and sooty; clearly they were in some kind of chimney, and soon they were all smudged black with ash.

A loud howl echoed down their tunnel, angry and urgent.

"Quiet!" the Seer hissed. "That must be a troll. Hel warned me about them. Draw your swords and stand ready; Norse myths describe trolls as formidable monsters."

Secretly, the Seer was alarmed. He had no idea what a troll really was, or how many of them were here. Norse myths referred to them only as vague rumors of fell beasts, evil terrors. Yet stealing Eric had committed them; they couldn't turn back.

The Seer considered hiding the moonstone, extinguishing Eric's glow. It would make them harder to see, but chances were that any trolls who lived here could see them even in total darkness. He decided to risk the light; the odds would be even and they could move faster.

Karl and Rafe led the way, sometimes crawling up the steep tunnel, when Roselyn stopped them all.

"Look!" Roselyn pointed at the blackened wall.

"Eric, come closer," the Seer said.

As Eric approached, passing right through them as they crowded together, the marks on the wall showed clearly; claw-marks of a huge hand: five deep scratches cut into the very rock.

"That's a troll?" Karl asked. "What do you expect us to do ... against that?"

"If I can, I'll use magic," the Seer said. "But I don't know what to use. These trolls live here; they must be able to see in the dark, so cloaking us in darkness won't help. I could make us look like trolls, but I've no idea what they look like. Either way, I couldn't keep up the illusion for long. It would exhaust me, and then I'd be no help when we need it."

"Make Garm," Seren suggested. "Trolls here must know Garm, and run from wolf."

"When should I cast?" the Seer asked. "A good idea, but I could become exhausted, and my spells fail, before a troll ever sees my illusion."

"We need to see them first," Karl said. "I could sneak ahead and spy."

"Without light?" the Seer rolled his eyes. "You can't see in the dark, and if you take Eric ..."

The Seer fell silent, and then they all realized it.

"Eric, can you see in the dark?" Rafe asked.

Glowing in the radiance of the moonstone, Eric tried to speak, his lips moving, but he couldn't make a sound. He shrugged and nodded.

"We'll wait here," Eloise said. "You go scout ahead."

The light failed as Eric walked ahead, around the corner. Standing in total darkness, the Seer tried to remain still and calm, despite the fear gripping him. He could use his magic to create a little light, but even that would quickly exhaust him. Then he remembered his little candle and reached inside his robe. They were in a chimney, so one tiny flame wouldn't raise any unusual smells. He pulled out his candle and focused his concentration, as he'd done many times while sailing across the North Sea. The tiny candle blazed suddenly, illuminating them all.

"Thank goodness," Roselyn said, and the others looked equally relieved.

Eric's return startled them all, his glow suddenly brightening the cavern. He pointed ahead and motioned for silence. They followed him for quite some ways farther up the tunnel.

Eric stopped suddenly and motioned for them to stay put. He waved the Seer forward, and then pointed ahead.

Understanding, the Seer handed his candle to Seren, then closed his eyes and drew on all of the magical strength that he had left. This had to look real; he'd only get one chance. But he wasn't worried despite being already tired from casting Eric's spell of Rejoining. Mimicking Garm had been Seren's idea, and she was never wrong.

Garm!

The Seer cast his illusion upon himself. The tunnel seemed filled with the head of the giant wolf, looking even more ghastly, backlit by Eric's glow. The Seer scrambled up the slope and wound his way through the passage, Eric right behind him.

Three trolls startled as the Seer stepped into view garbed in his Garm-illusion. The Seer almost smiled, imagining what he must look like to them, a giant wolf squeezing through their tunnels, massive, snarling teeth bared, shining with unearthly light; *Seren was a genius.*

The three trolls were monstrous, taller than Karl and wider than Rafe. They had tiny eyes, but huge noses and ears; a parody of human normalcy. They had pale, mottled skin, were covered in hair, and had huge, clawed hands and feet. They wore no clothes but seemed to decorate themselves by tying rags about their limbs.

Two of the trolls, both male, screeched and jumped to flee, but the third, a female, blocked their way. She stared, unmoving, and then closed her eyes, turned one ear to the Seer, and then sniffed the air.

Fear exploded in the Seer: illusions only worked on those who used their eyes. He hadn't considered that, living in darkness, these creatures might depend more on other senses. He wondered if he could modify his illusion without breaking it, and if it would do any good; he wasn't as practiced with illusions of sound, and he'd never even heard of an illusion of scent.

The female roared like a leopard and pushed the males out of her way.

The Seer broke into a panicked run, but soon he carried the moonstone too far from Eric and plunged into darkness. He fell, blind, hearing the monster rapidly approach.

"Eric!" the Seer cried desperately.

The Seer scrambled blindly, falling down slopes that he'd previously climbed. Eric's glow reappeared just as the female troll charged at him. It swiped a huge clawed hand at the Seer, but the Seer jumped back an instant before it raked his chest open. Her giant claws ripped through the fabric of his black robe, shredded it, and caught on a leafy cord around his neck.

The Seer fell back, terrified; he was no match for the monstrous troll. She loomed over him, but paused to look at the tiny treasure in her hand.

It was Titania's gift, the white crystal; the leafy vine had broken and left its white crystal egg in the troll's hairy palm. The Seer gasped to see it; he'd sworn not to let it fall into evil hands.

The Seer was going to die, and he'd failed his Lady: *he couldn't fail Titania as well.*

While the creature was distracted, the Seer leaped forward. He grabbed at the crystal, but only managed to knock it from the troll's hand.

The crystal fell, crashed to the stone floor of the tunnel, and shattered. Broken shards flew in all directions, harmless, but disastrous. The huge female troll growled angrily, seized the Seer in her clawed hands, and lifted him to the tunnel's ceiling.

'Forgive me, Lady!' the Seer thought, but he was glad that the crystal had broken; he'd promised to destroy it before he let evil possess it.

Suddenly two lights burst from the floor, not a glow like Eric's, but bright, piercing light. Gold and silver it shined, making the troll wince. The Seer gasped in wonder.

Out of the broken white crystal egg flew two of Titania's fairies, glistening on thin, sparkling dragonfly wings. One was male; he seemed to be made of pure gold, his skin glistening like polished metal. The other was female; brilliant silver, a metallic sheen over her whole body. Both were no taller than a handspan, too big to have fit inside the white crystal, but the Seer didn't stop to question it. Pressed against the roof of the tunnel, he squirmed in the angry troll's grip, fighting to free himself.

The golden male fairie suddenly flew up and hovered before him, right in front of the troll's face. A light greater than any burst from his gold body, brilliantly blasted, and filled the cave. The Seer clenched his eyes shut, covered them with his hands, and still the bright light penetrated; pure sunlight had descended into the cave to blind them with its brilliance. The troll and the Seer both screamed.

The sunlight faded suddenly, and then it was gone. The Seer blinked stupidly, blinded by spots before his eyes. When he could see again, the Seer gasped at the sight.

The troll had turned to stone. The Seer was still in her grasp, pinned against the ceiling, but she was no longer a living troll. Only her statue stood, her pained expression frozen forever as she was transformed into unliving rock.

"Ug-ly!" the golden fairie scorned. "Put her on top of a cathedral! What a gargoyle!"

"Glororil!" the silver fairie scolded. "Look what you did! How's the Seer supposed to get down from there?"

The Seer stopped struggling and hung in its stone grip.

"You ... know me?" he asked.

"Obviously!" the golden fairie sneered. "We've been with you since Titania's well, haven't we?"

"Glororil!" the silver fairie shouted. "Sometimes, I swear, you can be downright rude!"

The silver fairy flew up and hovered right in front of the Seer's nose.

"Forgive him," she apologized. "We didn't ask to go on this mission, but Titania insisted. I'm Silvana. We've been a part of your company all along; you just didn't know it."

The Seer stared at her, uncertain if he should. Silvana was beautiful, clearly equal of Eloise and Roselyn, but tiny, and sparking with silver light. Her skin was metallic silver, shining in Eric's glow, reflecting his own face as he gaped at her. Even her eyes and hair were silver, and he couldn't help but notice that she wore no clothes. The Seer felt like he should turn away, but he couldn't.

"I'm afraid that we can't get you down," she said, looking at the thick stone hands encircling his ribs.

"You've been with us ... the whole time?" the Seer asked.

"Since Titania made you swear the oath," Silvana said. "We watched everything; Grusshire, Bristlen, and the North Sea; that really had us worried."

"Us, too," the Seer said. "Ummmm, you were watching, even when ...?"

"Human love means nothing to us!" Glororil spat. "That was bad enough, but the privy ...!"

"He gets like this sometimes," Silvana smiled. "Don't worry; he's actually quite sweet."

"Not to humans!" Glororil insisted.

The Seer wanted to continue talking but stone claws were cutting into his ribs.

"I hate to ask ... but this is starting to hurt," the Seer said.

"I'll get your friends," Silvana smiled, and she flew off down the tunnel in a blur of silver sparks.

"Harrumph!" Glororil harrumphed.

The Seer looked at Glororil; he was tiny but muscular, and also not wearing clothes.

"How did you ...?"

"Turn the troll into stone?" Glororil asked. "Stupid human! Sunlight always turns trolls into stone; that's why they live down here, as far away from it as they can get. I can make sunlight, real sunlight, but don't ask me to do it again, 'cause I won't. Can't do it for long anyway. Takes a lot of energy to make sunlight, so I can only do short bursts."

"I understand," the Seer said.

"Sure you do," Glororil chuckled derisively. "You tried to frighten trolls with an optical illusion."

The Seer glared at the golden fairie, but he quickly turned away. He didn't like being talked to like he was an idiot. It especially galled him ... because that was how he talked to Karl.

Chapter 12

Troll Troubles

KARL

Everyone startled as a silver fairy flew into the candlelight.

"Hurry!" she said, their tiny candle-flame reflecting off of her metallic, silvery skin. "The Seer needs help! Follow me!"

The silver fairie flew back, paused just inside the edge of the candlelight, and then sped back up the tunnel. She vanished in a trail of silver sparks.

"What was that?" Rafe asked.

"A fairie!" Karl gasped. "Like ... Titania!"

"Who was she?" Roselyn asked.

"Go!" Eloise ordered. "Whoever she was, she said that the Seer needed help!"

Seren lead the way with the candle, lighting the tunnel. It seemed to go on forever, twisting and turning, and Karl helped her scrabble up the inclines. But he kept his sword drawn, in case he needed it, and he wished that he still had his shield.

Finally they saw Eric's glow, and his light revealed a strange scene: two small fairies, one golden, one silver, hovered before the Seer, who seemed to be climbing on top of a huge stone gargoyle.

"Get me down!" the Seer shouted.

"How you get there?" Seren asked, but the Seer ignored her.

Rafe pushed forward and let the Seer's dangling legs rest on his shoulders. Standing, the Seer managed to shift position, but he was still stuck.

"Give me a sword!" the Seer said.

"You're not going to ruin my blade cutting stone," Karl said.

"I need to use the pommel," the Seer said.

"Here," Rafe said, handing up his own sword, "just hurry!"

Holding the moonstone in one hand, the Seer pounded on one of the troll's thumbs with Rafe's pommel, banged until the stone thumb broke off, and then he squeezed through the gap. Rafe helped him climb down the monstrous statue, and then the Seer dusted himself off. The chest of his black robe was shredded, but otherwise he looked unharmed.

"That statue was a living troll a few moments ago," the Seer said. "Glororil, the golden fairy, can make sunlight, and that turned the troll to stone."

"You only knew that because I told you!" Glororil shouted.

"Stop it!" the silver fairie scolded both of them. "I'm Silvana. This is Glororil. Titania put us in the white crystal before she gave it to the Seer so that we could help when you needed us."

"That's why she told you to break it when you thought that you were going to die," Glororil grinned at the Seer. "You didn't know that either, did you?"

"Enough!" Silvana said. "We're still in the troll's lair, and we need to get out."

"What if we run into more trolls?" the Seer asked. "Glororil can't turn them all to stone."

The golden fairie glared at the Seer.

"Eric, lead us again," Eloise said. "Come back and let us know if you see any more trolls."

Eric led the way; his ghostly form vanished around the next bend in the tunnel. The light of his glow extinguished as he left the invisible radiance of the moonstone. The others followed more slowly in the light of Seren's candle.

Karl kept looking at Silvana, amazed; she was naked and very shapely, although tiny. Glororil was equally naked, but Karl tried not to look at him. Both shined in the candlelight.

"You can turn trolls to stone?" Eloise asked Silvana.

"Stupid ...," Glororil began, but Silvana silenced him with a gentle slap.

"Trolls naturally turn to stone in sunlight," Silvana explained. "They're creatures of darkness, and they regenerate quickly, if wounded. But sunlight kills them; that's why they live underground. Glororil can shine with sunlight, but it's very taxing; he can't do it for long."

Glororil hissed angrily and flew ahead, trailing golden sparks.

"In crystal, see and hear all?" Seren asked.

"Yes, everything," Silvana smiled. "You needn't be embarrassed; few humans could've faced the dangers that you've conquered; Titania chose well to let you come here."

"But our travels ... on horse and boat ...," Rafe said.

"We were there," Silvana said, "watching."

Karl felt embarrassed, wondering what they'd seen.

Soon Eric's glow brightened the tunnel. Eric was standing before a wide crossroad where two tunnels crossed. Pieces of bones lay scattered on the floor at his spectral feet, looking deeply gnawed, as if a dog had chewed them. Eric motioned to the numerous tunnels, obviously perplexed.

"Trolls ate here," the Seer said. "Which way do we go?"

Eric motioned for them all to remain. He pointed to Eloise and motioned for her to follow. Shrugging, Eloise did so, trailing as he vanished up one sloping tunnel.

"Candle soon gone," Seren said, holding out what was left of the Seer's candle. Karl was worried; he didn't want to be left in the dark again. Seren set the stub on the tunnel floor so that it could burn to its very bottom.

Eloise quickly returned.

"Trolls are that way," Eloise said. "Lots of them. But I saw a light. There's a big cavern ahead, full of trolls, and lots of other tunnels, but a bright light glows on the far side of it."

"Must be a way out," Karl said.

"We don't know that," the Seer said.

"The trolls can't see Eric," Eloise said. "I sent him ahead to check out the light. We'll wait here until he returns."

"How many trolls did you see?" Roselyn asked.

"Too many," Eloise said. "They were moving about a lot, going in and out of many tunnels."

"They probably know that we're here," the Seer said. "Two males saw me and fled before the female tried to kill me."

"Then they may be trying to ambush us," Karl said, looking behind them. "This crossroad's dangerous. Let's move closer to the cavern."

Eloise led as they entered the tunnel. They climbed up a sharp slope and then onto a narrow shelf. Seren moved slowly; the dripping candle was almost gone, just a melting stub in her hand.

Suddenly Seren cried out and dropped their spent candle. Its tiny light extinguished: total darkness blinded them.

"Rafe!" Karl whispered. "Move up to the front and keep your blade ready. If anything comes at us in the dark, we should at least be prepared."

Karl moved by feel toward the back, careful not to cut anyone with his sword. He heard Rafe move forward, whispering to the others to get a sense of everyone's location. Both tried to move quietly, but the 'shink' of their mail echoed down the inky tunnel. Karl understood why Eric had taken Eloise to spy on the trolls; she was small, quiet, and didn't wear armor.

The wait seemed interminable. Fear began to ripple up Karl's spine as he stared blindly into the darkness, imagining foes and wondering if they were real.

"Ssshhhh!" Karl hissed.

Up the tunnel came soft scratching sounds: claws on stone. Quickly the sounds grew closer and louder. Karl held tight to his sword, not knowing if they were watching him or not, wondering if they were out of his reach or inches before him.

Suddenly Silvana flew past Karl, spiraling in a shower of silver sparks. Eyes glowed in her trail's sparkling radiance, and growls sounded as two trolls climbed up the slope right behind them.

"Trolls!" Karl shouted.

Glororil spun past him, right at the trolls. Suddenly he exploded with light. Karl fell back, blinded by the brilliance, and covered his stinging eyes. A terrible wail cried out, lasting until the light faded.

When Karl looked again, the two trolls, and several more behind them, had turned to stone. All looked agonized, frozen in the fading sparkles of Silvana's silver sparks. Yet Karl noticed that Glororil was barely flying; Silvana held him aloft by both of his arms, keeping him from falling. Glororil looked exhausted, his wings barely flapping.

"That was great!" Karl said.

"Can he do it again?" Eloise asked. "If he did that in the big cavern then he could turn a hundred trolls to stone all at once."

"He must," Silvana said, "but he'll be of no use to anyone after that. One of you must carry him."

"Seren do," Seren said, and Silvana's silver sparkles illuminated Seren's upheld hand as she lowered Glororil onto her palm.

"Let's go!" Karl said.

"Shouldn't we wait for Eric?" Rafe asked.

"The tunnel behind us is completely blocked," Karl said. "We need to get out of here before they come at us from this side. If they come now, even if Glororil stones them, then we'll be trapped between their statues, unable to escape. That cavern's our only escape."

Silvana flew on ahead. Her sparks gave little light, but it was enough; they followed her up the narrow tunnel. Karl felt bad for the golden fairie; Titania had given him her favor, and he'd be ashamed if one of her people got hurt because of him.

Ahead of them glowed a dim light.

"Trolls!" Rafe whispered.

"That's the entrance to their cavern," Eloise said.

"Let me by!" Karl said, and he pushed his way to stand next to Rafe.

At the end of the tunnel stood numerous trolls, snarling and howling, saliva dripping from huge, hungry mouths. Karl and Rafe pointed their swords at them but to little avail; the tunnel was too narrow for proper sword-swings, and stabs and jabs would do little against these monsters.

Suddenly Silvana whizzed past, again carrying Glororil in her arms. Right between the hulking beasts she flew, dodging to avoid their clumsy grasps, and up into the center of the cavern.

Suddenly sunlight blazed inside the cavern, flooding them with light, illuminating a sea of trolls. Troll-screams deafened them all.

"Hurry!" Rafe shouted to Karl. "Now, or we'll be trapped!"

Rafe dashed forward as a troll pushed itself into the tunnel, fleeing from the light. The two collided, but Rafe struck hardest, and he knocked the troll back into the brightness. Karl followed, stabbing and pushing back another desperate troll, forcing his way out of the tunnel in time to see a hundred terrified trolls just as their writhings slowed and their flailing limbs began to stiffen. Their pale, mottled skin turned ashen gray, and then hardened; a hundred trolls turned to stone before Karl's eyes.

The light failed. Darkness swallowed them, save for a single spot. Far away, on the opposite side of the cavern, a bright beam of light shined down from the ceiling, illuminating a wide, empty crevice.

"Let's go!" the Seer cried, pushing from behind. "Hurry! Not all of the trolls were stoned!"

Moving anywhere was difficult; stone statues of trolls, frozen in anguish, blocked every path. Off-balanced, some tilted and threatened to fall over; a falling gargoyle could crush a companion.

Karl pushed through with Rafe right behind him. Easily Karl slipped between the statues, dodging shadowy stone troll-limbs, sliding his thinner body through gaps where Rafe had difficulty. Karl reached the edge of a tall ledge which the many trolls had attempted to climb to escape Glororil's sunlight. Seeing no recourse, Karl climbed down the troll statues to the cavern floor, using their arms and legs as rungs on a ladder. But the press of stone trolls was even thicker there and his going became slower.

A roar emitted from one of the numerous tunnels, followed by many more. The whole cavern echoed with the growls of living trolls who had escaped the powerful sunlight.

"Karl!" a shrill, tiny voice shouted, and Karl looked up. Poised on the stone arm of a troll was Silvana, Glororil unconscious in her arms.

"I'll get them," the Seer shouted. "Go on!"

"Hurry!" Silvana shouted.

Karl soon entered a less-dense region, free of troll-statues. Rafe joined him, his sword now sheathed, and the Seer came up behind Rafe, the tiny golden fairie carefully cupped in his hands. The women trailed right behind him. Glororil looked haggard, exhausted.

"This way!" Silvana shouted, and she flew past them in a glittering shower.

Suddenly many trolls roared. Karl spun to see dozens of trolls issuing out of the side tunnels, pouring into the cavern like giant rats. Furiously they howled, indiscriminately knocking over their statuesque brethren to give chase.

"Run!" Karl shouted, and he sprinted across the cavern floor. The others followed, but the illuminated crevice was a long way off. The trolls came fast, from every direction, climbing over their frozen fellows, snarling and howling.

"Faster!" the Seer cried.

"We'll never make it!" Roselyn screamed.

Suddenly Silvana flew up before them.

"Keep going!" Silvana cried. "Into the light! Don't stop, no matter what!"

Silvana flew up and hovered in midair. She spread her arms and legs wide, and suddenly a soft, bluish light burst from her silver skin. The whole cavern illuminated with her hushed, subtle glow.

The trolls faltered, fearing more sunlight, but Silvana's bluish glow wasn't sunlight. The trolls hesitated, but then chased faster.

"What is it?" Roselyn asked, still running.

"Moonlight?" Seren guessed.

"Moonlight?" the Seer gasped. *"Oh, no! Eloise!!!"*

The company halted, regardless of the rampaging trolls. Eloise had fallen; she writhed on the ground behind them.

"Eloise!" Rafe cried, and he started toward her.

"No!" the Seer cried, grabbing Rafe and pulling him on. "Run! It's the Wolfqueen!"

Trembling unbearably, Eloise ground her teeth, her eyes squeezed shut, her every muscle knotted. Finally she burst out an agonized, familiar howl. All of the trolls oriented on her, quickly closing the distance.

"Run!" the Seer cried.

Led by the Seer, Rafe and the others ran away, but Karl stood frozen. Tears welled in his eyes; he'd promised Eloise that this wouldn't happen again, but there wasn't anything that he could do to stop it. Blonde fur sprouted, and deadly claws suddenly burst from her fingertips. A short muzzle pushed outwards, gleaming with razor-sharp teeth. Horrified moments passed, and all too soon her excruciating transformation was complete. Despite Karl's promise, the Wolfqueen lived again.

"Run!" the Seer shouted behind him. "Karl, they can't hurt her! She'll be all right!"

Karl turned and ran; Eloise would kill him if he tried to help her. Inside his lair, the Wolflord had almost beaten them all, and back then they had Eric and Liz Apple; against the Wolfqueen they'd be helpless.

The steady light ahead grew brighter as they approached it. A narrow shaft opened in the cavern wall with bright sunlight beaming straight down inside it. They ran into the bright light to find that the shaft was only about twenty feet high. Handholds were scratched into its rough, rocky walls. The Seer pocketed Glororil and his moonstone inside of his torn robe and started climbing.

"Follow me!" the Seer shouted.

"What about Eloise?" Rafe demanded.

"What can hurt her?" the Seer asked, and he pushed up into the light. "Hurry! There's a big opening up here!"

Karl looked back as he reached the safety of the light; the Wolfqueen leaped up just as the trolls reached her. Dozens of the monsters swarmed over her, clawing and rending, but their fearsome roars quickly turned to howls of pain. In the dim moonlight, Karl saw them fall back and heard their yipes and scuffles. Karl tried to smile, imagining what the Wolfqueen must be doing to them, but he couldn't; Eloise was suffering.

The trolls fled. The Wolfqueen pounced on one, brought it down, and ripped it apart. Silvana's moonlight revealed her hellish wolf-form, her long blonde hair almost glowing. Mere moments the Wolfqueen spent rending the troll apart, and then she turned, ready to chase the others.

"No!" Karl cried. "Eloise! Over here!"

The Wolfqueen spun and her red eyes blazed. Even at this distance, Karl's good eyesight could make out the murder in her eyes as she oriented on him. Eloise snarled and ran toward him, clawing her way across the cavern.

"Climb!" Rafe shouted as Roselyn and Seren screamed.

Rafe grabbed both women and pushed them towards the wall. Instantly they began climbing up into the light, following the Seer, who was almost at the top. Karl pushed against their feet to help them, and then he grabbed Rafe and helped him up onto the rocks as Eloise charged closer.

"Look out!" Rafe cried.

Karl spun, terrified. Slavering, her eyes full of hate and fury, the Wolfqueen pounced upon Karl, claws and fangs eager for blood. Into the bright sunlight she leaped, right on top of him. Her sharp claws stabbed into his strong, silvered mail.

Suddenly the Wolfqueen howled in pain as the sunlight struck her. She flailed wildly, one arm striking Karl's helmet hard enough to stun him. Then she collapsed on top of him, cringing and screaming. Slowly the Wolfqueen transformed back into Eloise.

Amazed and terrified, Karl held Eloise as she changed; Eloise's familiar features slowly molded out of the Wolfqueen's savage semblance. One instant Eloise was blonde death, and then a trembling young girl writhing in unbearable anguish.

"Eloise!" Karl cried, clutching her against his chest. "Eloise!"

Tears poured from Eloise's eyes, but she couldn't speak. Karl held her, helpless.

Silvana flew into the bright light, her silver skin glistening yellow in its radiance.

"Climb!" the tiny silver fairie urged. "Trolls can't enter the light, but they can hurl big stones! Hurry, before they come back!"

Karl had no choice. He pushed to stand, still holding Eloise, and then lifted her over his shoulder and climbed. The warm sunlight felt good after the chill of Niflhiem and the tunnels of the trolls. But Karl had no idea where they were going, or what they'd face next.

Chapter 13

Radsvid

RAFE

Rafe scrambled up, determined to ascend the rough-stone vertical shaft quickly so that he could help Karl lift up Eloise. It wasn't an easy climb; Rafe's age and stocky build hampered him, and the weight of his mail dragged heavily. Yet Rafe pulled himself up, and then almost fell back when he spied the summit.

Seren and Roselyn grabbed Rafe's arms and helped pull him up onto the smooth, finished boards. A wide wooden platform lay atop the rough stone crevice, and bright sunlight shined directly upon it. Sparkling, Silvana flitted in the sunlight, hovering before the Seer, who was holding the unconscious golden fairie and chanting a spell of healing.

Before the crevice stood a great glowing gem, a magnificent diamond, hanging from an iron chain. Below it was a wide silver mirror, angled so that it reflected the diamond's bright glow to another silver mirror mounted inside the stony shaft. Its radiant sunlight beamed down into the troll's cavern.

Karl's appearance at the top startled Rafe from his fascination. Rafe quickly lifted Eloise's limp body off of Karl's shoulder, laid her on the polished deck, and knelt beside her.

The silver fairie flew over her.

"I'm so sorry," Silvana apologized to Eloise, although Eloise gave no sign that she heard. "We wanted to tell you, but Titania warned us that there might be no time. I shine with moonlight, as Glororil shines with sunlight. Moonlight takes much less energy so I can maintain it longer. Together, we can control your transformations."

"Why?" Rafe angrily glared up at the silver fairie.

"Owww!" Silvana cried out, and she fell back as if Rafe'd struck her.

"Rafe, stop it!" the Seer shouted. "She's fairie! Your eyes upon her are like Loki's eyes upon us! Don't glare at her with strong emotions!"

Rafe quickly subsided, turning his gaze from Silvana, but he was still angry.

"Titania wanted us to help you," Silvana gasped painfully, fearfully, her tiny, anxious face turned toward Rafe. "We fairies have little strength such as humans understand, so Titania sent us to bring out Eloise's wolf-strength when you need it."

Rafe glowered, but kept his eyes from Silvana. He didn't like anything that hurt Eloise; Eloise was his daughter as far as he was concerned. The Wolfqueen, and anything that empowered her, was the work of the devil. Yet Rafe knew that he'd pressed the girl-fairie too hard; Silvana was obviously frightened, and he couldn't blame her. Rafe was amazed to think of his eyes being like Loki's to anyone; he didn't want to hurt the fairie. As small as she was, he could probably crush her with ease, even accidentally. He'd have to be more careful.

Karl walked up behind him as Rafe touched Eloise's throat, feeling her blood pulse beneath his fingers.

"How is she?" Karl asked.

"Out cold," Rafe replied. "I think that she fainted."

"Small wonder," the Seer said, still holding the unconscious golden fairy. "Who knows what kind of a shock to her system that was? To transform into a lycanthrope, and then to transform back minutes later: that's probably never happened before."

"What can we do?" Roselyn asked.

"She needs rest," the Seer said. "We need a place to hide for a while, someplace safe."

"Glororil needs rest, too," Silvana said.

"Where we now?" Seren asked.

"Nidavellir, the land of the Dwarves," the Seer said. "I don't know anything about it, save what Hel told me. She said that we'd emerge on the Dwarf Ring; I guess that's where we are."

"Are we still inside the big tree?" Roselyn asked.

"I assume so, but I don't know," the Seer said. "Norse geography isn't very precise. Stories in both of the eddas that I read seemed to contradict each other on where some places were and how to get to them; relational perspectives don't seem to apply here. We saw Yggdrasil from its roots, and Niflhiem and the Well of Hvergelmir were both too vast to be contained by it. But, if we are in dwarf-land, then we're still underground, and have to go up."

Rafe bent and picked up Eloise; they couldn't stay here. Also, they needed to find fresh food. Their remaining supply of vegetables was small and going bad. If not for the invigorating water, hunger might turn them back. Perhaps they should've stayed in Niflhiem long enough to restock their provisions, but then, if they had, then they'd probably have remained forever.

"We'd best go," Rafe said. "Hel said that Loki would know when we left Niflhiem, and he could be anywhere. We're too visible out here in the open."

"Someplace with a hot bath would be nice," Roselyn muttered, wiping the black soot off of her hands as best she could.

Rafe ignored her and looked around. They stood on a wooden platform, which seemed to be widely curved against a tall, carved-stone wall. An ornate wooden rail rested on the inner edge of the deck and a strong wind blew on their faces. Rafe carried Eloise to the rail and looked over it.

Rafe froze and clutched Eloise protectively. Over the rail was a great drop, a view that could only be seen from the tallest mountain. Rafe seemed to be looking down through misty white clouds; far below lay hills, rivers, an icy coastline, and a wide sea. Islands dotted just off shore, looking tiny, too far away to see clearly.

"Where are we?" the Seer gasped.

Rafe couldn't turn to look at the others, who had crowded around, equally amazed by the view. Silvana fearlessly flew out over the edge of the rail, flying wide and free in the vast openness.

"You're on the fabulous Dwarf Ring," shouted a grating, gravelly voice, "and you're all my prisoners!"

Behind them stood a short man, a dwarf with long, greasy black hair and a heavy beard that drooped to his toes, wearing a dirty leather apron and thick boots. In his hands was a long, sharp spear, which he held pointed at them.

"Who are you?" the Seer asked.

"Radsvid's my name," he growled. "Drop your swords! You're my prisoners."

"Are we?" Karl asked, drawing his sword and stepping toward the dwarf.

"Black Spear, attack!" Radsvid shouted.

Karl froze, his sword ready, but nothing happened. Karl smiled, but then Radsvid snarled and pounded his stout speartip against the wooden deck.

"Attack!" Radsvid cried. "Darn contraption! Black Spear, attack!"

Suddenly the long black spear jerked, almost pulling itself from the dwarf's hands. Radsvid brandished it at Karl, who jumped back, avoiding the new threat. The deadly metal spear haft bent and flexed like the body of a snake, thrusting its razor-sharp point at Karl from strange directions. It moved like a living thing, and jabbed at anything that approached it. Rafe hesitated, wondering how Karl could defend himself against a magic living weapon, ready to set Eloise down and draw his own sword, but the Seer motioned for him to remain still.

"Ha!" Radsvid laughed. "It works! Now throw away your swords! You're my prisoners!"

"We need our swords," the Seer said, stepping calmly forward. "We're travelers passing through your land. Why would you want us as prisoners?"

"Not you!" Radsvid sneered, and then he glanced at Roselyn, Eloise, and Seren. *"Them."*

The lustful gleam in Radsvid's eyes left no doubt as to his intention.

"Like hell ...!" Karl raised his sword.

"Wait!" the Seer said to Karl. "Radsvid, if we were your prisoners, where would you take us?"

"You *are* my prisoners!" Radsvid said. "My home. Why?"

"How far is your home, and can we get there without anyone else seeing us?" the Seer asked.

"Sure," Radsvid said.

"Then lead on!" the Seer said. "We will keep our swords, but we accept our place as your prisoners."

"What?!?" Karl demanded.

Rafe grinned. Radsvid's home didn't sound comforting, but it was better than wandering lost. If a God and a half-goddess were after them, they mostly needed information so that they could get out of this land quickly and quietly; Radsvid was probably as good a source of the local geography as they were going to find. Rafe didn't like the way that he looked at the women, but the dwarf seemed to be a small threat, unlike Loki and his daughter. The Seer was being wise, although Rafe would never say so aloud. Like Eric, the Seer was a deeply religious man; he'd make a good Christian.

"Yes," Rafe interrupted them. "Radsvid, we surrender. Lead us away."

Karl turned and stared at Rafe, amazed and frustrated.

"That way," Radsvid said, motioning with his living spear, which was becoming more agitated, stabbing at the air faster and faster.

"Silvana!" Roselyn called to the silver fairie. "This way!"

"Radsvid, what is this precipice?" the Seer asked as they walked beside the rail.

"This is the great Dwarf Ring," Radsvid said. "See at that rainbow, up in the clouds? That's Bifrost, Heimdall's bridge. Below, that's Midgard."

"Midgard?" the Seer asked, looking down. "Earth?"

"You should know, human; it's your home."

"Home?" Seren asked.

"Incredible," the Seer said. "We must be looking down from the sky. That must be Norway, at least the western coast of it."

"Never been there," Radsvid said. "Don't want to go, either. We built a great slide, once, and covered the sunstone that keeps the trolls in their tunnel. We hoped to drop them all down to Midgard so that we could mine their tunnels. Didn't work."

"Sunstone?" the Seer asked. "You mean that giant diamond in front of the mirrors?"

"Yes, it soaks up sunlight during the day and shines it all night," Radsvid said. "Keeps the trolls down in their tunnels. Stupid stone-brains! We offered them your whole world ... and they tried to eat us!"

Radsvid struggled to hold his living spear. It was flailing wildly, jerking this way and that, almost pulling him off of his feet.

"Enough!" Radsvid cried. "Black Spear, stop!"

The spear kept stabbing, jerking harder.

"Stop!" Radsvid cried. "Halt! Desist! Terminate!"

Radsvid pounded his living spear harshly against the wooden deck.

"Stop, I say!" he shouted. "Quiet down!"

The jerking movements slowed and finally stopped with its haft twisted around, its deadly tip pointed back at Radsvid.

"Infernal contraption," the dwarf grumbled.

Rafe turned away so that the dwarf couldn't see his grin. As Rafe suspected, Radsvid was no real threat to them. Rafe glanced up the wide shaft at the clouds, seeing bright sunlight pour through the open roof far above, which followed the line of the rail around the wide ring. It seemed to be a great circle, but his old eyes couldn't see the far side. Karl might; Karl had great eyesight, but Rafe didn't ask. Then Rafe looked down at Midgard and wondered how high up they were, or if it were all some fantastic illusion like Skaldi had created.

Eloise moaned and shifted in his arms, but she didn't regain consciousness. Rafe held her tightly, feeling like a proud parent carrying his child.

"By the wall," Radsvid ordered, and they left the rail and walked to the stone wall encircling the Dwarf Ring. It was intricately carved with shallow pictographs, but solid, not a crack to be seen. Then Radsvid pressed on a secret spot, and a section of the wall swung out like a door. "Inside, and no tricks!"

Karl turned to glare questioningly at Rafe, but the stable-master gave him no response. Karl let out a heavy sigh and walked through the low doorway. Rafe shook his head; if he explained their surrender to Karl now then Radsvid would hear, and the dwarf probably wouldn't like it.

Inside, the corridor was made of blocks of rough stone, walling a passageway lined with extinguished torches. As they approached the torches, they ignited by themselves. Radsvid closed the secret door behind them, and as he walked, following them at a safe distance, the torches behind him extinguished.

They walked a short ways down the tunnel, and then Radsvid ordered them to stop. He pressed another, seemingly-random spot on the wall, and another secret door opened.

"Welcome to my home," Radsvid said, motioning with his bent spear. "Inside, all of you."

They entered a large, dimly-lit workshop. Everything was covered in soot and dust, and it stank of smoke. A bright fire burned in a large forge in the center of the room, and directly above it hung a great mirrored-spiral, anchored to the ceiling, pointing down at the fire. The forge's firelight reflected off of the mirrored-spiral to light the entire room, but the mirrored-spiral was blackened with soot and reflected the light poorly; it might've worked well if it weren't so filthy.

Silvana dashed in ahead of them as if eager to investigate. Radsvid's workshop was littered with forged metal, including some gold and silver, but mostly iron forged into strange tools and inventions, most of which had no purpose that Rafe could guess. Some were obvious, but had equally obvious flaws.

"What are these?" the Seer asked, motioning towards a pair of thick boots. Long, sharp spikes were coming out of the soles of the boots, and both boots were nailed to the wall.

"Wall-walking boots," Radsvid said. "That's what they're supposed to be. Wall-standing boots they turned out to be. The first step was easy. But I never got to take a second step; can't even pry them loose."

"Brilliant," the Seer smiled. "What about these heavy iron wings?"

"Never mind about those!" Radsvid snapped. "You're my prisoners!"

"By all means," the Seer said, "but even prisoners need to eat. It's been hours, and we're starving …"

"What?!?" Radsvid demanded. "I give the orders here! Put that girl on my bed. Then you men go over there, against the far wall, and stay there!"

Rafe glared at the dwarf, wondering if he really expected him to surrender Eloise. He made no move to obey.

"You want food?" Radsvid asked.

"Not that badly," Rafe said.

"You must want something else," Radsvid said. "Jewelry? Weapons? Armor? I can make wonderful things, valuable to have, yes?"

"What do you want in exchange?" Karl asked.

"Your women, of course," Radsvid said.

"We're not for sale!" Roselyn shouted.

In her armor, Roselyn stormed threateningly up toward the filthy dwarf. She towered over him, glowering, but Radsvid only reached out a hand and grabbed her leg.

"Hey!" Roselyn pushed him back, her eyes flaring angrily, and she made a fist of her gauntleted hand; Rafe smiled, hoping that she'd hit him.

"Warrior wench, eh?" Radsvid grinned wickedly. "I like that; feisty women squirm under the covers."

Roselyn swung hard, but the dwarf merely dodged back and retreated to a safe distance.

"Not with you, you grubby, disgusting little rodent!" Roselyn threatened. "One more word and I'll beat you senseless!"

Radsvid calmed, holding up his open hands, and said nothing. He slowly approached Roselyn again. She glowered down at him; his beady black eyes never left her.

"Nice armor," Radsvid said. "I could forge you better, of course. Invulnerable, that never rusts or grows dim, and a sword worthy of your beauty."

"I'll never pay your price," Roselyn said.

"Never's a long time," Radsvid grinned, looking up at her. "You'll change your mind once you see my ... skills at the forge."

Roselyn fumed, and finally spun around, turning her back to him.

"Never!"

"My, my!" Radsvid slavered, admiring her backside. "Such a pretty round one! Can't wait to get my hands on that!"

"Oh!" Roselyn shouted, and she swung her fist again, but Radsvid retreated under a table. Roselyn tried to run around the table, but piles of clutter blocked her passage.

"She can be first!" Radsvid said, popping out on the other side of the table and approaching Rafe. "I like them asleep ... when they can't object!"

Rafe glanced at Eloise, unconscious in his arms, and his fury rose. Smiling, Radsvid held out his arms as if he expected Rafe to drop Eloise into his grasp. Instead, Rafe drew back his foot and kicked the dwarf hard in the chest. Radsvid flew backwards and crashed into a pile of sooty junk, raising a thick cloud of dust.

"Hey!" Radsvid complained, clutching his injured chest. "Prisoners can't abuse their jailors!"

Karl stepped forward and pointed his sword at Radsvid, stabbing lightly into his greasy black beard.

"You're our prisoner now," Karl said. "Do as we say or I'll make you another head shorter. And you will never, ever, touch our women! Understand?"

"You can't kill me," the dwarf sneered. "You're my prisoners, like it or not. If you kill me, then you'll be trapped in here. Only I can open my door; in here you'll starve to death."

Karl and Radsvid glared at each other. Rafe feared that Radsvid might be telling the truth; he had no idea how to open the secret door.

"Don't kill him," Rafe said. "If we want information, I know ways to make him to talk."

"Yes, but will they be in time, or quiet?" Radsvid asked. "Loki was on the Dwarf Ring this morning asking about humans. Are you the ones that he's looking for? That makes you valuable. I could sell you, or you could appease me and I could help you escape ..."

"You won't get ...," Karl started.

"Wait!" the Seer interrupted. "Radsvid, we need to get to Jotunhiem, the land of the Giants. Do you know how to get there?"

"The Black River flows straight there," Radsvid said. "Of course, it winds through Svartalfhiem, where the murderous dark elves live, but it's the fastest way. The river's about an hour's walk from here, if you know the route. I can take you to the river directly ... for a price."

"Never," Karl said.

"Fine," Radsvid grinned. "Eat your swords when you're hungry."

"Don't be hasty, Karl," the Seer said. "We should rest and discuss the situation. There must be a less risky way of going on. If we get hungry, we could always see what roasted dwarf tastes like."

"Don't pretend that you're any different than me!" Radsvid laughed. "You don't want me to have your women because you want them for yourselves!"

"Lewd creature!" Silvana said, flying low, showering Radsvid with silver sparks.

"Need a cage to put you in, my pretty!" Radsvid said, and he tried to grab her, but Silvana '*eeked*', streaked away in a flash, and hovered safely near the ceiling.

"Enough," Rafe said firmly, but secretly he felt ashamed. Radsvid was partially right; they did want the women for themselves. He and Seren hadn't slipped away in Niflhiem only because there was no place to go and the stink of death permeated. Karl and the Seer were still contesting over Roselyn and Eloise, and they'd had even fewer opportunities.

At Roselyn's suggestion, they retired to a corner on the far side, where there was a large basin of water to wash in. Radsvid stayed on his side, leaving them alone. Karl cleared off a table with his arm, sending half a dozen strange devices crashing to the floor, and was obviously amused by Radsvid's shout of complaint. Roselyn draped her cloak over the dirty table and Rafe set Eloise, who moaned softly, onto the cloak to let her sleep in peace. The Seer set Glororil beside her ... but not too close, in case Eloise rolled over in her sleep.

Beside her, the golden fairie looked like an expensive child's doll.

The large basin had a pipe hanging above it, out of which fresh water was trickling. The excess water drained out of a spigot on the side of the basin, into a hole in the floor. The wide spigot was far bigger than the hole, so that the water splashed all over, but Rafe didn't care; it worked better than most of Radsvid's inventions.

At Roselyn's insistence, Seren washed first while the men looked away, standing shoulder to shoulder, blocking Radsvid's view; all were covered in soot from climbing through the troll tunnels. Seren stripped and scrubbed, then took a clean dress out of their packs. It was a fancy dress, one of Eloise's gowns from Castle Bristlen, more formal than their road merited, but they had no others. Then Roselyn stripped off her armor and washed down, and she picked out a clean undertunic, but put her gambeson and armor back on. She pulled an old rag from a pile of Radsvid's junk and used it to wipe the smudges from her armor.

Eloise finally awoke while the men were washing and changing. She went after them, and soon they were all clean and dressed. Glororil also awoke, yawning, stretching, and looking much better. The golden fairy still looked tired, but he glared at the humans with disgust, and then flew up to join Silvana near the ceiling.

None of the clothes from Castle Bristlen fit the Seer. He chose a bright red tunic, which fit him like a tent, because it was the last one. Then he searched through his dirty, torn robe, dug out a thin, yellow cord, and tied it about his waist; it didn't look proper but it helped. He wrapped his blessed moonstone in a silk scarf, tied it closed, and then looped it onto his yellow-cord belt.

When they were done, Seren had the Seer empty out all the rest of his pockets and then she threw his torn robe with the rest of their dirty clothes into the basin. Quickly she set to work, washing their clothes and ringing them out.

Although still tired, Eloise insisted on meeting with Radsvid, despite their warnings. Rafe consented only if she let him escort her; satisfied, they went in search of the dwarf.

Radsvid was also busy. They found him in a small alcove, hidden by a thick, heavily-stained curtain. Inside the alcove was a huge bed, and Radsvid was busy pushing piles of junk off of it and smoothing out its ragged, moldy blankets.

"Come join me, sweet-sweet!" Radsvid cried out when he saw Eloise, but he stepped back as Rafe pulled the curtain aside to reveal his presence.

"Cave-ins!" cursed the dwarf. "Go away! We don't need you!"

"Rafe is my guard and escort," Eloise replied. "I am Baroness Eloise Elizabeth Domwin du Harmonn. I'm the leader of this company. We need to get to Jotunhiem, the land of the Giants ..."

"Yes, I'll get you there," Radsvid said. "But you must pay my price."

Rafe fumed, but Eloise didn't even flinch.

"I understand that," Eloise said, "but surely you must realize that some things we can't give. If there's something else ..."

"Nope," Radsvid said. "My bed ... or starve."

"We could kill you ...," Rafe started, but Eloise gestured him silent.

"You can't kill me," Radsvid said to Eloise. "I know a secret route to the Black River, one seldom traveled. You'll never get there without me. Loki's offered gold for your capture; the other dwarves will report you the instant that they see you. I'm your only hope, and I can name any price that I want. Lie down on my bed and send that lummox away."

"You must be reasonable," Eloise insisted.

"Why?" Radsvid asked. "Loki's not looking for me. You can't go anywhere or survive where you are: you're trapped."

Eloise glared. Radsvid smiled, leaned against his bed, and patted its musty blankets, raising a small cloud of dust.

"A leader should put the safety of her company ahead of any personal reservations," Radsvid grinned. "Is my bed so repugnant that you'd die to stay out of it?"

"Yes, it is," Eloise said. "We have other things to offer; the Seer can do magic ..."

"You're all the magic that I need," Radsvid said. "Slip out of that dress and I'll show you my magic ..."

Rafe sighed; this was pointless. He wouldn't allow it, even if Eloise agreed to. But Rafe was equally perplexed; if they tortured him, then Radsvid's screams would alert every dwarf in Nidavellir. They could slit his throat and silence him forever, but then how would they get directions to Jotunhiem? Radsvid held all of the daggers. They could break him, in time, but time was one factor that they had little of. With Hel loose, angry, and Loki already looking for them, they had to flee quickly and quietly.

"Let's go," Eloise said to Rafe, and she turned with indignant airs and stormed back to the others.

Seren washed and hung their clothes to dry. Rafe smiled as he watched her; Seren was sturdy and strong, more useful than Eloise or Roselyn. Raised without servants, Seren was accustomed to caring for herself and didn't stand idly by while others worked. Circumstances had kept them apart; Niflhiem was no place for lovers; Rafe wished that they could have a few hours alone.

Eloise insisted on discussing their predicament, in which Rafe only absently participated. Talk was useless; they should kill Radsvid and hope for the best.

"I doubt if any of my illusions would fool Radsvid," the Seer said. "Most of my spells would do little to him that Karl's sword couldn't do more easily. I could mesmerize him, if Radsvid cooperated, but I doubt if he'd consent to it, and I couldn't force him to act against his will."

"We could send Eric ahead, like before, to scout for safe passage to the Black River," Roselyn suggested.

"Hel wasn't in the troll caves," the Seer said. "Her eyes can always see Eric, and he'd be hers to command, if she saw him. She'd make him betray us; Eric's one of her dead; he'd have no choice. Loki can probably see Eric as well as Hel, since he's a God and her father. Eric would be invisible to the dwarves, but it'd be a great risk. Sending the fairies would be about the same; Hel and Loki couldn't command them, but anyone could see them."

"There're no risk-free methods," Karl said. "We'll just have to take our chances."

"Why?" Seren asked, looking up from her tub, her sleeves pushed back past her elbows, wringing out a wet tunic. "Pay Radsvid, follow him to safety."

"I will not sleep that ... *thing!*" Roselyn snapped.

"Nor will I," Eloise insisted.

"Not you," she replied. "Seren do."

"*No!*" Rafe shouted so forcefully that he surprised even himself.

"O-Only way risk-free," Seren stammered, glancing at Rafe.

"*You will not sleep with that ... that ...!*" Rafe bellowed, pointing across the room toward the curtained bedchamber.

"I been with worse," Seren said.

Rafe glowered, bristling. No matter what she'd been before, Seren was his lady now, and he wouldn't let her debase herself, not for anything. No one spoke. Rafe glared at them all, daring anyone to refute him.

"Rafe," Seren said.

"No!" Rafe cut her off.

"Please ..."

"Never!"

Rafe glared down at her. Seren stared up at him, her face uncomprehending, almost pleading. *Why?* Did she want that dwarf inside her? To foul her with his lowborn filth?

"You fight for company," Seren said. "Karl fight. Even Roselyn fight. Seer do magic. Eloise lead ..."

"You do plenty," Rafe said.

"You do," Eloise confirmed, and the others all nodded in agreement.

"Cook, wash clothes," Seren said. "Not important."

"You stopped me from killing them in Grusshire," the Seer said.

Rafe glanced at the Seer, then back to Seren; they'd found them together back then, in the freshly-dug grave, but he'd never suspected why. Seren had probably done other things as well, small things that he didn't know about. There was no question about her value to the company, but that wasn't the issue. Seren was his, although he hadn't declared her so publicly; he hadn't thought that there was any need. Seren had proven her worth during the bar fight when she'd saved them from murderers in the street. *He wouldn't let her ruin herself!*

"What if take chance ... and fail?" Seren asked. "Die, never get home?"

A long silence ensued. Rafe ground his teeth together, determined not to relent. Finally an idea struck him.

"I can solve this right now," Rafe said.

Rafe drew his sword. With Radsvid dead, any talk of appeasing him would be over. It might even be the Christian thing to do; killing such a foul and perverse creature would surely be the Lord's work. That he'd enjoy it was just a side-benefit. Rafe turned toward the musty curtain, determined to murder the dwarf.

"Halt, Sir Rafe of du Harmonn!" Eloise shouted. "Put that away! I'm still your baroness!"

Rafe hesitated, but he didn't sheath his sword. He slowly glanced back.

"Rafe, obey me," Eloise said. "You've trusted me this far, all the way to another world. You won't kill Radsvid until I say so."

"Then say so!" Rafe insisted.

"We took a chance and followed Eric into Grusshire," Eloise said. "Look what happened because of that! We're alive today because we don't take chances unless we must. You won't decide this by yourself."

Karl placed a hand on Karl's shoulder.

"Easy, Rafe," Karl said. "When the time comes, you may strike the blow."

Rafe heaved a heavy sigh and let his breath *hissss!* between clenched teeth.

"Seren's right about one thing," Roselyn said to Rafe. "I remember standing on the hillcrest watching as you, Karl, and Eric went down to fight in the war. I was afraid that all of you would die there, that both sides would turn on you the instant that they saw you. How did you think I felt, not knowing if I was about to lose the three men that I loved most in the world?"

Rafe looked down, unwilling to meet her eyes.

"You and Karl walk into danger, risking yourselves, at the drop of a hat," Roselyn continued. "Each time you're risking all of our lives; where would we be without you? Then you return and pat yourselves on the back for your bravery. What of our suffering, watching helpless ... while you fight?"

"You've fought, too," Rafe muttered.

"Only when I had no choice," Roselyn said. "You wouldn't let me risk myself when one of you could fight in my place. Well, I don't want Seren to give herself to that ... rabid worm, but if she's willing to sacrifice herself, as you do, then I'll honor her for her courage."

Rafe raised his eyes to stare at Roselyn. Surely she was joking, but Roselyn's countenance belied her intent. *How could she?* Roselyn was willing to let Seren foul herself, as if she could ever be cleansed of it. Rafe didn't falter but remained resolute, steadfast in his convictions. It was an honor for him to spare them suffering, and seldom could he spare them with as much delight as he'd get from beheading Radsvid.

Perhaps they'd done wrong, treating the women like equals and letting them take command. Rafe didn't make the world, neither the Earth nor this blasted giant tree, but he had to live in them. Most women were weaker than most men, and he'd never met one that could've out-muscled him in his prime. By letting them be equals, Rafe was letting them make sacrifices as well.

"If you think this is noble, then you sleep with Radsvid," Rafe said to Roselyn.

Roselyn flinched as if Rafe had slapped her.

Rafe regretted his words at once. Roselyn wasn't trying to be mean, and he had spoken dishonorably. Men and women were different; no one was to blame. God made them that way. It was every man's lot to protect women, who were needed to bear children. That meant that women had to let men do the fighting. Never should men hide while women fight; God and nature rebelled against it.

Rafe didn't sheath his sword. If they wanted to test his stubbornness then they were welcome to try.

"It my decision, no?" Seren asked.

Again, no one spoke. Karl and the Seer looked away, unwilling to address the issue. Rafe chagrined; Karl and the Seer wouldn't let Radsvid touch Eloise or Roselyn. *Did they expect him to do less for Seren?*

"We need speak to Rafe," Seren said, wiping the wash-water off of her hands. "Alone."

Rafe turned to look at her, but Seren looked down, avoiding his gaze. Rafe didn't want to speak in private; there wasn't anything to talk about. As the others turned away, Rafe fumed, wanting to shout *'Come back!'*, but he only brooded in silence as they slowly walked to the other side of Radsvid's workshop.

"There's nothing to discuss!" Rafe said when they were alone.

Seren said nothing. She raised her eyes to meet his, and Rafe was surprised to see small tears dripping down her cheeks. Seren faced him, and then she stepped slowly toward him. She never looked away, just stared into his eyes, and Rafe stood speechless, not knowing what to say.

Seren had amazed Rafe countless times. From living in a brothel, she'd walked away from her familiar life into insanity without even a backwards glance. She'd faced giants and armies of undead, Eric's ghost and the Goddess of Death, all without flinching or trying to flee. She'd huddled by him on a leaky dragonship during a storm at sea that would balk the toughest sailors. Yet he'd never seen her truly afraid.

Seren leaned against him, her sallow cheek pressed against Rafe's rough, cold mail. Seren slid her arms around him and held tightly, and Rafe felt torn in two. He loved her, despite her previous profession, but he didn't think that he could endure another man

193

touching her, let alone that filthy, disgusting vermin of a dwarf.

Rafe refused to put his arms around her, not willing to show any sign of relenting. He stood straight, rigid, but inside he was melted butter dripping onto the floor. Rafe wished that she'd say something, anything to break the uncomfortable silence, but she only trembled slightly as she pressed against him. Words Rafe could argue with, but he couldn't resist her silent touch. Like a statue he remained, but tears began to flow from his own eyes, unbidden and unwanted.

"When time come," Seren whispered, "my Rafe must be brave."

Rafe gritted his teeth and closed his eyes; some things he simply couldn't endure. Trouble would come of this, even if he had to cause it.

Chapter 14

Sacrifice

ELOISE

Eloise felt her throat tighten as Seren approached. Rafe was standing where she'd left him, alone, unmoving, his back to them. Eloise knew what Seren was going to say but didn't want to hear it.

Seren slid between the junk-cluttered tables and approached her directly. Roselyn was close by, but Karl and the Seer stood a ways apart. Radsvid was still in his bedchamber, no doubt waiting for them to come to him; he had them trapped like a mice in a tankard. The fairies were hovering near the ceiling, probably oblivious to their problem; Eloise envied them.

Seren approached seeming stern and business-like; Eloise felt ashamed for her thoughts, but she couldn't help thinking that whoring had been Seren's business for more years than either she or Roselyn had been alive. Yet Eloise said nothing, waiting for Seren to speak.

"Tell Radsvid need food and strong drinks," Seren said. "Say one of us be his, once him bring new food, and then he take all to river. No tell him who; he no show interest in me. Just say hurry, and him get what he want."

Seren stood there, tall and imperious, as if she were the leader, with Eloise merely her servant. Eloise slowly nodded; for what she was about to do, Seren could act in any way that she wanted. In some ways, Seren always was in command; whenever she spoke, however poorly, they all listened. Whenever she advised, Seren spoke wisely, and they always followed her suggestions. Seren was an old whore, while Roselyn was a countess and she was a baroness, but that didn't seem to matter. Seren never tried to command; she just knew when and what to recommend, and let others see her wisdom. Eloise had prided herself on her leadership since their first visit to Grusshire; now she was beginning to see what real leadership was. Seren may have been a whore, but she and Roselyn weren't timid virgins; any of them could have suffered Radsvid's demands to save all of them. Seren was willing to endure his filth for the sake of the company. It put Eloise's vaunted nobility in

perspective: in many ways, Seren the Whore was far
superior to Eloise the Baroness.

Eloise walked slowly, composing what she was
going to say. Eloise wished that she was a sword-fighter
and could rashly run Radsvid through, but she could
barely lift the heavy blades and would never consider
wearing steel armor like Roselyn. She'd wondered why
Roselyn kept wearing it; she could have any dress that
she wanted. Eloise had laughed when Roselyn had tried
to punch Radsvid; if Roselyn had carried a sword, then
they wouldn't have to do this.

Eloise stopped outside his bedchamber. She'd
never before felt like a slaver bartering human flesh, and
the sensation sickened her. Yet she was their appointed
leader and had to do her part.

"Radsvid!" Eloise snapped. "Come out here!"

Radsvid was grinning ear to ear as he slowly
pulled aside the heavy curtain. Eloise's stomach turned;
Radsvid was acting like Lancelot stealing his way into
Guinevere's garden, while in truth he was a disgusting
extortionist willing to torment a woman who'd only
suffer his rape to save her comrade's lives. Eloise
loathed Radsvid; he was no better than her stepfather, or
Sir Guldwin, or the dozen that Roselyn had endured
under threat of her bastard father. Eloise felt ashamed
again; both Seren and Roselyn had been whored, Seren
by birthright, Roselyn by her father's ambitions. If
Baron Vandislidge du Harmonn had lived, doubtless
she'd eventually been whored as well, married her off to

a man that she didn't love. Eloise was the only one of
them who'd had every chance to remain a virgin, and
she'd let herself be seduced by Captain Sir Gunderson,
whose love she never trusted. She should be the one to
suffer this damnation, but she couldn't do so willingly.

"You win," Eloise said reluctantly.

Radsvid smiled, displaying dark, crooked teeth.

"But we need supplies for the road. Bring us
plenty of food, and the strongest ale that you have, and
you may sleep with one of us. However, right
afterwards, you must take us safely to the Black River,
agreed?"

"Agreed," Radsvid said. "Wait here, my
delectable golden morsel; I'll be right back with food and
drink."

Radsvid reached under a table and pulled out a
greasy woven basket. He carried it back to the door,
which the Seer was standing beside, and pressed a
hidden spot on the wall. The door opened and he
vanished through it, closing it behind him.

The Seer grinned, waited a few moments, and
then pressed the same spot on the wall. Nothing
happened. The Seer's grin vanished. He tried again,
using different hand placements, but all failed. Radsvid
had been telling the truth; without him, they'd never
leave his workshop.

Eloise glanced back at Rafe, who sat upon the
table, head bowed, his back to them. She considered
going over to him; he'd come to her aid after Karl and

Roselyn had first made love in that little deserted farmhouse outside of Madrone. But she suspected that he wanted to be alone; if he didn't come and join them soon, then she'd go to him.

Eloise glanced at Seren. Like Rafe, she'd turned her back to all of them. Looking at her, Eloise might've guessed that she was studying the strange devices hanging from the wall, but Eloise knew better; it wasn't her upcoming torture with Radsvid that Seren feared, it was the wedge that this would pound between Rafe and herself.

Eloise's situation was little better than Seren's. She and Roselyn both wanted Karl, and had gladly avoided the subject, but where would their contest lead? Would it split the company? Would Roselyn stand aside for her, or could she give up Karl to her best friend? What would the Seer do? So much had happened since the storm, and so quickly, that such matters had been dropped. What would happen when they could relax again? They'd survived so much; *could their company survive not being in danger?*

Eloise bowed her head. She was their leader, and it was her turn to sacrifice. Eloise loved Karl, and would do anything to have him, but hers was the responsibility for keeping the company together. If it came to it, Eloise would have to give Karl to Roselyn, even if it tore her heart in two.

"Let me try," Karl said irritably.

Both the Seer and Karl were inspecting the wall, pressing on it, trying to open the door. Eloise smiled; not long ago they would've killed each other, fighting like dogs for dominance. Now they were companions, if not friends, but who knew what could come of it? Perhaps their situation wasn't as bad as she thought; if the men could quell their animosity then perhaps there was hope for all of them.

Eventually the door opened, long after Karl and the Seer had given up trying to open it. Radsvid came in, his greasy basket full of bread loaves, strange fruits, and several red-clay bottles. He'd taken longer than Eloise had expected but brought more than she'd hoped. Radsvid set the basket on top of a pile of junk cluttering a table, and then he turned to Eloise.

"Now, my pretty, it's time for us," Radsvid grinned.

Eloise shuddered, but held her ground as Radsvid approached, drooling, his eyes wide with anticipation.

"Go into your bedroom," Eloise ordered him. "One of us will be with you momentarily."

"We have an agreement!" Radsvid complained. "I brought you food ...!"

"You won't have to wait long."

Radsvid cast a distrustful glance at them, and then stepped behind his curtain. Eloise closed her eyes, dreading this moment as she had the second rising of the full moon in Grusshire.

Without a word, Seren brushed past her and followed Radsvid into his chamber.

"Hey ...!" Radsvid's voice sounded disappointed, but almost instantly he laughed wickedly.

Eloise started to cry. She should've done more, found some other way. Now Seren would suffer for them all, and she'd bear the guilt forever.

Radsvid made a disgusting sound, as if his mouth was watering before a delicious meal, and Eloise couldn't bear it. She feared what Rafe would do when he heard, and realized that soon it'd be loud enough for them all to hear.

Eloise snapped her fingers loudly and motioned for everyone to follow her. She walked quickly and firmly toward Rafe, who was still sitting alone, downcast, facing away from them.

"Silvana!" Eloise called to the fairies who were flitting about the ceiling. "Glororil! Come down here."

Silvana flew down instantly in a streak of silver sparks and landed on Eloise's shoulder. Glororil came more slowly, spinning in wide circles, never landing. Eloise walked right up to Rafe, and after a moment, placed her hand over his. Rafe tensed under her touch but he didn't move. The others gathered around them.

"We'll be leaving soon," Eloise said. "Karl, you and the Seer fill our packs with food from the basket. Roselyn, we'll have to carry our clothes, even if they're still wet."

"Yes, Baroness," Roselyn said.

Eloise glanced up at her face, surprised to hear Roselyn use her formal title. Roselyn was standing tall, formal despite her heavy armor, but tears were streaming down her cheeks; Roselyn knew what was going on, as did they all.

"Seer, where will the river take us?" Eloise asked, trying to keep the discussion going.

The Seer opened his mouth to speak, but just then Radsvid's grating voice sounded from behind his curtain. It was too muffled to hear clearly, but Rafe shuddered and his breath seethed between his teeth in a soft growl. Rafe seemed like a bear arousing from hibernation, about to attack the stranger in his cave.

Suddenly Silvana flitted down to a small table before them. She looked up at them and raised her silver arms. Beautifully, Silvana began to sing.

Silvana's voice sounded like birdsong and wind chimes and tinkled like silver bells. Silvana sang no words, only notes so high that no human voice could reach them. Her song was merry and gay, melodies of scales rising and falling, and trilling notes clear and sharp that hung long in the air. She filled the mind with images pure and innocent, wholesome and happy, yet a note of sadness wove amid her joy. Eloise briefly wondered about the fairies, what they knew and understood, and now she saw the truth; the sadness in Silvana's song came from within. Silvana was tiny, silvery, and almost alien, yet she knew everything that was happening, what Seren was suffering, and why Rafe was fuming. Eloise had thought that the fairies were like the crystal talisman that they'd been sealed in: just an item to be carried, a tool to use when they must. She'd tried to not think about them at all; they could force her terrible, painful transformation to bring out the Wolfqueen.

Glororil flew suddenly down and spun quickly around and around Silvana, showering her with golden sparks. Glororil moved as gracefully as Silvana and proceeded to dance around her, reaching out to touch her outstretched hands only to zip away on his translucent dragonfly wings. He used his whole body, spinning and tumbling, never once landing or touching any object, although he flew so close to the piled junk that Eloise feared that he'd crash into it. But always Glororil slipped past, buzzed free, flew back to Silvana, and gestured lovingly to her.

Silvana's song was mesmerizing. Eloise couldn't tell how long she sat listening or heard anything but her high, soft, sweet voice. Glororil's dance was equally enthralling; it never detracted from Silvana's music, but blended with it, as if they were one. No one moved or spoke, watching and listening as if they had no strength or desire to turn away. Silvana's song went on and on, never repeating but hauntingly familiar, like a forgotten childhood dream retaining only a faint memory of the pure joy that it gave.

Eloise finally shook herself, as if awakening, only to realize that Silvana's song had ended. Glororil was holding her in his arms, and the fairies were kissing, oblivious to the stares of the others. Eloise had no idea how much time had passed; Silvana's song could've lasted minutes or hours.

The approaching clomp of Radsvid's boots made Eloise turn around. The dwarf grinned widely as if completely satisfied; Eloise hoped that Rafe wouldn't turn to look, but he did. Suddenly Rafe lunged and charged the dwarf as if he'd pound him even shorter.

Karl, the Seer, and Roselyn tackled him, knocked Rafe against a sturdy workbench, and pinned him there. Rafe struggled with unguessed strength, but Karl held him in a headlock and the Seer clung to his back. Roselyn, with her armored weight, pressed them all against a table, clutching its wooden edge with both of her hands.

"Can't take it back!" the dwarf laughed.

Rafe shouted, cursed, and threatened until the Seer cupped a hand over his mouth.

"Hel and Loki!" the Seer shouted at Rafe. "Remember? They'll hear you in Niflhiem if you shout like that again!"

Rafe slowed his resistance. They held him, and Eloise pushed past, around the table, and stood between them and Radsvid.

"Stop it, Rafe!" Eloise ordered. "We're leaving at once. Stay as far away from ...it ... as you can. Karl, let him go. Gather our things. We're leaving!"

Slowly they released their hold on Rafe, who stood bristling, but made no further move to advance on Radsvid. The dwarf seemed amused by the whole affair, as if Rafe was no threat to him. Eloise turned to face Radsvid, furious, barely maintaining her control.

"Take us to the Black River right now."

"Sure," Radsvid grinned, leaning against a broken table. "Why not? I've had my fun."

Eloise glared; she detested the dwarf. Fortunately, her agreement with Radsvid was only valid until they got to the river in safety. Once there, if Rafe chose to kill him, then Eloise wouldn't stop him. In fact, she might even hold Radsvid down still while Rafe took his time.

Karl picked up the whole basket of food and brought it with him while Roselyn pulled down their wet laundry. The Seer went to the curtain hiding Radsvid's bedchamber; Seren was there, standing just outside of it, looking miserable. Eloise wanted to comfort her but feared to leave Rafe and Radsvid with no one between them.

Silvana and Glororil flew down from the ceiling as Radsvid approached, though staying as far from him as possible. Radsvid ignored them and began digging through a pile of junk on the floor. Finally he lifted up a large square mesh, folded flat.

"What's that?" Eloise demanded.

"This is my fishing net," Radsvid said. "Since I'm going to the river, I might as well do some fishing."

"A metal net?" Eloise asked suspiciously.

"It's magnetic, like my ring, which opens my door," Radsvid said. "Folded, it opens easily, but once it closes, nothing can get out."

"Your net must be magic," the Seer said, approaching the dwarf with one arm supporting Seren. "Simple magnetism wouldn't do that."

"Just good dwarven forging," Radsvid boasted. "I'm the best."

Eloise doubted if any of Radsvid's crazy inventions worked, but that wasn't her concern. She had to get them to the Black River, if she could, before any of them killed Radsvid.

"Seer, is Eric with us?" Eloise asked.

"I'll check," the Seer said, and he untied his silk pouch and held it up. Eric appeared, glowing as always under the moonstone, so close to Eloise that she startled; she was still unused to his ghostly silence.

"Gather all of our things," Eloise said to everyone. "Bring it now or leave it behind. Radsvid, fulfill your promise: take us to the river."

Radsvid opened his door and Eloise followed as he stepped out into the hallway. A darkened torch hanging on the wall blazed aflame as they stepped near it, and soon they were walking single-file down the hallway, the torches igniting themselves as they approached, snuffing themselves out as they passed. The fairies followed, flying over their heads.

Radsvid took a burning torch down from the wall and led them through another door into a musty, darker passageway filled with cobwebs and thick dust that puffed up as they walked atop it.

"Must we go this way?" Eloise complained.

"This is the only way, unless you want to parade down the central hall with every dwarf in Nidavellir watching," Radsvid said. "Come, we've a long ways to go."

Radsvid held the torch before him, burning a path through the spidery strands as he went. The webs singed and melted before him, but he only cleared a path big enough for himself. Eloise had to duck to get through the holes that Radsvid made, and winced each time that the ghostly, wafting strands brushed against her. Behind her, Karl drew his sword and cut a wider, taller opening for himself and the others. Eloise would've liked to travel behind him, but she didn't trust having nothing but webs between Radsvid's back and Karl's slashing sword.

The dark tunnel seemed endless. The slate floor was broken, uneven in places, and some of its tiles tilted under their feet.

Soon they came to a wide opening. A round room appeared with a gentle wind blowing the cobwebs about, making them dance in the torchlight. Web-blocked passages led off in all directions, and in the center of the room stood a great circular stone staircase spiraling up and down through wide holes in the floor and ceiling. The fairies dashed into the center of it, flying sparkling circles in the vast openness.

"This is the Great Spiral Stairs," Radsvid said. "Once, this was the heart of Nidavellir, the pride of the dwarves. My grandfather remembered when they still used it, despite its crumbling stone. I haven't been here for almost a century. Few travel here, so we should be safe enough."

Eloise looked up and down the shaft; the wide circular stairway rotated around the edges of a great open pit with no rail, and many of the steps were cracked and broken. She couldn't see the bottom or top; outside of the torchlight, darkness consumed all. Ordinarily she wouldn't have stepped foot on such a crumbling structure, but she was their leader; it was her duty.

Chapter 15

Betrayal

ROSELYN

Stumbling in near total darkness, Roselyn walked behind Seren, the last in line. Roselyn felt gravely concerned; Seren was walking very slowly, almost blindly, and Roselyn suspected that she'd purposely fall back and get lost, if not watched. Rafe had utterly rejected her attempts to walk beside him; he wouldn't look at her. Without surveillance, Roselyn suspected that Seren would just sit down and cry until she starved to death.

Pushing through the filthy webs, Roselyn shuddered, imagining tiny spiders crawling all over her armor where she couldn't feel them. Roselyn detested spiders; as a child she'd run screaming from even the smallest of them. Finally she'd discovered that she could squish them easily, and had done so ever since. Roselyn still held a secret dread of them, but she tried not to think about it.

Seren and Rafe were so perfect for each other that it hurt to see them fighting. Roselyn didn't agree with Eloise's solution: Roselyn would've let them kill Radsvid and trusted to luck to find the river. She never would've let Seren sacrifice her body to Radsvid's lusts, knowing what it'd do to Rafe. Yet she'd made Eloise their leader; if Roselyn defied Eloise openly, how long would the women retain command? Athelwynne would regain control, and like Eric, he was too zealous to consider what was best for the company.

Walking in armor now felt easy; Roselyn was growing stronger. The first day that she'd worn armor, running away from her father's camp, it'd been torturous. But Roselyn's armor was her symbol, proof that she'd left her old life behind; she wasn't Countess Roselyn anymore. Roselyn was a warrior; warriors didn't have to bow to anyone as long as their sword was sharp. Walking in armor felt powerful, after she'd gotten used to it. She'd always been a scrapper, even as a rebellious child. Whenever her father had beaten her into submission, which he'd done many times, her spirit had never died, for Roselyn had remained willful in her heart, defiant to the last. The men that she'd bedded with had used her only as container, like a flask of precious wine passed around by unworthy men, constantly opened but never tasted.

Karl alone had tasted her, and she prayed that he wanted more. Roselyn had never thought that she'd love so deeply, but Karl had welcomed her rebellious spirit with open arms, inside which she had nothing to rebel against. The long nights in Niflhiem, sleeping alone, close to him but not close enough, had been arduous. Roselyn had slept only after hours of frustration. Yet she dared not touch Karl; Hel had always been watching always them, jealous, and it might have proven fatal to provoke her half-goddess anger by flaunting their love in her face. Hel surprised Roselyn when she released them; Roselyn had suspected that Hel would keep them, at least Karl, forever. Hel must've truly loved them, in her own way, to let them go. How they'd betrayed her was inexcusable, despite that it was Eric's only hope.

Roselyn stumbled as a loose flagstone unexpectedly tilted beneath her feet and pushed her through a curtain of cobwebs, almost making her drop the heavy pack containing their wet clothes. Roselyn hated walking in the dark. Why hadn't she stolen a torch?

Radsvid was the culmination of all that she hated in men. To Radsvid, Roselyn was a source of pleasure, a tool for his ego, a toy to be discarded after use. All women were the same to Radsvid; it hadn't mattered to him that it was Seren, not herself or Eloise, who'd come to his bed. Roselyn had thought that utter blatancy like

Radsvid's would be preferable to the flowery lies that the insincere courtiers in her father's castle had whispered to her, but she'd found Radsvid's unconcealed lusts insulting beyond measure. The lies and flatteries of the young knights were at least attempts to appear suitable; never before Radsvid had Roselyn met anyone so disgustingly obvious, so honestly lecherous. How strange it was that Karl, who spoke neither flowery nor blatantly, only truth, was the man who'd stolen her heart.

Roselyn felt sorry for Seren, guilty that she'd suffered Radsvid's bed to save them. Roselyn had done much the same by sleeping with Athelwynne in Bristlen. She liked Athelwynne; he thought deeply, mechanically, but all of his disdain was a cover for deep feelings that he seemed afraid to share. Someday he'd have to choose; would he live for his passions or let his bitterness consume him?

The torchlight grew brighter and Roselyn pushed out of the musty webs into an open chamber. Many passages led into darkness, but cobwebs choked their entrances. In the center of the room rose a great spiral stairway circling up into gloom. In the gold and silver sparkles of the fairie-trails, the stone stairs looked ancient, crumbling and cracked, but Roselyn cared only that she was out of the dark, web-choked tunnel.

The others had stopped. Eloise and Radsvid were talking, but Roselyn couldn't hear their words. She hated walking last in line, but someone had to watch Seren.

Seren walked up beside Rafe. Roselyn held her breath and hoped, but when Seren reached out her hand to him, Rafe walked away from her. Seren looked as if Skaldi had crushed her with his giant fist. Seren had been so strong; Roselyn had been impressed with her ever since she'd watched her deal the final blow on Skaldi, splitting open the evil giant's head. Countess and whore: despite their differences, their lives had a lot of similarities. Roselyn burned with fury at the way that Rafe was treating her, but her interference would only make it worse.

Radsvid and Eloise led the way up the stairs and the others followed. The fairies didn't bother with the stairs but flew straight up the open space in the center. Radsvid held their only torch out over the edge, lighting the stairs much better than he had the dark passageway. Yet Seren didn't move until Roselyn took her by the arm.

The stairs rose on and on upwards. Roselyn placed each foot upon the next step, trying not to think of the depth of the fall; she could see no bottom.

They stopped for a rest, just in time, for Roselyn was certain that both she and Seren would've collapsed before long. Athelwynne handed out bread, grapes, and made everyone drink from his canteen. Roselyn drank first; the refreshing, invigorating Water of Life flowed into her, washing over her tiredness and lightening her mood.

No one spoke as they ate and rested, still gasping for breath. The dry, musty tunnels left them wheezing in the stale, acrid air. Each landing looked much the same as the others; some had side-tunnels that were obviously recently used, but most remained heavily curtained by ancient webs layered with dust. In the torchlight, it was hard to tell the levels apart.

All too soon they resumed their trek. At Roselyn's urging, Seren wearily rose and climbed. Roselyn shouldered their wet-clothes pack and followed. The fairies, especially Glororil, seemed more annoyed by their rest-stops than relieved; they quickly flitted around the stairs while the rest slowly climbed.

Finally Radsvid led them off of the stairs, although Roselyn couldn't imagine how he knew which landing to take. The stairs continued upwards into darkness, and Roselyn could only guess at how high it went. This landing looked the same as all of the others save that two of the side tunnels looked well-used, free of cobwebs, and countless footprints in the dust showed recent usage. They rested again and drank more water.

"We're near the river," Radsvid said. "If we walk swiftly and silently then we'll be there shortly."

"Will there be boats at the river?" Athelwynne asked.

"Yes, but I won't help you steal them," Radsvid said, picking up his metal fishing net. "That's your concern, not mine; I'm here to catch other things. Once you're on the docks, our bargain's complete."

After passing around a canteen one last time, they headed down a well-used tunnel. This tunnel was in much better condition than the other, but again the shadows of the others blocked the torchlight, leaving Roselyn mostly in darkness. Still, without the cobwebs, the way was much easier.

Just when Roselyn felt that she couldn't take another step, they came to a wide open chamber with double-doors facing the end of the tunnel. Beyond it, the rush of a mighty river softly roared.

"Here it is," Radsvid said. "These doors open onto the docks of the Black River. You may want to draw your weapons; there're likely to be many dwarves here."

"What's the river like?" Athelwynne asked. "Is it wide, broad, ...?"

"Underground rivers aren't like surface waters," Radsvid said. "The Black River's narrow and swift. We have to tie our boats securely or the current drags them away."

"That's what we need," the Seer said. "We should do this as quickly as possible. Karl, Rafe: you lead, with the rest of us right behind. We'll frighten any dwarves back, pile into the closest boat, and cut the tether. We should be out of Nidavellir before anyone has the chance to sound the alarm."

Karl and Rafe nodded and drew their swords. Radsvid and the Seer grabbed the handles of the twin doors, ready to open them. Roselyn and the others crowded behind them.

They pulled open the doors and dashed into the chaos. Karl and Rafe shouted as they charged onto a well-lit wooden dock, waving their swords; nearby dwarves screamed and fled. Roselyn pulled Seren with her and the fairies buzzed over their heads, showering them with glittering sparks.

Suddenly a tall, black-haired woman turned to face them. Karl and Rafe stopped in their tracks, and Eloise screamed in horror.

Hel glared at them, furious, her countenance of beauty twisted with rage. The force of her eyes burned them all. Hel opened her mouth as if to speak and reached out one graceful hand to seize Karl and lift him off of his feet.

Suddenly Glororil buzzed down from the ceiling. Hel's gaze faltered as she hesitated, surprised as the tiny golden man on dragonfly wings sparkled, hovering before her face.

Sunlight exploded from Glororil, blinding them all. Roselyn quickly shielded her eyes; even in the tunnels of the trolls Glororil hadn't shown this brightly. They all turned away, protecting their vision, as Karl fell from Hel's grasp.

The bright sunlight failed almost instantly, more like a dazzling flash than the steady beams of the sun. Roselyn looked back as Glororil zipped away, avoiding

Hel's reaching hand, Hel's other hand still covering her dazed eyes.

Karl sprung up with his sword, poised to bring it down with all of his weight. Roselyn gasped; *could Karl's sword slay the Goddess of Death?*

Karl froze, not swinging his weapon. Instead, Karl threw himself against Hel and shouldered her hard, too fast for Hel's dead legs to balance; Hel fell backwards onto the wooden dock, still blind from Glororil's attack.

"No!" Radsvid cried, running to help Hel. *"You promised me gold, a net full of gold!"*

Rafe swung his sword hard. Radsvid cried out and threw up his net as a shield; Rafe's sword hammered into the folded steel mesh, but it couldn't cut through. Twice Rafe swung, hard enough to cleave the dwarf in two, but Radsvid's net blocked each blow. Then Rafe reached down with his left hand, seized the filthy dwarf by his tunic, and lifted him off of the ground.

"Father!" Hel shouted angrily, her godly voice booming loudly across the river.

Roselyn's breath caught in her throat. They'd blinded Hel, perhaps long enough to escape, but against Loki they'd have no hope. She doubted if the God couldn't hear his only daughter cry; *Loki was sure to come fast.*

"Hurry, to the boats!" the Seer shouted, and he ran to the river's edge.

The others followed as quickly as they could. Rafe came last, still holding Radsvid in one hand and beating his filthy, bleeding head with the pommel of his sword. Blood streamed down Radsvid's screaming face.

Karl, Athelwynne, and Eloise virtually fell into the nearest boat and piled atop each other, with Roselyn and Seren right behind. The small wooden rowboat tilted wildly, but Rafe paused on the edge of the dock and even stopped hammering his pommel into Radsvid's head; Rafe looked upstream, horrified.

Loud, beating wings flapped, and a giant emerald-green falcon suddenly flew out of the shadows, straight at them. Its cry shrieked in anger; the falcon was Loki, catching up to them at last.

Rafe's pommel hammered into Radsvid one last time, and then Rafe knocked the heavy net from the dwarf's grip. Rafe swung Radsvid back, and then tossed the dwarf at the giant green falcon. Radsvid hurtled through the air, out over the river, and suddenly collided with the great bird. With matching cries they struck, and both fell splashing into the dark rushing waters.

Quickly Rafe tossed his sword into the boat beside the others. With a single great shake, he flung open Radsvid's magic fishing net, unfolding it to a vast width. Then, like a fisherman, Rafe flung the metal net out over the water, onto the very spot where Radsvid and Loki, in his falcon form, had disappeared into the river. The heavy iron net splashed loudly and sank beneath the surface.

"*No!*" Hel cried as she struggled to rise, her angry eyes clear again.

Rafe stepped into the boat, snatched up his sword, and slashed its tether in two. Freed from the dock, the boat lurched into the current and quickly floated away. Hel staggered to the edge of the dock, her red eyes glaring painfully, bearing down upon all the companions, just as they floated out of her range into the center of the river. The fairies dashed ahead down the great dark tunnel that the river flowed into, leaving only sparkling trails as they fled the wrath of Hel's stare.

Roselyn and the others cried out, helpless against Hel's glare, but the current quickly dragged them away.

"*Liars!*" Hel shouted. "*Betrayers!*"

Roselyn winced at Hel's words; Hel's hate was justified.

An echoing roar resounded as Loki broke the surface, again back in his human form. Loki seemed gigantic, even bigger than before, standing waist-deep in the middle of the river, soaking wet, and furious. Entrapping him was a metal fishing net, clinging tightly all over him, and upon his chest, also trapped in the net, was Radsvid the Dwarf, looking very frightened of the God of Evil roaring in anger.

The fear in Radsvid's eyes was the last sight that Roselyn had of Nidavellir as the fast current of the underground river swept their boat into the narrow, lightless tunnel.

Chapter 16

Fighters

ERIC

Relieved, Eric sat still in the boat as the others passed through him. If not for Glororil, Hel would've captured them all. Eric had been lucky; Hel had looked right at him on the dock in Nidavellir. Her anger must have befuddled her; if Hel had ordered him to remain, then he'd have obeyed.

Eric wondered what the Seer was planning; it was hard to hear the others unless they spoke directly to him, yet he had no way of telling them that since he could neither touch nor make any sound, and not even be seen except in the light of the moonstone, which glowed like a shining lantern to his dead eyes. Yet Eric was content;

they were grasping at their one last chance to get him into Valhalla, and that was all that mattered. Having seen Niflhiem, Eric knew the horror that awaited him if he didn't make it to the Warrior's Afterlife. No matter what, Eric had to stay with the company.

Shifting places, Eloise sat right through him, and then she ducked when they swung an oar over her head and right through his face. Eric ducked slightly; a trained reaction to his days at sea, but the oar passed through him. Eloise didn't even seem aware that she was sitting inside of Eric, oblivious to his ghostly self. Eric wished that they kept the moonstone uncovered; being visible was at least slightly better than being nothing.

Finally both oars splashed in the water. Karl paddled, keeping them in the center of the river, where the current was strongest. The others settled themselves as best they could; Rafe and the Seer in the fore, Eloise, Seren, and Roselyn aft. The fairies flew ahead and darted between the thick, glistening stalactites that pointed down at the river like great stone spearheads. Eric wished that he could do something useful, but being invisible and intangible, he could do nothing.

They seemed to be having some difficulty, and Eric finally realized that they could barely see. The tunnel must be pitch black, but to Eric's ghostly eyes it was merely dim, as if veiled in shadow. Eric wondered how Karl could see to keep them in the center of the river and guessed that he was merely keeping them where the current pulled strongest. The glimmering trails of the fairies led; Karl must be fixating on them.

Finally the Seer pulled out the moonstone and all eyes turned to Eric. Sitting inside of him, Eloise startled, but Eric obligingly stood as his glow lit their rowboat. Standing in the tiny rocking boat didn't bother him; he had no body to balance with.

Eric turned to the Seer and began gesturing, trying to be understood. He cupped an ear with his one hand, in a gesture of helplessness, and after several guesses, the Seer grasped what he meant.

"You can't hear us?" the Seer asked.

Eric held up his one hand, his forefinger and thumb extended close together.

"You can only hear a little?" the Seer guessed.

Eric nodded.

"I see," the Seer said. "We'll try to speak more plainly. You know that we're still trying to fulfill my duty to the Lady?"

Eric shook his head.

"I believe that my Lady wants for you, Hel, and your arm to be brought together at the Gates of Valhalla," the Seer said slowly, loud enough for Eric to hear. "The Well of Mimir is on the way; I should be able to confirm my suspicions there."

Eric nodded, displaying that he understood, but secretly he was full of doubts. Eric wasn't a Druid; why would the Lady of the Britains care if he were interred in Valhalla? His welfare couldn't be her true intent. *What hidden purpose did she have?* Also, the Valkyrie had said that he could enter Valhalla, not that he would enter Valhalla; an important difference. Also, how did the Seer plan to gain knowledge from the Well of Mimir? Mimir was all-powerful, but he charged even Odin a heavy price.

The Seer was right: if they hadn't betrayed Hel then she never would've left Niflhiem. Eric wondered if they'd planned to steal his spirit before they left. If so, then they were wise to conceal their secret. If Eric had known, then Hel would've known, and she would've never given them leave to depart. Yet Hel had released them, and Eric couldn't imagine why: that troubled him. Often the Norse Gods, in many myths, acted irrationally, only to discover that their actions were being directed by the Norns, the Weavers of Fate. Were those three evil witches, Urd, Skuld, and Verdandi, manipulating their company? If so, then they were in grave trouble; the Norns had their own grim purposes and accounted to no one.

Eric shuddered, recalling Niflhiem. He'd been worse than a slave, his very thoughts raped, his every movement absolutely controlled. On Earth, even the lowest of thralls could think for themselves and remained masters of their private thoughts. In Niflhiem, Eric had been little more than a puppet, moving only by Hel's wish, gathering information for her ears alone. She hadn't needed to hear their tale; Hel had perused Eric's memory, all of his adventures, his every thought and feeling throughout his long life. It was the ultimate invasion, a total humiliation. All that Eric was, and ever had been, was Hel's, and he'd been powerless to resist.

Valhalla: Eric had to enter its gates. Hovering in his ghostly form, needing neither food nor sleep, what was Eric but a dim lantern for the others, a tool that only the moonstone activated? Whenever they put the moonstone away, when Eric vanished from their eyes, his existence became worse than anything he'd ever imagined. Unable to touch, smell, or taste, unable to affect anything at all tortured him worse than Svenson Two-Sword ever could. It was so unfair! All his life he'd sought to earn the respect of the Valkyrie. *Why had they rejected him?*

"Seer, where are we?" Eloise asked.

"We're rushing toward Svartalfhiem, the land of the Dark Elves," the Seer said.

"What's a dark elf?" Karl asked.

"You will know as soon as I do," the Seer said. "I recall nothing about them in the Norse myths. Hopefully we'll never find out: Loki and Hel will be after us again; I doubt if we can brook any more delays."

"We'd best try to get some sleep," Karl said, yawning. "It feels like days since we left Niflhiem."

"Who knows what time it is in this subterranean nightmare?" the Seer asked. "As far as I know, Svartalfhiem is the Norse realm closest to the surface, since Jotunhiem is described as wide fields and rolling hills. But that means, if this river leads there, that this water is flowing uphill."

"Isn't that impossible?" Karl asked.

The Seer merely shrugged; they'd seen so many strange things that water flowing uphill was just a minor amazement, and they were too exhausted to care.

Their tunnel's width widened and narrowed, changing its current, and several times Karl had to steer their boat around stalactites that hung midstream, almost to the water's edge. Exhausted, Eloise curled up against Roselyn and Seren, and soon all were resting.

Eric felt bad for Seren. Rafe was wrong to reject her because of Radsvid; *did he think that she was a virgin?* Whoring wasn't considered respectable, even in Norway, but it wasn't a dishonest way for runaway peasant girls to make a living. Many soldiers took them for wives, and sailors purchased them for voyages; a good whore could often retire after renting herself out to an entire ship. Most nobles, especially wives, looked down upon whores, but Eric seldom heeded the opinions of those born to wealth or power. Once they'd struggled in the dirt for scraps of food then they might understand the lives of the lower classes. But Rafe was neither rich nor noble; for him to deny Seren for sleeping with one more paying customer made no sense.

"Halt!" cried a high, challenging voice. "Light elves! Halt and be recognized!"

Suddenly gold and silver trails streaked back into the boat, the fairies flying too fast to be seen.

"Dark elves!" Silvana squeaked.

"Murderers!" Glororil warned.

Instinctively Eric tensed and donned his fighting awareness: Eric focused his concentration and opened his peripheral senses to everything around him while scanning the darkness for any danger. Everything became suspect, a possible threat, and anything that he identified as non-threatening was instantly disregarded. A moment ago became as unimportant as a moment from now; Eric existed totally where he was, mindful only of the world around him and every potential danger.

Fighting-awareness was the secret of Eric's skill, in which his heart raced and time seemed to pass slowly, allowing him near-instantaneous reactions. All true warriors had their own inner-warrior, a mindset reserved only for combat. The inner-warrior was a high-energy state; anyone who tried to maintain it always was doomed to fail, and constant usage when it wasn't needed dulled it until it grew weak and slow. Fighting-awareness ruined normal life; the pleasure of company, even the ease of good beer, became hated distractions when one's life was in peril. The inner-warrior was a sacred state, utilized only in great need, quick and deadly, ready to kill, to survive at any cost. Vikings revered its state, the secret power behind every berserker. In its heightened awareness, a man could move instantly, ignore pain, and even stare down death.

Yet no heightening swelled Eric's senses. His heart didn't pound. Breath didn't heave his chest or rush through his widened nostrils in forced, rapid puffs. Eric was dead, his spirit-body pale and hollow, empty and useless. Eric was a warrior no more; a shade, a shadow, impotent and helpless, even less than those fool farmers and townsmen that he'd scoffed at all his life. All that Eric felt was shame and regret; all of his other senses seemed void. If he couldn't get into Valhalla, then he'd have no choice but to return to Niflhiem; even that cursed slave-life was preferable to this living hell.

"Look out!" the Seer cried as their boat ran into a black net hidden in the darkness, its top hanging just above the waterline. The current frothed through its thick web of ropes, but their boat crashed into it. The companions toppled forward, and suddenly a large metal hook on the end of a wooden pole reached out of the darkness and snared the side of their boat. Eloise screamed and jumped away from the sharp iron hook that stabbed into the inner hull of the boat.

Eric recognized the hook; sailors, especially pirates, often used it to pull ships together. Eric reached to grab the hook, to free their boat from its grasp, but his ghostly hand passed right through it.

"I'll do it," Karl said. "Get back, Eric."

Eric moved away although there was no need; Karl could've reached right through him, if he'd thought of it. Yet Eric couldn't blame his companions for not wanting to reach through him. To them, he was a walking ghost, a constant reminder of death. *Who would want to touch such a thing?* Yet Karl's reluctance made Eric feel better. By making allowances for him, while they could see him, they were at least acknowledging his existence.

"Easy!" cried the voice from shore. "Don't pull off my hook! I'm just bringing you close so that I can inspect you."

Eric saw the figure clearly. He was about Eloise's height but thinner, almost skeletal. His face was stark pale white as if he'd never endured sunlight. He had thin, pointed ears, like Titania's fairies, but he was wearing a suit of articulated metal plates, blackened and polished like new. At his side hung a thin sword, and he was pulling them hard toward the wooden dock that he was standing upon. Behind him was a small cave with a single tunnel leading off into darkness.

"No!" Silvana cried. "Beware!"

"He's a Dark Elf!" Glororil shouted. "He'll kill us all!"

Eric stepped toward him, right off of the boat, onto the water. He might as well: being dead, Eric could no longer be harmed. As he stepped near the dock, his glow illuminated the stranger for them all to see.

"These light-elves are deceiving you," the figure said, pulling the boat toward the dock. "I don't intend to harm you, if your business is honest. My name is Ruthedhel; I'm the border guard, and my duty is to inspect all who enter Svartalfhiem."

Karl pulled off the hook but to no avail; their ship was already close to the dock, close enough that Ruthedhel could've easily stepped into their boat.

"He lies!" Glororil hissed. "His people invaded our land, started a war ..!"

"What?" Ruthedhel demanded. "The Elvin Wars ended a thousand years ago! How dare you deceive these humans?"

"He lies!" Silvana insisted. "That's why Titania led us to Midgard, to escape the devastation."

"Titania?" Ruthedhel asked. "The legendary Queen of the Lost Elves? You claim that Titania went to Midgard?"

"We met her at a gathering of her folk," the Seer said. "Titania assigned Silvana and Glororil to travel with us."

"This is news indeed, if it's true," Ruthedhel said. "Our legends say that Titania was a great queen of light-elves who vanished without a trace in the Elvin Wars."

"She led us to Midgard when you attacked," Glororil said. "Obviously she never learned that the war ended, if it has. The war could still be raging, and you could be lying about it."

"Dark Elves don't lie," Ruthedhel said, narrowing his eyes.

Eric watched the dark elf carefully, suspiciously, as if he were an enemy. His instincts urged him to don his fighting persona, but it was useless. What could he do but wave his ghostly arm before the dark elf's face? Yet something nagged at him, something that he couldn't name. Ruthedhel looked like a child, small, smooth-skinned, and delicate. If not for his tight-fitting armor and austere, confident manner, Eric might've thought him a boy of ten or twelve.

Ruthedhel set his pole onto a pair of hooks on the cave wall. Beneath it was a sword rack with several well-polished blades of different styles. A round metal shield lay beside the swords with several other types of weapons; axes, a mace, and several long, slender spears. The small cavern was sparsely furnished with a tiny bed, two chairs, a table covered with scrolls, and several unlit candle stands. As Eric watched, Ruthedhel faced them. Something was strange about him, about the way that he moved, which troubled Eric.

"How can you remember this war?" Karl asked Silvana and Glororil suddenly. "If it was a thousand years ago ..."

"Light-Elves don't count years," Ruthedhel said. "Dark Elves do, but only because of our annual tournaments. We live far longer than humans, of course. I remember the Elvin Wars clearly; some of the greatest fighting that I've ever seen happened back then."

"It was horrible, savage ...!" Silvana said.

"Beautiful and heroic," Ruthedhel said. "Light-elves never appreciate the elegance of combat."

"Dark elves waste their artistry on violence," Glororil said.

"There's no point in arguing," Ruthedhel said. "I'll take you to our king, and you may convince him of your tale."

"We're in a hurry and can't abide detours," the Seer said.

"I'm afraid that you must," Ruthedhel said. "I don't have the right to grant light-elves and humans free passage through our lands."

"I lead this company," Eloise spoke up, and she carefully stood in the boat. "I'm Baroness Eloise Elizabeth du Harmonn. The Seer is my trusted advisor, and he speaks the truth; we must go, now and quickly."

"Forgive me, Baroness," Ruthedhel said, "but what pursues you so quickly that you must travel so? The Caverns of the Dark Elves are beautiful and wondrous, our feasts a delight. Surely you wouldn't want to miss them."

"They sound delightful," Eloise said. "Were our mission not so urgent then I'd gladly come, for all that we've seen of your world is Niflhiem and Nidavellir."

"Poor traveling you've done to see only our worst," Ruthedhel said.

"I'm glad to hear it, for worst it has been," Eloise said. "Yet Hel and Loki are chasing us, and are doubtless not far behind."

"Hel and Loki?" Ruthedhel exclaimed. "Such names are accursed in Svartalfhiem! You'll find little welcome anywhere with such fiends on your heels.

What's your mission? Speak quickly, for I must spread the alarm, if such foes truly approach."

"Our business is of no consequence to dark elves," Eloise said. "Our fallen friend, Eric, must be taken to the Gates of Valhalla. There we must go, even if all of the foul beasts of this world pursue us."

"Loki and his daughter are two of our foulest," Ruthedhel said. "Yet all the more I'm bound by my office; you must come with me and bargain for passage before our king."

"Please?" Roselyn asked. "Please let us go. Hel and Loki will kill us, if they catch us."

"I wish that I could," Ruthedhel said. "I don't believe that you're spies or thieves, but by our laws of fealty, I'm commanded to lead you to the royal presence."

"Is there no other way?" Eloise asked.

"None, I'm afraid," Ruthedhel said.

"He lies!" Glororil hissed. "He can be challenged!"

"Challenged by humans?" Ruthedhel asked. "Are you mad? My training days alone were longer than five mortal lives!"

"All dark elves must honor a challenge," Silvana said.

"What's a challenge?" Eloise asked.

Ruthedhel paused, amazed or offended, as if Eloise had questioned his very existence.

"A challenge is call to fight," Karl spoke up, answering her. "I'll challenge him. What are the stakes?"

"Stakes?" Ruthedhel asked. "The loser of a challenge becomes the servant of the victor until the next Royal Tournament. Then all fealties are released and reformed on the field of battle. If I win, you'll be my servant and I'll order you to lead your company to the presence of our king. If I lose, then I'll be obliged to let you pass, as you wish. But I beg you to reconsider: I've been honing my fighting skills for centuries. Even if you're the greatest of your kind, you have no hope against me."

Karl bristled, glaring, but Eric understood at last; Ruthedhel had seemed odd since Eric's first sight of him, strange, as if he bore some hidden secret. Now Eric saw, to his amazement, Ruthedhel's secret. When Eric had first seen Karl, Eric knew that Karl could become a great fighter; the way that Karl stood, moved, and the focus in his eyes told Eric all that he needed to know. The size and strength of Karl's body was only a bonus. Eric had seen thousands of warriors, including the best in all of Europe. He'd trained since early childhood and lived a mercenary life of war and murder; Eric could spot a fellow warrior at a glance.

Ruthedhel surpassed all of the warriors that Eric had ever seen. His movements flowed slowly, fluidic, with a control that even Eric hadn't mastered. Ruthedhel moved so gracefully that Eric hadn't recognized the obvious skills hidden in his deft, coordinated gestures. His self-mastery was excellent; with control such as his, Eric would've needed no companions; even armies would've given him little difficulty. Eric could've wielded his sword into a crown of his own and the Valkyrie would've vied for the honor of claiming him. Ruthedhel, despite his size, excelled Eric's best fighting skills as a berserker surpassed an irate child.

"I challenge you," Karl said, and he stepped out of the boat and drew his sword.

"Please don't," Ruthedhel said. "It would be unfair of me to accept, yet I must, because of my duty."

Eric moved between them, waving Karl back with his one hand; Eric would've sat upon Karl if he'd had a body to sit with. Karl was at a difficult stage in his training: skilled enough to know that he could fight well, but not experienced enough to recognize fighting skills in others. After raw ability, sword fighting was mostly experience and dedication. As skilled as Eric was, he'd fought only for one human lifetime, a fraction of the practice that Ruthedhel had experienced.

"Eric, move aside," Karl ordered.

"Wait!" Eloise said. "Eric's trying to tell us something."

Eric turned to Eloise. He pointed to Karl, then to Ruthedhel, then slashed his hand across his chest, palm outward in a gesture of rejection. Eloise had to trust him; there was no way that he could explain it to her, and Karl would never accept that Ruthedhel, who was physically smaller than the Seer, was too great a fighter for him.

"Eric doesn't want Karl to fight," the Seer said.

"I have to," Karl insisted. "We have to keep moving or Hel and Loki'll catch us."

Eric bowed his head. Karl was right, but he couldn't defeat Ruthedhel, and fighting when there was no need was pointless. Worse, Karl could get killed, and the company wouldn't get far without him. But they couldn't afford to waste time like they had in Nidavellir with Radsvid. Despite any warrior skills, even the most protected halls of the dark elves couldn't withstand Loki for long.

There was only one way to defeat Ruthedhel, but Eric knew that they'd all object. Eric pointed at Eloise, and then at Ruthedhel, his expression grave.

"You want ... Eloise to fight Ruthedhel?" the Seer asked. "Eric, are you mad?"

Slowly Eric raised his arm; he pointed at Silvana.

"Not Eloise," Roselyn gasped. "Eric wants ... the Wolfqueen to fight Ruthedhel."

"No!" Karl shouted as Eloise paled. "I won't allow it. I'll fight him!"

Karl pushed right through Eric's ghostly form, raised his sword, and faced the slender, armored elf. Ruthedhel didn't move or speak, but his smile belied an unspoken amusement.

"Defend yourself," Karl warned.

"A dark elf is always defended," Ruthedhel said.

Eric would've bitten his lip, if he could. Eric wondered what Karl was watching, if he'd noticed that the dark elf's eyes were fixed on Karl's drawn sword as any experienced warrior's eyes would. Ruthedhel had shifted his weight to his back leg, almost imperceptibly, arched his back, and straightened his shoulders. Ruthedhel was tensed for combat, although he appeared to be standing relaxed and off-guard. Eric fretted; the elf was a master of deception.

Again Eric stepped between them, but this time Eric turned his back on Karl. Eric faced Ruthedhel, standing still, just looking at him. Part of being a great warrior was the ability to read your opponent; surely a fighter as skilled as Ruthedhel wouldn't ignore that. There was no need for gestures or plaintive pleas for a warrior who'd survived a thousand years.

To Eric's relief, Ruthedhel held him in his gaze, and then nodded slightly; they needed no words to understand each other. Eric stepped away, giving them room.

"Whenever you're ready," Ruthedhel said to Karl.

"I'm waiting on you," Karl said. "Draw your sword."

"I'll draw it when I need it," Ruthedhel said. "Attack, if you're determined to do this."

Karl hesitated, then stepped forward. He raised his sword, then unceremoniously swung hard.

Ruthedhel never moved. Karl's sword slashed the air before his face and missed him by inches.

"You're out of range," Ruthedhel said. "Try again."

Karl's face flushed; Ruthedhel was obviously toying with him. Karl wouldn't tolerate being insulted, and pride would be his undoing; infuriated, Karl would become rash, more determined to end the fight quickly. Over-extended efforts to damage one's opponent causes amateur mistakes and leaves the attacker vulnerable to counter-attacks. By insulting Karl, Ruthedhel was controlling the fight, which was always the key to winning.

Karl stepped closer and raised his sword again. Eric silently shook his head; already Karl was flustered. He was repeating the same blow, which an experienced warrior would never do. Karl was even going into stance too early, showing his opponent what he was about to do. Ruthedhel stood calmly, seeming oblivious to Karl's threat, and only Eric's skillful eyes could see how prepared the dark elf really was. The way that Karl was holding his sword, only one attack was possible; Ruthedhel could counterattack in a dozen different ways, and Karl would never see it coming.

Karl swung again, harder; too hard, the force of his swing pulled him slightly off-balance. Eric would've instantly taken advantage of his opponent's mistake, stepped close, and won the fight. But Ruthedhel merely stepped backwards, out of range, and again Karl's sword sliced nothing but air.

"Are you going to fight me or not?"

Eric hesitated, confused. Why hadn't Ruthedhel ended this? Only fools dragged out a fight unnecessarily long, and Ruthedhel couldn't be a fool: foolish warriors always died young, as had Thorland, Svenson's son. Yet Eric couldn't be too sure of his facts. Despite his lifetime of training, every new fight held a valuable lesson. *What lessons would a thousand years of combat teach?*

"I am fighting," Ruthedhel answered Karl. "As you challenged me, I have no choice. It would be dishonorable to lose on purpose, so you won't leave here undefeated. But while I must fight, I'm not required to harm you. I can simply wait for you to tire yourself out, as you eventually will, throwing useless attacks like that. Unlike you, I have all the time in the world. If you wish to end this now, then you should surrender."

"I can't surrender," Karl said. "All of our lives depend on me."

"How sad," Ruthedhel said.

Karl jumped forward at the rebuke and swung as hard as he could. With blinding speed, Ruthedhel drew his sword at an impossible angle, such that it blocked Karl's blow almost before it cleared its scabbard. Their swords clanged, echoing down the river tunnel in both directions, but Ruthedhel's block didn't stop Karl's swing, just lightly deflected it. Karl fell forward, toppled by his own momentum, and Ruthedhel swept his sword down and stabbed lightly into Karl's boot. The leather wasn't pierced, but Karl's foot was pinned so that Karl tumbled forward onto the stone shelf and landed hard on his chest. Instantly Karl rolled over, but Ruthedhel slapped the flat of his blade hard against the bare knuckles of Karl's right hand. Karl cried out and dropped his sword, and Ruthedhel pinned him against the ground with his elvish blade at Karl's human throat.

"This challenge is over," Ruthedhel declared.

"No!" Roselyn cried, and she jumped from the boat and charged the dark elf, barehanded, ready to avenge Karl.

"Easy!" Ruthedhel ordered, stopping her with a warning glance. "You dare challenge me without a weapon? Are all humans mad?"

"I don't care how good a fighter you are," Roselyn warned. "If you hurt him, I'll kill you!"

Roselyn stood just outside of Ruthedhel's range, poised to charge in, no matter what.

"Ah, you're his lover!" Ruthedhel said. "I see it in your eyes. A lucky man he is to be loved by a lady of such spirit! Dark-elf maids would delight to teach one such as you. Don't die foolishly; I've no desire to harm anyone. Come meet my king and you'll be treated as honored guests."

"Stand aside, Roselyn," Rafe said suddenly, carefully balancing, trying to exit the boat without falling into the rushing river. "I'll challenge him next."

"No," Eloise said. "Sit down, Sir Rafe. Eric's right: I'll fight this warrior."

"No!" Rafe said. "I can't let you sacrifice ..."

"Why not?" Eloise demanded, glaring at Rafe. "Seren sacrificed herself; *will you treat me as badly once I've saved our company?*"

Rafe startled at her vehement tone, and then averted his eyes.

"Help me up," Eloise ordered, and Rafe obediently held out his hand and helped Eloise balance as she stepped across the boat. Roselyn came back and helped pull Eloise up onto the wooden dock.

"Back in the boat, all of you," Eloise ordered. "I'll challenge this dark elf."

Ruthedhel withdrew his sword, allowing Karl to stand. But Karl remained prone.

"Eloise, please ...," Karl begged.

"I'm not making half of the sacrifice that Seren did," Eloise said bluntly. "Back into the boat ... now!"

Slowly Karl retrieved his sword and stood. Head bowed, he slunk back and followed Roselyn down into the boat.

Eric looked at them with pity. The company had been through so much, so quickly, that it was a wonder that they weren't at each other's throats. He'd seen entire crews mutiny for less, and watched superior armies fall just because their morale was low. Karl was humiliated, defeated with ease by a fighter half his size. Rafe was miserable, torn between his love for Seren and his hurt and jealousy. Seren was the worst of all, having willingly suffered Radsvid's depravities only to be unjustly condemned. Roselyn was doing the best, but she was also the most reserved; the success of the company would be her undoing; Roselyn could never return to England, not even under Eloise's protection. Succeed or not, Roselyn couldn't stay with the company forever, and if Karl chose to stay with Eloise, then Roselyn would be truly alone.

Eloise circled Ruthedhel, putting him between her and her friends.

"Silvana," Eloise said plainly, without emotion. "Do it."

Slowly the silver fairie rose on fluttering wings from her hiding place in the boat. Glororil rose with her but remained below her, awaiting her radiance.

"Are you certain?" Silvana asked.

"It's for the good of the company," Eloise said, but her voice cracked as she said it. Slowly Eloise reached down and lifted up her skirt, pulling off her outer dress and letting it fall to the ground. She kicked off her leather boots and stood before the dark elf wearing only her chemise.

"What are you doing?" Ruthedhel asked suspiciously.

"Challenging you."

"You have no weapon or armor, and even less musculature than your lovely friend ..."

"Glororil, shine the instant that he yields."

"I will," the golden fairie promised.

"I won't be deceived," Ruthedhel warned.

"I've no wish to deceive you," Eloise said. "Please yield before you die; I don't want your blood on my hands."

Even in his wispy nothingness, Eric felt sorry for Eloise. Ruthedhel tensed, as Eric would, prepared for anything.

Silvana burst with light; her soft, bluish radiance illuminated the chamber far better than Eric. Silvana's moonlight reflected off of the moist stalactites and rushing waters, and showed intricate etched patterns decorating Ruthedhel's armor, too subtle to be seen in Eric's glow. Silvana's moonlight illuminated them all, casting stark shadows on the cavern walls and boat.

Eloise convulsed, but gritted her teeth and fought not to scream. Then the pain seized her: Eloise fell onto the rocky cavern floor, her blonde hair covering her face. There Eloise writhed, and finally her screams burst forth, deafening them all. Twisting and flailing, her arms and legs sprouted blonde fur and a wolfish muzzle pushed out of her face. Fangs filled her mouth and claws stabbed out of her fingertips. Eloise's cries became inhuman ... and finally agonized howls.

The Wolfqueen rose slowly, hate-filled eyes glaring red as she glanced about. She snarled viciously and growled, spied Ruthedhel, and oriented on him.

Startled but never slow, Ruthedhel lunged forward before the Wolfqueen even rose. He stabbed her cleanly, right through her shoulder, deep into her chest, but the Wolfqueen only howled and fell back. Reeking black vapors rose from her wound and the stinking dark mist covered her shoulder, then dissipated. No trace of the wound remained when the smoke cleared; the Wolfqueen snarled at Ruthedhel.

Instantly she pounced, without warning, right at Ruthedhel. Eric startled; he'd forgotten the fury of Eloise's curse. Eloise was pure beast, more deadly than any forest predator. In the wild, fangs and claws, beaks and talons, deadly horns, and even size and swiftness never guaranteed victory. Savagery ruled the wilds, and sheer ferocity dominated all combats of beasts. Ruthedhel was doomed: nothing boasted the ferocity of the Wolfqueen.

Ruthedhel slashed even as he ducked the Wolfqueen's raking claws. He threw himself down and rolled beneath her, throwing himself to lie where she'd first risen, exchanging places as the Wolfqueen fell upon the spot where Ruthedhel had started. Black mists were already covering her right breast, which Ruthedhel's diving slash had opened. As before, the Wolfqueen healed instantly.

The Wolfqueen attacked before he could rise. Ruthedhel rolled aside and futilely stabbed, but the Wolfqueen leapt upon him. His thin blade didn't seem to bother her, yet Ruthedhel kicked with a suddenness that even Eric hadn't expected, and the Wolfqueen toppled onto her back.

Eric gaped amazed; no human could face such a horror. That Ruthedhel had survived three attacks was amazing, but no one could keep it up for long. The Wolfqueen never tired, fueled by pure evil.

Ruthedhel leapt to his feet and ran. The Wolfqueen pursued, inches behind. Ruthedhel dashed straight at the cavern wall, then suddenly jumped high. Propelled by his momentum, he ran two paces up the wall before back-flipping. The Wolfqueen crashed into the wall, rebounded unhurt, and spun to face him. Yet Ruthedhel had the advantage; with strength unguessed, Ruthedhel's blade struck at the Wolfqueen's neck and sliced clean through. Eloise's severed wolf-head twirled and fell back. Her decapitated body collapsed.

Roselyn screamed, and would've jumped from the boat had Karl not restrained her. Even Eric's phantasmal jaw fell open; he didn't know what this would do to Eloise.

Ruthedhel stepped away, panting, sweat drenching his face and dripping onto his metal breastplate. Yet he kept his eyes focused on the fallen body, his sword raised and ready.

The black mists rose, stinking the most foul and pungent odor, and covered the severed head and body. Both turned black, shiny, and melted into a liquid pool. The Wolfqueen arose whole and angry from the puddle, howling in murderous fury.

"I yield!" Ruthedhel shouted, but just then the Wolfqueen attacked; she bounded upon him in a single leap. Their collision carried them out onto the docks, their heads hanging out over the water, right by the boat. Ruthedhel's sword was knocked from his hand, his arms locked around the Wolfqueen's neck, fighting to keep her savage fangs from his unarmored face. Karl jumped to help him, almost capsizing the boat as he fell atop the Wolfqueen, wrestling to pin her raking claws.

Glororil's blinding light exploded upon them; dazzling as the sun, he shined inside the dark cavern, reflecting up from the rushing waters. All squeezed their eyes shut and the Wolfqueen howled in pain.

Writhing, shrieking, the savage Wolfqueen melted back into their sobbing, trembling baroness. Eloise collapsed, sandwiched between the horrified dark elf and Karl, who held her arms pinned.

"Don't hurt her!" Karl shouted at Ruthedhel.

Slowly Karl gathered Eloise up in his arms and cradled her to his chest as he sat on the edge of the wooden dock. Roselyn and the Seer got out of the boat to help him, and tried to comfort Eloise as she cried.

Eric bowed his head. Like the Seer's methods, this one was evil, costing his companions pain and grief. Despite their love for each other, they were still Saxons, unaccustomed to the violence of warrior-ways. They'd won; Ruthedhel had yielded, but it wasn't a victory to boast of.

Eric mused over the change in himself as much as the change in the others. This victory was much like Grusshire, the town that he'd sacrificed to slow Svenson

Two-Sword. The others were now more acclimated to violence; they'd all grown greatly since he'd first met them. Yet Eric wasn't unchanged, either. Once, the anguish of his companions hadn't bothered him; harsh, violent lessons had taught them to understand truth, courage, and confidence. Now Eric felt their suffering deeply, as if their agonies were his. He loved them, each and every one, and as they'd grown to be like Eric, he'd grown more like them. Eric was no longer an ultimate warrior; the best didn't let sentimentality bind their sword-hand. In loving them, Eric was accepting a weakness, a weapon that could be used against him.

Yet he'd have it no other way. Eric's life was already over; for good or ill, he was dead. He'd still strive to reach Valhalla, his only hope, but he wasn't as single-minded as he'd once been. Valhalla would be empty for him now if his entrance cost the lives of his companions. If all hope failed, then he'd sell himself to Hel to save them, and accept doom in Niflhiem, if by his sacrifice his companions could be spared.

Never before had Eric placed the security of others over his godly reward. Eric was amazed that he felt so now. It'd take him time to consider this strange, new feeling; perhaps someday he'd even understand Saxon hearts. His glow in the moonstone brightened; somehow that thought warmed his ghostly form.

Ruthedhel rose slowly, knelt before Eloise, and held out his sword.

"Mistress, my servitude is yours," Ruthedhel said. "That was amazing! Such perfect fighting, incredible speed, direct attacks ...! I'm awestruck! You must explain ...!"

"Leave her be," the Seer said, his voice deep with concern, such that he startled even Eric. "Her transformation is painful; you don't know what she's suffered to beat you."

"I must know," Ruthedhel said.

With a nod, the Seer took Ruthedhel aside, just inside his dark tunnel. Eric wandered with them as they stepped away from the others.

"It's Lycanthropy, the curse of the Wolf-Moon," the Seer said. "Eloise was wounded by another such creature, but not killed. Its curse infects her now, and in the light of the full moon, she transforms into the Wolfqueen, and stays as such until daylight restores her."

"The lights of the fairies control her?" Ruthedhel guessed. "A fearsome curse ... and a marvel; I've never seen such magical healing, and only trolls and giants wield such physical strength. But they lack her swiftness and control."

"She's a terror, when changed," the Seer said. "But she has no consciousness. She'd have slain us all, after you were dead."

"All of my life I've longed for such power," Ruthedhel said. "I'm one of our best, revered by many.

Yet my fighting skills come from discipline, which she seems to lack entirely. I don't know if it'd be worth it."

"One of our reasons for coming here was to find a cure for her," the Seer said. "Until now, we haven't met anyone whom I dared ask. Do dark elves know of anything that might help?"

"I'm not learned in the ways of magic," Ruthedhel said. "Skills such as mine don't develop through divided dedications. There are dark elves who study such things; I'll speak to them when I may. When your errand is completed, I'll tell you all that I learn, if you return this way. But don't expect too much; I've never even heard of such a curse, even in our oldest tales."

"If I can, I'll return," the Seer said. "I'd appreciate meeting those dark elves whose studies mirror my own. If their skills excel mine as yours does of human fighters, they've much that I'd like to learn."

"I'd be honored to introduce you."

"Ruthedhel?" Eloise called weakly.

Ruthedhel hurried to Eloise's side. Eloise lay still in Karl's arms as Roselyn held her hands. Tears still wet Eloise's cheeks, but she was otherwise restored.

"Yes, Mistress?" Ruthedhel knelt before her.

"We have to go," Eloise said.

"At once," Ruthedhel promised.

"I ... hope I ... didn't ...!"

"I'm unharmed, Mistress," Ruthedhel said. "I can't say the same for my armor. Your ... claws ... have scored it deeply, clean through my pauldrons."

"I'm sorry."

"Be not!" Ruthedhel smiled. "To witness such ... perfect fighting, gladly I'd sacrifice a dozen suits of armor! It was my honor to combat someone so masterful. Accept this gift of mine in repayment for the honor that you've done me."

Ruthedhel pulled off of his wrist a small golden band and slid it onto Eloise's wrist. He pushed it up onto her forearm, where it fit snugly.

"Thank, you," Eloise tried to smile, but she couldn't. "We must go at once. I don't wish to tax your servitude, but if there's anything you have that we need ...?"

"Food?"

Eloise glanced at Roselyn.

"We've got enough to last for days," Roselyn said, looking at Ruthedhel. "However, if I may ask, since you have so many: I need a sword."

"Take any that you wish," Ruthedhel said, gesturing to his weapon's rack. "Yet if there's anything that you'll need most, it's my company. The Black River winds through the heart of our realm, and without me, I don't know how far you'll get. Also, there's the guard at the other end, who won't let you pass unchallenged."

"But that would leave your border unguarded!" Karl said.

"Unguarded from what?" Ruthedhel laughed. "Trolls? Cowardly dwarves? My people would love an invasion; give us a chance to do some real fighting. This post is just an honorary position which I accepted so that I could have some privacy to work on my studies."

"We accept your company gladly," Eloise said.

Ruthedhel helped Roselyn select a sword that best fitted her; it had a soft-leather grip made of braided suede, a gold-chased pommel and hilt, and a slender, razor-sharp blade. Roselyn swished it through the air flamboyantly and thanked Ruthedhel many times. Then they all climbed into the boat, Ruthedhel in the fore. He unhitched a mechanical linkage and the dark net fell beneath the surface; the swift current pushed them on, and Karl levered with the oars to help push them away from the wooden dock.

Back in the center of the current, the flowing water carried them quickly downstream with Eric's glow lighting their boat. Glororil and Silvana flew ahead, again illuminating their way, revealing the massive stalactites hanging low from the ceiling. Soon they came upon many bright lights, and in places they emerged into large caverns where the Black River was lined with elegant stone buildings and wide patios. Trees towered, growing in flowerful gardens, and they passed many dark elves, all of whom paused to stare at the strange company as it sailed down their river. Yet Ruthedhel waved at the other dark elves and they went back to talking, eating, or simply walking on peaceful paths set beside the cool river.

The dark elves' realm was fascinating and delightful. Much of it seemed peaceful, but they passed more than a few armored combatants too engaged in sword-practice to notice the companions. Much of Svartalfhiem was dark, but lights abounded, especially by the river, and Eric wished that he had the time to explore their realm. He envied their skills, yet he wasn't concerned; in Valhalla, the Einherjar fought every day, and doubtless there were many there even older than Ruthedhel. If Eric made it to Valhalla, there he'd learn all that he wanted.

"Do all dark elves fight?" Eloise asked.

"No, some don't," Ruthedhel said. "Many fight for a while, but then take a few centuries to rest. Dark elves live long, according to your human ways of counting time. Fighting gives us a purpose, a goal of perfection that can never be fully achieved."

"Surely many are wounded or killed," Roselyn said.

"Accidents happen, but fewer than you'd think," Ruthedhel said. "Control is the key to excellence; a fighter who knows that their blow can kill always stops before it does and accepts the yield of their opponent. In time you'll understand, if you make use of that sword."

"Roselyn's already proven herself in combat," Karl commented.

"I'm not surprised," Ruthedhel said. "She has potential; I can see it in her eyes and by the way that she moves. I was more surprised to see your friend Eric with you; I didn't know that humans traveled with their dead."

"That's a long story," Eloise said. "Perhaps, if all turns out well but we can't get across Bifrost, then we'll come back this way and tell our tale."

"If so, then you'll discover the bounty of our tables," Ruthedhel said. "Dark elves delight in long tales of combat and richly reward those who narrate well."

They sailed past many more caverns, some more vast than the great troll cavern, although none compared to the immenseness of Niflhiem. Ruthedhel pointed out many special places that he loved and the houses of his dearest friends, and he called out to several dark elves on the shore as they sailed swiftly through the dark realm.

The fairies flitted freely and were waved to by many of the dark elves. Finally they flew down, close to the boat.

"The Elvin War must truly have ended," Silvana said. "Many greet us warmly."

"Their cities are vast," Glororil said to the companions. "You should see it from above; their streets are wide, though dark."

"You see," Ruthedhel said to Glororil, "our ways are not too different."

"Your ways are as dark as your hearts," Glororil rebuked. "Light-elves delight in our power to live, not our power to kill."

"One is the other, when the world's violent," Ruthedhel said. "Life is best lived on the edge, where it's precious beyond measure. Nowhere can any feel as alive as in the pitched heat of a raging battlefield."

"You waste your lives fighting."

"You waste your lives dancing and singing."

"Enough!" Silvana silenced both of them. "I've just learned that the Elvin Wars are over, and I'd appreciate it if you two didn't start them all over again!"

The current drug them into longer tunnels and less frequently into populated caverns. Finally Ruthedhel spoke up.

"We're approaching the border," Ruthedhel said to Karl. "Paddle out of the current to the left. There's a net across the river; we need to slow down."

When they emerged into the last cavern, their speed lessened and Karl maneuvered their boat against the wooden dock before it struck the taut black webbing. Beside it stood a beautiful elf maid in armor much like Ruthedhel's.

"Stand and be challenged!" she cried.

"I'll accept the challenge for all," Ruthedhel answered. "These humans have already earned their passage and are pressed for speed."

"You're Ruthedhel, are you not?" she asked, and he nodded. "I am Lilana, the Black River border guard."

"I'm honored," Ruthedhel said, standing in the boat and bowing.

"You have to fight her?" Karl asked in a whisper.

"Indeed, a lucky battle," Ruthedhel smiled. "Even to lose is to win."

Ruthedhel jumped upon the dock, unlatched the net, and instantly drew his sword. Lilana's blade clanged against his an instant later. As the net fell, the Black River's strong current caught them again, but they all sat watching as the two dark elves slashed and stabbed in their deadly game.

"They're crazy," Glororil remarked, and Eric wished that he could respond. To him, it looked like paradise.

Ruthedhel knocked Lilana's sword from her hand and stepped on it, but she kicked him hard and then jumped atop him. They fell together grappling, locked in combat. Amazed, the rest of the companions watched silently as the current swept them unwillingly down the tunnel and out of Svartalfhiem.

Jay Palmer

Chapter 17

Citadel of the Giants

SEREN

Clear sunlight blinded Seren as they emerged above-ground. Familiar trees and bushes surrounded; they were out of the dark tunnels at last, the fresh air like wholesome perfume reviving them after the chill, stagnant underground. Yet, as the others cheered the warm sunlight, Seren felt no joy.

I should have stayed a whore, Seren thought darkly. Laying on her back for coins, open for any man with money, Seren was invulnerable; no man was long enough to reach her heart.

Love ruined everything. Love had trampled her mother, who'd taught Seren the truth of romance. Seren had watched dozens of whores lose their hearts over and over, crushed each time that their idolization ended. Worse, those who married for love soon complained about their lazy husbands so often that, eventually, complaining became their only joy. No good ever came of love.

Seren had always refused love, avoided it like a plague, and scoffed at the romantic bardic tales told before fireplaces for young, naive girls dreaming fancies too ridiculous for words. They were whores, born of whores and destined to bear daughters who'd become whores. Any other belief was idle nonsense and an invitation to pain. To believe in love was to accept inevitable disappointment; Seren had carefully shielded herself from any man offering more than coppers.

Then she'd met Rafe, a lonely man with bags of gold and jewels; a prized commodity for any whore. Seren had been suspicious of his young companions, but quickly learned that they were no threat to her. Close friends, protectors, they'd seemed glad that Rafe had someone to spend his nights with. At first, Seren had assumed that the beautiful young girls were glad to be rid of Rafe's aged attentions, but she'd quickly learned that her assumption was wrong: either of them would've gladly slept with Rafe, if he'd asked. That Rafe hadn't asked was the first thing that had really attracted Seren, the first crack in her armor against love.

Rafe was a good Christian. He certainly wasn't cowardly: how many times had Rafe faced death without flinching just in the short time that Seren had known him?

Radsvid was already just a bad memory, one evil face among the thousands who'd lain atop her in the dark. Seren didn't regret sleeping with him; someone had to ... or they might've never escaped Nidavellir.

She'd chosen wrong. Seren had let a bag of gold and unbelievable bravery blind her. Now where was she? Trapped in another world, risking death at every turn, because she'd stupidly dropped her guard and let love seep in like a sickness, infecting her with childish dreams. After all her years, all of the lecherous men of Madrone, Seren's determination had availed her nothing. Love had claimed her, and as always, betrayed her.

Seren had no idea what to do. She'd never get home from here, alone, unaided. She needed them, no matter how she felt. She wasn't even sure that she could find other humans in this realm, save the dead in Niflhiem. Alone, she'd be lost, helpless until she starved.

All of the others seemed supportive of her and angry at Rafe. Eloise had surprised her, yelling at Rafe in Svartalfhiem. Yet Rafe was their friend; without him, what did they need with an aging whore? Karl and the Seer had eyes only for the young women, and both girls were nobility: they wouldn't want her. That hurt Seren the most; she'd begun to think of them as family. *Without Rafe, they'd no longer want her.*

A yellow flower gently floated past them as Karl rowed, the tiny splash of his oars guiding them. Seren looked up at the blue, sunlit sky, amazed at how relieved she felt to feel the sun's warmth and see its comfortable familiarity. She'd never even seen a cave before the company; now she never wanted to see another.

"Look out!" the Seer called to Karl. "Pull aside! There's a tree across the river."

The fairies flew in glittering circles over a tree that had fallen into the river, its thick branches blocking their path. It must've fallen recently; its fluttering leaves were still green.

"We'll have to lift the boat over it," Karl said, rowing them swiftly toward the bank.

"Here you are!" shouted a deep voice. "I thought I heard you!"

From behind a stand of trees stepped a powerfully-muscled giant. He didn't look like Skaldi, the misshapen giant that they'd fought on the Druid hilltop in England; this one was younger, well-dressed, his short brown beard unkempt but not unclean, and he was smiling. He was built like Eric except that he was enormously tall, and his bulk matched his height. He was wearing a brown tunic with matching breeches, and he walked toward them easily, seeming neither sinister nor loathsome.

Seren stared at him briefly, then looked away, taking a deep breath of the fresh, fragrant air, free of the musty odors of the Norse underworld. Another giant:

Seren wasn't impressed. Seren was sick of monsters and elves and ... dwarves. All that she wanted was to go home.

"Halt!" the Seer cried. "What do you want?"

"Forgive me," said the giant. "I'm Blathanoir, son of Blakkakar, at your service. I've been ordered to bring you to Heid."

The Seer paused, glancing at the others.

"Who?" he asked.

"My Mistress, Heid," Blathanoir the giant said. "She commanded me to bring you to her."

"Why?"

"She didn't tell me why," the giant shrugged. "She never does. But I must obey her. Stay in your boat; it'll be faster if I carry you to Jotunhiem."

"We can't go to Jotunhiem!" Eloise said. "We're in a hurry ..."

"I'm afraid that I must insist," Blathanoir said.

The giant reached the edge of the water and stepped into the river. Suddenly Eric stepped out of the boat, silently waved his arm and stump, and blocked the giant's path. Blathanoir stopped and looked at Eric; even lit by the moonstone, Eric was pale and almost transparent in the bright sunlight.

"What's this?" the giant asked.

Eric turned to the Seer, shaking his head fiercely, warningly.

"Eric says that we shouldn't go with him," Karl interpreted.

"I heard nothing!" Blathanoir insisted.

"Eric can't speak," the Seer explained. "Outside of Niflhiem, he's dead, a pale shade."

"Well, let's hear what he has to say," Blathanoir said, and he waved a hand at Eric.

"Don't you think that I wish I could talk?" Eric shouted suddenly.

"Eric!" Roselyn gasped. "You talked!"

"How'd you do that?" the Seer asked.

"He's not talking," the giant said, smiling. "It's an illusion, a simple one. We giants are masters of illusion. If we wish to hear him talk, we can grant sound to his voice."

Eric turned to the giant. "You said Heid; do you mean Heid the Gleaming One, who was once called Gullvieg?"

"You know my Mistress," Blathanoir bowed to Eric.

"Enough to know of her madness," Eric said. "Heid's lust for gold started the first war between the Vanir and the Asier."

"The .... what?" Eloise asked.

"The old and the new Gods," the Seer interpreted. "Norse faith is unique in one important aspect: it remembers before itself. Odin, Thor, and the rulers of Asgard weren't the first Norse Gods. The Vanir existed first, the Norse Gods of fertility ..."

"Bah!" Blathanoir scowled. "Lies, all of it!"

"Truth!" Eric contended. "Wrongly told, but ..."

"We're the master race," Blathanoir grumbled. "All others are usurpers."

"You?" Eric laughed. "The giants?"

"Yes, we giants!" Blathanoir boomed. "We're the first-born. Our great father Aurgelmir first awoke in the springs of Ginnungagap formed by the great melt where the ice of Niflhiem and the fires of Muspell met, and Aurgelmir first nursed from the teats of Audumla, the giant cow, who licked Buri the Idiot out of the ice. Aurgelmir would have killed Buri then, had he known the evil that Buri would cause!"

"I thought Ymir was the first giant's name," the Seer said.

"It is, in Asgard," Eric said, "but his tale is twisted wrong. Buri was no idiot; he was the grandfather of Odin, Vili and Ve. Ymir, whom the giants call Aurgelmir, was the totally evil one. Alone he fathered the race of giants out of his sweat. But Bor, Buri's son, married Bestla, the fair daughter of the frost giant Bolthor."

"Bestla the Cursed!" the giant spat. "Bestla the Bitch! She spawned Bor's three cursed sons, Odin, Villi and Ve! They killed Aurgelmir because they were jealous of him, and tried to drown all of his children with his blood."

"They killed Ymir because of the brutal giants that he kept fostering, who were attacking the Vanir," Eric argued. "The death of his race was accidental, caused by the flood of Ymir's blood as it washed over the lands.

Bergelmir the Lucky and his wife were the only giants that survived."

"It was the wisdom and foresight of wise Bergelmir that he'd hollowed a tree into a boat, in which he and his wife escaped the treachery of Odin and his brothers," the giant scorned, "but first-born Aurgelmir isn't the only credit to our master race. After their evil ambush, Odin and his brothers built the world of Aurgelmir's flesh and the mountains of Aurgelmir's bones. From his teeth and jaws came all boulders and stones, and his blood filled the sea. Lifting his skull, they made the eternal sky, and they flung his brains high to become all clouds. The world itself is made of Aurgelmir, and so only to the giants it belongs!"

"Those who chop the wood and build the house own it, not those who grew the trees," Eric said.

"Peace!" the Seer interrupted. "The giant has a right to his own beliefs, Eric, same as you. We Druids have never understood your strange religion. I think that the giants were born first, but they weren't Gods. They were savages, as everybody's first ancestors were. The Vanir were the first civilized Gods, back when Odin and his brothers were still young; the Vanir embody fertility, praised by all new races because of their necessity for birth and growth. Yet once their race became strong, the Aesir, Gods of Asgard who were warriors, assimilated the older Gods after long years of pointless war. The giants remained separate, but the three races have shared an unbroken peace since then."

"Lies!" Blathanoir shouted.

"You Druids know nothing!" Eric said. "There's never been peace between giants and the Aesir!"

"Only because the frightened Asgardians hide inside their giant-built wall, which they lied, cheated, and murdered to obtain!" Blathanoir sneered. "Yet we giants only laugh. It's their second wall; their first wall we giants destroyed!"

"You didn't!" Eric shouted. "That wall was destroyed in the great First War."

"We started that war!" Blathanoir laughed. "Giants sent Gullvieg to Asgard knowing that the young Gods would kill her, since no one can stand her lusts for long."

"Gullvieg is dead?" Eloise asked. "But ... you said ... that she wanted to see us."

"She does, and we should get going," Blathanoir warned.

"But if the Gods killed her ...?" Eloise argued.

"She's a Goddess," Eric said. "Gullvieg drove them crazy with her gold-lust, and they killed her. The Gods tortured and pierced Gullvieg with many spears, and then threw her body into a great fire. But after being burned to death, Gullvieg stepped out of the fire whole and alive. Three times the Gods killed and burned her, but Gullvieg always returned. So they renamed her Heid, the Gleaming One. Ever after, Heid was a Seeress, the most evil of women. Heid enchants staves and casts wicked spells."

"Now she lives with us," Blathanoir said. "You must come to meet her ... or suffer her wrath."

"What can she do to us?" Karl asked.

"The nicest thing that she could do would be to hand you over to Loki and Hel," Blathanoir said. "As a Seeress, she can find you wherever you go."

"True, but they'll find us anyway," the Seer said. "They know where we're going, so they need only arrive first. What could Heid do if she weren't being nice?"

"Enchant you all," Blathanoir frowned. "You'd all become her personal slaves, and be tormented forever, as I am."

"And to think, we could've gone with Ruthedhel!" Roselyn grumbled.

"Gods and giants!" Karl sneered. "Sounds more like a children's story than a religion."

"How did Heid know that we were coming?" the Seer inquired.

"All in Utgard know of you," Blathanoir said. "Loki and his evil daughter arrived yesterday in a silver chariot pulled by black wolves. Utgard-Loki refused them admittance to Utgard, but he listened to their pleas. We know of your journey and from where you came. Loki promised us much gold and secret information to capture you. But Heid overheard all, and then used her enchantments to find you, and sent me to fetch you."

"Loki and ... Utgard-Loki?" Roselyn asked.

"Utgard-Loki is king of all Jotunhiem," the giant said. "Loki is but an Aesir."

"Aesir is better than any giant," Eric said.

"There's no point in arguing," Blathanoir said. "Even if you puny humans could defeat me, Heid would simply enchant you and make you walk all the way to Jotunhiem. That would take you many days, for it's far from here. I can carry your boat as easily as the river and have you there by nightfall. Will you resist me? I've no desire to injure you; Heid would be upset."

The others exchanged nervous glances.

Seren said nothing, looking away; she wanted nothing to do with giants or sorceresses. She didn't say a word, determined to keep her silence, but Seren already knew that they'd let this giant take them to Jotunhiem. What would be the point of resisting a sorceress that could enchant them into slaves?

"We've faced giants before," Karl reminded Eloise, turning his glare toward Blathanoir, "and we won."

"It was an expensive victory," Roselyn reminded him, "and Eric says that this Heid can do more than make illusions."

"Much more," Eric said. "She doesn't have honor like Ruthedhel. We'll go to her, willingly or not. I say that willingly is best. Once Heid enchants you, you're hers forever."

"Since there's no other choice, speed would be best," Eloise said. "The sooner that we get to Jotunhiem, the sooner we may continue. Eric, get back in the boat. Um ... Blathanoir, was it? We're ready to go."

"I'll carry you there with dispatch," Blathanoir said. "Hold tight; the faster I go, the bumpier your ride."

Eric stepped back inside the boat, flickering as the companions moved between him and the blessed moonstone. Blathanoir waded out to his knees, then reached down and lifted their boat, hoisting all of them high into the air. He set their boat onto one of his massive shoulders and then he walked back up onto the shore.

Seren clung tightly to the side of the boat as they were lifted and spun. Their momentum tossed her, and she feared that Blathanoir would fling them all from the boat. Yet no one fell, and suddenly the muscular giant bounded off, running, bouncing them on his shoulder.

Everyone but Eric clung for dear life, bouncing up and down as the smooth, hard hull of the boat dropped, rose, and slammed against them until they were fighting to hold their posteriors away from the slapping impacts. Seren tried to do this, but her strength soon failed. It was like riding a wagon pulled by galloping wild horses with all four wheels notched and broken. Silvana and Glororil flew around them as they were carried, refusing to land in the jostling boat. Seren had no choice but to grit her teeth and endure, but she'd never felt more like dinner being carried to the table.

Blathanoir jostled them the whole way, hour after hour, seeming to enjoy their discomfort. His strength and endurance amazed Seren, for neither steep slopes nor long runs bothered him. No mortal man could've kept pace with him, and no man could've lifted the heavy boat containing them, their armor, and their weapons. Seren was almost glad that she was hungry again; if she'd eaten anything recently, surely this ride would've made her lose it.

"Be warned," Eric's voice whispered, though he was unseen because the Seer had quickly pocketed the fragile moonstone. "Utgard's a dangerous place. The giants there are the largest and fiercest. Both Thor and Loki were humbled by its king."

"By illusion," the Seer said, "but we've faced illusions before."

"Skaldi was a wandering fool, a peasant giant!" Eric warned. "Utgard-Loki is the wise and wicked King of Giants, the greatest master of illusion. Utgard's the giant's chief citadel. We won't get out of there unscathed."

Soon a great many-towered fortress loomed in the distance, taller than the mountains, its crenellations almost touching the emerging evening stars. Made of huge blocks of marble, its magnificent hall was surrounded by tall towers, each topped by wide flags blowing in the wind. Its long shadow under the setting sun eclipsed the shade of the mountains. The wall around it rose taller than the Gates of Niflhiem, formidable and immensely strong. Blathanoir ran right up to the giant standing guard before the gates.

"I have them," Blathanoir smiled. "Let me pass."

"Take them straight to Utgard-Loki," the guard warned, looking curiously down into the boat, for he was much taller than Blathanoir. "The King must see them before Heid does."

"I will," Blathanoir promised, and as the taller giant opened the gates, Blathanoir sprinted through the evening gloom. The massive door opened for him and they were helplessly carried inside.

The guard at the gate was huge, but the giants and giantesses in the hall easily dwarfed him. The room was gargantuan, rising above them until it was lost in the gloom of distance. Blathanoir brought them to the room's center, then set their boat down on the stone floor at the feet of the largest giant, wearing a crown of gold, who sat in a mammoth carven chair. Sick from the ride, they crawled out of the boat and fearfully stood around it.

"So you found them!" the crowned giant laughed. "Good boy, Blathanoir! You've beaten all of my searchers, despite your youth; I'll remember this. Run play now; I'll see to them."

"Y- Yes, your Majesty," Blathanoir stuttered. "B- But what of ...?"

"Heid will know that they're here," Utgard-Loki grinned. "You've done well. Perhaps, when you grow up, you'll be allowed to join us, if you continue with such feats."

Blathanoir bowed, but he didn't exit through the main doors. Instead, he ran to a side door and disappeared through it.

"Poor boy!" Utgard-Loki sighed. "A fine lad; too bad that Heid caught him. How I wish that I could free him! But that doesn't matter now. First I must decide how to punish you trespassers."

Utgard-Loki glared down upon them. They stood frozen before him, trembling beside their useless boat. His eyes didn't seem potent like Hel's or Loki's, but he was towering, threatening.

"W- We didn't mean to trespass," the Seer implored. "Let us go and we'll vanish and never bother you again."

"Why does Loki seek you?" Utgard-Loki demanded. "Why has Hel left her place of imprisonment? What powers have you that Yggdrasil itself should turn upside-down at your coming?"

"We can't ...," Karl began.

"Please!" Eloise said. "I'm their chosen leader, great king. I'll speak for all. Our answer is simple: we aren't trespassers, but victims. Blathanoir found us skirting the borders of your land, which we never wanted to enter, and he forcibly carried us here. He kidnapped us."

"Any of my men would've done the same," Utgard-Loki growled. "Within sight of my lands, all foreigners are trespassers and must pay with their lives, as Loki will pay with gold and answers."

"Wait!" the Seer cried. "Eloise is right; let us prove this to you."

"How?" Utgard-Loki asked. "As long as you're trespassers, you can prove nothing. Now answer my questions or I'll have you cooked for supper. Why does Hel and Loki chase you?"

"What can we do to become not-trespassers?" the Seer asked.

"Nothing," Utgard-Loki said. "Nothing ... unless you can earn the right to be here, as these giants have."

"How?" the Seer asked. "Tell us and we'll do it."

"Impossible!" the giant king laughed. "To earn the right to be here, you must perform some manly deed greater than we! You might as well admit your loss; no mortal could match against a giant of Utgard!"

"But can we try?" the Seer asked. "If we're as weak as you say, then it can do little harm."

"If you wish," Utgard-Loki chuckled. "If only to prove that you're helpless and amuse my guests. I'll give you this much: If just one of you can prove greatest at any manly trait, craft, or skill, then I'll pardon and free you all. Is that fair?"

"Fair as I think it'll get," the Seer sighed, "but we'll need a moment. We must choose our tests wisely."

"Truly spoken," Utgard-Loki said, "but take not over-long. Should Loki return before the test is over, I'll sell you all for his gold after you've told me what I want to know, which you will, if I have to squeeze it out of you."

"Hurry," the Seer said, turning to the companions. "All right, start thinking. What can we do better than they?"

Seren looked about, wondering. Surely no feat of strength would win out here. It had to be something ... human; something they alone shared in common.

"I can see better than anyone else," Karl said.

"You do see well," the Seer said, "but Utgard-Loki is bound to use illusions against us. Do you think that you can beat him?"

"I can try," Karl said. "It's all that I can think of."

"Very well!" Utgard-Loki said. "You've chosen wisely! Good eyes are useful in many ways, and some giants have no better eyes than humans. Let's see how you fare against us. Gundi is a giant well known for his sight. Defeat him and all of your lives will be spared!"

Utgard-Loki called the giant forward. Gundi was less tall than the king, but his eyes were bright and shining.

"Look up there, out of that tiny window," Utgard-Loki directed them. "See the clear night's sky? Fast as you can, tell us how many stars you can see between the shutters."

"Three score and seven," Gundi said quickly.

"What?" Karl demanded. "I can see clearly: there are only, eh, three, four, five, eight! Eight stars shine through that window!"

"Eight is all that you can see," Utgard-Loki smiled. "I hope that this isn't the best that we can expect; my people will be insulted to compete with you."

"That's not fair!" Karl argued. "If I can't see the stars, how do I know that they're there?"

"Perhaps you're right," Utgard-Loki said. "Let us try a closer test. Is that acceptable?"

"It is," Karl said.

"Then look down at the tiny hauberk you wear," Utgard-Loki said. "Fast as you can, tell me how many rings make up its harness."

"What?" Karl cried.

"Six-thousand, four hundred and twenty-two," Gundi said.

"Wait!" Karl cried. "I said that I could see better! This is a test of counting!"

"It seems to me that they're the same," Utgard-Loki said, "but I do wish to be fair. Perhaps you're slow-witted and can't count what you see. Very well, but this last test shall prove all. Fast as you can, point to your own dead companion, Eric Bjornson."

"The moonstone!" Roselyn shouted.

Karl gasped, looking about, but the dim shadows revealed nothing. Gundi pointed before the Seer yanked out his moonstone and held it up; Eric appeared, glowing exactly where Gundi was pointing.

"I'm here!" Eric shouted, but too late.

"So, your eyes aren't the treasures that you thought," Utgard-Loki said while his guests laughed. "Don't fret yet. There are many of you left to try."

"I'll try last," the Seer said as Karl scowled. "My meager magics are no threat here, and there's nothing else that I can do."

"I know what I can do!" Roselyn said. "During courts, I used to do fine delicate needle-work, and I'll bet I can do that better than any giant!"

"Perhaps you can," Utgard-Loki laughed, "but such womanish skills win nothing in my hall. Perhaps there's some other test that you'd try; I see that you bear a sharp elvin-sword ..."

"No!" the Seer said. "Whatever we do, we mustn't choose contests that risk our lives. I'm sure that Karl was cheated by illusion, though I don't know how."

"Then there's nothing I can do," Roselyn said.

"I can challenge him!" Glororil shrilly cried. "I can shine brighter than any other!"

"To shine is no man's talent!" Utgard-Loki laughed.

"It is, when it's used to defeat enemies!" Glororil shouted. "Hel herself wasn't an arm's reach away when I blinded her, and we all escaped because of it!"

"That was a brave and manly deed!" Utgard-Loki declared. "Very well; Thyrnn, come here! Face this noisy elf and teach him what brilliance is."

"Cover your eyes," Glororil whispered to the companions. "This is going to be bright!"

Thyrnn, whose face and arms were dark red, came forward from his place at the tables. No hair graced his chest, arms, or head, not even eyelashes. Thyrnn took a stance before Glororil, grinning evilly. Slowly he began to glow red as flame, then quickly turned white hot, as molten steel in a forge. The companions covered their eyes with their hands, but the bright light shone right through their skin.

Glororil waited until Thyrnn was burning blinding-white, then released his power. Golden light exploded upon the hall, and Utgard glowed with striving lights, one blinding white, one radiant gold, and both glowed like suns, glistening through everything. Even covered, Seren's eyes stung painfully; she prayed that she wouldn't be blinded.

Suddenly the golden light failed. None was brighter than Glororil, but the golden fairy's power was short-lived, while Thyrnn shined bright as ever.

"Enough!" Utgard-Loki shouted. "Thyrnn, spare our eyes! This contest is over, and again these strangers have lost!"

The guests laughed loudly and clapped their hands.

"I'm ... sorry," Glororil apologized, weakly gasping for breath.

"You did well," Roselyn said. "Thanks for trying."

"Titania told us ... to use our lights to help you," Glororil confessed. "I- I thought ... I was ... brightest."

"You are, I suspect," the Seer said. "I detected some illusion, but I couldn't tell what. The power of Thyrnn's light was truly real."

"I'd be glad to try," Silvana chimed, "but I don't know what I could do. I've only my fairie talents."

"Perhaps they'll help," Roselyn said. "You can fly ..."

"Utgard-Loki won't accept that," the Seer said. "Flying is a fairy ability, not manly at all."

"Then I must try," Eloise said. "I can't fail."

"The Wolfqueen?" Roselyn asked. "Eloise, no! The giants are cheating with magic. If you should lose, you could die."

"Eloise need not fight," the Seer said. "Being fearsome is a very manly art, and none can beat Eloise at that."

"Glororil will need a moment," Silvana flew down to them.

"So be it," Eloise said, turning to Utgard-Loki. "I'll face your test, but I need a moment to prepare."

"The longer that you wait, the sooner Loki will return," smiled Utgard-Loki.

"Seren, snap out of it!" Karl whispered, grabbing her arm and shaking her. "You're our smartest; we need you!"

Seren raised her head to look at Karl, then slowly turned away; this wasn't her fight anymore. If they killed her, then she'd die, and she wouldn't even try to resist.

"I whore," Seren berated herself, tears welling in her swollen, unblinking red eyes. "Excel only at whore-skill. That Seren no do, maybe never again."

Seren looked up; Karl's surprise would've amused her if their situation weren't so dire. Karl was an honest, simple man, so young that she could anticipate almost all of his reactions. But Karl was Rafe's friend, not hers.

"I'm alright now," Glororil said finally.

"And I'm ready," Silvana smiled.

"We're ready," Eloise said to the King of Utgard. "I'll face your test, for I'm more fearsome than anyone else here."

"I'd hardly call you fearsome," Utgard-Loki smirked.

"I will be," Eloise said. "Bring forth you champion and I'll defeat him."

"As you wish," Utgard-Loki said. "Kasdnir, come, let us look at you. Let's see who can out-frighten the other."

A tall, dark giant shuffled forward, his teeth clenched and snarling. Already he was a fearsome sight, but Seren knew to expect worse. Even Utgard-Loki glanced fearfully at Kasdnir and edged back in his throne.

"Begin!" he said.

Silvana moved first, flying up high, then bursting with her glowing bluish light, soft and relaxing, soothing after the war of brightness between Glororil and Thyrnn.

Eloise screamed. She didn't fall, as she always had before, but stood trembling as the moonlight drilled into her, conjuring its dreadful effects. Eloise exploded with fur and fangs, her delicate hands knotting into claws more deadly than daggers. Howls and shrieks echoed in the hall as her transformation completed and the Wolfqueen stood revealed in her evil fury. The Wolfqueen faced Kasdnir and snarled.

But Kasdnir only snarled back and, seeming of his own will, began to change. Huge as he was, he fell forward within reach of the angry Wolfqueen, but in a flash Kasdnir was gone, changed into a form that no curse could match. Kasdnir grew greater than before, his face truly wolfish, more like Garm than the Wolfqueen, but darker, meaner, glowing with evil radiance. Kasdnir's eyes were the worst threat; like Loki's, they burned down and struck the Wolfqueen in a blaze of visible agony. Eloise howled in pain and fury, too pressed to fight but resisting to her last. Slowly Kasdnir bent down and opened slavering jaws that could swallow the Wolfqueen whole.

"Enough!" the Seer cried, seeing Eloise about to be gobbled. "Draw him back! We admit to losing! Glororil, save her!"

Glororil burst forth his golden sunlight, and this time the Wolfqueen screamed and fell, overcome by the sunlight combined with the power of Kasdnir's eyes. Eloise slowly transformed back. Utgard-Loki shouted at Kasdnir, and angrily the great wolf-shape snarled, but slowly he melted back to giant-shape that he'd worn before. The glare of his eyes faded, and soon he was Kasdnir, standing grimly triumphant before the throne of Utgard.

Roselyn, the Seer, and Karl ran forward as the brilliant sun-glow faded to pale yellow. Soon Eloise was sobbing in their arms.

"It seems that your chances are running out," Utgard-Loki smiled as his guests resumed laughing. "If you'll end these silly games then we can continue with our other business. You might as well give up; you'll never win."

"I'll win," Eric said suddenly, still glowing in the radiance of the moonstone. "I can pass through walls leaving no holes, and walk on any surface."

"You can do so only because you're dead, and that's nothing to boast of," Utgard-Loki sneered. "You must choose something that you could've done in life, if you'd be tested."

"All right," Eric grumbled. "I was raised listening to stories about you and Odin's folk. There's nothing men know that I don't. That's not only a manly deed, but illusions won't affect its outcome."

"Indeed," Utgard-Loki said. "Yet that'll be hard to prove since I have no human servants for you to compete with. You must match yourself against me and trust that I'll be fair."

"You haven't been fair to begin with, but that can't stop me. Ask me nine questions, and then I'll ask you nine, until one loses."

"Very well," Utgard-Loki said. "Answer now my first question. Tell me this, Eric Bjornson, if you are wise. Who are the Twelve who assemble around the Well of Urd each day?"

"Odin, Thor, Baulder, Heimdall, Loki, Hod, Vidar, Tyr, Bragi, Vali, Ull, and Forseti are the Twelve. With them sit Njord, Frigg, Freyja, Gefion, Eir, Vili, Ve, Lofn, Sif, Saga, Aegir, Freyr, Idun, and others of great wisdom; these are they who gather each day before the Well of Urd."

"Answer now my second question," Utgard-Loki said. "Tell me this, Eric Bjornson, if you are wise. To whom did the Terrible One sacrifice himself, and why?"

"Odin sacrificed himself to himself, Odin to Odin, hung by the neck upon the great tree Yggdrasil," Eric recited. "Odin's reward was the treasured Nine Secrets of the Dead, and with the Nine Secrets of the Gods, eighteen powerful sorceries they combine to make, and with them Odin can cure the sick, heal wounds, unlock fetters, divert arrows, steal any weapon, reverse curses, douse flames, undo hatred, calm tempests, deceive witches, revive the weary, hear the whispers of hanged men, bless mortals, recognize all elves, grant wisdom, make women swoon, shackle with love, and the power of a secret; these are the charms of Odin."

"Answer now my third question," Utgard-Loki said. "Tell me this, Eric Bjornson, if you are wise. What treasures did Loki carry from Nidavellir, and what price did he pay?"

"For a prank, Loki cut off Sif's beautiful golden hair," Eric laughed. "Thor threatened to kill him, but Loki went to the dwarves, to the sons of Ivaldi, for magical hair of gold to replace the shorn locks of Thor's wife. As he bargained honestly, the dwarf-brothers gave Loki not only hair of gold, but a great ship called Skidbaldnir for Freyja and a magic spear called Gungnir for Odin. Believing these to be the greatest gifts, and always greedy, instead of bringing them right back, Loki bargained his head against two other dwarves, Eitri and Brokk, that they could make no finer gifts. Eitri and Brokk forged Draupnir, the golden armband that drops eight rings its own size every nine nights, Gullinbursti, Freyr's silver-bristled boar, and Mjollnir, Thor's magic hammer. Odin favored the gifts of these dwarves, for he prized most Mjollnir, the hammer that could kill any giant with a single blow. In retribution, Brokk laced Loki's mouth shut with strong thongs of leather, and the Gods of Asgard laughed at him."

"Answer now my fourth question," Utgard-Loki said. "Tell me this, Eric Bjornson, if you are wise. What names have the homes of Gods and elves?"

"In Asgard live the Aesir and the Vanir who dwell not elsewhere. Odin rests in Gladsheim and Saga shares the peaceful land of Sokkvabekk, Thor dwells in

Bilskirnir, and Heimdall rests in Himinbjorg. Baulder sleeps in Breidablik, Foresti abides in Glitnir, and mighty Njord swims in the harbor Noatun. Njord's wife, fair Skadi, daughter of Thiazi, dwells in Thrymhiem. Freyja blesses the land of Folkvang, and Vidar rests where no man knows in the lovely forests of Vidi. The light-elves dance in Alfhiem, and Svartalfhiem is the battlefield of the dark elves."

"Answer now my fifth question," Utgard-Loki said. "Tell me this, Eric Bjornson, if you are wise. What names have the rivers that flow across Asgard?"

"Hear the names!" Eric said. "Thund near Valhal, Slith, Ifing, Sekin and Ekin, Sid, Vid, Fjorn, Rin and Rinnandi, Gipul and Gopul, Old, Vin and Hol and Tholl, Grod and Gunnthorin."

"Answer now my sixth question," Utgard-Loki said. "Tell me this, Eric Bjornson, if you are wise. What names grace the Valkyrie, who choose the worthiest from the slain, and what do their names mean?"

"Hail the Valkyrie!" Eric shouted. "Their names and meanings I could never forget: Hrist and Mist, Skeggjöld and Skögul, Hildr, Prudr, and Göll, Herfjötur and Hlökk, Geirahöd, Randgríðr, and Róta. In the Saxon tongue, Hrist means Shaker, Mist the Fog, Skeggjöld means Axe Time, and Skögul means Raging. Hildr is the Warrior, Prudr is Might, and Göll means Shrieking. Herfjötur means Host Fetter, Hlökk means Screaming. Geirahöd is the Spear Bearer, Randgríðr the Shield Bearer, and Róta is the Wrecker of Plans!"

"Answer now my seventh question," Utgard-Loki said. "Tell me this, Eric Bjornson, if you are wise. What steeds do the Gods ride?"

"Sleipnir, Loki's child, bears Odin where he wills," Eric said. "The others ride Glað the shining one, Gyllir, Gils, and Glen, Skeiðbrimir who gallops, silver-maned Silfrintopp, sinewy Sinir, shaggy Falhófnir, golden Gulltopp, and Léttfet the Light-foot."

"Answer now my eighth question," Utgard-Loki said. "Tell me this, Eric Bjornson, if you are wise. According to Odin, what things do only fools trust?"

"A creaking bow," Eric said. "Fires unwatched and wolves unseen, boars in the brush, dark clouds, a calm sea, arrows in flight, a starving beggar, new ice, snow on a sunny mountain, slithering snakes, the kisses of a seductress, a repaired sword, a playful bear, any crown-wearer, an angry slave, kindness from a witch, coincidences and unexpected meetings, rotten wood, racing horses, and the whispers of a dying enemy; these are that which only fools trust."

"You've done well," Utgard-Loki said. "All my questions you've answered wisely and true. I was a fool to think that I could stump you!"

"These things I've known since I was a lad," Eric laughed. "Ask now your last, that I may begin mine."

"As you wish, but I see no point to it. Answer now my ninth question. Tell me this, Eric Bjornson, if you are wise. Does Loki own a falcon-skin coat?"

"Yes!" Eric laughed. "I've seen it, and so I've won. You surprised me, King of Utgard, for your last question was your easiest."

"But you answered wrong!" Utgard-Loki laughed. "Fool mortal! Loki often borrows it, but Odin's wife Frigg owns the famous falcon-skin coat! You failed to answer all nine!"

Eric paused and his mouth fell open, but he quickly recovered.

"Deceiver, you tricked me. I may be only a ghost, but I'll make you rue it. You still have my nine questions to answer."

"Ask away!" Utgard-Loki laughed. "You've only heard tales of all these things; I've seen them. You can't know more than I."

"We'll see," Eric said. "Tell me now, Giant-King, if you know all. Answer this first question: Who are the Norns, and from whence do they hail?"

"From Jötunheimr they came, three evil witches, giantesses who bring death: Urd, Skuld, and Verdandi," Utgard-Loki said. "Urd the Spinner draws forth the threads of each life, Skuld the Weaver enmeshes all into the tapestry of life, and Verdandi the Slayer severs each thread and dooms all to die."

"Tell me now, Giant-King, if you know all," Eric said. "Answer this second question: What words of wisdom does Odin give?"

"Odin is the font of wise cunning," Utgard-Loki said. "Heed no witch's words, cuckold no neighbor, nor journey far without supplies. Shun evil men, yet befriend all who are true. Heed the wise, and strain not their friendship. Waste no angry words on those witless or evil. Precious is that which serves you well. Let no evil thrive in shadow. Guard your eyes. Speak honest to strangers. Admire lusty women. Beware ale-sodden thoughts, a thief's smile, and strange woods in moonlight."

"Tell me now, Giant-King, if you know all," Eric said. "Answer this third question: What are the objects that hover in the sky?"

"Moon, son of Mundilfari, leads Bil and Hjúki among the stars," Utgard-Loki said. "Sun, daughter of Mundilfari, steers the horses Árvak and Alsvið to warm and brighten the world. The brains of Aurgelmir were hurled skyward to form all clouds. Bifrost is the rainbow bridge that the Valkyries travel."

"Tell me now, Giant-King, if you know all," Eric said. "Answer this fourth question: What are the races spawned by the stranger called Rig, and of whom were they born?"

"Heimdall disguised himself as Rig the Traveler," Utgard-Loki said. "Wandering in secret, Heimdall strode across Midgard and slept with those who succored him. Ai and Edda were Great Grandfather and Great Grandmother, and from them was born Thrall, who married Thir the Drudge, and of them was born the race of thralls. Afi and Amma were Grandfather and Grandmother, and of them was born Karl, who married

Snor, and of them was born the race of peasants. Fathir and Mothir were Father and Mother, and from them was born Jarl, whom Rig raised as a son and shared his wisdom, and Jarl's descendants became the kings of men."

"Tell me now, Giant-King, if you know all," Eric said. "Answer this fifth question: Who stole Mjollnir, and how did Thor recover it?"

"Thrym the Giant stole Mjollnir and buried it eight miles beneath his fortress," Utgard-Loki said. "Generously he offered to return Thor's hammer, asking only for Freyja, the Goddess of Beauty. But the Aesir cheated; the Son of Earth arrived swathed in a bridal gown, a veil hiding his angry eyes. Bedecked as Freyja, Thor bowed before the giant, and Thrym honored his oath and brought forth Mjollnir as a pledge of love to his bride. But Thor betrayed the bargain of the Aesir, seized the hammer, murdered Thrym, and stole back Mjollnir."

"Eric, what are you doing?" the Seer interrupted. "I could've answered that! Your questions must be harder!"

"They will be," Eric promised. "I should've known that the King of Utgard would know all about the past. Now I'll ask of the future, and let's see if he's as wise as he claims."

"Ask away, dead viking," Utgard-Loki laughed. "There's nothing that I don't know!"

"Tell me now, Giant-King, if you know all," Eric said. "Answer this sixth question: What warning will come to the Gods that death approaches?"

"The dark dreams of Baulder shall trouble all," Utgard-Loki said. "In the guise of Vegtam the Wanderer, Valtam's son, to Niflhiem shall Odin ride, where he shall conjure a dead Seeress to interpret Baulder's dreams. The dead Seeress shall predict the death of Baulder, but Odin's disguise shall be uncovered, and the Seeress shall turn him away ere he learns more."

"Tell me now, Giant-King, if you know all," Eric said. "Answer this seventh question: Who shall doom Baulder, and what shall be his fate?"

"From the lips of blessed Frigg, who sought to protect her son from all things, Loki will eavesdrop Baulder's secret weakness, and coerce Baulder's brother, Blind Hod, into casting Loki's dart at brave Baulder, who shall instantly fall," Utgard-Loki said. "All of the Gods shall ride to the realm of the dead to recover him, but Hel in Niflhiem shall refuse to release Baulder unless all things weep for him. Then the Aesir shall send out messengers to force tears from all things, from men, Gods, and giants, and even plants and rocks. But Loki, in disguise, shall refuse, and Baulder shall remain with Hel.

"Revenge the Gods shall have, binding Loki by the entrails of his youngest son in a deep cave. A venomous serpent whose fangs drip burning poison shall be hung above him. Weeping Sigyn, Loki's wife, shall catch the burning poison in a cup, but when her cup is full and she goes to empty it, the acidic venom shall drip onto Loki's face, and his writings shall shake all of Midgard."

"Tell me now, Giant-King, if you know all," Eric said. "Answer this eighth question: When will Loki break his bonds, and how shall fall both men and Gods?"

"Ragnarrok ends the worlds of men, giants, and Gods," Utgard-Loki said. "Tormented to madness, Loki shall shatter his bonds, and all the hosts of evil shall join him. Fenris shall break his dwarven fetter and rise in savage fury. The giants, trolls, and the vast legions of Niflhiem will wage final war against the Aesir and the Vanir. Heimdall shall witness their rise and blow upon his great horn; the warriors of Valhalla shall rise and battle all. Odin shall be swallowed whole by Fenris the Master-Wolf, whom Vidar shall slay. Thor's mighty hammer, Mjollnir, shall slay the monstrous serpent Jormungand, but Thor shall stagger back nine steps, covered in poison, and there die. Viciously Garm and brave Tyr the One-handed shall contest, and both shall die from their wounds. The oldest and bitterest of enemies, Loki and Heimdall shall duel without quarter, and both shall slay the other ere their longest of combats end. Then shall Black Surt come from fiery Muspell with his flaming sword; Freyr shall rise to stop him, but Freyr gave his sword to his servant Skirnir for the love of the giantess Gerd, and his love shall doom all. Black

Surt shall fling fire at all of the nine worlds, igniting Yggdrasil itself. The blackened Earth shall sink into the boiling sea, and all shall die, save only a few, but if those survivors are of good heart or evil, not even the Norns can say."

"So now we come to the last," Eric said firmly.

"True, and I'll answer your last question as all others," smiled Utgard-Loki. "Then I'll have beaten you, Eric Bjornson."

"We'll see. Tell me now, Giant-King, if you know all," Eric said. "Answer this ninth question: What words shall Odin whisper in his dead son's ear at the funeral of Baulder?"

"Not fair!" Utgard-Loki cried. "No man knows what Odin shall say to his fallen son, Baulder the White!"

"Then you can't answer," Eric grinned widely. "We are even, eight and eight."

"Not so!" Utgard-Loki laughed. "I can answer: 'It is for the best!' Odin shall say. 'Now the giants can rule as the Master-race that they are!'"

"Odin won't say that!" Eric shouted. "He'd never ...!"

"I have answered!" Utgard-Loki laughed. "Fool shade! If I'm wrong, then you must prove me so! Can you? Do you know what Odin shall say?"

"No," Eric confessed angrily. "But ...!"

"Then you've lost!" Utgard-Loki said. "Summon Loki and tell him to bring much gold! We have prisoners awaiting his attentions!"

"It's my turn, giant-king!" the Seer shouted. "I'll take up where Eric left off, for I think I can beat you. I'll ask first, nine questions of mine, then answer nine questions of yours."

"Ask away!" Utgard-Loki laughed. "But take care; I see that you're no Viking. If you ask secrets from your strange world, then I'll ask things known only to giants!"

"These questions will be easy for you, I suspect," the Seer said. "Here's my first question: Why do you risk losing to us in these games when you don't have to?"

"That's not a standard question!" Utgard-Loki said.

"I'm not a standard questioner," the Seer smiled. "You'll have your chance to get back at me when you ask your questions."

"Indeed I will!" Utgard-Loki growled. "You'll have no chance! But to answer your question, I can't lose. Heid will make you see her whether I win or not. Wisely I made her the guardian of my treasury; her powers and gold-lust make her perfect for the task, and she won't let you go without gaining Loki's gold. Even if I wanted to, I've no power to stop her. Whether she collects Loki's gold or I do, it'll rest in my treasury, so I can't lose."

"That's worth much to know," the Seer said. "Here's my second question: Is there a way that we can avoid meeting Heid?"

"None that I know of," Utgard-Loki laughed. "Heid is Vanir. Once you entered Utgard, you were trapped.

If you don't go willingly, then she'll change your will to thoughts that suit her."

"That's worth much to know," the Seer said. "Here's my third question: Is there any way that we can keep her or you from turning us over to Loki?"

"Now I understand these questions!" laughed the giant-king. "Yes, if you can defeat me in contest, then I and my subjects won't turn you in to Loki or Hel. No, Heid will sell you out, and no power in Jotunhiem can stop her. Your pleas will fall on deaf ears; Loki has offered gold, and Heid listens to nothing else."

"That's worth much to know," the Seer said. "Here's my fourth question: What is the quickest way for us to get from here to the Spring of Mimir?"

"Mimir?" Utgard-Loki asked. "Why do you go there?"

"It's my turn for questioning," the Seer said. "The sooner that you answer, the sooner you may ask."

"Oh, all right," Utgard-Loki shrugged. "Due East of here is a path that leads to the Great Drop, a steep cliff that slopes sharply down to the edge of Yggdrasil. From there, you'll see an overgrown grotto. Mimir lies there, where none dwell. Beside the Drop is an old farm, unused and falling to ruins. There lies the only route down. The path is treacherous and slow, leading far out of the way, yet there is no other way."

"That's worth much to know," the Seer said. "Here's my fifth question: How can I summon the spirit of Mimir and gain its wisdom?"

"There's nothing to summon," Utgard-Loki eyed the Seer curiously. "Mimir's head is set on a rock beside the bottomless pool; you'll be spoken to at once. Beware the voice of Mimir, for he'll seek to draw you into deals most dangerous! His prices are steep and few come out better than they started."

"That's worth much to know," the Seer said. "Here's my sixth question: From the Spring of Mimir, what's the quickest way to get to Valhalla?"

"There's no easy way," Utgard-Loki said. "If you climb back up here, and then head for the three valleys of Thor, you'll come to the rocking sea. Cross that and you'll be near Asgard, not far from Valhalla. Or you can follow the tributaries of Mimir up the winding way past the Well of Urd, but then you'll draw near to the deserted city of Vanahiem, and pass by deadly Alfhiem, where the light-elves live. Neither way is easy or short."

"That's worth much to know," the Seer said. "Here's my seventh question: What shall be our greatest danger along the way?"

"What won't be?" Utgard-Loki laughed. "Mimir is omnipotent, Jotunhiem won't welcome your trespassing twice, Vanahiem is haunted, Alfhiem is filled with wicked light-elves, in Asgard live the lying Aesir, and Loki and Hel will be chasing you all the way! Every danger is more than you can handle."

"That's worth much to know," the Seer said. "Here's my eighth question: Is there any way that we can defeat Loki, should he face us?"

"Only one," Utgard-Loki said coldly. "Slit your own throats and die before he overcomes you, as he surely will. You're only mortals; against Loki you have no chance, no matter what you do, as you've no chance against me. You've failed, all of you! Admit that you've lost and end this game!"

"Not until I ask all nine," the Seer said, unmoved by the giant-king's laughter. "Here's my ninth question: How can we return to Midgard upon the Rainbow Bridge?"

"What makes you think that you can cross the Rainbow Bridge?" Utgard-Loki laughed. "Heimdall guards it ceaselessly, save when his wisdom is needed elsewhere, and then his personal elite guardsmen prevent any passage, Aesir or giant. Heimdall alone can recite the spells to allow you to walk the translucent bands, but he won't; mortals aren't allowed to return after they've visited Yggdrasil. Should you try, Heimdall need only utter the counterspell and let you sink through the bridge and plummet to your deaths."

Seren's heart sank. They were trapped here, she'd known, but she'd always assumed that they'd find a way home. But just as well; she'd long since given up any real hope for their quest. All that they could do now was plod along until their strengths gave out, or one of their many enemies squashed them like the insignificant annoyances that they were.

"That's worth much to know," the Seer sighed. "You've answered well and true, King of Utgard. I thank you. There's no need to ask your nine; I've known all along that I can't match you, and I accept my loss."

"You never meant to win?" Utgard-Loki roared.

"I knew that you'd win, fairly or by cheating, as you've already proven," the Seer said. "I used my loss to answer important questions that might help us finish our quest and escape alive, but your words have dissuaded my hopes. I know now that we're doomed."

"Not yet," Utgard-Loki said. "Tell me freely why Loki wants you, instead of making me squeeze you from it, and I may let you live."

"We can't," the Seer said sadly. "Loki made us the same offer. In a choice between death and honor, we've already made our decision."

"So be it," Utgard-Loki said, and he reached down and grabbed the Seer about the chest with one enormous hand. "You've all lost, but you challenged best. I deem you, wizard, are the most knowledgeable of your group, and therefore the most dangerous. You'll suffer first."

"Wait!" Rafe cried, speaking for the first time since leaving Svartalfhiem. "I'll have my chance!"

"Why?" Utgard-Loki sneered. "My guests grow weary of this game! You'll fare no better than the others."

"Honor your promise!" Rafe growled. "I'll have my turn."

"Very well, but be quick about it," Utgard-Loki sighed, and he released the Seer and leaned back in his throne. "What will you challenge?"

Rafe walked forward, assuming a bold stance before the throne of Utgard.

"I challenge with the virtue of trust," Rafe said.

"Trust?" Utgard-Loki asked. "How will you challenge for trust?"

"This lady here," Rafe explained, motioning to Seren, "this lady I trust above all others. I trust her, as all warriors must trust their fellows in battle, with all that I hold dear. Into her hands I place my very life. This is my challenge: Seren, I love you and I always will. Here and now I ask for you to forgive me, and return my love, and should you not, I offer my life to these giants to end in any way that suits their fancy. If you don't love me, stay silent, and soon I'll trouble you no more. Yet say that you love me and I'll be spared to be your faithful servant forever."

"No!" Karl gasped, but Rafe ignored him.

"That is my challenge, Utgard-Loki!" Rafe shouted, turning to face the giant. "Trust! My life ... in the hands of another. A death of slow torture if she won't design to love me. That's the trust that I put in her hands! Will you, giant, dare as much as I? Will you place your life into the hands of another?"

Utgard-Loki hesitated, looking askance.

"Normally I wouldn't allow this, but I see the red anger of her eyes when she looks at you. You're not friends, at least, not anymore; I sense that you're challenging her more than I. You're indeed a brave man if you dare the vengeance of a woman betrayed. This is undeniably interesting. I'll allow it on one condition; if she should refuse you, then you must tell me freely that wisdom which Loki most wants to know."

"Agreed," Rafe said.

Seren glanced up at Rafe. *Was he mad? She'd stabbed men for less than he'd done to her! Must he betray Titania, too?*

"Behold the fury in her eyes!" Utgard-Loki said. "Indeed, this is a great challenge, deadly and daring. But before I call for a challenger, you must prove to me that these words aren't empty wind. Speak now, maiden, if you love this mortal. Or be silent. Choose."

Slowly Seren looked up, her furious gaze sliding from Rafe to the giant, then back again. Seren pursed her lip. Rafe had hurt her, denied her, and humiliated her. *Why had he put his life in her hands?* He could easily have done so with any of the others, who would've laughed and said anything to save him. But she couldn't speak the words. She was still justly enraged over how he'd treated her. Yet his challenge had caught her unprepared; Seren sat leaning against their useless boat dumbfounded, uncertain, and confused.

What did it matter if Rafe loved her? Love was the enemy, the beast that gnawed at Seren's armor and tricked her into following Rafe. Seren hated love and all the lies and deceits that came from it. Love was the greatest lie of all.

Seren looked up at Rafe and met his eyes. *She wouldn't be defeated by love!* Seren would stand defiant, and damned be anyone who claimed to love her.

"Of course I love you!" Seren finally shouted at Rafe, "but I had to ...! Don't you see ...?"

Rafe stood proudly before Seren, smiling with tears on his cheeks.

"I do now," Rafe said. "I regret everything. Forgive me, Seren!"

Seren held out her arms, and Rafe embraced her.

"A worthy challenge," Utgard-Loki confessed. "Neither I nor my subjects would dare as much as this brave mortal. Very well; it has gained you nothing, but you've won. You're free to join us in our feasting this evening, and we giants won't betray you to Loki. Your fate is still sealed: Heid won't risk losing her gold."

"One step at a time," the Seer smiled, watching Seren and Rafe hug once again.

"We can't stay," Eloise said to the giant-king. "We must be gone before Loki returns. We should see Heid now, since we must."

"But we'd appreciate some food to spare our supplies," the Seer said. "We haven't enough to travel all the way to Valhalla."

"Of course," Utgard-Loki smiled. "I'll have my servants bring you food; your tiny packs hold less than a single bite for giants."

"We couldn't carry more," the Seer said, "but tell me, Utgard-Loki, if you would: what illusions did you use to trick us? It won't matter now and we'll hold no grudges."

"Why do you wish to know?" Utgard-Loki asked.

"The sting of loss lasts forever," the Seer said. "I don't mind, for I never thought to win, but my friends may not feel as bad if they knew their true opponents."

"I understand," Utgard-Loki said. "Here is the truth: Karl has good eyes, but Gundi was really Hraesvelg, the eagle who sits on the uppermost branch of Yggdrasil, whose wings make the winds that blow across all worlds. Only Odin and Heimdall can match his keen sight. No mortal stood a chance."

Karl smiled; a magical eagle was no opponent to be shamed by. Utgard-Loki glanced at Karl but kept on talking.

"Glororil was indeed brightest, and I feared that even Thrynn might not be able to match him. Luckily, Glororil couldn't hold his full power for long. Thrynn had no difficulty there, as he is eternal Muspell, the Land of Fire, where Black Surt sits. No elf could outlast that."

"I knew I was brighter!" Glororil shouted down at them.

"Eloise was more fearsome than any giant," Utgard-Loki continued, looking down at Eloise. "I marvel at her terror, for only Thor and Odin could strike such horror among my subjects. But Kadsnir was in reality bound

Fenris the Master-Wolf, and no half-beast could match him."

"I wish that nothing so fearsome existed," Eloise said.

"It's a great and powerful magic," Utgard-Loki said. "But it was Rafe who amazed me most. He's earned a place in Utgard, for he has shown us a virtue sadly lacking among our kind. For his victory, I name him Rafe Giant-Bane, so that he may brag and we must suffer his taunts. But I warn all of you against coming here again, for my people won't welcome his presence twice. Only the honor of my promise shall let you leave, if you can."

"Since we're trapped by Heid," the Seer finished, grinning as if he alone held some secret. "You are most honorable, giant-king, yet we'll see; the test of honor comes not when it's easy, but when it's strained. Perhaps your honor shall be proven this day."

Utgard-Loki's servants brought them only a tiny plate of food, yet it was piled with more than they could eat in a week. Ravenously they gorged, stuffing their mouths and what little they could into their knapsacks. The amount on the plate dwindled only slightly before they were done.

Utgard-Loki directed them to a golden door behind his great throne. The door was huge, standing partially open, and inside it stood a woman no taller than Roselyn, peeking through the door. She was gold all over, like Glororil but not metallic, even her skin, eyes and hair were colored gold, and she was as beautiful as Roselyn, wearing a golden gown and layer after layer of intricate golden jewelry; without introductions Seren knew that this was Heid. Her eyes glared at them with a look not-focused, seeing but blindly, and the radiance of her presence tingled against Seren's skin. Her unpupiled, golden eyes even glowed like Loki's; this woman was Vanir, a real Goddess. As they walked within the range of her vision, the power of her eyes struck Seren like a cold slap on the face. Heid's presence radiated about her like a tangible glow and her eyes blasted like invisible crossbow bolts. Unwillingly they stepped closer.

Heid pushed open her golden door and stepped back as they approached, motioning for them to come in. They entered her room, Silvana and Glororil hovering behind them. Then Seren suddenly froze, staring as her jaw fell; only her first sight of Yggdrasil had ever stunned her more.

Heid's vast chamber was stacked with gold: gold furniture, gold cups, gold crowns, scepters, jewelry, and everything else that Seren could imagine, heaped in piles that would've filled every tavern in Madrone. Never had Seren dreamed that so much gold existed! It lay in huge mounds with only narrow aisles leading back into darkness between precarious cliffs that threatened to collapse upon anyone fool enough to brave them.

Yet ... who wouldn't dare? It was so beautiful, so tempting; what fool could resist? But Heid stood between them and her vast treasure trove, and Seren didn't think that any of them wanted to examine her fantastic hoard bad enough to risk getting close to Heid.

Slowly Heid approached them, her wide, glazed eyes staring, fingers outreached as she advanced. Eloise stepped back, but Heid quickly closed the distance and grabbed at the gold armband that Ruthedhel had given Eloise.

"Mine!" Heid screamed, and she wrenched at the band, hard and again, until Eloise screamed and willingly surrendered the golden trinket to get away from the crazed Vanir. Heid clutched the gold armband protectively against her chest, glared jealously at them, and then swiftly ran back to a gold-inlaid table and, with a sharp glance at them, Heid stashed the treasure in a large box made of the same precious metal.

"Completely insane," the Seer remarked.

"What we do?" Seren asked desperately, not liking the gleam in Heid's eyes.

"This should be easy," the Seer grinned at Eloise. "Mad people are no challenge for sane. Turn around and let me dig some of those trinkets out of your pack; I'll get us out of here."

"What trinkets?" Karl whispered as Eloise pivoted and the Seer dug into her pack.

"I stole some gold from Radsvid's workshop," the Seer whispered. "I thought that we might need it. Wait until she turns her back, and then move."

"Must we kill her?" Roselyn asked.

"No!" the Seer hissed. "The Aesir did that and it started a war! Here she comes; just follow my lead."

"Gold?" Heid's raspy, grating voice creaked. "More gold? What have you? More gold for Heid?"

"Wait there!" the Seer said loudly. "Wait! I'll give you gold, if you wait!"

"Gold!" Heid shrieked, and she ran forward, but the Seer jerked out a few small gold rings and tossed them high, arcing over Heid, flying behind her. Heid screamed and chased the baubles as they bounced with loud 'pings!' among her collection.

"Now!" the Seer whispered, and he ran out the door. The companions followed in a rush and ran past Utgard-Loki and his equally shocked guests.

"Good-bye!" Eloise shouted, and she waved at the slack-jawed giant-king.

The guards at the door moved to intercept them, barring their way with massive halberds.

"Utgard-Loki!" the Seer cried, turning around. "Now is the true test! Upon your honor, you swore to set us free!"

"Say no more!" Utgard-Loki shouted, breaking into a smile. "Let them flee, if they can!"

"What do you ...?" Karl's voice choked as he glanced behind.

Seren looked back to see what had widened Karl's eyes; she screamed in horror. Out of Heid's door poured two dozen large, twisting, slithering snakes. The giants erupted with laughter. The snakes slid over the ancient floor and chased after the companions.

"Run!" the Seer cried, and out of the door he led them, toward the gate under pale twinkling stars. Yet the snakes moved faster than any living thing. Before Seren could react, coils swarmed around her shoes and tumbled her to the ground. Eloise and Rafe fell next, and then the others toppled, becoming even more entangled by the serpents streaming up behind them.

Karl unsheathed his sword as he hit the ground and rolled to strike, but under the starlight he hesitated; his snake had no head. No, it wasn't a snake; it was ...!

"Heid!" the Seer screamed.

"What are they?" Rafe shouted over the screams of the girls.

"Wood!" the Seer shouted. "Living sticks! Enchanted staves of Heid!"

Heid's charging out of Utgard convinced them that the Seer was right. Though they moved and twisted like snakes, their coils had grain where scales should be, and gleamed of shining wood. These were polished branches, no more, brought alive by Heid's magic. But Karl's sword was all that he had. Viciously he sliced and chopped one stave in half, but its severed ends coiled tightly around his blade. Karl tried to shake them off, but as he did, other staves slid up his mail, wrapped around his arms, and tightened until Karl was pinned, locked amid woven wood.

"Gold, bad people!" Heid laughed. "Stay! Stay! Loki wants you. Gives gold to Heid! My gold! Mine!"

"Please!" Eloise cried. "We can give you more gold later if you'll just let us go!"

"No later!" Heid shouted. "Gold now! All gold now!"

"Forget it, Eloise," Rafe said. "She's mad; you'll get no mercy from her."

"We've got to try something!" Roselyn screamed, fighting with a branch tightening around her throat.

"Beware, Heid!" the Seer shouted. "Utgard-Loki will cheat you! He means to take his gold away from you, if you don't let us go!"

"No!" Heid laughed. "Utgard-Loki is my servant! Giants have no gold! All mine!"

"Moonstone!" Seren gasped desperately. "Seer, make Eric seen!"

"What?" the Seer asked, but he reached inside his robe, not waiting for Seren to answer.

"Heid!" Seren cried as the Seer pulled out the moonstone and raised it high. "Ghost steal Heid's gold! Ghost steal gold-room!"

Shimmering under the moonstone, Eric appeared, white and ghostly under the pale stars. Heid screamed and stepped back, shocked by Eric's sudden appearance. Eric looked at Seren, seeming confused.

"Go, Eric!" Seren shouted. "Lead Heid away! Rejoin at Mimir!"

With a wink, Eric turned to the Vanir queen, wailing as he had in Bristlen, and he charged at Heid, waving both his arm and stump. Heid screamed and pointed at Eric, but her power was useless; Heid was Vanir, a Goddess of fertility. Only over the living was her power useful, and Eric passed right through her unscathed, a howling, mournful phantom flying back inside Utgard toward her priceless treasure room.

Heid screamed and chased after Eric, who vanished inside Utgard's massive, guarded doors. But the company wasn't safe yet.

The giant standing guard at the gate folded his huge arms and looked down upon them with open amusement. The snaky branches had stopped moving now, returning to hard, thick wooden branches. Seren strained, but her poor strength was no match for the hardwood staves.

"I can't get out!" Eloise cried over Rafe's grunting struggles.

Roselyn coughed, choking against the coil that had closed upon her throat. Seren twisted hard, but futilely. Glororil and Silvana flew down to help, but their puny strengths did nothing.

"Cursed stick no break!" Seren swore.

"It's no use!" Rafe said. "We're stuck!"

"We can't be!" Karl cried. "Roselyn's being strangled to death!"

"Help ...!" Roselyn choked.

Silvana and Glororil pulled on the branch coiled around her throat, but the power of the fairies wasn't physical strength.

"Roselyn, hang on!" Rafe shouted. "If just one of us can get free ..."

"Roselyn no breathe!" Seren cried. "She no breathe!"

"Roselyn!" Eloise screamed. "Karl, do something!"

"Silvana!" Karl cried. "Moonglow! Now!"

"But ..."

"Now!"

At once the beautiful silver fairie leaped into the air and exploded with a soft, blue-white glow.

"No!" Rafe shouted, too late.

Eloise screamed. The bluish rays burned into her cursed flesh as her transformation began. Long yellow hair sprouted from Eloise's pores and her bones cruelly twisted out of shape, painfully bending to her inhuman form. Agonizing seconds later, Eloise was gone, the Wolfqueen howling in her place. Worriedly Seren noticed how much faster her transformations occurred; if they didn't find a cure for her soon, it might be too late.

The Wolfqueen broke free with ease, rending the thick branches like straws, hurling their splintered fragments into starry night's darkness. Shocked and surprised, the giant-guard jumped back, wielding his deadly axe. The Wolfqueen jumped up and turned, slavering, and looked down with satanic delight upon the helpless companions still pinned in the coils of their staves. A growl escaped the Wolfqueen's lips as Eloise almost smiled. She gathered to pounce and rend their trapped bodies like the monstrous killer that she was. Her red eyes glowed with bloodlust, anticipating her glut of flesh.

"Glororil!" Karl shouted. "Sunburst! Now!"

Glororil's golden brilliance flamed out, banished the twinkling stars and all of night's darkness, and stabbed through the Wolfqueen like a blast of Greek-naphtha. Howling in unimaginable torment, the Wolfqueen staggered, faltered, and failed, blonde hairs singeing from her flesh into flying ash caught on the night's wind under the solar glow. Bones crushed inward and claws lessened to nails. As Glororil dimmed, his fiery sunlight fading to a yellow glow, the Wolfqueen was expelled. Human once more, Eloise collapsed. Prone, Eloise sobbed loudly, but they couldn't let her rest.

"Eloise!" Karl cried. "Roselyn's choking to death! Only you can save her! Eloise!"

Roselyn was gagging, her face totally blue. Blubbering, Eloise crawled toward Roselyn, grabbed one end of the branch choking her, and pulled with a leverage that Roselyn couldn't manage. Slowly the wood bent; Roselyn coughed, gasping clean air, but Eloise lay spent. Her strength gone, Eloise placed her knee beside Roselyn's head and let the branch squeeze against her thigh, leaving Roselyn's neck unbound.

"She did it!" Rafe shouted. "Roselyn's breathing!"

"Eloise, I'm sorry!" Karl pleaded. "I didn't ...!"

"No," Eloise coughed weakly. "You did ... what had to be done. Thank ... you."

"You saved Roselyn, not me," Karl said.

"Eloise all right?" Seren asked. "Change quick, look bad!"

"I ... feel bad," Eloise said, trembling with sobs. "Hurts ... inside, somehow. I seem to be ... changing quicker. Oh, help me! It hurts so bad! I don't want to change anymore!"

"She's changing back and forth too often," Karl said. "Seer, remember what you said would happen eventually? I think we're speeding it up. If we're going to find a cure for her, we've got to do it soon!"

"Sooner!" Seren said. "Glororil bright! Loki see light, come fast. Eloise free all now!"

"We may not live long enough to be freed," Rafe said, ceasing to strain against his bonds. "Listen! I hear wheels; someone's coming!"

"Loki!" Seren gasped.

"I don't hear anything," Karl said.

"Rest your head against the ground!" Rafe said. "Press your ear to the dirt and you'll hear wheels rumble!"

"Eloise, help us!" Karl shouted. "We've got to get ..."

Suddenly the branch-halves enveloping Karl's sword loosened and fell against his hilt with a sudden *'clack!'*. The wooden limbs came to life again and writhed, twisting as they had before. Like snakes, they squirmed and slithered off them. Seren kicked to fling hers off, but the staves were already moving, slithering back into Utgard. In seconds, they were all free.

"What happened?" Karl shouted as he jumped to his feet, and began helping the others up.

"Eric pretend steal gold!" Seren said. "Up! We go now!"

Roselyn, still catching her breath, lay unmoving, despite Karl's attempt to help her up. Eloise, still sick with the pains of her violent transformations, also couldn't rise. The rest of them stood ready to go, but the girls were too weak to move.

"We'll have to carry them," Karl said. "Rafe, take Eloise. Seer, help him. We've got to get off the road!"

Seren helped pull Roselyn to her feet, and then Karl bent and threw her over his shoulder. He strained under the weight; both of them were wearing armor.

Rafe lifted Eloise up with a strained grunt as the Seer helped him, each pulling one arm over his shoulders to help her walk. Between the two men Eloise hung exhaustedly, trying to walk but barely able to stand. The giant-guard watched silently as they limped out of the Gate of Utgard, instantly turned off to one side, and wearily trudged down the outside wall. Glororil and Silvana flew beside them. They passed over a small wooded rise and then threw themselves down to hide behind the hilltop, peering back between some bushes.

Instantly the roar of spinning wagon-wheels grew loud as Loki rolled into view steering a silver-etched chariot drawn by fast-running wolves. Clinging to the chariot beside him was Hel, searching for the companions as furiously as her father. Neither glanced at the hill, both intent only upon the open Gate of Utgard, and as the giant-guard hesitated, Hel and Loki raced forward, and the wolf-chariot thundered inside just before the guard slammed the gate shut. Onward they rode, wolves and chariot, father and daughter, right into the citadel of Utgard; the God and his daughter vanished inside the citadel's great door.

"Come on!" Karl urged. "We won't get a second chance! We've got to get away before they come after us!"

"But Eric inside!" Seren argued.

"We can go back," Glororil offered.

"No, Eric can fend for himself!" Karl shouted. "He can pass right out of the back wall, if he has to, or sink into the floor. If he can't, then there's nothing that we can do for him. Come! Run ... while we can!"

But running was impossible. Roselyn was rubbing her sore throat underneath her gorget, still gasping, and Eloise was almost unconscious. Barely they managed a fast walk, which weakened them with every step. Heading eastward, they plunged into a thick forest and hurried to get out of sight of the towering giant's citadel. Yet how much farther they had to go Seren couldn't guess.

Jay Palmer

Chapter 18

The Well of Mimir

THE SEER

We'll never escape, the Seer realized. Roselyn had almost choked to death and could barely walk. Eloise was unconscious, now hanging over Rafe's shoulder like a limp grain-sack. They were all exhausted; how long had it been since they'd last slept? Days, he suspected, but the Seer had lost all reckoning of time in the eternally-dark tunnels of the Black River. Loki and Hel, in their fast chariot, could catch them easily, and Heid could enchant them and bring them back, if Blathanoir had spoken truly.

They needed something, something big ... or they'd never escape, but what were his meager Druid skills compared to the wisdom of Gods?

As the Seer led their way into immensely tall pines, grave doubts gnawed at him. Mimir was their next stop, if they made it there. Mimir was all-knowing and all-powerful; Mimir would know the Lady's purpose for their errand, if anyone in this strange land did. Her purpose was really all that the Seer could afford to care about. He liked Eric, and would gladly help him enter Valhalla, but if the Lady's true purpose was otherwise, then he'd have to oppose him.

The Lady: She still hadn't reached out to him, not once since he'd passed through the Hidden Portal. Never in his life had he gone so long without sensing Her; even as a youth, before he went to the Magic Isle, he'd always felt Her spirit supporting him. Had She truly abandoned him ... and what would he do if She had?

Eloise's condition concerned him; the Seer had no idea what effects the rapidity of her transformations would have on her body. Were there unknown differences between Silvana's glow and real moonlight? Was Eloise's curse intensifying? Or, were her abrupt transformations tearing her insides apart? Any mistake on his part, action or inaction, could kill her. He'd hoped that they could limit her changes, but the Wolfqueen was their strongest weapon, their only last resort.

The Seer bowed his head; his concern for Eloise had little to do with her curse. He missed their trysts under the canopy before the storm had struck the North Sea. Never before had the Seer been so happy as during those lazy days. The Seer knew that he was a fanatic, a self-driven man, too serious for his own good; Eloise had made him forget all of that.

He still wondered why she'd slept with him; perhaps because Roselyn had. Sometimes Eloise and Roselyn seemed to be sisters, othertimes competitors, but always friends. He'd never known a friendship that deep. He and Hel had understood each other; it had wrenched his heart to betray her, to knowingly crush their tender bond. Yet the Seer had to follow his Lady's will; no other purpose was as great to him as Hers.

Dimly the Seer recalled Eloise's second transformation, their last night in Grusshire, after his failed attempt to restrain her. The fairies had rescued them, which left them in grave danger, so the Seer had used a simple spell and created illusionary dancing lights that distracted the Wolfqueen long enough for them to escape. Could such a trick deceive Loki, Hel, and Heid? It wouldn't last, but anything would help.

"Are we stopping?" Karl asked, almost bumping into the Seer from behind.

"Oh!" the Seer exclaimed. "Sorry; I was thinking of casting a spell, creating an illusion of us going off in another direction, to lead Loki and Hel away."

"Do it!" Karl said, as if it were the only logical choice.

"There are risks," the Seer said. "Hel and Loki may not be fooled by mortal magic. It'd take all of my strength, and then I'd have to rest."

"We're going to get caught anyway," Karl said. "It may be our only chance."

"Very well," the Seer said. "Put the girls down and rest. You may have to carry me when this is over."

The Seer turned back and faced the massive citadel of Utgard. He took a deep breath ... and suddenly yawned. He felt as exhausted as the others, more tired than he could remember. When he got back to England, he'd have to find a rich patron until he was rested enough to earn a living on his own. That might not be easy; most of the royalty had converted to Christianity, but some Saxon households hadn't forgotten the Lady. Memories of Farmer Tiller and his family sprang to mind; with his magics, the Seer could easily make their simple crops grow tall and plentiful.

Argh! His thoughts were drifting; a clear sign that he wasn't concentrating. It wasn't unexpected; back in Madrone, the Seer sometimes rested for days before attempting a difficult spellcasting. He grinned, thinking of how much he'd learned since Garm attacked them outside of Niflhiem. All of the books in his library were nothing compared to what he'd experienced since coming to Yggdrasil. When he got back, he'd have to spend a whole year just writing it down. How delightful it would be to see the expressions on the Druid High Council when he presented ...

The Seer's grin vanished. He was failing, his concentration gone. He was too tired to cast properly, too weak to summon the powers that he needed.

'Back to the basics', the Seer thought, trying not to feel ashamed. It'd been years since he'd required the simple chants. Mostly they were nonsense, incantations with no real power, used to train novitiates with neither talent nor brains. Yet chants were easy to focus on, a tool for concentration, and useful at need. The Seer took a breath and began to mumble one of his favorites, a prayer to the Lady for Her blessing. He recited it under his breath and paused only a second before repeating it.

On his forth recitation, the Seer began to feel the familiar alignment as his thoughts properly channeled. Slowly the subtle sensations stood out as he focused on his chant, dimming out his normal, mundane senses. He let all other sensations fade away and opened his awareness only to the quiet fabric of Nature and Spirit.

The Seer delved deep inside himself. He reached out his fingers, feeling for currents of power like the long roots of a great tree reaching into a magic river; the Seer drank as deeply as he could. The Seer stood in Jotunhiem, the land of giant illusion-masters, and he was trying to cast a deception upon Gods; he had to push himself to his limits.

The Seer's eyes rolled back. He was barely aware of his balance. He had to keep enough hold on reality to cast his spell; falling would break his concentration. He'd often conjectured that the schism between reality and magic was the true power that folded both, that made them one. If he lost his hold entirely, at this depth, he'd drown in madness.

The Seer raised his arms and cast his spell. What they'd see, and how they'd see it, the Seer visualized both in the real world and the magic realm. Details he sought, the sensations that they needed, so real that they wouldn't doubt. The Seer saw himself and the company, on horseback, riding fast into the distance. He saw the backs of their heads ride away. The company rode away: small because of the distance, mail gleaming dimly in the starlight, heads bouncing, helms glinting, flicking brown horsetails trailing behind as they galloped over hills toward the horizon.

His teeth clenched under the strain. The Seer focused, flexed, and bent his will; everyone must feel the same sensations that he did. *He had to see! He had to believe!*

Pain struck the Seer like a searing wave. It blinded him like lightning from a starless sky; he fell into his spellcasting, refusing all else. He struggled to ignore his agony, to focus through it, to follow the steps of mental leaps in their proper order. Energies electrocuted him, flashed through his being in two worlds, and tore him apart. *He was burning with energy!*

Dimly he heard screams, distant and agonized, but hauntingly familiar, as if they were his own voice.

"Seer!" Seren shouted, and she slapped his face.

The heat of her palm on his cheek burned, but the Seer recognized it as her normal body temperature meeting his own. Spellcasting twisted the senses, and they took a while to return to normal. His head was pounding, more than he could ever recall, and he felt deeply drained, worse than he had after his battle with Skaldi.

Had his spell worked? The Seer couldn't tell. It didn't matter; he couldn't do it again. It'd be days before he could spellcast again, before his strength recovered.

Again Seren's palm slapped against his cheek, and the Seer realized that he was sleeping. He coughed and tried to move his arms, but he couldn't. He pried open his eyes; the effort stung, but it was better than lying still while getting slapped.

"He's coming out of it," Rafe's voice thundered all around him.

"Seer!" Seren shouted. "You dead?"

The Seer groaned, secretly wishing that Seren was right: *the dead don't hurt this much.*

"Alive," the Seer whispered, although the effort exhausted him even further.

"Seer, wake up!" Karl shouted in his ear. "You've been out for half an hour, and we can't carry you anymore."

Carry? Half an hour? The Seer turned to Karl only to find that he was standing several paces away, looking back through the trees.

"Loki?" the Seer asked. "Hel?"

"They rode off long ago," Rafe said. "The charged out of Utgard as soon as the gates opened, riding their chariot. We saw them through the branches; they rode off down the road, shouting and pointing at those hills over there."

The Seer relaxed and yawned. *His spell had worked.* It wouldn't last for long, but they were safe for the moment.

"Seer, wake up!" Seren shouted again.

"Athelwynne?" asked Roselyn's voice. "Are you alright?"

"Fine," the Seer breathed. "Just tired. Help me up."

"Eloise?" Roselyn said. "Please wake up. It's time to go."

The Seer looked over as Rafe and Seren helped him to stand; Eloise was lying on the ground, her head in Roselyn's lap. She looked haggard, too pale for one so young. Eloise's mouth was hung open and the Seer noticed her large teeth; her incisors were definitely bigger. Her face looked no longer innocent, but somehow ... feral.

Or were his senses still befuddled? He couldn't tell. He hoped that they were, that Eloise's transformations hadn't yet left a permanent physical mark on her. He'd read something, somewhere ... his brain still hurt ..., that described the stages wherein lycanthropy devoured its victim until only wolf remained.

The Seer stepped forward ... and suddenly his legs buckled beneath him. Rafe caught him before he fell; the Seer felt weak as a newborn, yet they had to keep going; Hel and Loki would soon perceive his deception.

Rafe put a beefy arm around the Seer's waist and helped him walk. Karl lifted up Eloise in his arms, and Seren helped Roselyn to stand. Slowly they limped deeper into the forest.

"Where we go?" Seren asked.

"East," the Seer said, clinging to Rafe to keep from falling. "Utgard-Loki said that there was a path that led to a cliff; we have to descend that cliff."

They struggled along for about a mile, moving slowly, before they found a trail heading east. It cut across their path, straight through the woods, the bright starlight clearly illuminating it. Walking down the path was considerably easier, so they traveled faster.

Dawn gradually lightened the sky, revealing strange damage overhead. Above their path, all of the tree branches were snapped off, even high up; tall giants must've walked this way. The path was just wide enough for gigantic feet, which meant that they could walk in pairs with ease.

The sun rose, peeking above the horizon ahead of them. Their path went on for miles before the woods opened out into wide fields of yellow grass. Massive rotten fence posts ran beside these woods; once this had been a giant's farm, unused for so long that little remained of it. The companions rested again, and Seren passed around their canteen and made sure that everyone drank some of the last of their water.

Mile after mile they walked in the hot sun, until they almost longed for the cool, shaded tunnels of the Norse underworld. The Seer regained some of his strength once his senses returned to normal.

Their trail led straight as an arrow across the vast field. At its far end stood a large, tumbled shack of what must've been a small giant's cabin, but even from this distance, the ruin of its crumbling walls and half-fallen roof were clearly visible. Their trail led right past it, but beyond it was nothing but distant hills.

"That's must be the cliff," the Seer said. "Just as Utgard-Loki described it: the Great Drop."

"We'll check it out," Silvana said, and she flew on ahead. Glororil glanced back at them, frowned, and then dashed after her. Soon they both returned.

"It's not a bad cliff, not straight down," Silvana said.

"It won't be easy," Glororil said. "It's all loose dirt. You'll slide down it more than climb."

"Uh, oh," Roselyn gasped, suddenly looking back. "Do you hear something?"

"Sounds like Loki's chariot!" Rafe said.

"Run!" Karl cried, and he virtually leapt forward, taking the lead, Eloise tight in his arms. Eloise clung tightly, awake, but still too weak to walk.

"*No!*" the Seer cried, stumbling after. "We've come so far! We can't lose now!"

"We can, if you wait to talk about it!" Rafe shouted, and he grabbed Seren by the arm to help her balance. "*Run!*"

They ran, crossing the field as fast as their legs could push them, but just when it looked like they'd make it, a fierce cry rose behind them and the distant tingle of Loki's eyes stabbed at their backs. The Seer risked a quick glance back: emerging from the woods, bouncing over their trail, Loki's wicked smile gleamed as he urged his huge wolves faster, Hel clutching the rim of his shaking chariot. The companions would reach the cliff before them, the Seer gauged, but no further.

Loki's gaze burned like hot coals before they reached the Great Drop and looked down the steep, dangerous slope to the forest below. Falling down that cliff would kill them, but there was nowhere else to go. A tiny, crumbled path, little more than a narrow ledge, led downward at a sharp angle, but they'd never make it; Loki and Hel were closing fast.

"Make it stop!" Eloise cried. "It hurts so bad!"

"Hurry!" Seren cried. "In house!"

"Why?" Karl asked.

"Only place!" Seren shouted, and for no other reason they followed her inside. There the pain of

Loki's stare was cut off, but the ruined house offered no escape or defense.

"We're trapped!" Roselyn said.

"I'm sorry," the Seer said. "I hoped that my spell would last longer ..."

"Shut up!" Karl shouted. "I'm trying to think of a way out of here."

"Brother, there is none," Rafe said sadly. "Karl, my friend, this is the end."

"Fly!" Seren shouted at Glororil and Silvana, who circled above them. "Go now, be safe!"

"We can't leave without you!" Silvana shouted, flying between the few remaining rafters. "Titania made us promise!"

"Flee!" the Seer shouted. "Your powers can't stop Loki! Go now, while you can!"

"Stay behind me, my love," Rafe said to Seren, touching her cheek. "No matter what happens, I never stopped loving you."

"That's it!" Karl cried, looking at the crumbling back wall. "Roselyn, give me your sword!"

"Why?" Roselyn asked, but Karl snatched the strong, sharp elvin-sword from her scabbard and ran to the back wall.

"They're here!" Eloise shouted, looking out between the cracked walls. "Loki's slowing his chariot just outside!"

Karl hacked at the wall and chopped through its rotten boards, cutting out a huge square.

"What're you doing?" Roselyn shouted. "Karl, Loki's here!"

"Loki's getting off!" Eloise shouted. "He's helping Hel down!"

Karl swung as never before, frantically chopping. Splinters and wood-chips rained upon him, but he ignored them all, madly attacking the ancient wall. The whole crumbling shelter began to shake, threatening to cave in.

"Rafe, help me!" Karl shouted, throwing the sword down and using his fists on the severed boards, breaking the last fragments. Rafe joined him, although the Seer had no idea why. The huge section of wall collapsed, falling outwards, and crashed to the ground just on the edge of Great Drop.

"They're coming to the door!" Eloise cried. "They're coming in!"

"Get on!" Karl cried, and he grabbed Seren and the Seer and threw them onto the flat section of wall. "Eloise, get over here! Roselyn, hurry! Rafe, grab the edge! Eloise, hurry! Trust me: my brother and I used to do this on snow!"

Roselyn snatched up her precious elvin-sword and jumped onto the wooden square beside the Seer and Seren. Eloise, not a second behind, ran across the room and jumped through the square hole as Karl bent down and grabbed the edge, and Rafe followed his example.

"Lift and push!" Karl shouted.

Grunting, straining against all of the weight of the companions and their armor combined, Rafe and Karl lifted. At that instant, Loki's burning gaze hammered upon the Seer's face. Rafe screamed, but pushed hard. The square section of wall tilted up, toppling the seated companions, and the men stepped out of the shack, pushing with all their might. But the pain overwhelmed; Rafe and Karl fell, and the wooden square of wall dropped back to the ground, exposing all of them to the wrath of the angry God and his daughter.

Suddenly Glororil flew from the rafters down to the corner-post. Glororil slammed against it and hugged its wooden frame tightly. But the golden fairie screamed, caught in the straight burning intensity of Hel's vengeful stare.

Abruptly Glororil exploded with all of the bursting power of the raging sun. Light blasted out of the dark corner in waves of expanding brilliance. The rotting beam cracked, giving way under the crumbling strain. The house began to tilt, trembled with its sudden failure, and rained a pelting hail of dirt and splinters. The rest of the roof collapsed and crashed down on the God and his daughter as two tiny, winged figures darted out through newly-opened holes.

The force of the evil eyes failed.

"Again, Karl!" Rafe shouted, and they lifted, desperation giving way to enormous strength. The others screamed as the square section of wall tilted. Karl and Rafe pushed harder, edging them over the steep cliff. At the last moment, Karl jumped on, grabbed Rafe, and drug him onto the square as it began to slide, scraping down the steep hillside.

The crumbling house fell to ruinous timbers as the remaining walls toppled. Hel and Loki screamed, wood burying them as it fell, but Loki was a God, ancient and powerful, steeped in evil magic. Suddenly the house exploded into dust, blown into nothingness by the fury of an enraged God.

But the companions were too busy to care. Their homemade sled careened wildly down the rough slope, totally out of control, showering them with dirt and rocks. The cliff fell almost straight down, sloping just enough to keep them from flying off, not enough to slow them down. A sharp bump smacked hard beneath them and boards cracked loudly, splintering, but it was too late. They flew down, leapt over gullies, and crashed into rocks in showers of dirt and wood-chunks, their only salvation tearing apart beneath them.

The Seer doubted the wisdom of Karl's brainstorm as he realized that he was screaming, that they were all screaming, scared to death and coming closer. Rocks and grasses tore free as sharp stones dug chunks out of their careening lifeboat. The patchy forest before them grew bigger and clearer as they jarred and bounced downward. Every second brought them closer, but tore the wall beneath them apart.

Suddenly they struck an outcropping boulder and their wooden land-raft shattered and broke into splinters and flying boards. The Seer tumbled onward, rolled head over heels alongside the others, and crashed down the hill.

At the bottom of the cliff, the Seer ungently, painfully slid to a stop over a patch of rocky sand, and then he splashed into a filthy puddle. Dimly the notion came to him that he was alive, and slowly he stretched his limbs, bending every joint to make sure that he wasn't broken. He was scratched and bruised, bleeding all over, his clothes in tatters.

Seren screamed and clutched her shoulder, and Eloise sobbed as blood streamed from her knee. The Seer tried to stand, but only fell, splashing into a shallow pool as Roselyn unsteadily pushed up in the middle of the dirty water. Rafe lay unmoving on the hillside, just shy of the water, face-down, his legs buried by a small avalanche of dirt still trickling down the hill.

An angry cry screeched behind them; looking up, the Seer saw Hel and Loki fuming at the top of the tall cliff, staring down at them.

"We've got to go!" Karl shouted. "Now!"

"We can't!" the Seer shouted. "Karl, look at us! Eloise's losing blood, and Seren's shoulder may be broken. Rafe may be dead ...!"

"How far is Mimir?" Karl shouted.

"Just over there!" the Seer shouted back, pointing at the nearby trees.

"Let's go!" Karl shouted urgently.

"We can't!" the Seer shouted. "Eloi ..."

"I don't give a damn about Eloise!" Karl shouted loudly in his face. "Pick her up! Carry her, or leave her behind! Hel and Loki won't wait up there long! We've got to get to that spring of yours and get some weapon that can save us, or we die! Move! Roselyn, help Seren. I'll get Rafe. *Now!"*

Karl was right. The Seer hesitated, not sure if their terrible ride or Karl being right stunned him the most. Quickly he shook himself and started helping the others up. This was his last chance to accomplish his quest for the Lady. Amazingly, if he did succeed, he might have Karl to thank for it.

The Seer carefully lifted Seren, who was covered with mud, trying not to move her sore arm. He wanted to inspect her injury, but they had no time. The burn of Hel and Loki's stares were distant but painful. After helping Seren up, the Seer pulled Roselyn to her feet, and then lifted Eloise in his arms. All of the ground before them was muddy, boggy, but he pushed across it.

Karl kicked the dirty water and splashed a filthy wave onto Rafe's head, making him cough and sputter.

"Sir Rafe!" Karl shouted, and he grabbed his arm ungently. "Up! Get up! Now, while you can!"

Karl pulled Rafe to his feet and drug him into and across the squishing muck.

Eloise in his arms, the Seer headed straight for the nearby woods, with Roselyn helping Seren right behind him; Seren was crying loudly.

"Seren!" Rafe shouted, and he pushed Karl aside, running to assist his love.

"Hurry!" the Seer shouted. "Loki's coming!"

Ahead of them all ran Karl. He pushed into the thin woods, the Seer and Eloise right behind him. Their feet splashed mud as they ran, yet they pressed on. Hanging branches blinded them and low bushes tangled their footing, but Karl pushed through and squeezed out into an open area.

Before them appeared a wide, gently bubbling pool surrounded by massive boulders in the shade of towering trees. Atop the foremost stone pinnacle sat a bodiless, decapitated head, tanned and healthy as if alive; it smiled down upon them.

"Greetings!" it laughed, its voice loud, as clear and musical as Silvana's, though deep and resonating. "I am Mimir. Welcome to my well. Sit! Relax! Tell me what brings you here and I'll aid you!"

"We're dearly pressed, great Mimir," the Seer said, pushing through the branches. "Forgive our sudden intrusion, but ..."

"Get on with it!" Karl shouted. "Loki will be here any second!"

"Shut up!" the Seer screamed. "This has to be done just so! Or do you know more about this than I?"

Glororil and Silvana slipped through the branches, gasped at the sight of Mimir, and slowly settled to stand weightlessly upon Karl's shoulders. Rafe and the others pushed through closely behind them.

The Seer handed Eloise to Karl before turning back to the living head overlooking the well.

"Hail, Mimir!" the Seer shouted. "We're pressed for time, so forgive me if I fail in the pleasantries and customs. We come in great need all the way from Midgard to beg a boon of you. Help us, if you will, Great Mimir, and all of our blessings will be yours!"

"Gladly!" Mimir smiled evilly. "For the customary price, I'll be delighted to help each and every one of you."

"Your price," the Seer grimaced, and he pulled out a small knife. "Yes, I know: an ounce of flesh. One finger will serve well, will it not?"

"One finger?" Mimir laughed. "An ounce of flesh? Fool mortal! That demand I made of Odin the Terrible-One, for it was all that I dared! Odin is Aesir, his flesh divine! You are only human! To earn a favor of Mimir, you must cast yourself into my hungry pool! That is the cost of Mimir's wisdom to mortals: your life!"

"No ...," the Seer whispered, realizing the fullness of his folly. He turned, gaping, toward his companions, then back to Mimir, stunned speechless.

"Seer, you idiot!" Rafe shouted. "I'll kill you!"

"No!" Roselyn screamed, but Rafe pushed forward.

Karl stepped in Rafe's path and stopped him, struggling not to drop Eloise.

"At ease, Sir Rafe," Karl said. "You don't have to kill the Seer. He's going to die all by himself. There's no other way out. If one of us doesn't die here, then

Loki'll kill us all. The Seer promised that he'd pay us for coming here, and now it's time to collect."

"No!" Roselyn screamed. "Athelwynne, you can't!"

"Karl, I can't be bothered with Loki!" the Seer shouted. "The Lady sent me here! I must know why!"

"Damn the Lady!" Rafe shouted. "You've got to help us! Don't try to fight Loki! Send us back to Earth!"

"No!" Glororil warned. "Loki can travel to Midgard! Send us to Alfhiem; we'll all be safe there!"

"What about me?" Eloise cried. "You said that you'd cure me! You promised!"

"Loki's coming!" Silvana shrilly screamed.

"Hold it!" Karl cried. "Everyone shut up! Seer, whatever you're going to do, do it, or step aside! One of us must die for the sake of the rest!"

"Do you want to?" the Seer seethed.

"No," Karl said, "but I will, if need be! The girls must be saved!"

"No!" Eloise cried. "I forbid you both!"

"Silence!" the Seer commanded. "I must think! The Lady sent me here: *why?"*

"Loki say he send," Seren interjected.

"Loki lies, as always," the Seer said, and he turned his back on them. "All right, Mimir, I'm game: my life for one boon of your magic wisdom, if you can do as I ask."

"With the right magic words, there's nothing that I can't do," Mimir smiled, his eyes ablaze with evil delight. "Fortunately, I know all of the words! I accept!"

"With one condition!" the Seer shouted. "You must prove your part of the bargain first, and then take my life afterwards!"

"Agreed!" Mimir said. "But don't think that you can escape me! No one escapes a bargain with Mimir!"

"So I expected," the Seer said. "Here's my challenge ..."

Suddenly a pillar of green fire erupted behind them, just outside of the ring of trees. Leaves crashed and branches cracked as Loki pushed through the trees, coming towards them.

"Loki!" Silvana screamed.

"Use your magic now!" the Seer shouted to Mimir. "Speak your words! I'm a Druid! I worship a Goddess called The Lady! Find her, in whatever world or universe she dwells in, and ..."

"Freeze, mortals!" Loki shouted. "You're mine, and I'll chase you no farther! Tell me the secret way to Midgard, now, or die!"

".. AND BRING THE LADY HERE TO ME NOW!"

"As you wish!" Mimir smiled as Loki focused his blazing eyes upon them.

Suddenly the gentle pool splashed upwards, and leaves and twigs fell from shaking branches as the ground trembled with a thunderous rumble. An earthquake erupted and cast everything about the grotto like twigs, shook the tall trees and massive boulders, and tossed the companions down to helplessly bounce upon the shuddering ground. Even Loki lost his footing and fell, shocked and frightened, as the world trembled beneath them. All Yggdrasil quaked as if their universe were tearing itself apart. Only Mimir remained calm, unmoved, laughing at them for the puny fools that they were.

"What have you done?" Roselyn screamed.

Suddenly Yggdrasil calmed; the rocking stopped, and they all looked up.

Above the Well of Mimir hovered a tall, magnificent woman in a gown of softest blue, glowing of golden radiance, not of color like Heid, nor of light like Glororil, but like the glow of the real sun, shining of purest warmth and kindness, the very essence of life.

"Peace," She smiled, looking down at them, and the power of Her presence, emanating from Her eyes, didn't blast them. Instead, it healed all of their hurts and worries. Pain vanished before the Lady and suffering didn't exist. Even the branches beside them sprouted new buds before Her, flowers blossomed, and new grasses grew. The Lady of the Druids had come to Yggdrasil, and life came with Her.

"My Lady!" the Seer cried, and he scrambled to his knees. Then another light shined upon them, only slightly less bright but definitely more fell. Loki choked and dove back into the muddy bushes, crawling away like an odious snake in the grass.

"Behold!" Mimir laughed. "The sight of Odin spies upon us. The Master of Battles comes!"

But the Lady ignored the raving head and bent slightly to smile down at the Seer, groveling at Her feet.

"Rise, my child," the Lady sweetly spoke.

Slowly the Seer lifted his head, smiling with awe upon the face of his Goddess.

"My Lady!" the Seer whispered.

"I am She," the Lady smiled. "You've done well, my son, as I wished."

"But the quest ...!" the Seer pleaded.

"You have achieved my will," the Lady smiled. "I knew, when you reached here, that you'd call upon me. That was your true task, which I appointed for you long ago."

The Seer sat stunned, listening to her words, but doubting his very ears. *Had he truly done Her will?*

"Then ... I served you well?" the Seer asked.

"None has ever done me greater service," the Lady smiled, and the Seer virtually glowed.

"That's all I ask for!" the Seer smiled, and tears leaked from his eyes.

"Well, I could ask for more!" Karl spoke up, interrupting the silence. "Forgive me, Great Lady, but we've journeyed far and suffered much! Why? Why would you want anyone to bring you here?"

"This isn't my realm," the Lady explained, gazing full upon Karl. "I couldn't just appear here, for there are amenities to consider with the Gods of this world. Yet I wished to speak with them, for they face the same danger as I and my Lord. So I sent you.

"I come seeking survival, possibly salvation for all my people, the whole Druid race. As was foretold long ago, after many centuries, the son of the Christian God was born and a new spring began for His people. Somehow the Christian God had survived His winter and found himself remembered, though His people were enslaved and cursed by many. But that was long ago by mortal reckoning, almost a thousand years. Yet a new, second spring arose for the Christian God, and His followers became strong and many. Now the spring of the Christian God is passing, and soon His summer shall come. Then we older Gods must fade, as others did before us, the old giving way to the new. Yet someday, in the far distant future, a thousand years from now, His summer will end, and fall shall return to His people, as it has now come to Mine, to the Druids, and to the worshippers of the Gods of Yggdrasil. I must not fade in My winter and let My people die. I must live through the long, cold loneliness and return in another spring. The Gods of Asgard face the same doom as My Lord and I. Alone, I know not how We will survive, but together? Who knows what powers We may mingle, divinities of different worlds? That is what I've come to discuss with the Gods and Goddesses of this world. That is why I led you to my faithful servant Athelwynne, to help him bring Me here. All the thanks and blessings that I have I bestow upon you, My children. You've all done well. Blessed be, My sons and daughters."

"Blessed be, Great Mother," the Seer smiled. "Now I can die happily, having lived to gaze upon you."

"Yes, so you must, to be loyal to your word," the Lady said to the Seer. "Yet fear not death, for I'm with you, and I still need your loyalty. So well have you served Me that I can't let you die unrewarded. Honor your promise, and trust to Me, and you'll never know darkness again."

"Beside you I could never fear," the Seer smiled.

Slowly the Seer stood, and then he reached up and took off the long black case holding Eric's arm. Smiling, he slipped the black case over Eloise's head. Although healed by the power of the Lady, Eloise shuddered, hating the morbid case, but she didn't refuse. Then the Seer untied his pouch containing his blessed moonstone and gave that to her. Eloise accepted it far more eagerly, and the Seer bent and kissed her softly; *his last kiss.*

"Please take care of my friends," the Seer said to the Lady, smiling at all of them. "Beside your service, they're all that I truly love."

"We will," the Lady smiled.

The Seer steeled himself. He, too, had been healed by the Lady's presence, yet his task was greater than ever. No magic was required, but nothing in his training had ever prepared him for this: his first human sacrifice. The Seer looked at the deep pool in the center of the boulders beneath the severed head of Mimir: *this would take all of his strength.*

337

"Mimir, I'm ready," the Seer said gravely.

"No!" Eloise screamed, but Karl grabbed and held her back. No one wanted to see the Seer sacrificed, but these matters were greater than they should interfere in.

Wet, huge tears streaked down the Seer's cheeks; he wasn't alone. All of the companions, even Karl and Rafe, stood crying, frozen, sharing the knowledge that before the Lady of the Druids, their wills meant nothing. The Seer inhaled deeply and tried to appear content.

"Good-bye, my loving friends," the Seer said to them. "Forget me not, and may blessings shower upon you!"

"Seer!" Eloise screamed, but he took a wide step back, and then looked into the deep water. It looked cold, and the Seer felt mildly amused, as if chill water were all that he had to fear. His loneliness, his isolation, his endless training and fasting, practicing and studying: all was about to end. Yet he'd done everything for his Lady, and She'd promised to care for him. He could feel Her again, not only before him but inside of him where She'd always been, and he felt Her now in every fiber of his being. She flamed inside his soul.

The Seer raised up both his hands and reached out to Her.

"Blessed be the Lady, may She live and rule forever!" the Seer shouted.

With one leap, he splashed deep into the still pool of Mimir. The water was icy; it drenched him instantly with freezing cold. He tried to relax, to trust the

Lady, but the hungry power of Mimir greedily seized and pulled him down. The Seer panicked, opened his eyes, and looked up at the streaming circle of wavering light far above him, rapidly diminishing as Mimir's undertow dragged him deeper.

'*Help them*', the Seer prayed to the Lady.

The frigid waters stabbed and numbed his limbs. The pressure in his chest built up and finally burst the air from his lungs. The Seer choked and convulsed, thrashing helplessly until his sight grew dim and darkness closed in.

Jay Palmer

Chapter 19

The Gathering of the Gods and Hel's Chase

RAFE

Rings danced upon the frothing water, but nothing else. Rafe held his breath and silently counted the endless seconds until too many had passed. Roselyn and Eloise burst out weeping and Karl scraped away tears with his bare, muddy hands. Rafe waited in silence, just staring, unwilling to accept; *it was a game, a trick to cheat Mimir.* The Seer had magic, could do almost anything, and he had saved them so many times that the Seer must have some secret, some trick, some plan to escape. But as the long, still moments passed, slowly reality forced its way through Rafe's skull. The waters stilled, calm and unmoving, and the tiny bubbles returned as if it'd never been disturbed. The Seer didn't emerge *... and never would.*

The Seer was dead.

Rafe's breath choked and tears wet his eyes, yet he remained rigid. The Seer had sacrificed himself for his Lady, not for them, but the result had been the same. Rafe had never really liked the Seer, the pagan mystic with his snotty, small-guy grudge against the world, but he'd proven himself in the end. Rafe felt humbled; Rafe was a good Christian, but he didn't know if he could martyr himself. He hoped that he would, but one never knew such things until one was put to the test. If it ever came to that, Rafe hoped that he would show the courage of the Seer.

Seren buried her head against Rafe's mailed chest and sobbed. Rafe held her tightly, but he resisted crying, allowing no sign of weakness. The Seer had proven his strength, and the hysterical blubberings of an old horse-trainer would only dishonor him.

The Lady of the Druids watched as the waters splashed, rippled, and finally stilled, only tiny bubbles disturbing its surface. Sobbing, Eloise collapsed upon the grass and Roselyn fainted. Karl caught Roselyn before she hit the ground, and then he lowered her gently. Karl tenderly patted Roselyn's cheek, forcing her eyes open, but he kept his gaze upon the pool. Karl looked shocked, as if he expected the Seer to surface at any second, but it was too late.

"Lady, help him!" Karl shouted suddenly, breaking the silence. *"He's your man!"*

"Athelwynne needs no help of Mine," the Lady smiled. "He served Me faithfully, honoring all the vows of his youth. Now he's honored his vow to Mimir, as he knew he must, for no trickery could I use to cheat the one whose wisdom brought Me here; things have gone too far for Me to risk fading back. Though I can't stay long, I must be here when the Gods arrive."

"The Gods?" Rafe asked. "Here?"

"They approach even now, and when they're gathered, you must all be ready to leave," the Lady smiled. "They come to see me, and our dealings must be uninterrupted. But I bless each of you, and with those blessings you may journey in peace. You've each shown great skill and courage, and if you aren't slow, perhaps you may yet achieve your goal. Hurry now and prepare; you still have far to go."

"We'll never make it," Rafe said sadly. "Loki will hunt us down and kill us; he seeks the secret route back to Earth."

"Loki shall be required here," the Lady smiled. "He's one of the Twelve and must be present during our council. But as I can't stay long, let me give you this gift to speed you on your journey."

The Lady waved her hand and five flowers upon the ground beside them burst upward, growing and brightening until they were flowers no more, but stable horseflesh. Five large white horses the flowers grew into, tall and strong beside them. Rafe whistled, amazed, for never had he seen such magnificent stallions.

The Lady waved her hand again, and from the trees fell ten green leaves, gently floating down to the ground. There they transformed to polished bridles and saddles, each inlaid with silver in the forms of leafy vines.

"These are that which you are accustomed to needing," the Lady smiled. "Take and use them well. These horses are strong and never tire; they will carry you to Valhalla swiftly."

"Thank you," Rafe said sadly, "but I don't think that they're needed. Our friend Eric parted from us in Utgard and we haven't seen him since. Without Eric, we've no reason to seek Valhalla."

"Mortal eyes see only the living," the Lady smiled. "Your lost friend stands beside you, as he has since Loki departed. Speak, Eric Bjornson; I give you voice."

"At your service, Great Lady," Eric's voice rumbled, coming from near Rafe's left shoulder, "but if I may be so bold, before I seek immortal Valhalla, there is one other boon that I would ask of you. Our darling Eloise, whom I love above all women, is cursed by the wolf-moon, and I beg your mercy upon her."

"I wouldn't consider her gift a curse, so many times it has saved you," the Lady smiled, "yet I do understand how a young girl may find it unpleasant in her life, and so I'll take this gift away. It shant be destroyed, for it holds a fraction of the strength of My Lord, the Horned Hunter. Her curse shall be placed into the hands of My most-trusted servant, to give and take as he pleases. Arise, Eloise Elizabeth du Harmonn, Baroness still, but Wolfqueen no longer."

"Oh!" Eloise gasped, her eyes wide and bright as never before. *"Thank you! Thank you, my Lady!"*

"You've earned it, My daughter," the Lady smiled. "You all have. But now you must go. Upon the winds I hear the thunder of Sleipnir's hooves, and his master rides him as never before. Good-bye, and blessed be!"

"No!" Roselyn shouted, stirring as Karl tended her, fighting to sit up. "We can't leave without Athelwynne!"

"You must," the Lady smiled. "Athelwynne served Me all that he could in life, and now he shall be with Me forever. I shall protect and treasure him always, and We shall never forget you. Now go, and don't tarry, lest more of your company fall."

"Come, Roselyn," Rafe said sadly. "We've been saved and blessed. Let's ask for no more."

"But Athel ...," Roselyn sobbed, bowing her head and wringing tears from her eyes.

Eloise cried, too. They all did, except Rafe. Rafe held his pain tightly inside; it'd be undignified to break down before the others.

The white horses, as if by unspoken command, walked toward the trees, pushing their way out of the grotto exactly where the companions had come through. Sniffing back his tears, Rafe eased Seren off of him and picked up one of the beautiful leather saddles in each hand. Karl did the same. Eloise respectfully adjusted the

Seer's black leather case across her back and tied the pouch holding the moonstone to her belt, and then picked up the last saddle. Her wounded knee was smooth and unscarred, and even the lost blood was gone from her clean, pale leg. Her shoulder completely healed, Seren stepped forward and gathered up all of the inlaid bridles.

"Blessed be, Great Mother," Seren said, looking up at the Lady.

"Blessed be," She smiled.

Seren bent in reverence, half-bowing, half-curtsying, and then gently took Roselyn's hand and led her away. Beside her, Roselyn stumbled blindly, following as they pushed into the trees.

"Behold!" said Eric's voice beside them. "Odin rides the sky!"

Amid their grief, they all turned to look. Among the stars twinkling against the black sky of night flew a golden sun shining brighter than Glororil had ever dreamed. The magnificent, vibrant glow of Odin preceded his passage, and such was his godly presence that all who saw him knew him. Odin was tall and strong, solidly built, encased in gleaming golden armor, wielding his mighty spear Gungnir in one hand and gripping Sleipnir's reins with the other. On each of his shoulders sat a flapping raven, talons dug deep into Odin's heavily-mailed shoulders, and a leather eye-patch hung strapped across his rugged face. His reins wrapped around the tossing muzzle of a huge, powerful horse, black as jet and running swiftly over empty sky. Sleipnir it was, the greatest of horses. Eight legs galloped beneath him and no winged bird could match his speed. As a meteor, Sleipnir fell shrieking from the sky, and Odin cried out glad greetings in a thunderous voice as he rode to land not ten yards from them. Rafe grabbed a thin tree trunk, bracing for the impact, but none came. Sleipnir slammed to the ground with graceful leisure, eight hooves landing gently with practiced ease.

Odin was huge, but he dismounted in a sudden but sure leap from Sleipnir, who whinnied and stamped, eager to ride again. Odin brandished Gungnir, wielded it high in his right hand, and shook it with a violent war-cry. Then Odin tossed Gungnir to his left hand, crossed his right fist over his chest, and bowed to the Lady, almost a smile breaking between his great bushy mustache and thick beard.

"Welcome to Yggdrasil!" Odin shouted. "Welcome and well met!"

Gracefully the Lady smiled and lightly bowed in return.

"Greetings to Odin, All-father and King of the Aesir, mightiest in battle, wisest in lore," the Lady said sweetly. "Forgive My sudden intrusion! I was brought here by a lost servant, but let us not waste this strange chance! News I bring, as affects both Our worlds, and well it would be that We should share this wisdom. Pray gather thy council, for My tale must not be secret."

"Not all of the giants could stay them now," Odin grinned, staring at the great Lady in blue. "Behold! Forth come the Aesir!"

"Baulder the White!" gasped Eric's voice as another rider burst into the clearing. The brightness of his splendor shone throughout the nine worlds, emanating from within; a crystal glow that radiated wisdom, honor, and gentleness beyond the conception of man. Fairest he was, riding a white stallion with a mane of brightest gold. From his horse he leapt, more graceful than any winged fairie, and Baulder knelt in reverence before the Lady, greeting her with words glorious and proud.

"Look!" Seren cried. "Another Lady!"

"Nay!" Eric shouted. "Behold Freyja, Pearl of Asgard!"

Indeed, no other could she be, but as Freyja came at them across the sky, riding a chariot drawn by white-winged swans, Rafe had to cover his eyes. The golden glow around her dress of deepest blue dazzled, not of brightness but of purest warmth and kindness, the very essence of life. As Freyja landed in the clearing before them, flowers came alive anew, bursting with colors and fragrances that no Earth-born buds could match. Sweetly Freyja bowed to the Lady, and the Lady bowed back, and Rafe looked from one to the other as if twin suns had descended from the sky to grace each with the other's presence. Rafe wiped his eyes as tears streaked down his cheeks, his sad mourning interrupted with the joyous sight that only twin beauties, the greatest Goddesses of two universes, could inspire.

A thunderous bolt of lightning shattered the serenity. Thor, the Son of Earth, the Thunderer, clattered into the already crowded clearing. His war-chariot was gleaming gold and drawn by two burly mountain goats. Thor looked quite different from the others; his aura was electric, almost tangible, but his eyes were clear and bright. Thor's red beard was thick but trimmed, and he wore a crested Viking cap. Mail was his garb, shining rings of etched steel, each forged and welded without rivet or split, all gathered with a belt of the tendons of frost giants. Upon his hands rested gauntlets of iron more threatening than any gaze of Loki, yet less than one thing. In one hand, Thor carried Mjollnir, the fabled dwarven hammer of Asgard. The dread of that weapon no words could encompass.

Suddenly a squeezing grip seized Rafe by the back of his neck and snatched him off of the ground.

"Loki!" Eloise screamed.

Helplessly Rafe was lifted and turned to face Loki's evil eyes, mercilessly blasting him, though not painfully. Under the force of Loki's stare, Rafe could barely see Karl trapped in Loki's other hand.

"Run while you can!" Loki whispered. "Soon you'll all die horribly, I swear! You'll regret refusing me for some fairy bitch!"

Loki roughly tossed them onto the water-soaked ground, and then stepped past them, out into the clearing. Rafe's neck felt like it'd been twisted off and Karl complained no less.

"We'd best get out of here!" Eric whispered.

"One minute!" Karl groaned as he slowly twisted and rubbed his neck.

As they waited, more Aesir and Vanir arrived. Heimdall entered, his sleepless, watchful eyes red and weary. Njord, the Vanir who ruled the sea, marched in behind him. Frigg, Odin's wife, entered next, with brave Tyr the One-handed, poetic Bragi, and Idun, carrying her large basket of life-giving golden apples.

Then Vidar came. A hush fell momentarily upon all gathered; Vidar's helm and armor were darkest black and a somber gloom hung over him as he bowed slightly before the Lady. Freyja introduced him, and Rafe could tell from his emanating power that Vidar spoke only with deeds. Rafe didn't need to guess how he knew such things; the presence of the Norse Gods was unlike the feelings of peace and serenity which flowed from the Lady of the Druids. The Norse Gods seemed darker, more fell, their essence too strong to be contained in physical bodies. To look at a Norse God was to know them.

Wise Foresti came next, then laughing Saga, who drank with Odin, and Eir, who was the greatest healer in all the nine worlds, and the virgin Gefjon, and Fulla, her long beautiful hair streaming out from beneath her golden circlet. Vali and Ull walked in, each sporting bows as was their want, for never could they decide between them who was the better shot.

Others came, Aesir and Vanir alike, Gods and Goddess, until Rafe and the others were forced to back up farther into the trees. The last God that they saw enter was Hod, the blind-god, whose trusty horse led him to the Lady. Hod bowed deeply and spoke long to her, but his words were lost in the clamor of the crowd.

Rafe turned away at last, his red eyes stinging, and pushed through the mud, between the thin bushes, and out of the clearing. The others followed, still crying for their lost companion. The gathering of immortals was fascinating, but they could bear no more. The Seer was gone, and with him went all of their magic and all of their hope.

The Lady's five white horses stood waiting outside the clearing. Rafe had no saddle blankets but he suspected that none were needed; the gifts of the Lady were surely as strong as they required. He slapped the saddles upon their bare backs with experienced ease and buckled their straps.

"Go on without me," Eric's voice whispered from the trees. "I'll catch up when I can. Ride for Valhalla; I'll meet you at its gates."

"Eric?" Karl asked, but no answer followed.

"Hel!" Seren warned, and they all looked up.

In the distance, on the top of the cliff, was Hel, rapidly driving Loki's chariot south across the ridge.

Rafe frowned. Eric couldn't come within sight of Hel; being dead, he belonged to her, and if she ordered him to return to Niflhiem, then he'd have to obey. Rafe had hoped that Hel would be required for the council with the Lady, but he recalled that she was only Loki's bastard daughter, not a full goddess.

"We'd best go," Rafe said. "If Hel catches us, it'll be little worse than if Loki does."

"She must be riding around to another trail," Karl said. "The cliff's too steep for that chariot."

"Let her go," Rafe said. "She's almost out of view. Then we can ride out without her witnessing our route."

"Lady say meeting no last long," Seren warned.

The white horses of the Lady were the most muscular stallions that Rafe had ever seen; he doubted if even the twin wolves pulling Loki's chariot could match their speed. Quickly he saddled them while Hel drove away, but Rafe wasn't worried about Hel anymore. The only thing that Rafe really cared about was Seren, that they were together again. She met his eyes and a wide, troubled grin spread across her face; they'd just lost the Seer: *now wasn't the time for unbridled joy.*

Hel slowly disappeared over the crest of the hill.

"Let's go," Rafe said. "Lean forward in your saddle, your face into their manes."

Leading the way, Rafe steered his horse straight at the cliff. The horse didn't balk at all, just headed straight up the steep, crumbling cliff. Their hard, wide hooves were better suited to this terrain than boots, but Rafe suspected that terrain was irrelevant. Having seen the Lady, and felt her presence, Rafe never doubted that her horses could take them wherever they had to go.

The powerful stallions drove up the steep hillside, stomped and kicked the loose dirt, and never once faltered. Leaned forward, Rafe twisted to look back, to make sure that the others were following his instructions. Eloise and Seren weren't even holding their reins, their arms clamped tightly about their horse's necks, their faces buried in mane. Roselyn and Karl, both armored, were almost standing in their stirrups to keep from sliding off, leaning hard with their faces between their horse's white ears. The fairies flew far above them in circles, sparks glittering.

The white stallions topped the rise and seemed ready for more. Rafe waited until everyone was ready, reins in their hands ... and then Rafe realized his error.

"Uh ... does anyone know the way to Valhalla?"

"Die with a sword?" Karl asked, and he chuckled at his own joke.

Eloise closed her eyes and Roselyn began to cry again; the Seer had been their guide. "Lady say horses take us where we need go," Seren said.

Rafe looked doubtful; he'd known horses all his life. Some were dumb as rocks, others smart enough to escape from sturdy pens or break open barrels of grain. All were infuriatingly stubborn. He'd fed, washed, nursed, and trained horses, and cursed them with every foul word that he knew. Never once had a horse understood him.

"Horse," Eloise said to her stallion, "take me to Valhalla."

Eloise's white stallion bolted forward so quickly that Eloise let out a little cry of terror. Her horse galloped away, back down the path they'd come on, across the ruined farm between the tall yellow grasses. The others watched Eloise ride for the woods, clinging for dear life, through the cloud of dust raised by her horse's hooves. Silvana and Glororil spun, high in the air, and then darted after her, silver and golden trails twinkling in her wake.

Rafe sat dumbfounded.

"Valhalla!" Karl cried to his horse, and he charged after Eloise, thundering away. Seren and Roselyn glanced questioningly at Rafe, but he only shrugged; Rafe was no wizard, nor would he make any attempt to explain the oddities that he'd seen since Karl, Eric, Roselyn, and Eloise had charged into his stables the day that Castle Bristlen was sieged.

"Valhalla!" Seren and Roselyn shouted together, and their horses dashed forward as if racing down the path. Rafe sat alone, watching them leave.

Some things just shouldn't be, Rafe thought to himself. Gods, giants, elves: all that he could accept, but *horses that understood English?* That wasn't just impossible, *that was wrong!*

Rafe looked back down the hill. The glow of the council, of the Lady, Odin, and the other Gods lit the grotto; light streamed out between the tall trees that blocked Rafe's view of Mimir. Rafe sat perplexed: where was God ... and his son, Jesus? Was the Lady's story of repeating Divine Seasons true? What did it mean to him?

Rafe had never felt at ease with this whole quest. What would Christ say if he knew that Rafe had left Earth to deliver a friend's soul to a bunch of pagan deities? Such questions were beyond him. What Rafe knew was, if their positions had been switched, would Eric have led the company on a quest to Heaven to see that Rafe's spirit reached the Gates of St. Peter? Rafe suspected that Eric would've, if the Seer had agreed to lead him. Eric would've loved an adventure like that, and Rafe owed him no less. Rafe would rather explain to Christ about helping Eric enter pagan Valhalla than explain how a Norse mercenary was a truer friend than a Christian.

Rafe's horse snorted nervously, and Rafe instantly looked around; even the dumbest horses were aware of most dangers, and Rafe had learned not to ignore them. His eyes widened as he saw the black wolves charging toward him, pulling Loki's chariot, with Hel steering. Already Rafe could feel the uncomfortable tingle of Hel's stare.

"Valhalla!" Rafe said to his horse, and it burst from standing still into a gallop so fast that Rafe clutched at his reins wrong and almost fell off. Yet his white horse ignored his fumbling and dashed to catch up with the others.

Quickly Rafe's horse left Hel's wolves behind. He glanced back, before he rode into the woods, and spied Hel's chariot still closer to the ruined barn by the Great Drop than to him; Loki's wolves were no match for the Lady's horses. He looked forward, down the trail, but saw only clouds of dust.

Rafe pressed his horse, leaned into the wind blowing past him, and professionally balanced his weight between his saddle and his stirrups. Expertly he rode, and his horse seemed eager to please him, delighted to run faster. The Lady's horse galloped faster than any horse that Rafe had ever ridden, and with a smoother gait, even at incredible speed. Rafe kept expecting the horse to slow, to tire, but it never did. The horse ran as if it would never stop.

Soon Rafe caught up with the others. The woods ended, and opened on wide, grassy fields and small hills. Their trail cut a nearly straight line, winding only around the tallest hills and thickest clumps of trees.

Silvana and Glororil buzzed past him, circled around, and flew ahead, matching the horses' speed with ease. They darted so quickly around the companions that Rafe only saw them by their glittering trails, sparkling gold and silver in the starlight. Rafe wondered about them; they didn't seem to have great depth, at least not how humans equated depth. They were creatures of beauty, content with what they were. To Rafe, they were more than just companions; they were little angels; proof that some beauty was eternal.

Soon Rafe caught up with Seren, who looked terrified, the thin lines on her face taut, her hands clutching her reins as tightly as she could, almost blinded by the whistling wind. Rafe smiled at Seren, and she forced a grin back, but she remained too frightened to do anything but cling tightly while her white horse ran.

"Just hold on!" Rafe shouted to Seren over the wind. "These horses won't let you fall, and Valhalla can't be far away at this speed!"

Seren nodded that she understood, but never said a word. Rafe smiled again and wryly winked at her. Seren looked surprised, and then glared disapprovingly.

Rafe motioned ahead and pressed his horse for more speed. Seren nodded, and Rafe leaned forward, racing for the others. These horses were all infinitely strong and incredibly fast, but Rafe was the best rider, even better than Eric. Rafe knew best how to time his rhythmic movements to his horse's, freeing it to gallop faster.

Rafe quickly caught up to Roselyn. Roselyn was riding hard, not frightened at all. Rafe admired Roselyn; of them all, she'd changed the most. Roselyn's first day in armor had been a sore trial; now she wore armor with confident ease and looked natural in it, like some Greek Amazon from the ancient legends of Rome.

Roselyn nodded firmly to Rafe just like a man would. Rafe understood instantly; she needed no help of his. In fact, Rafe had little to offer her. Roselyn had become a warrior, and in a short time, she might excel even him.

Rafe rode on and slowly caught up with Karl. He wasn't surprised to find him yawning; Rafe was tired, too. Yet they were almost to the end of their road. Soon they'd live or die, and Rafe had no idea which fate they'd endure. Against Hel in her fury, Rafe suspected that they'd have little chance, and the Lady had said that Loki wouldn't be long detained. Against Loki they'd have no chance at all. Yet any other destination would only prolong their suffering while ruining their only remaining purpose, Eric's sole prayer.

"How far?" Karl shouted at Rafe.

Rafe only shrugged. Perhaps the Seer might've known, or Eric, but the Seer was dead, and none of them knew where Eric was.

"It can't be too far!" Karl shouted. "We saw Yggdrasil from the roots; it's vast, but not infinite."

Rafe laughed out loud; Karl sounded like the Seer, who he'd hated at first. Despite their rivalry over the women, Karl and the Seer had been good for each other. Karl had learned to think deeper, and might even become a scholar, if he survived the rest of the day. The Seer had certainly reconsidered his disgust for common soldiers, seeing Karl's honor and chivalry. In time, Rafe suspected, they would've become close friends.

Rafe saw Karl's puzzled look and quit laughing. Recalling their rivalry, Rafe suddenly remembered that their company wasn't paired up evenly anymore. With the Seer dead, both Eloise and Roselyn had only Karl left to choose from. If anything could still break apart their company, the girl's romantic rivalry could. The instant that Karl chose one girl over the other, their companionship would fail.

Rafe rode faster, clinging so lightly to his horse that he was amazed that the wind didn't blow him off. Slowly he pulled ahead of Karl into the dust cloud kicked up by Eloise's horse.

Next to his, Eloise's horse was traveling the fastest. She was no better a rider than the others, but she was the smallest and wore no heavy armor. Rafe slowly pulled abreast with her and glanced to make certain that she was all right, surprised to see Eloise motion him back, behind her. Rafe was taken aback; with the Seer gone, he'd assumed that he'd have to take the lead. He was the oldest, and in his mind, best suited to assume command after the Seer had fallen. Yet Eloise and the Seer had always contested for leadership of the company; with him dead, Eloise seemed determined to rule.

Rafe slowed his horse's pace. He could easily out-race Eloise, but why should he? She'd made him a knight, elevated him to nobility, and even if she hadn't, Eloise was noble-born, his baroness, and his friend.

Rafe wouldn't challenge her leadership; Eloise was the daughter that he'd never had.

Rafe blew Eloise a kiss and fell in behind her. Eloise laughed when she saw the kiss, and Rafe wondered if she was thinking about the ruined farmhouse after Grusshire where she'd promised him anything that he desired. Afterwards, Rafe had tried not to think about that moment, except how he'd nobly refused her. He was glad that she'd never tried to kiss him again: Rafe was happy with Seren, and Eloise was too desirable to deny twice.

As they topped a rise, Rafe saw a wide, starlit river cutting across their trail. Rafe knew that they'd have to slow down to see how deep it was before they dared to try and cross it. Unknown rivers were dangerous; many strong men had died trying to cross strange rivers. His one consolation was that Hel, in Loki's chariot, would have even greater difficulty. She might even be forced to go another way, around to a bridge or narrower crossing. Yet that would only delay the inevitable; once they got to Valhalla, they'd have to wait for Hel to arrive.

The white horses slowed as they approached the river. They reined in at the water's edge.

"We're far ahead of Hel, aren't we?" Roselyn asked, yawning. "Maybe we should rest."

"No, we continue," Eloise said. "We're too close to slow down now."

"We can rest once we're there without fear of getting caught," Rafe said.

"Too bad we have to go there," Glororil said, flying down and buzzing between them. "Valhalla's a terrible land, full of violence and death. To get there, we must pass by golden Asgard, city of the Aesir, and Alfhiem, where Silvana and I were born."

"You know the way to Valhalla?" Rafe demanded. "Why didn't you tell us?"

"You never asked us," Glororil smiled.

"We thought that you knew," Silvana said, giving Glororil a disapproving stare.

"How far it away?" Seren asked.

"Not far," Silvana said. "Jotunhiem is the largest land atop Yggdrasil, and we're nearly out of it. This is the first of the many rivers that flow across Asgard; once we cross it, we'll be out of Jotunhiem. There'll be many more rivers, but most are covered with magnificent bridges. The road will get easier for you."

"I think that I should cross first," Rafe said. "Rivers can be tricky."

"Of course," Eloise said, and Rafe bowed slightly to her. Eloise tried to bite back a smile and failed utterly.

Rafe dismounted, wondering if the water was cold, but he wasn't frightened; fording rivers wasn't new to him. As far as he was concerned, they'd already made it. All that they needed was to stay awake until the

Lady's horses carried them to the Gates of Valhalla.
Then, for good or ill, all would be decided.

Chapter 20

The Gates of Valhalla

KARL

The Gates of Valhalla gleamed tall and bright in the first rays of the rising sun. Ancient skulls layered in beaten gold decorated its high arch and walls made of spears twenty feet tall. Valhalla's magnificent gate was built of smaller golden spears, wide enough to march whole armies through, and polished round-shields adorned it. A wide road led to its entrance and beyond, white as chalk, paved with the powder of crushed human bones. A short, wide bridge arched over a torrential river streaming just outside its gates, yet they didn't cross it; its gates were closed, barred, and Valhalla wasn't deserted. Past the golden gates, the white road of crushed human bones led high up a great hill to a mighty hall roofed with golden shields. Viking warriors milled about it or walked away from it to face a grim day's fighting.

The company reined in at last before the great gates. Karl sighed heavily; they'd won the race, but the real battle had yet to begin. Karl jumped off of his saddle, unable to keep from yawning. The others seemed equally tired; Seren was almost asleep in her saddle.

"Rest now," Eloise yawned, letting Rafe help her dismount. "Silvana, are you and Glororil as exhausted as we are?"

"Fairies don't tire like humans do," Glororil smirked.

"Glororil! Really!" Silvana scolded him. "Fairies don't sleep while the sun's bright. Actually, just seeing Alfhiem was refreshing enough for us. We'll go there, when this is over, for it's our ancient home."

Karl smiled, recalling the sights that they'd ridden past. Vanahiem was deserted, a crumbling ruin of a city, tucked between huge mountains, barely visible in the starlit distance. Asgard towered impressive beyond words, a sparkling jewel of a city, with glorious towers and brilliant mansions shining even under the starry sky, so tall that their roofs easily peaked over a fortified wall that dwarfed the massive barrier around Niflhiem. One great hall stood out from all the others, roofed with plates of glistening gold, and Silvana had told them that it was Odin's hall of feasting. Karl had been tempted to slow down, to investigate the marvelous city, but that would have to wait.

Then they'd ridden past what seemed to be a distant forest. Silvana had cheered and excitedly flown between the companions, making sure that that they all noticed it. Alfhiem she named it, the ancient home of all Fairie. Even the dark elves had originally come from there, she said. It seemed like any other deep forest, but looking closely, Karl spied an order and symmetry to the trees, and around the vast forest grew a tall, thick hedge, wider than any river that he'd ever heard of, with long, thick, natural spikes: deadly thorns encircled Alfhiem. His keen eyes could see little else, but he suspected that tens of thousands of fairies could live inside that hedge, unseen by passersby.

"We need to sleep," Eloise said flatly. "Silvana, you and Glororil must stand guard and awaken us when Hel or Loki arrives."

"We will," Silvana promised.

They unsaddled their horses and let them roam free, and the horses went to the river to drink. Under the warm sun, the companions spread out on the thick, fragrant grass, and sleep came almost instantly.

Karl startled awake to find Silvana hovering over his face. He'd almost swatted her away, like he would any insect, but he caught himself in time. The sinking sun told him that he must have slept all day.

"Hel's coming," Silvana warned, and then she flew over to Roselyn. Eloise was already awake, sitting up and blinking.

"This is it," Eloise said plainly.

"I guess so," Karl replied.

Karl didn't know what to think. All of their travels had been poised for this moment. He could've used a few more weeks of sleep, and he was hungry, but that didn't matter. Karl twisted his head, stretched his neck, and stood up. Instinctively he placed his hand on his sword hilt to make sure that he was still armed, although he doubted if any sword would help. Why should Hel forgive them? Loki certainly wouldn't.

Loki's silver chariot rattled loudly as Hel crossed the last bridge and rode into the valley, her face twisted with rage. The wolves of Loki skidded to a halt, panting and seething, before the companions.

"Hel, wait!" Karl cried. "We have something for you!"

Hel turned all of her focus upon Karl's flesh. Her stare burned into him and stabbed with immortal, overwhelming hate, yet Hel withheld the savage pain. Karl turned to Eloise, who carried the black leather pouch with Eric's arm, though Karl suspected how useless it would be.

Then an unexpected voice made Hel turn away.

"Hel, stop!" Eric's voice cried. "It's me you want, not them!"

"Eric!" Hel cried, turning to stare at a nearby spot where Karl's eyes detected nothing. "Stand there and never move again! You're mad, Eric! Dare you face me now, after all that you've done?"

"I did what I had to, Hel," Eric said. "I had to get here ... to see if the Valkyrie's words were true. Don't blame my friends; ply your vengeance upon me."

"I'll do both!" Hel screamed. "You're just another lying, insignificant subject, though you've tasked me worse than any have ever dared. But these puny mortals! These ... Saxons! They came into my home and lied, offering false love and friendship, baited me, and kept me on a string! They abused my loneliness, and when I returned what they'd offered, they cheated and stole you ... as they'd to planned to all along!"

"Hel, that isn't fair ...," Karl said.

"How dare you speak to me!" Hel shrieked. "I'm not some mortal wench! I am as I was born, Hel, monster-daughter of Loki! What do I care about what's fair? Look at my legs? Is that fair? But I'll be fair! You took my one weakness and flaunted it before all Yggdrasil. Now you'll regret it! You forced me here, and now your warm, fresh blood will heal my stiffened legs that I may return home! Five mortal deaths for punishment! That's fair! That's the cost of angering Hel!"

The full shock of Hel's rage slammed into Karl like a giant's fist. He crumpled onto the green grass, which started to wilt under the force of Hel's glare. Her glower bombarded him, boiled and broiled Karl's flesh inside his heavy mail, scalding him with invisible flames. Yet, for all his suffering, Hel wasn't Vanir or Aesir; Hel's power couldn't kill them, merely torment them for all eternity. Their lives she'd have to end herself.

Slowly Karl's pain faded; it didn't vanish, but diminished. Karl wrenched open his eyes; dimly, through a blur of tears, Karl saw Hel reach down and snap the thick leather thongs binding her stiff legs to Loki's chariot. He'd forgotten how strong she was, how with her bare hands she could tear them apart like the wings off of a butterfly.

Slowly Hel stepped down, carefully making her way off the ornate chariot. Firmly Hel clutched its sides and edged, inch by inch, gritting her teeth with effort just to move her dead, hardened legs. Finally Hel slipped off Loki's chariot down onto the white road, almost falling over as she did. For a second, her glaring gaze left Karl, but he lay too weak to move. If only she'd give him a few moments; if they could all make it to the tiny river, then maybe the rapid current would float them away. But instantly Hel's arresting glare returned and flamed mercilessly down upon them.

A burst of solar brilliance erupted above them, but Hel had seen that once too often. Raising her eyes, Hel blasted Glororil from the sky, and Silvana screamed as Glororil fell like a flaming meteor to the ground. Then Hel returned her full vision upon them and Karl writhed as never before, helpless as death inched towards him.

Karl prayed that the others were better off than he; he could no longer see, barely hear, and feel nothing but the searing intensity of Hel's hate racking his body and mind.

A dead, skeletal foot brushed his arm, and dimly Karl was aware of the rasping of Roselyn's elf sword scraping from her scabbard. Karl tried to look, but it was as if he'd stared into the midday sun; only the blinding red glare of Hel's eyes colored his sight. Karl pictured her standing over him, raising the deadly elf sword high, ready to bring it down.

Suddenly an explosion rocked the ground beneath them, and a pillar of emerald flames burst from the road, reaching high into the darkening sky. Wrapped in Frigg's falcon-skin cloak, Loki stepped from the pillar as it vanished in a cloud of black smoke, his dark eyes beaming the outrage that he radiated, the vengeance that he demanded.

"Stop!" Loki screamed at his daughter. "Stay that blade! These mortals are mine! They have information that belongs to me!"

"They humiliated me, father!" Hel raved. "It's my right to kill them!"

"Obey me!" Loki upbraided, and he turned his merciless power upon his own daughter.

Hel screamed; Hel was no goddess, no match for her father. Under Loki's gaze, Hel was as helpless as Karl was under hers. With an anguished scream, Hel teetered and fell upon the grass.

Furiously, Loki turned on the white horses and stared. They neighed and reared, but Loki forced them back into the stream with the force of his eyes, burning into them as Hel's glare had burned into the companions; but Loki was Aesir, his power far greater. Where they merely felt fire, their horses became engulfed in blistering red flames. Faltering, the horses fell splashing onto their sides, futilely kicking, whinnying in pain. Cruelly Loki concentrated, pressed down upon them, and the precious white horses, gifts of the Lady, strong beyond the words, shriveled back down into the flowers from which She'd made them. The flowers turned brown, then black, and finally crumbled into ash and were washed downstream by the current. The Lady's great, powerful, tireless white horses were gone.

Only the companions were left to deal with, and they had no hope of escape. Loki looked down upon them and glared evilly.

"Now!" Loki cried. "Tell me where the Hidden Portal lies or you'll suffer torments unimaginable before you slowly die!"

Godly eyes fell upon them; the tortures of Loki's stare no agony of Hel's could match. Another world claimed Karl, one that no human could ever willingly conceive. Blinding torment was all that existed and agony was all that offered. Only one escape existed; no matter what, Karl had to take it.

"Stop it!" Karl cried. *"All right! All right! I'll tell you! I'll tell!"*

Slowly Karl became aware of the world around him; soft, green grass replaced the burning coals of the other world. Hel was crawling away on her elbows, her teeth gritted, but Loki stood triumphant. Despair shuddered within Karl; *they'd failed.* Loki was too powerful, too cruel to be resisted by mere mortals. Karl would have to break his promise to Titania, to the Lady, to the Seer, and to himself. If he didn't do it willingly, Loki would simply force him, with no more effort than crushing an ant. Gasping for breath, Karl looked up at Loki, trying to speak through the pain.

"Tell me, mortal!" Loki seethed.

"The ... Hidden ... Portal ... lies ..."

"Somewhere where you'll never find it!" boomed a deep, startling voice.

Across the road appeared a strange pale figure, floating down from the sky. Light glowed from his sparkling white robes, which dimmed the first few evening stars shining in the darkening sky above them. Down the newcomer floated, and lightly he touched the ground as if gravity held no sway. As he touched down, at his feet grew new grasses and tiny flowers burst into bloom. Something familiar shined from him; behind the brilliance of his white robe, he had coal-black hair and eyes, and his face ...! Karl gasped. His face ...!

"Seer!" Seren screamed.

"No!" Roselyn screamed. "Yes! *Athelwynne!*"

"Seer!" Eloise squealed. "You're alive!"

"Seer, help us!" Rafe wailed.

"Relax," the Seer smiled. "Help is on the way. The Lady arranged it."

"But ... Seer, you're alive!" Karl shouted. "We watched you jump into Mimir's Well! How did you survive?"

"I didn't," the Seer smiled. "I died, and gave my life to Mimir in exchange for his service, as I promised. But my soul still belonged to the Lady, and into Her bosom She took me, as She does with all of Her loyal servants. But She wishes for my services to continue, so She gave me a new form. I am now Her emissary to Yggdrasil, and as such I shall serve Her forever."

"Mortal wizard!" Loki cried. "Shut up!"

Loki glared, but the Seer stood against him.

"Beware Her power!" the Seer warned, glaring threateningly. "I'm Her messenger and most-trusted servant. The power of the Lady flows through me."

"I am Loki!" the evil God scoffed. "Brag not before your betters, if you'd continue your pitiful servitude! I can destroy you with a single thought."

"Once you could have," the Seer said. "No doubt you can yet destroy me, but not easily. Yet before those who come now even your boasts pale! Behold the sky!"

Suddenly a great presence filled the sky. Shining upon the clouds came the magical aura that had come at once to the Lady in the grotto of Mimir. Odin the Terrible-One approached, again riding the skies on Sleipnir, his fabulous eight-legged horse. The radiant awe of his glory burst upon them as he rode nearer.

"No!" Loki cried. "He was in deep conference when I left!"

"Forgive me, great Trickster, but my Lady noticed the instant that you left," the Seer explained. "At once She concluded the proceedings, promising further talks between Her world and yours, to be arranged through me. Her last act was to explain to Odin how you cheated him of one of his best warriors, and She asked him to come here soon as She left, to take back what's his."

"No!" Loki shouted, but it was too late.

Galloping across the sky, Odin steered Sleipnir down fast, landing smooth and surely before the closed Gates of Valhalla. Leaping off of his marvelous steed, Odin brandished Gungnir threateningly.

"Loki, what mischief have you done this time?" Odin demanded. "How dare you interfere with my Valkyrie? Where's this warrior?"

"Here!" Eric cried. "Oh, Alfather!"

"Eric, be silent!" Hel ordered, struggling to her feet.

"You be silent!" Odin growled at Hel. "What're you doing out of Niflhiem? Have you grown content with your infirmity, or have your poor subjects run out of blood?"

"I came after my own!" Hel snapped. "Those who come to me are mine, whether Loki sent them or not!"

"It's no doing of mine!" Loki argued. "I'm not responsible for the fumblings of your shield-maids! If they don't choose a one-armed corpse, that's not my fault."

"We shall see!" Odin said, and he turned toward Valhalla and shouted in a loud and terrible voice. *"Hail the Valkyrie! Hear now and come, bids Odin your master! Ride at once! To the gates of your land, come now! Tarry not when Odin calls!"*

Hearing Odin's command, a great crowd poured out of the golden shield-roofed hall on the hill and rushed towards them. They were the Einherjar, the fierce warriors of Odin, who rose each morning to fight and die upon Odin's battlefield, yet no matter what wounds or death they suffered, they arose whole and well each evening, and wandered back to Odin's hall to drink and feast all night. Right up to the wide gates they ran, pressed against the golden spears, and looked out across the river. All were Vikings like Eric, some younger, some grimmer, but all strong, fierce, and stout of heart.

But even more impressive were the shadows flying above them. Over gate and river, winged horses that only Sleipnir could outrace flew high and landed near the road. Twelve winged horses landed before them, and each bore a beautifully-armored Valkyrie. As they touched ground, their riders leaped from their magical steeds and saluted Odin with weapon and shield. Two of the Valkyrie were exactly as Karl remembered from before, from on Earth when Eric had died.

The Valkyrie were all stern and beautiful with sharp, defined features and dark, grim countenances. Well they bore their polished, battle-scarred armor as if they'd been wearing it forever. Each was like a cross between Roselyn and the female dark-elf that they'd left Ruthedhel fighting. Indeed, they reminded Karl of Ruthedhel, trim and muscular from centuries of fighting. Odin smiled upon them, his chosen elite, while everyone else fell silent.

Quietly Karl scrambled over to Roselyn and helped her and the others up, then backed away from Odin's powerful radiance. Eloise reached inside her bodice and brought out the Seer's moonstone, lighting Eric up like a candle in the growing twilight. Sobbing, Silvana flew up to them, Glororil clutched in her arms, looking thin and translucent, almost dead. Hel had stunned him hard, and he was only a frail fairie. Roselyn caught them both in her hands and held them close to her breast, shielding them from the fury of Odin's being.

"That's her!" Karl shouted, and he pointed at the Valkyrie surrounded by the white, hazy cloud. "That's the Valkyrie that I spoke to on Earth! She told me to come here with Eric's arm!"

Odin ignored Karl, facing his twelve fearsome shield-maidens.

"Hail the Valkyrie!" Odin shouted. "Hail to those upon whose choices all our fates are doomed! Hail Hrist and Mist, Skeggjöld and Skögul, Hildr, Prudr, and Göll, Herfjötur and Hlökk, Geirahöd, Randgríðr, and

Róta! Answer now, and speak true: who has seen this shriven mortal before?"

"I have, but I don't know from where," said the Valkyrie that Karl had pointed at, her icy voice the same as he remembered.

"Speak, Mist," Odin commanded. "Tell us what you know."

"I can't recall," Mist answered. "A dimness clouds my mind."

"It was you!" Karl shouted. "You ..!"

"Beware the Valkyrie, mortal," Mist hissed, her cold voice cutting through him like a glacial chill, and the fog around her turned icy blue.

"Bound to the weapon by a bond of flesh, you said," Karl remembered. "So it was written."

"So it is," the Valkyrie said slowly, "but how ...?"

"You told me that when I showed you Eric's arm," Karl said, "but you wouldn't take him. Only Hel, should the arm and sword be brought to her at Valhalla, could admit him now, you said, and you told me to bring it here!"

"Beware the Valkyrie!" Mist warned, her dark eyes flashing, but her voice faltered. "I do remember those words, but it's as if another said them, not I."

"They're Loki's words!" the Seer said to Odin. "He used your Valkyrie to trick these poor mortals into following their lost friend here in hopes of causing great mischief on Midgard!"

"He lies!" Loki shouted.

"Silence!" Odin boomed. "I'll decide what's true or false! Speak, messenger. How do you know this?"

"I witnessed it all," the Seer said. "As did these humans, just outside Niflhiem. Loki met us there, bragging about how he'd brought us here to show him the secret Portal by which we came. But Garm chased him off, and we've been running from him ever since."

"Dog!" Mist shrieked at Loki. *"You dare mock the Valkyrie?"*

Mist glared, her enveloping cloud turning red as flame.

"All lies," Loki grumbled.

"It does sound like you, Trickster, but it matters not," Odin said. "We'll speak about this passage later, you and I, and harsh shall be my words, if you live that long. If you've trifled with my Valkyrie then you must face their wrath. But there's no punishment for toying with mortals. The only matter of importance is the fate of this deceased warrior. Show me his arm!"

"I have it!" Eloise said, and quickly she handed the moonstone to Seren and unshouldered the Seer's long black leather pouch. Untying its laces, Eloise popped open the lid and the horrible, putrid smell of rotting flesh poured out. Eloise grimaced, holding the reeking pouch away from her, unable to stand the stench.

"Here, let me," Rafe offered, and gingerly he reached his fingers inside and pulled out the gangrenous arm, hand, sword and all. Eric's dead arm was black and crusted, but the stiff dead hand still grasped Eric's heavy Viking broadsword.

"What's this?" Odin demanded. "Wounds such as these are but scratches in Valhalla! Did he not die in battle? Was this man a coward?"

"No!" said Mist, looking towards Eric. "Bravely he lived and bravely he died! Loyal Viking he was, well deserving of reward. I swooped to claim him, but then I didn't. I can't remember why."

"It wasn't me!" Loki sneered with an amused smile.

"It matters not," Odin said. "This man was a warrior and he belongs in Valhalla. So it is decreed. You must surrender him, Hel, for he has earned reward."

"No!" Hel cried. "You seek precedence! Once a soul enters Niflhiem then they're bound to me forever! You can't make me give him up!"

"Hel, I seek no precedence," Odin said. "When comes Ragnarrok, all men of valor must march from Valhalla. You'll have the rest. So it is written. But this man was wrongly sent to Niflhiem. You must give him up; the walls of Niflhiem are too low to risk the anger of the Aesir."

Hel turned to face Karl. Their eyes met momentarily, and Karl was almost slain by the hate that she dared not blast him with before Odin. But Hel lingered upon him only a moment. Then her gaze shifted to Rafe and Seren, to Roselyn and Eloise, and finally to the Seer, who looked so different, so noble and lordly in his glowing white robes. Hel was a proud woman, a half-goddess; Karl knew that she'd refuse. At last, Hel turned her angry glare away from them and focused upon the one who'd started it all: Loki.

"You!" Hel cried. "This is your fault! You made me do this, father, so if I must pay, then you must also! I won't suffer this humiliation alone! Hear me, Odin! Hear me, all! *This fallen warrior, Eric Bjornson, I'll release if, and only if, he and those who stand with him can defeat my father Loki in combat this day!* Else he's mine forever! So says Hel, Queen of Niflhiem, Goddess of Death!"

"No!" Odin cried. "Loki's Aesir; mortals can't defeat him!"

"Nonetheless, that's my challenge!" Hel smiled. "Either Loki accepts the humiliation of defeat or I won't suffer surrendering my own. Accept my terms or forfeit your claim."

"But Loki can't lose!" Odin argued. "Eric can't disobey Loki!"

"He can, if I will it, and I do," Hel grinned. "Eric shall fight with my powers of the dead! Let the battle begin!"

Karl hesitated, unsure. Loki laughed, greatly amused. Karl wanted to help, but what could he do?

"I'll fight," the Seer said. "I'm backed by the power of the Lady and don't fear Loki. I'll fight with Eric, and Eloise shall join me."

"What?" Eloise gasped. "What good would I be?"

"Don't you remember the words of the Lady?" the Seer smiled. "Your curse wasn't destroyed, but placed in the keeping of her most-trusted servant. I'm that servant, Eloise, and I can give and take back your curse at will. Join us, Eloise, and let us fight together one last time!"

"You mean ... just this once?"

"Once, for Eric, and never again!"

"V- Very well," Eloise said, though a little unsure. Yet, as the Seer held out his hand, Eloise stepped forward and stood by the Seer and Eric.

"And I'll fight with the mortals!" Mist shouted angrily, and she strode forward. "I must avenge my disgrace; it's my right!"

"No!" Loki argued. "The Valkyrie can't join them!"

"You made these enemies, Loki," Odin grinned. "Now pay for your interference. The Valkyrie are my chosen, blessed with my power! Your enemy grows stronger, Loki!"

"These few are no match for me!" Loki laughed. "You're a fool, Odin, to let your precious Valkyrie die so easily. You barely have enough of them to carry your precious warriors to Valhalla!"

"That's my business!" Odin growled, flaring his flaming eyes at Loki. "Mind your own! You have enough to deal with!"

"So I do," Loki sneered, "but only for the moment!"

Fast as a striking snake, Loki turned and blasted his full force upon Eric and those who stood with him.

Loki's eyes glared, and he pointed his long fingers at his foes, unleashing visible beams of hate. Mist jumped in front of Eloise, blocking Loki's beams with her silver shield, and the Seer returned a blast of his own pure, white radiance. Eric was stunned, but held his ground.

Loki was strongest; his eyes flamed like Thrynn the giant as his power slammed into the crumbling few who stood against him.

"Karl, do something!" Roselyn shouted. "We've got to help them!"

"How?" Karl asked, motioning to the blasting godly powers.

"No!" Rafe cried, grabbing Roselyn's arm before she charged forward. "We can't help! This battle's out of our league!"

"Silvana!" the Seer suddenly shouted. "Now! Hurry!"

Out of Roselyn's hands burst the tiny silver fairie, only glancing back once at fallen Glororil, her dying lover, curled unconscious in Roselyn's palm. Torn between anguish and fear, Silvana spewed forth her fairie-light, silver-blue and pale in the gathering darkness.

As before, Silvana's glow struck Eloise, and she screamed and fell to her knees. The awful change came rapidly, trembling at first, then exploding into fur and fangs and claws.

As the change hastened, Mist stepped aside, withdrawing her Valkyrie shield. Flames from Loki's hands cascaded down upon Eloise, already racked with unimaginable torment, and she screamed as no human ever had before or would again. Eloise fell writhing, helplessly tortured by two agonies, each greater than the other, seared apart by flame and transformation.

But Eloise faded; against the power of Loki, the Wolfqueen rose snarling and furious. Her curse was more steeped in evil than Loki, older than Aesir or Vanir, part of the unknown wickedness that prowled Ginnungagap when Yggdrasil was young, before ever God or giant walked. The Wolfqueen was born of evil's true heart from ages past and realms of darkness.

Loki hesitated, pondering his new foe but a moment, but it was enough. Eric leaped forward, reaching out with his one ghostly hand, and the Mist the Valkyrie advanced with practiced caution, warily stalking her foe. The Wolfqueen leaped right at Loki while the Seer flamed his own bright power, the pureness of the Lady, concentrating all of Her might at the evil God.

But Loki took the blast unharmed, barely scathed. Instantly Loki resumed his attack, pouring out all his potency. Eric stopped in his tracks, straining against Loki's unholy dominance, but able only to slow his retreat to inches at a step. Mist staggered, but ducked beneath her shield and pushed forward, one strained step at a time. The Seer was clearly stunned; he stumbled a few steps back, but held out, stoutly pouring all of his strength into resisting Loki's might. The Wolfqueen had been struck in mid-leap, and fallen only to scramble back to her feet. She dug her claws deep into the white road and howled in pain, but pushed forward.

Loki increased his strength. Despite all else, Loki was a God, one of the Twelve, and his mastery was as divine as he. He was Aesir, born of giant-stock, half-brother of Thor, the most cunning of all in Asgard. Few powers in the universe were greater than he.

Yet his opponents were of no single power. The Wolfqueen was perhaps the strongest, being the oldest and least understood, coming from a source of purest evil. Eric wielded the power of Hel, Loki's daughter, the inescapable maw of death. By dying, he'd suffered the worst that any mortal soul could, and Loki's power could harm him no further. Mist the Valkyrie upheld the power of Odin; she could be slain, but not easily. Odin was clearly more powerful than Loki, and while Mist hadn't all of his power, she was an immortal warrior, trained in battlefields going back to the creation of Midgard. Her skills weren't feigned, and her sword, forged in Gladshiem, could kill any God, Aesir or Vanir.

But clearly Loki's greatest threat was the Seer. Robed in white, the Seer embodied the energies of a whole other universe and the Goddess who ruled it alone, submitting to none but Her own bestial Lord. The Lady had chosen Her mightiest warrior, Her most masterful subject, and given him powers beyond human conception. The electricity that poured from his radiance stung even immortal Loki. The Seer was almost a God himself.

But Loki was a God! His strength was pure and whole, undeniably his. Theirs were but echoes, shadows of their true sources of power. Loki pushed harder and strained himself to his absolute limit. Karl bit his lip; with of all that power raging, they couldn't hold out long. This fight had to be won now, or he, all of them, everything, would be lost forever.

Suddenly a cloud of darkness swarmed over the Seer, straining to collapse his field of bursting energies. The beams upon Eric increased in intensity, and Eric stepped back, yielding to keep from being blasted out of the clearing. The Valkyrie Mist bent lower, straining against the flaming raw power exploding from Loki's eyes and fingers, stalwart behind her shield. Her slow steps forward halted, and Mist found herself being pressed back, down, almost crushed beneath her shield, her icy cloud trailing behind her. The Wolfqueen fared the worst; naked before Loki's intensity, she held her ground, refusing to yield, howling in anger and agony as his outrage burned through her, singeing off every hair, charring layer after layer of flesh, almost lost in a cloud of reeking black smoke as it fought to heal her back together while Loki blasted her apart.

Yet they didn't yield. No matter the pain or torment, the four stood their ground, fighting, although as long seconds passed, Karl realized that they couldn't win. Loki blasted forth all of his godly power, threatening to disintegrate the whole valley and everything in it. Even the Einherjar backed away from

Valhalla's gate, fearful of Loki's ire. Never before had such energies been unleashed in Yggdrasil.

"*No!*" Roselyn screamed, and she dropped Glororil and jumped forward, snatched up her elf-sword from where Hel had dropped it, and suddenly Roselyn berserked and charged into the fray. Instantly Karl jumped after her, but Roselyn moved too fast and dashed forward with her elf-sword raised.

Karl charged after her. He had to stop Roselyn, to make her understand! *Roselyn could do nothing against Loki!* They were just humans, powerless against the brutality of the angry God.

Dimly Karl heard Rafe and Seren rushing up behind him. He wanted to turn around, to tell them to go back, but he couldn't waste the moment. Headlong Karl rushed into the fury of Loki's power, seeing only Roselyn charge ahead of him: *Roselyn had to be stopped!*

Too late! Loki spotted Roselyn charge in berserk fury and bent his eyes upon her. All of Loki's godly fury streamed through his eyes and struck Roselyn cleanly. Her thin elvin-sword couldn't block Loki's might; Roselyn screamed, brandished her elvin-sword high, and fought with her last effort to get to Loki, to strike him, cursing him with her last breath.

But Roselyn's charge was futile. Her attack was ineffectual, and in one instant, everything became meaningless. Loki's power washed down upon

Roselyn's perfect form, seared the skin from her bones, and wholly melted her loveliness into nothingness.

Roselyn's beauty, her charm, her love, and Karl's life ... was gone in an instant.

Karl froze, shocked beyond words, totally uncaring as Loki's eyes raised slightly, focusing on him, Rafe, and Seren.

Roselyn was dead; Karl didn't care anymore.

Instantly Loki exploded his power upon them, but an instant too late. Loki had been at the limit of his power and pushed it one smidgen too far. The Seer broke free, blasting his first clean shot right across Loki's eyes, searing them shut in a sea of purest white, backed by all of the power of the Lady. The Wolfqueen broke free next, pain and anger pushing her strength so high that no God could resist her. Straight at Loki she pounced, twenty claws stabbing deep into his divine godly flesh as her fangs ripped open his throat. Mist dove forward and sliced her sword deep into Loki's thigh and slammed her shield hard into his gut. Lastly came Eric himself; his one ghostly hand reached right through the Wolfqueen and deep into Loki's chest, seized Loki's evil heart, and squeezed to crush the life from it.

The wave of pain that struck Karl was incomparable, but before he evaporated, Loki's power vanished, overcome by the other's attacks. Seething, Karl, Rafe, and Seren raged forward, and together they body-slammed the giant God. Loki screamed and wavered, and finally, furiously, Loki toppled backwards, overcome at last.

"Stop!" Odin laughed, and with a wave of his hand an irresistible force gripped Karl, and all of them were raised up into the air. They cursed and shouted; all that they wanted was to be released, to get back to Loki, to return to him all of the shame and anguish that they'd suffered since this whole episode began. But Odin held them back, helpless and impotent. The Seer ceased his attack.

"Enough!" Odin cried. "Loki is defeated! Though I'd rather see him suffer what he deserves, greatly would the Norns punish me if I knowingly allowed Loki to die and ruin their plans. But well pleased am I with such fierceness! May you all be chosen by my Valkyrie someday!"

"Glororil!" the Seer shouted, seeming unusually energetic after using his magic. "The Wolfqueen, quickly! Shine your light!"

But looking back, all that Karl saw was Silvana, tiny on the ground, sobbing, holding golden Glororil pressed to her silver breast. Glororil lay unmoving, surely dying.

"Glororil!" the Seer shouted, and he ran to the fairies and scooped them out of the grass into his hands. Slowly the Seer looked down upon them and a soft white glow brightened his hands. Both fairies became enveloped in his light, and when it faded, Glororil looked much better, almost as if he were sleeping.

"Hey!" Seren shouted. "Much trouble! Wolfqueen, no Glororil, no Eloise!"

"Don't worry," the Seer smiled. "I'm so weary that I almost forgot; I can remove Eloise's curse at will."

The Seer raised one hand and pointed at the snarling Wolfqueen, who was still fighting to get back at Loki, and the Seer blinked. The Wolfqueen suddenly twisted around to face the Seer, then froze. No horrible change or painful transformation wrenched her; as gently as starlight appearing in the evening, the Wolfqueen faded out and Eloise faded in, garbed in a simple dress of pure white. Slowly Eloise blinked, and then she smiled; her wolf-curse was gone again, this time never to return.

Odin lowered his hand, and slowly they descended back to the road. Loki lay stretched out on the grass beside his fallen feathered cloak, clutching his bloody throat and thigh, badly wounded, though mostly ashamed and humiliated. But Karl didn't care. His eyes were fixed on one thing:

"Roselyn!" Karl gasped.

When Roselyn had berserked forward, they'd all given chase, Seren forgetting that she'd been holding the moonstone. Now dropped and forgotten on the road, the moonstone was still lighting Eric, but not just he. Ghostly glowing, Roselyn stood translucent and white, hovering over her empty mail coat and fallen elf-sword. Roselyn was as dead as Eric, standing only as a phantom.

Dead.

"Roselyn!" Eloise screamed. "No! *Roselyn!*"

Tears welled deep in Karl's eyes. Karl had loved Roselyn since the first moment he'd seen her. Now Roselyn stood bodiless, looking down at the road, a ghost like Eric, just as dead. He'd truly lost her forever.

"Oh, Roselyn ...," Karl whispered.

"No!" Seren cried; her knees buckled and she collapsed onto the grass.

"No! Not Roselyn!" Eloise screamed, and she rushed forward, but Rafe caught her in his arms and held her back, though blind with his own tears.

"No!" the Seer gasped, and he stared disbelieving.

They'd just defeated Loki. The Seer now wielded the strength of the Lady, was almost a God, yet powerless to change the event that he feared most, the death of a beloved.

"N-n-no ...," Rafe stammered, his cheeks flooded with tears. *"Don't weep. W-w-we m-m-mustn't w-w-weep..."*

"No!" Karl shouted, shocked and grief-stricken. "Roselyn, *why?* Why not me?"

"Karl, don't!" the Seer shouted. "Don't make it any harder! It was her choice: Roselyn saw that we were losing ... and sacrificed herself!"

"You could've told me!" Karl shouted at Roselyn's phantom. *"I would've ...!"*

"She knows!" the Seer answered for Roselyn. "That's why ...!"

Slowly Roselyn looked up. As their eyes met, Karl saw anguish wring from her ghostly face, eyes that would never again know tears but would beg to weep even in death. Roselyn was all that Karl cared for, and in her forlorn glance Karl saw that all that Roselyn ever wanted was him and a chance to live free of the royal prison that she'd been born to. But Roselyn had known, faced with the same choice that the Seer'd been, that if she hadn't sacrificed herself, then Karl would've, and that thought Roselyn couldn't bear. Had Roselyn done nothing, then Loki would've won, and none of them would've had any hope.

But for Karl, no hope existed. Roselyn, his life and his love, was dead, and nothing that he could do would change that.

But Karl wasn't the only one present.

"Hail, Odin, my rightful liege!" Mist cried, her cold voice loud and clear over the sudden silence. "Behold! A warrior has fallen, bravely and with honor, in the act of saving many lives! This warrior deserves reward!"

Slowly, carefully, Mist lifted the point of her sword out toward Roselyn's glowing spirit. Her icy fog grew golden as it flowed from her blade toward Roselyn; close, but not touching.

"No!" Odin shouted. "Mortal women can't enter Valhalla!"

"Yes, she's mine!" Hel cried.

"No!" Mist shouted boldly at Hel, and then Mist turned back to Odin. "The worlds are changing, my liege; Midgard, Yggdrasil, and all the others that we know of. Perhaps this should change as well. But never will Mist deny her liege his will! Instead, I offer that this brave maiden join not the Einherjar, but the shield-maids of Valkyrie! Well has she earned this right, for never have I seen such a fearsome foe more bravely attacked!"

Cheers erupted from the other Valkyries, who shouted fiercely and shook their weapons high. Odin looked at his Valkyrie, and then paused to consider, and glared down at Roselyn's eerie spirit. Harshly Odin fixed his one eye upon Roselyn's wavering figure, concentrated, and burned into her. Roselyn staggered, faltering under the intensity of Odin's omnipotent gaze beaming directly upon her, helpless, unable to resist. Karl wanted to scream, to cry out, but why should Odin heed him?

Roselyn foundered and crumbled. Her glow dimmed; her entire ethereal form began to fade, to diminish. Roselyn's incorporeal form failed, deteriorating, withering into nothing. But just then Odin ceased his powerful, relentless stare, and a wide smile spread beneath his bushy mustache.

"Indeed, Mist, she is worthy!" Odin said. "Her heart is true, her spirit fierce, and her loyalty eternal. So be it! Kneel, specter!"

Still ghostly white and dim, Roselyn lifted her fading, spectral head to gaze silently at Odin, and then she turned to look back at her companions; at Karl.

Clearly Karl could feel Roselyn's phantom eyes contact his, beaming out as Hel's had, not holding Karl by will or pain but through their bond of love. Even death couldn't sever that eternal fusion. Somehow Karl felt Roselyn's shock at Odin's offer, her need for help and council, but in this Roselyn stood alone. Only her wishes did Odin care to hear, but Karl could've told him: Roselyn wanted to be with Karl. Alive or dead, it didn't matter. And Karl wanted to be with her. That was all that either of them cared about.

Slowly Roselyn turned to face Odin, and silently she sank to her intangible knees. Odin held out Gungnir, his sacred spear, and lightly touched Roselyn's head.

"Speak, specter," Odin said. "Do you now hear and vow loyalty to Odin as your liege, forgetting all others, and acknowledge him as your true and rightful master, forsaking all wills that aren't his, and swear to be true and loyal to him, surrendering all worldly cares and worries save for the duties that he appoints for you, and that you will serve him well and be as his right arm, doing always as he deems best, obeying his rightful commands in thought and word and deed from now until the end of time?"

Roselyn silently nodded.

"Then pick up thy weapon, and never again be seen without it!"

Glowing ghostly white, Roselyn bent down and reached out her wavy transparent hand. Yet, as it closed upon her grip, Roselyn's ghostly glow faded and was gone. Roselyn's hand was real and alive. Roselyn was real and alive. Roselyn smiled, and Karl exploded with joy; life had returned to them both.

Roselyn stood and raised her blade high in salute, first to Odin, and then to her new sisters. The Valkyrie cheered, and so did the Einherjar, and the companions rejoiced just to see Roselyn again.

"Oh, Roselyn!" Eloise shouted gladly.

The Seer smiled widely as Rafe and Seren cheered. But, as quickly as Karl's joy had returned, it faded. This wasn't Countess Roselyn, whom Karl had loved and treasured and wanted to spend all eternity with; this was a Valkyrie, a Chooser of the Slain. Roselyn had belonged to Karl. This Valkyrie belonged to Odin.

The others dashed forward and embraced and congratulated her. Roselyn hugged all of them, smiling brightly, until she looked at Karl. Then all of their smiles broke.

Tears still ran down Karl's cheeks. Nothing had changed. Karl had lost Roselyn forever. The wall that had temporarily risen between Rafe and Seren was nothing compared to this.

"Karl ...!" Roselyn gasped, suddenly aware. "Karl, I'm sorry ..., but there was no other way!"

"Karl, it can still work out!" Eloise said carefully.

"You needn't be parted forever," the Seer insisted. "As a Valkyrie, Roselyn is immortal, and she has the power to choose from all the dead! You can still be together forever, her as Valkyrie, you as Einherjar!"

"Karl, my brother," Rafe said, "don't lose yourself in mourning. Roselyn's alive! Come, touch her!"

Roselyn smiled and held out her arms to Karl. Everyone froze, smiling, awaiting the glad moment when Karl rushed into her arms.

But Karl turned away. He understood what they were saying, but it was too ... incredible, impossible! All that Karl wanted was Roselyn, his Roselyn. This Valkyrie he couldn't bear to look at.

"Karl," Eloise came close, gently taking Karl's arm, "it's all right. Roselyn still loves you, as much as I do. But ... but she's known all along ... Roselyn could never go home. Not like the rest of us. You and Rafe are knights now; you belong on Earth. The Seer has a whole new home, and even if he hadn't, his old teachers could never refuse him now. Silvana and Glororil can return to Titania or Alfhiem. Seren was always free. And I, with my father dead, can go back anytime, for now I'm only responsible to the king. But Roselyn's father's still alive, and she'd be his property, if she returned. Even the king wouldn't dare change that. But now ...!"

Slowly Eloise turned Karl around, and there stood Roselyn, only an arm's length ... *and an eternity* ... away.

"I wanted to tell you," Roselyn confessed, crying. "I couldn't! I love you so! Things will work out! I'll come for you! I promise!"

"And I'll be with you until then," Eloise promised.

"We all will," Rafe said.

"Promise," Seren agreed.

Sobbing, Karl flung himself into Roselyn's arms, and his tears drenched her shoulder. Comfort fell upon him from all directions, but it was hollow. Inside, Karl still felt empty.

"We'll be together!" Roselyn whispered in his ear. "Forever!"

"Don't mourn what you haven't lost," the Seer smiled at both of them. "Someday the wait will have seemed short, when you've been together for centuries. In some ways, Karl, we're lucky. We fought Loki, and thanks to Roselyn, the cost was only one of us. And we beat Loki! Even I wouldn't have dared pray for such a miracle!"

"I ... I loved you!" Karl stammered to Roselyn.

"And you will again," Roselyn vowed, and she held him close, and Karl knew that she meant it.

Suddenly another stepped behind him. Slowly Karl turned and glimpsed the cold, beautiful Mist surrounded by her eternal vapors. Karl stepped back, as did the others, though it tore his heart in half. From now on, even if things worked out, he'd always be stepping away from Roselyn, her new life and her new duties. But Karl would have to learn to live with that or give up any hope of happiness ever again.

Roselyn, suddenly self-conscience, raised herself tall, regally, and lifted her sword in salute.

"Hail, Mist!" Roselyn shouted. "Words can't express my thanks. I pray that I may prove worthy of your trust."

Suddenly Mist jumped forward, steel flashing as her sword struck, but Roselyn, elf-sword in hand, flinched to block, barely crossing the Valkyrie's sword in time. Her defense had become instinctive: *she'd learned well.*

"You shall!" Mist warned, her encircling fog icy blue. "I've risked much of my honor to reward you."

Roselyn froze, uncertain. Then a fell light, like Hel at her angriest, lit Roselyn's eyes. Roselyn lunged with her own sword and slashed straight down at Mist's unhelmeted head. But Mist was a Valkyrie, skilled and experienced to give even Ruthedhel sport. Easily Mist blocked the blow, stepped back and softly laughed.

"Not bad," Mist smiled, looking her new sister over, and her vaporous shroud turned bright white. "That mortal armor will have to go, but we'll make you better. Soon you can even get rid of that flimsy elf-blade; we'll make you a real sword. But that will come in time. You're one of us now, and we Valkyrie support each other."

"Then ... you'll help me?" Roselyn asked. "Even if I have to beg a favor so soon?"

"Keep no secrets from your shield-sisters!" Mist laughed grimly. "If Odin allows it, we'll all help you!"

"But it's not me who needs help!" Roselyn smiled. "It's my friends; I won't rest until I know that they're safe on Earth, at home in their own lands. That's the only thing that I need right now."

"So be it!" Mist laughed. "We always fly to Midgard, and all of our horses carry more than one. With Odin's leave, we'd be glad to take your friends back, and you can go with us, just to be certain."

"Really?" Rafe gasped. "You can take us back to England?"

"There's nowhere that we can't fly!" Mist snapped, eyeing Rafe coldly. "Come, let's ride now, before the feasting begins in Elvidnir! We've much to celebrate this evening!"

"But ..," Karl stammered, " ... but Roselyn! This means you ... you have to stay here!"

"I'm afraid so," Roselyn said. "But Karl, I did it for us! It's our only chance! Now I'll be here when you ... die. Just be sure to keep a sword in your hand! That way I can find you, when the time comes; then we'll be together forever!"

"And I'll watch over all of you, as often as I can," the Seer smiled. "But now, I must go. I've got to get Glororil back to Alfhiem before I leave; he's badly hurt, but I suspect that they can heal him there. Eventually you must all go back to the Fairie clearing and tell Titania what happened, and that, no doubt, she can expect messengers from Alfhiem in the near future. But right now, fly straight to the king; you won't get much argument about your story if you arrive on magical flying horses."

"That's right!" Rafe gasped. "A treasure! We forgot to find something for the king so that he'd confirm our knighthood!"

"A treasure?" the Seer laughed. "What do you have in your canteens? Ymir's blood! The Water of Life! What greater treasure do you want?

"Good-bye, my friends!" the Seer said, and he quickly hugged each of them. "Blessed be! May the love of the Lady always shine upon you! And don't worry about Roselyn! Eric'll be here with her, and I'll check up on both of them every time that I come over from my Lady's realm!"

"Thank you, my brother!" Rafe smiled weakly at the Seer. "But don't you forget about us, either. If you ever need any help, just come and get us, all right?"

"Count on it," the Seer grinned. "Good-Bye! Bye, Eric! Good-bye, everybody!"

The Seer cupped Glororil and Silvana close against his chest. Silvana smiled and waved.

"Good-bye, human friends!" Silvana shouted. "We love you!"

The Seer's robes shined until both he and the fairies became enveloped in its growing, glowing whiteness. When the light faded, all three were gone.

"I really don't want to leave you behind," Karl said to Roselyn.

"Don't worry," Roselyn smiled. "It won't be as long as it seems. I'll be waiting for you, and meanwhile, you can take care of Eloise."

"Eloise?" Karl asked. "But ..."

"But what?" Eloise demanded. "What's your problem, Karl? Every time that anybody tells you anything, it's 'But' this and 'But' that! You'll have to stop that to be a decent baron!"

"Baron?" Karl exclaimed. "Me?"

"Who else would marry a baroness?"

"Me?" Karl asked again.

"Karl, you're so naive!" Roselyn laughed. "Of course you'll marry Eloise, and the two of you will be very happy together. You'll take good care of her, and she'll tell you exactly how to do it."

"But ... wait!" Karl stammered. "This is all happening so fast! What about Eric?"

"Oh, my God!" Rafe shouted. "We almost forgot!"

Sprinting back to where it had been dropped, Rafe bent and picked up the smelly, rancid arm, still holding its sword, and presented it to Hel.

"Here is the arm of Eric the Viking!" Rafe shouted to Hel. "Keep now your promise and set Eric free!"

"Get away from me!" Hel scowled. "Eric, too! I want no part of you lying hypocrites!"

"Yes, you do," Karl said firmly, and he lifted his sword and turned to face Loki, who was still sprawled on the ground, weak from his wounds. There was still one debt left that Karl could cancel, and he meant to pay it in full. "Behold, Loki! You've been defeated! Now you must pay the ransom of your challenge!"

Karl reached down beside Loki, snatched up his fallen falcon-skin cloak, and carried it away.

"Don't ... don't think you'll get far with that!" Loki snarled, nursing his wounds. "There's nowhere that you can hide that cloak from me, and when I find it ..."

"But I won't have it!" Karl laughed, and he walked straight up to where Hel stood, and handed her the feathered cloak. "Here, Hel. I don't know if you can keep this or not, but I want you to take it for now. It'll help you get home, as I know you must. I just wanted to say ... how sorry I am for deceiving you, but surely you gave us no choice. I do care for you, Hel. I hope that we're still friends."

"Friends?" Hel sneered, honestly shocked. "Your friendship is all lies and betrayal! You expect me to believe you ... *after all this?"*

"After all this," Karl affirmed. "We ... We love you, Hel. I do. I couldn't help loving you from the first moment that I saw you. I wanted you to come with me then, as much as you wanted me to stay. No one's to blame, and friends shouldn't quarrel. You're a beautiful woman, Hel, and you deserve every happiness. The Seer and Roselyn will be able to visit you now, as often as their duties allow." Karl stared into Hel's dark eyes, and then looked down. "I really was tempted to stay, you know. You could've given me everything that I ever wanted, but I guess ...," Karl glanced back at Eloise and Roselyn, "... I guess I was just being dense in not realizing that I'd had it all along."

"T- Then .., then I guess I ... can't blame you, either," Hel growled, and slowly an unwanted, but very welcomed smile spread across her face. "Thank you, Karl, ... *my friend.*"

As Hel leaned forward, Karl flung the famous falcon-skin cloak over her shoulders, and to Karl's surprise, Hel kissed him, and their lips pressed together warm and passionately, and Karl found himself more attracted to Hel than ever. He'd forgotten about Hel's presence of mind, how quickly she could change her whole outlook once her mind was made up. Karl returned Hel's kiss with all of the love and passion that he felt, but they each had their separate dooms. When finally they broke, they both had tears in their eyes.

"Beware, Eloise!" Roselyn laughed. "You can't take your eyes off of Karl for a second while there's another woman around!"

Everyone laughed, even Hel, and then Eloise, Seren and Rafe came forward. All embraced Hel with honest warmth and love. Hel and Eric even bowed deeply to each other, though no words passed between them. When at last they were done, Hel spun suddenly around and her human form dropped away. Hel became a huge pale-pink falcon, sleek and beautiful, flapping her graceful wings as she flew back to Niflhiem. Underneath Hel hung tiny greenish-black talons, but they didn't bother her at all. After a few days back, Hel would be as good as new. Better, because now Hel had friends.

Suddenly the Gates of Valhalla opened wide. Rafe crossed the short bridge and walked up to its entrance, leaned over ceremoniously, and placed Eric's arm inside. Eric smiled triumphantly and proudly strode forward. All of the Einherjar cheered wildly.

Without a word, Eric walked boldly through the gates, stopped just inside, and bent over. Quickly he fumbled with something, and then his paleness hardened to full color. Eric stood and faced them all, smiling wide, standing as flesh and blood once again, both living hands thrust high above his head, his healed and reattached right arm still gripping his heavy Viking blade. Eric gave a joyful shout.

The quest was over, and the Einherjar cheered. One ran forward before the others, before all of the other Einherjar swarmed over them, and that lone warrior snared Eric in a brotherly hug that only Karl's could have vied with. Unexpectedly Karl recognized him from their adventures on Earth, his long yellow hair and twin swords instantly identifying him: King Svenson Two-Sword, Eric's greatest friend and enemy, laughing and smiling, and Eric hugged him back gladly. Then the cheering Einherjar flooded over them and lifted them both high on their shoulders: Eric was home at last.

Loki scowled and vanished in a puff of emerald flame, but no one seemed to notice or care. Odin turned back to mount Sleipnir. For Odin, now that his warrior had been returned, everything was over. Karl was just beginning a lifetime without Roselyn.

"Odin!" Karl called, falling to his knees on the grass before the Alfather, reaching up to take Roselyn's hand. The Terrible One paused and looked back at Karl, almost blasting him with the force of his one-eyed gaze. "Forgive me, Alfather, but ... Roselyn! I mean ... you will take care of her, won't you?"

Odin smiled knowingly at the lovers.

"As if she were my own daughter," Odin promised, mounting Sleipnir. "Reginleif my new Valkyrie shall be named, and in your tongue that means Kin of the Gods."

Odin shook his reins, and Sleipnir leaped into the starry sky and galloped back to Asgard. All of the Valkyrie and the Einherjar cheered after their lord and king, and Karl cheered with them.

There was little time for congratulations, but they shoved a lot into a short space. They wanted to say goodbye to Eric, but the Einherjar had already carried him and Svenson up to Elvidner, and it might be weeks before they stopped celebrating. Roselyn promised to carry their goodbyes to Eric, though they knew that it was unnecessary. After all that they'd been through, Eric knew how they felt, and they knew that Eric felt the same.

Finally, Mist had Eloise mount her winged horse behind her, and Roselyn had Karl mount behind her on a borrowed magical steed. Two other Valkyries, muscular Skeggjöld and Skögul, had Rafe and Seren mount behind them. Karl kissed Roselyn on the cheek, snuggling close, saving their full good-byes until she had to fly back, hoping that they could sneak off for a last few hours alone. Someday they'd be together forever; *Karl could hardly wait.*

"It's kind of strange," Karl said, still crying, though he wasn't sure if his tears were from happiness or not. "We've lost so many good people! First Eric, and before him Liz Apple, then the Seer, and now you, Roselyn, and we almost lost Glororil. But it seems as if no one has really, truly died!"

"I noticed that, too!" Eloise happily agreed.

"Of course!" Mist laughed icily. "Why do you think they call these 'The Immortal Lands'? You have been part of a great tale, a moment of importance to all of the wise: the birth of a new Valkyrie. You shall live forever on the tongues of storytellers."

Not exactly the form of immortality that he'd choose, Karl smiled, but then a subtle, strange sensation filled him. Fame was its own reward, in many ways, and was he not now free to seek it? The husband of Baroness Eloise, the betrothed of Countess Roselyn, now Reginleif, Kin of the Gods, immortal Valkyrie of Odin: it was Karl's duty to seek fame. He could amaze others with his bold and reckless adventuring; *what harm could any sword do to him, save to send him to Roselyn, his greatest love?* Determined to die with a sword, Karl felt a strange excitement warm him; *Karl was free, finally free, to take any risk, to dare any danger.*

Karl turned back, gazed through the open Gates of Valhalla, and spied Eric's distant figure still being carried up the wide hill atop the shoulders of the Einherjar. Finally, Karl understood the wily old Viking, and that was the strangest thought of all.

THE END

ABOUT THE AUTHOR

Born in Tripler Army Medical Center, Honolulu, Hawaii, Jay Palmer works as a technical writer in the software industry in Seattle, Washington. Jay enjoys parties, reading everything in sight, woodworking, obscure board games, and riding his Kawasaki Vulcan. Jay is a knight in the SCA, frequently attends writer conferences, SciFi Conventions, and he and Karen are both avid ballroom dancers. But most of all, Jay enjoys writing.

37784056R00228

Made in the USA
San Bernardino, CA
25 August 2016